SPLINTERED REEDS

JODIE CAIN SMITH

For Bay

*One day, you will be old
enough to read this book.*

PROLOGUE

Once Clayton Vancleave knew what he needed, it was easy to find. The dusty padlock snapped off with one squeeze of his trusty bolt cutters. Alone in the warehouse, the creak of the steel cage went unnoticed. He lifted one of the five-gallon barrels stored in the cage—thirty-five identical barrels lined up on metal shelving and marked for disposal—and set it down on his rolling cart. Then he occupied the empty space with a barrel of water, one harmless dupe among so much poison.

The night before, Clayton'd sat in his favorite lawn chair, a Dollar General special faded by the sun, felt the river lick his bare toes, cracked open a beer, then set the barrel on the water's edge. As the brackish water filled the barrel, Clayton finished the Bud. A couple of taps of a hammer secured the lid, and a fabricated label produced what he viewed as a dead ringer to the stockpile of banned chemicals. His Liberty's Guard contact had been right. A string of government suits had neglected hundreds of gallons of the deadly toxin, left in oblivion in the storage facility of the Vector Department of the Mobile County Health Department.

Damn fools, he thought, then closed the cage and replaced the busted padlock with an identical one purchased at Ace the previous month. Clayton'd even rubbed the lock around in his oyster shell driveway, then let it sit on the stoop of his single-wide trailer, which did away with any hint of new-and-shiny. He wondered how many days, weeks, or months would pass before someone, his boss maybe, tried the lock only to discover their key no longer worked. He hoped the frustration would drive the man-boy wild. It'd take a damn genius to recognize his padlock switcheroo, and as far as Clayton was concerned, no such genius worked for the Mobile County Health Department, especially not that twenty-five-year-old kid in the manager's chair. Must be nice to have a rich and powerful daddy. Clayton didn't have a rich daddy, but he was smarter than all of them.

As a teenager at B.C. Rain High School, every teacher thought Mr. Vancleave was college material, but back then Clayton had no interest in spending a shit ton of money to sit around a classroom with a bunch of Oxford shirt-wearing preppy boys, then spend his life in a suit and tie. Ten years after earning his diploma, he still preferred actual work with a steady paycheck, just enough to pay for his trailer, gas for his bass boat, and a few nights a week singing karaoke at Jack-O-Diamonds.

Clayton exited the warehouse at 4:34 a.m. He loaded the barrel into the back of his MCHD truck and clamped it into place. He donned an N95 mask, then pried the barrel's lid open and attached it to a wide hose that fed the chemical through the sprayer. Soon enough, the liquid would transform into a fine mist.

A laminated route card lay on the passenger seat, unnecessary for guidance. Clayton knew all the routes by memory, being the senior staff member. He'd driven this truck for a decade, east to west and north to south and back again through Mobile County, protecting the fine citizens against pesky mosquitoes because they were too dumb to stay inside at dusk and dawn or use a bit of

OFF! If he cared to speak to any of them, Clayton would have thanked them for their stupidity.

Clayton cranked the engine, slid it into reverse, and was on Congress Street heading southeast in seconds. The only red light he hit between Congress and his route of choice was at Ann Street and Government Boulevard. He nodded to the nighttime attendant at Griffith Shell, who was beginning his shift by spraying the parking lot with a garden hose. The light turned green and Clayton cruised past the stately homes on the outskirts of Oakleigh. *You'll have your turn soon*, he thought while driving past the bungalows, creole cottages, Greek Revivals, and Federal style homes with their manicured yards and porch swings.

At a four-way stop, he reached into a duffel bag on the passenger side floorboard. He felt around past a clean shirt, towel, and small cooler bag of Gatorades. His fingertips identified his gas mask, purchased from an Army surplus store with cash, two months prior. No, Clayton Vancleave was *no dummy*. He'd known this day was coming. Although his Liberty Guard contact proved stingy on details, he had the good sense to be prepared. So, when he lifted the gas mask off a cluttered shelf and the attendant remarked, "That thing still works perfect," he bought it.

Clayton secured the mask straps around the back of his head, rolled his window up tight, closed the AC vents, and pressed the gas pedal. As he crept toward the Birdville Projects, he switched the mosquito sprayer to on. In the truck bed, the machine choked before releasing its familiar sound—the sound every Mobilian from the southern tip of Dauphin Island all the way north to Creola knows. Everyone knows the whirring and whooshing of the Bug Man. And everyone takes comfort in the sound.

It took thirty minutes for Clayton to cover the Birdville projects, then Maysville and the nearly all-Black Williamson High School. He crept past the dilapidated homes, feeling his jaw tighten beneath the mask. "Nothin' but welfare mamas and no-good thugs," he thought. "Ya can't pay your own rent, but you can afford that new Benz."

Clayton used the last of the barrel's potent concoction, cruising nice and slow along the shallow shoulder of Broad Street. He chuckled as a young man—one hand keeping his pants from falling down, the other clutching a Dollar General shopping bag—scurried under a slipshod awning at the sight of him. "Enjoy your last meal, ingrate." Adrenaline pumped through his veins as he imagined all those Black bodies convulsing in the streets.

The next day Clayton repeated himself, every step minus having to break the padlock. Knowing the combination made entering the cage of banned chemicals even easier. Between his two runs that day, he listened to the ambulance sirens and nodded his agreement when coworkers commented on the increased meat wagons that day. *Yep. Sure are.* Clayton resisted the urge to smile, despite the temptation that tugged at his sallow face. Instead, he feigned concern and confusion before hopping back behind the wheel of his truck.

At 5:50 p.m. he left the Vector parking lot and cruised the tree-lined streets of Oakleigh, the historic garden district, just in time for cocktail hour at Callaghan's. He drove nice and slow past the Irish pub, glaring at the woke motherfuckers with their vodka sodas and bourbons on the rocks and White Claws. "So much smarter than me, huh? If you was smart, you'd know to run from my truck." If any of the patrons noticed Clayton's gas mask, none flinched at the discovery. One dog walker paused as he drove by, but then bent over in her overpriced leggings to collect little Fifi's turd in a green plastic bag.

Clayton hit two more uppity Midtown neighborhoods, passing joggers and cyclists, each outfitted for safety with their helmets and reflective gear. Although, they didn't think of every precaution. Then, he drove back to Congress Street via St. Francis, one block from the best outdoor dining in Mobile and the closest Clayton could get to all the bankers and lawyers and engineers and their spouses and mistresses and the girls they're all pretending not to bang in the executive bathrooms. He'd love to hose them down with the nerve agent, make them lick it off their lips right before they fall to their knees and writhe on the street. Piss themselves on the sidewalk.

With another empty barrel, Clayton pulled into his usual spot in the Vector parking lot. He turned off the engine, checked off his completed routes on his clipboard, and stuck a note under the metal clip. He tossed the clipboard on the driver's seat as he exited the truck.

In his own car, an old beater of a Buick if you ever saw one, Clayton polished off a Wendy's Double Stack—extra bacon—a large coke, and large fry. At home on the river, he grabbed a six-pack from the fridge. Back in his favorite spot, he sunk low into the lawn chair, naked toes in the water again. After the last swig of his third beer, the pre-paid phone in his lap buzzed.

"Yeah," he said into the phone. "It's done."

Three more beers down. He was out of beer and out of tasks. The job was complete. He wondered if the others had accomplished their mission as well. Charleston, Jacksonville, Baltimore, Tampa, New Orleans, Galveston. Had it all gone as planned? Breathing in the question, he exhaled the pride of a victorious hero, having fought the good fight. Then, he lifted his daddy's pistol to his right temple and pulled the trigger.

The next day, when Clayton didn't show for work, his supervisor opened the driver's side door. He'd have to drive Clayton's route, seeing that Clayton was too lazy to show up to work. The big bosses would ride his ass if the routes weren't driven every day, Monday to Friday, from June to September. He grabbed the clipboard to verify yesterday's completed routes. Clayton's note waved at him as a sharp breeze flapped the paper up and down. If not clipped down, it would've blown away.

Scribbled in black ink were two sentences:

They took my history from me, so I took their future from them. My life mattered.
— Clayton Vancleave, LT Liberty's Guard

1

I'm no fool. I never expected utopia. But I did expect fewer broken promises.

———

"Ules, Ules."

Eighteen inches from my face, the door shakes. The door shouldn't shake. Not at this hour. Not this door. Not because my sister's kid is banging her little fists against it.

"Ules!"

"Just a minute, Mallie," I call back, snatching a piece of packing paper from the top of the crumpled stack. Having run out of toilet paper months ago—I guess the hoarders were the smart ones—we're now rationing the paper that kept Christmas ornaments safe. "What are you doing out here? Where's your mom?" I say through the latched door.

"Mama sleep," Mallie says, then to my absolute horror, slides four chubby fingers under the door. "Ules make a stinky?"

"No," I snap back. "Get your hand off the ground. Ground gross. Ground gross!" *Now who sounds like a toddler?* I stand, pull up my panties and shorts, and spritz my hands with Mama's homemade sanitizer—vodka mixed with witch hazel and the last of my vitamin E capsules. None of us have died from E. coli since being reduced to using an outhouse, so I guess this stuff does the trick.

Mallie's fingertips still rake the ground beneath the door. "Ules, come out."

"I will just as soon as you get away from the door," I call back, then add a serious, "And do *not* stick your fingers in your mouth!"

The fingers disappear from beneath the door, so I creak it open. "Heaven forbid I have a little privacy for my morning piss," I tell the child who stands gazing up at me and pointing her nasty fingers at me.

"Bad word! Ules say bad word. Pott-ee word."

I snatch both her hands in mine and soak them with the sanitizer. "Yes, yes. Auntie Jules said a potty word."

"I tell Mama."

"Yes, please. Go right ahead. Then I can ask your mother why you are out here by yourself." Mallie responds with a crinkling of her nose. I guess toddlers don't get sarcasm.

I glance around, but Kate, my sister and Mallie's mother, is nowhere. Just Mallie and me. The back door of the house is wide open. "Did you open that door?" I am certain I closed it all the way. I had heard the *click click* noise of the door when I came out.

"Yes!" Mallie throws up her arms, pride brimming on her face. "I do it!"

"Wow. Such a big girl who can open the door all by herself now."

"Yes!"

I'm sure for Mallie this is a major accomplishment, one we should celebrate with treats and tickles. She can get out of the house now. By herself. With none of us aware. Just out into the great wide open. Out here with all that south Mobile County has to offer. Bobcats, alligators, the bay that she can't swim in, about a million types of snakes and spiders and creepers of both the insect and human kind. She can get out of the house on her own. *We're going to have to tie her to her bed at night.*

"Mallie, you are, under no circumstances, to walk out of the house by yourself." I stoop down to her eye level. "You got it? Do not come outside by yourself. Under no circumstances are you to come outside by yourself."

She shakes her head, which makes her blonde curls shudder, and her big, blue eyes cloud with tears.

"I'm not mad at you. I promise," I say, wrapping her in my arms. "Auntie Jules is not mad. I just need you to be safe. It's not safe out here by yourself. Not safe."

Mallie wriggles out of my embrace and takes off toward the front of the house. The front of the house faces Mobile Bay—item number one on the "Things that can kill Mallie List." The list seems to grow every day. And Mallie, with her blonde curls and bright blue eyes, is the only source of genuine joy and light for the Martin family these days. So, I think we've all become protective of her. I know I have. Always encase her in bubble wrap and tether her to one of us. We've already lost so much. Losing Mallie would break us.

So, I hurry after her.

At seventeen, I ran as fast as I could from this small fishing village on the southern tip of Alabama, and the 1,200 square feet of my childhood home. Seventeen-year-old me yearned for secrets and privacy and neither existed here, then or now. When I met Jacob, I thought I had left home for good.

"Mallie, stop!" My right flip-flop slides off my foot as I dash down the hill toward the rock bulkhead. Three feet deep, brackish water against barnacled rocks awaits Mallie if she beats me to the rocks. "Stop," I yell again and come to an abrupt stop as I swoop her up. Or, I try to stop. My left foot slides forward on the dewy grass, causing me to land hard on my back.

"Again! Again," Mallie giggles, then grabs my face. "Again Ules! Again!"

I pant on the ground, my arms still wrapped around Mallie. "No. I didn't do that on purpose, Mallie." Without letting her go, I hobble to my feet, then march up the hill for my other flip-flop. "Little girl, you know you are not to go by the rocks without an adult. You know that." My words sting. Mallie looks at me then folds in on herself, hiding her face from me.

"I'm sorry, honey. I'm sorry. But you can't run down to the rocks like that." Sitting on the front porch steps, I hold her on my lap and stroke her hair. She sucks her thumb and probably plots how to get to the rocks next time.

Mobile Bay, my childhood playground, spreads from right to left in front of me, sparkling in the sun, casting sequins with every ripple. Then, the sun hits the tin roof of the boathouse and sunbeams explode around the pier as if heaven itself opens its doors.

Sitting on the stoop, shielding my eyes from the sun with Mallie's warm little body against mine, I can dismiss my new life. I breathe in and try to let each disturbing element go. Blackouts. Cold showers. No blow dryers. Domestic terrorists. Empty grocery shelves. No takeout dinners. Bombings. Poison. No job. One outhouse for thirteen people. I think I can accept all of it, except one.

I look out over the water, past the end of the pier, to a man in a kayak. Squinting my eyes, my vision blurs until I imagine the kayaker as a Chickasaw from long ago; another time when searching for sustenance beneath the brackish water was how each day began. My ancestors knew exactly how to survive. I wish that I, like the Chickasaw that fished these waters a century ago, didn't know any different. I wish I didn't know how easy life can be with all the modern conveniences of electricity, grocery stores, microwaves, and delivery pizza.

But I do know differently.

The man in the kayak isn't Chickasaw. He's probably just like me. Trying to survive the best he can. Trying to catch enough this morning to feed his family tonight. Maybe tonight the knowledge that his family will not go to bed hungry will help make up for everything else we know.

We know what Clayton Vancleave did. We saw the news coverage and all those people poisoned. Our people. Friends from college and high school. Distant cousins. They're all dead. We know what Liberty's Guard did in the name of patriotism; witnessed the calculated chaos they created and the chaos they maintain. Explosions at power stations. Bullets flying in grocery stores, churches, and city buildings. And I know what we didn't do. We didn't listen to the warnings. We could have prevented every death, but we ignored the signs. We ignored their rage, their commitment, their abilities. We thought we were too big, too strong, too special to fail, but we were the exact right size, right weakness, right attitude to implode.

"Jules!" My brother Matt's voice bellows from inside the house. "Grab the nets! Mullets runnin'!"

I spring to my feet, scoop up Mallie, run across the porch and fling the door open, meeting Matt nose-to-nose.

"Have the mullet been calling to you this morning, Fish Whisperer?" I ask him, referring to his ability to know what is under the surface of the Bay by lying on the pier and listening, how a fish cuts or slaps the water. Or maybe he felt something in the air, or the wind sent him some secret signal only he and the sharks hear.

"Come on!" Matt pushes past Mallie and me, charging toward the pier.

I don't know how he knows, but sure enough, when I look at

the bay, little splashes break the glassy water, and they're heading our way.

I plop Mallie on the kitchen floor and call to my sister sleeping in the rear of the house, "Kate, come get your kid!" Grabbing the nets by the counter, I turn and rush outside, pulling the door closed behind me to Mallie's screams of protest. She is not a child who accepts being left behind. Any more of this and I will lose my "favorite aunt" status.

"Jules! Move your ass!" *Flop, flop, flop, flop.*

Matt moves fast, even in flip-flops. If I moved that fast in flip-flops, I would bust my ass on an uneven plank and end up face first in the water—or ass first on the ground, as was the case earlier. To look at him, Matt should be slower. He should be weaker, but he moves with the same athleticism he displayed as a teen on the baseball field. On the diamond, he shocked spectators as his stubby legs and 150-pound frame flew around the bases. First basemen winced at Matt's throw from third to first as it slapped the leather of their gloves.

By the time I catch up to Matt at the end of the pier, he's lowered the ladder into the waist deep water. A large, galvanized pail sits next to him on the lower dock. His rifle hangs from a strap slung across his chest and back. Although small, Matt is well-skilled at scaring the shit out of anyone daring to fish the water that surrounds our pier. I wonder how intimidating he'll be when we all run out of bullets. I watch him scan the horizon, then lay the rifle on the crab pier and slide down the ladder.

Kicking off my flops, I toss the tub and one long-handled net to Matt, then climb down the ladder, careful not to drop the other net. Nothing pisses Matt off more than lost fishing equipment. We've already lost enough to looters. We don't need to lose more to my clumsiness.

After a minute in the cool water, the mullet ping my legs. I hate mullet. They taste too fishy for me, but they aren't the turtles or gamey possum I will find in the swamp traps, so I'll fish while the mullet is here for the taking. Maybe I can trade some for salt. And I'll check the citrus trees. Even a small lemon would improve the flavor, although it's still a bit early for lemons.

In the water, I focus on my net and watch for sharks eager to feed as well. Here I can't think about my former life or my current life. I've no space for comparing old reality to new reality. All I can do is scoop up mullet and dump them in the tub. Scoop, dump, scoop, dump. After a half hour, my arms are sore, my stomach grumbles, and the tub is full.

"Looks like we're having a fish fry tonight," Matt grins, hoisting the tub of flopping mullet up onto the lower dock. His grin fades as a boat appears in the distance, heading for our pier. Water sprays behind the vessel as it pops up and over the deep-water chop. "Jules, be ready on the bell if these jackasses start something."

I hop up from the crab pier to the main boathouse and position myself near the jubilee bell, the brass bell intended to signal neighbors of a fishing jubilee, but, of late, rung out in alarm rather than celebration.

"Must be nice to have that kind of fuel, huh?" I ask. "Wonder what they're doin' to get the gas for a dual engine?"

"I don't think you really want to know that, Jules."

As the boat approaches, I see the large K on a shield, a symbol of The Knights painted on the front hull—our very own red-blooded, all-American, homegrown militia. One man stands at the helm of the boat, a pair of binoculars hanging from his neck. Three other men, all in camouflage pants and T-shirts, sit in the bow. Dread tingles through my muscles.

The few rumors that float our way of The Knight's compound paint a picture of an Al-Qaeda-style training camp meets *Little House on the Prairie*. The men and boys train for combat, clean guns, and prep explosives while the little ladies bake bread and make pies. *They're doing God's work*, some say. *Men like The Knights will save this country*, their supporters assert. My mind flashes to a billboard on the highway near to here: *The Ancient Path is righteous. Join God's Knights.*

I know, I know. The Knights aren't Liberty's Guard. They didn't pull a Clayton Vancleave and poison whole neighborhoods. They're one of many pocket militias that rose up all over this country out of fear. But they think they're answering a divine call to arms. That strict adherence to their ideology is what will "save this country." Now that the United States has some big, fucking holes in its armor, The Knights aim to fill every one of those holes with Christians, which doesn't sound so bad until you realize they mean only one type of Christian. No Catholics, Mormons, Methodists, Baptists, Jehovah's Witnesses, Presbyterians, and on and on. None of *those* Christians need apply. They're not *real* Christians, and therefore not real Americans. Fundamentalist. Radicalized. White. Yeah, they're not too big on black and brown people either. They are true believers in America as a White Christian Nation. And that scares the shit out of me.

"Do you think they have some secret stash of camo T-shirts?" I ask Matt, trying to stave off panic with lame sarcasm.

"Probably. Probably use 'em to hide all the stolen fuel." Matt picks up his rifle, holding it down by his side with his right hand. "Ya need some help?" Matt asks the men as they idle up next to the pier, having reduced the engines to burps and sputters.

"Know any good spots this morning?" The captain looks from Matt's rifle to the full tub of mullet.

"Nope," answers Matt.

"Looks like you got pretty lucky," the man says, still eying our morning catch. "We thought maybe you had a jubilee going." He stares at the scaly creatures, flopping and gasping as bubbles of wet air leave their tiny mouths.

"No, man. No jubilee. You woulda heard the bell," Matt

shrugs off the man's suggestion that we kept news of the mysterious, fishing free-for-all called *jubilee* to ourselves. Such selfishness is taboo in Bellefontaine. A jubilee may be the one thing The Knights care about more than God's eventual wrath. "The mullet were runnin' this morning, but they've gone on." Matt points his rifle to the left, indicating the direction of the mullet. "Ya might try some of the old pylons further down. They're headin' that way."

"Yeah, we were out at Middle Bay Lighthouse just now. Ain't nothing biting out there."

"Looks like you didn't leave empty-handed though," I say and gesture toward the stack of shiplap, the white paint nearly stripped clean from years of standing against the wind and water. "Which commandment is *thou shall not steal*?"

The captain cuts his eyes at me, then turns back to Matt. "Y'all sure have a pretty spot here, don'chya." Scanning the front of Daddy's property, the men in the boat exchange a look I can't quite interpret, somewhere between appreciation, lust, and rusty wheels turning.

"You don't want to keep the fish waiting." Matt's hand adjusts around the forearm of his rifle. "Or the repairs you must be making to the lighthouse. Let me know if you're looking to get rid of that old lumber. Might trade you for it."

I cut my eyes at Matt. No way in Hell are we trading anything with The Knights and he knows it. Daddy won't allow it.

"Um, yeah. I'll keep that in mind." The captain, who seems in no hurry to fish, tilts the throttle from idle back to trolling. "Well, I guess we better get to it. Gotta get these boards repaired and back out there."

Sure, you do.

As the boat pulls away, one man in the bow winks at me from under a filthy white hat, then flicks his tongue against his teeth, never dropping his stare. His pit-stained T-shirt and oil and algae-rubbed camo pants add to my revulsion. My stomach turns at the thought of his long, pale, tattooed arm ever touching me. Keeping his gaze on me, he removes his baseball cap to reveal thinning, blond hair with wet wisps creeping below his shoulders. He licks his bottom lip as his gaze drops from my face. To my boobs. Then to my hips.

"Not a chance in hell." I take a step backward, moving as far away from him as I can without falling into the water.

"We'll see!" he calls back to me as the boat floats south.

"What a bunch of d-bags," Matt says. He grabs a mullet out of the tub, throws it down on the cutting board and chops off its head with a cleaver. "I wonder what's left of the lighthouse. They can't really be stripping it for scrap?"

"There's something wrong with that guy, Matt."

"Well, yeah. He's drank his fill of The Knight's Kool-Aid." Matt affects his best Gomer Pyle accent. "Join us as we fight the demons! The vampires in DC want to eat your children and corrupt your women. Beware! And whatever else those dipshits believe in."

"Matt, I'm serious."

"If you wanna safeguard your heritage, sponsor a dead Confederate General today. Just five dollars a day can get ol' General Lee back in the saddle." He hocks a loogie over the railing for emphasis.

"Dammit, Matt. I mean, there's something more the matter with the blond guy. And notice they didn't go off toward the mullet. They weren't here for mullet, Matt."

"I don't think that's what they're fishing for this morning, sis." Matt winks at me, then grins. "I think that blond one wants to show you his fishin' pole."

"Matt, stop. I'm being serious and you think it's all funny. I'd like you to have someone like that do what—" I cut myself off and stave off the panic. Or try to at least. "All I know is every fiber of my being is screaming to keep an extra eye out for that guy."

"We will, Jules. And they're gone now. No need to freak out. Just forget about it."

Oh, if I could forget. If I could stop freaking out and start forgetting, I would forget the hell out of all of this.

Because there are moments of forgetting. Glorious forgetting. The kind of forgetting that sweeps you away into the unconscious abyss. In those moments, I find a familiar bliss, a joy I remember. Cool, white sheets rumpled across a king-sized bed. The knowledge of morning, although no light breaks through the blackout curtains. The smell of coffee, freshly brewed. Kisses on my cheek. Kisses on my neck. Although I'm only pretending to sleep. I open my eyes to his—big, brown with flecks of gold and long, thick lashes. In those precious best of moments, I forget to panic and remember Jacob.

If I could forget forever, I would. I would forget and forget and forget until the end of time. I'd forget how much he loved me. I'd forget how our bodies fit together. I'd forget that Jacob's hands and lips and eyes are gone. But I can't forget forever. And when the forgetting ends, I face the same damn truth: My Jacob is dead. Quick and cruel, that truth snaps back at me. It slaps me, punishes me for daring to forget. *My Jacob is dead. My Jacob is dead.*

Now nearing the end of May, the crushing ache of September has lessened a bit, but the truth of Jacob's death is still too much to accept. The fact that I don't know exactly what happened that day on Fort Stewart, Georgia, grinds at my edges. It sharpens what used to be soft and easy about me. It lays bare three things I know for sure. The first is that Savannah had a bug man, one just as fucked up as ours. The second is that the Army ordered all bodies of the victims on Hunter Army Airfield cremated over concerns about polluting the soil. The third truth is that the waves of grief crashing into me, then exploding into rage and pain, will never end. It's turning me into someone I don't know. Someone I don't like. Someone failing. Someone who freaks out all the time.

And that's what Matt and no one else around here seems to get. I never freaked out before. Sure, I knew the world was dangerous to a certain extent. I knew not to walk to my car at night by myself or go for a run by myself or meet the cable guy or a plumber at my house by myself. Basically, anything by myself, especially after dark, waved a big freaking "Proceed with caution!" sign. But I had Jacob, and he made me feel invincible. Because Jacob believed I was strong, I believed I was strong. No man's victim. Badass in pointed-toe boots, stiletto boots. But I don't have Jacob anymore. All my trust and faith and badassery died with him. The boots remain, but they're nothing more than a useless costume now.

"Matt, I wish—" I cut myself off when I see Kate and Mallie walking on the pier. I turn away from them and breathe. In and out. In and out. Slow the wave. Lessen the impact.

As I turn back to Kate and Mallie, two US Army Blackhawk helicopters appear on the horizon. They float closer and closer until water kicks up all around the pier. Kate holds Mallie close to her body to hold her steady against the rising wind.

"Here, boys, I caught this special for you!" Matt tosses a severed mullet head toward one chopper.

"Matt," I caution, "Don't get them started!" I breathe slowly, count my inhales and exhales.

"Oh, please, what are they gonna do? Accuse me of assault with a deadly fish head?"

"You don't want to be on their radar. Just play nice." *Inhale-one-two-three-four. Exhale-one-two-three-four.*

"Jules, what do you think they've been doing with all the patrols and flyovers of the last nine months? We live smack dab in the middle of their radar."

"I feel like we're in the middle of everything." *Exhale-one-two-three-four.*

As the helicopter hovers above, Kate walks against the wind, trying to get herself and Mallie under the boathouse roof. "Kate! Just stay there," I call, worried that if she loses her balance, she'll tumble into the water and Mallie isn't wearing her life jacket. Kate ignores me.

The helicopter overhead turns, and the shift in the air causes the roof to shudder and creak. I see it hovering just outside the small tin roof now. On an exhale, I catch the stare of a soldier sitting in the open door of one helicopter. He looks at me then adjusts his rifle, resting it on his knee; the barrel pointed in my direction. *Inhale-one-two-three-four.* Then he leans forward a little, shifts his rifle again. I follow the direction of the barrel across the water, down the wooden planks, to Kate and down her tanned arm to Mallie. That sweet girl, that precious baby, has not an anxious bone in her body. She simply raises one chubby arm and waves.

And I want to scream.

2

If you are listening to this, congratulations. You're still alive.

The voice, part shock jock, part televangelist, belongs to Preach. It breaks through the static pops of the hand-cranked radio propped on the windowsill of the garage, my oven of solitude. Listening to this show is proof of how starved for entertainment one woman can be. But, after my breakdown on the pier earlier, I need something mindless.

You've made it to month nine of this awful new normal. Yes, devoted listeners, nine months since those bastards, Liberty's Guard, took matters into their own hands. Not that I blame them for being so angry. I'm angry too. But I didn't go off killing people and destroying property. Oh, I bet they're all running scared now.

This, I decide, is inaccurate. Liberty's Guard isn't running scared. They're probably living the high life in Mexico. Except for those that took the suicide-martyrdom route.

And I've got one question for the snowflakes: Was kowtowing to a bunch of communists, ripping down our statues, and canceling our history and heritage worth it? Are you proud of yourselves?

Woah. That took a turn. And, really, who thought statue removal would be so triggering?

Well, all you blue wussies out there, you godless cowards, are you happy now that you're hiding under your beds? Cause I know you ain't got the means to defend yourselves. Guess what? I live in Red America. And in Red America, we value our history, our God, and our freedom. And we have the skills to survive this. Do you?

Why, yes. Yes, I do. I guess not all Blue Americans are a bunch of pacifists. Some of us know exactly how to survive and are praying like hell I don't have to impersonate Annie Oakley much longer.

So, the bad news is still the bad news: the lights are out. Again. Whoever picked up the cause of destroying this country after Liberty's Guard went to hide in their caves is doing a fine job of extendin' this fiasco. But don't fret. 'Ol Preach is gonna bring you up to speed on the latest and greatest happenin's all around Mobile.

Preach clears his throat of what sounds like a decade's worth of mucus. The spitting sounds that follow are a really pleasant touch. Provides a nice "alone in the basement" feeling—if people here had basements, which they do not because of all the water.

Sources tell me downtown is a ghost town, deserted save for a few bums and strays, and with every tweak of the grid, they get about two days of 'lectricity before the system goes down again. But I promise you, my devoted listeners, you brave sons of bitches out there, they're working on it. Last thing we need right now is for any of you to panic. Keep at it. Keep doing what you're doing. Obey the curfew, behave in those ration lines, and be vigilant. Just cause most of the Libtards wouldn't know a rifle from a rattlesnake, don't mean some of 'em aren't looking to take aim at you and yours. One freedom martial law doesn't take away is our patriotic duty to protect ourselves. So, hold on—

"My fra-ends," Matt exaggerates a country accent as he walks through the garage door. "Hold on to the Lord and hide your shi-it."

"I always do." I jingle the keys I keep on a piece of leather twine around my neck, then flip off the radio.

"Did he say anything worth hearing?" Matt asks. Even though Daddy doesn't like the gossip spilled over the radio, none of us ever leave the house without first checking the radio for warnings. At least Daddy's letting us leave at all now. Baby steps. Teeny, tiny baby steps.

"Nope, just the usual. Blackouts, 'I like what they did, kill the Libs,' oh, and for your own good, play nice with the Army and shoot straight."

"So helpful," Matt says. "So, we good to go?" he asks but doesn't seem to expect a response as he eyes then flips back the worn cover of the *Army Survival Guide* resting in its usual spot on the table. The black lettering is fading into the dingy white cover and is two read-throughs away from the spine losing pages. "What does this thing say about hunting seasons around here?" Matt may be the Fish Whisperer, but he's far from a wizard on dry land.

"Not much," I tell him. "Just what traps and shit are good for different prey. I don't think they intended for you to live off the land for this long, and it wasn't written specifically for lower Alabama."

Hunting on land was quickly becoming my area of expertise. My new-normal job. Soon after returning to Bellefontaine, I started making stuff: traps, snares, nets, and some crude weaponry. At first, I built them to keep my fingers and mind busy, and the small traps reminded me of Jacob and a specific memory, one that brought more comfort than pain.

"Probably not." Matt rubs his thumb against the top right corner of a page.

"Matt, your hands," I say.

"Oh, sorry." He lays the book down on the table and looks at his hands. Little shimmers of fish scales show around his knuckles, and bits of red peek out from under his nails. "I loaded the crab traps before I came in."

"It's fine," I say, placing the book on a shelf, brushing scales off a corner. I've bartered or repurposed many of Jacob's belongings, but not the manual. It remains mine, securely behind the locked door of the garage. Earlier, while Matt cleaned the fish on the pier and I retreated to my workspace in the garage, I ran my fingers over the cover, felt the worn cardstock, velvety from his hands as an ROTC cadet long ago and my hands after months of looking for Jacob in the pages.

It was our first and last camping trip together when I first saw the guide. Jacob had wanted to teach me to rappel. I had no idea why my life would ever require such a skill, but I went along on the trip, hoping that I would magically become one with nature and discover my inner daredevil. I watched Jacob descend the seventy-five-foot cliff, skipping from right foot to left, flying against the rock backdrop like Spider-Man. Then I promptly refused to attempt the cliff myself, deeming rappelling to be an absurd mode of transport.

Jacob offered a ten-foot boulder as a compromise. "Just get used to the rope," he said. "All you have to do is lean back. The harness will hold you."

"Bullshit," I told him and then, like a ninny, sang show tunes to myself and cried and tried to calm myself before plummeting to my imminent death off the boulder, which felt a hell of a lot higher than ten feet as I leaned back. The only thing I was sure of was my incompetence. Jacob stood beneath me and did his best to coax me down. "Come on, Jules. I promise I will catch you if you slip."

The harness strangled my upper thighs and waist, framing my

ass and surely giving Jacob the most unattractive view with my feet planted against the rock and my hands clutching the rope. When you're facing death, it's hard as hell to suck in your stomach and hold your shoulders back and all that posture nonsense drilled into your brain as a girl raised in the South. And, anyway, there was no way I could "suck in" my ass, it being on display in the harness for all to see. When two climbers a few yards over told Jacob to "Get your girl to shut up, will ya?" I sobbed louder, trembling from the sure-as-shit fall waiting to break both my legs and my neck. After hanging there, frozen for several, extraordinarily long minutes, God intervened and conjured up a thunderous downpour, forcing an end to my rappelling lesson. Jacob reached up and pulled me to safety, just as he said he would. I decided then and there never to question the existence of a higher power.

With all the gear soaked from the rain, Jacob spent day two of our trip making small animal traps. This is when I first saw the survival manual. Following little black-and-white diagrams, Jacob whittled sticks into tiny spears and tied 550 cord to rocks as triggers and counterweights. I spent the day reading and praying that Jacob wouldn't catch anything. By the end of that trip, I had accepted the knowledge that I'd found my forever partner in a man my complete opposite.

For years after that trip, the manual sat with Jacob's other Army manuals on a shelf in our home office—unopened once we had the money for comfy hotel rooms and Jacob realized my need for a hot shower, a blow dryer, and nature-free sleep. I never thought I would have reason to read the manual or that it would become one of my most valuable possessions. But if I hold it close and smell the pages, I am back on that boulder, in those woods, in that tent. I feel his hands on my waist, strong and secure. The hands that loved me more than anyone ever had or will again. Jacob's hands.

"Hey, Jules," Matt says, snapping me to the present. "Are we going or what?"

"What? Oh, yeah. Yeah. Sure." I slip back into my flops. When Matt passes me in the doorway, I swallow hard against the look of pity in his eyes.

———

Mama and Daddy's property weaves through the swamps and marshland along a half-mile stretch of Mobile Bay's western coast. Years ago, when developers and real estate moguls leveled sections of forest along the waterfront, Daddy bought several acres known as Goat Island and several more surrounding a small lagoon. Mama fought him on spending a sizeable chunk of their life savings on the land, but in the end, he won the argument and bought the land. Doing nothing with it was the best way Daddy could protect the coastline he loved, the Little Amazon that is our beloved Bellefontaine and surrounding communities. To this day, at five p.m., you'll find him and Mama swinging back and forth on one of the wooden swings on the pier, surveying their small kingdom, a glass of Mama's homemade wine sloshing with every slant.

The best way to reach most of Goat Island and the lagoon is by kayak. In a kayak, you avoid any psycho doomsday-er hidden in the woods and won't end up with a snake around your ankle or ticks hiding in your clothes or a bobcat stalking you from tree-to-tree. This is my problem with nature. There are far too many ways to die.

Today, our constant search for food means a trip for Matt and me through the wetlands to check the mist net. Most of the geese flew north by now, but the off chance that we snagged a straggler is the perfect opportunity for Matt and I to exchange the main house for kayaks and open water.

Paddling south along the coast, Matt and I bob up and down over the choppy water of Mobile Bay, past dozens of abandoned pylons, stripped by hurricanes until bare except for barnacles. At the first coastline point south of Daddy's pier, a sharp right turn leads straight into the marshland.

As our kayaks skim through the narrow opening, the water changes. The lagoon snakes through the tall grass and around the dense, sulfur soil separating the Bay from the swamp. The water here is smooth as glass, and tall grass blocks the wind and the sounds of the bay's chop. Floating on the lagoon, seagull squawks give way to buzzing cicada and gurgles of water easing in and out of thick reeds. The reeds are so tall that the lagoon feels transformative, both mind and soul. Life is manageable while floating here in my kayak, meandering further into the lagoon, heading toward the complete stillness of the swamp.

"Bubbles, Jules!"

Matt's warning launches me from my blessed quiet.

"Where?" I ask, scanning the water for the alligator waiting to turn my boat over, sink his massive teeth into my leg, and drag me to the bottom for a death-roll finale. "Matt, I don't see him!" I slap the water with my paddle, hoping to scare the beast away. I twist in my seat, then find Matt doubling over in his kayak, laughing. "Jesus Christ, Matt! You scared me half to death!" I jab at him with my oar but come up a foot short.

"That's why it's funny." Then he stops and sucks in air. He looks over my shoulder and moves his chin in my direction. "Just behind you," he whispers. "Not shittin' you this time."

I whip my head around to see nothing but grass waving at me.

"Every time!" Matt laughs.

"Let's just get to the lookout, jackass."

"Sure, Jules," Matt says, still laughing, seemingly impressed with himself.

Matt and I guide our kayaks up onto the shore nearest the

lookout, a ten-by-ten-foot raised deck encased by a waist-high railing. It's all that remains of a housing development gone wrong, then abandoned, allowing Daddy to sweep in with a low bid. A single, narrow staircase leads from the ground to the deck. Standing on it, the view is magnificent. Trees, reeds, the snake-like, watery path of the lagoon, then the untouched and wild Goat Island, and the mouth of Fowl River. Beyond that, the tip of Mon Louis Island breaks the horizon, all bordered by the expanse of Mobile Bay.

No matter the season, bird droppings cover the entire left side of the structure, signaling which side the birds prefer, whether pelicans, gulls, or the geese we hope to snag. So, tying the mist net off the left stilts had served us well through the winter months. In late December, as we sat down for Christmas Dinner, Kate had affected a British accent while carving the Christmas Goose, then Garrett, her husband, made a lame attempt at humor with "God bless us everyone." I longed for a neat and tidy way to kill myself rather than continuing life as a pioneer woman who hunts her meals. I did not get my Christmas wish.

As we approach the lookout, I see the damage. It's the kind of damage only human hands can make. Weeks of my handiwork, tying the thick fishing line into dozens of squares until my fingers burned, fighting with Matt over every inch of precious fishing line used. Weeks of my damn life. Now hanging in tatters. Two large gashes—top to bottom, binding to binding—render the net useless.

"What the hell kind of bird did this?" Matt asks as he puts his entire arm through one gash.

"The kind with opposable thumbs. It was cut, Matt." I rub my fingers against a string, the end a blunt nub against my thumb. "No bird is going to cause two identical gashes of this size."

"Jules, Matt, wha'chya doin'?" A voice comes from the other side of the deck.

Matt swings his rifle around till the butt is in his shoulder and the nose points toward the voice.

Reaching for my knife sheathed in my belt, I turn, but stop short upon seeing Billy Roberts, an old friend, and another man walking toward us. Both men don Army uniforms.

"Billy, since when were you back in town?" Matt calls, lowering his rifle.

"I joined this unit a few weeks ago," Billy says, one dimple forming in his right cheek as it always did when he smiled at a teenage version of me. He steps toward me and gives me the all-too-familiar head tilt. "Jules, Mama told me what happened. I'm so sorry for y—"

"Why are you with him?" I ask Billy and indicate the man standing next to him—Captain Johnson. "He will never have permission to be here."

"Do you have a permit for that?" Captain Johnson asks, now walking toward us.

Blood pounds in my ears. "No, I don't have a permit for this," I answer. "I don't need one. And you need to get off my family's land. Now. You're trespassing."

Matt tugs at my arm, trying to pull me close to him. I shrug him off and take another step toward Johnson.

Johnson brushes off my warning, then stops and looks at me, hard. "Have we met?" Johnson asks.

"Met? Yes, we've met. I've got the scars to prove it."

3

The first explosion woke me. The second rocked the house. The third met with Mallie's screams. The cries were not her angry cries for food or vengeful shrieks for autonomy or sleepy whimpering. That morning, her screams were of terror. Like the rest of us, she was unaware of what just reduced to rubble. She only knew something terrible happened. And the terrible was close.

That morning, only four months ago, but what now feels like a different lifetime, I ran to the end of the pier, followed closely by the entire Martin clan. Down the shoreline, seagulls darted from smoke rising over the trees. Bells clanged from every pier along the western shore, but they rang out of disaster rather than joy.

"Daddy, was that the marina?" Mama asked.

"I hope not." Daddy looked through his binoculars toward the smoke.

The Fowl River Marina was the one fuel stop between the Industrial Canal and Alabama Point. It housed shrimp boats and yachts, crabbing vessels, and even a few house boats too battered to travel up and down the river anymore. Add in a convenience store and a small burger joint. The Renauds, the family that had owned and run the operation for fifty years, were a mainstay of Bellefontaine and the marina, a major landmark second only to the Holy T intersection that held two of the four churches in the small town.

"Could the fuel lines explode? Maybe leftover gasoline in them?" I asked.

"Possibly," Matt said, "but what would trigger that?"

Standing shoulder to shoulder on the end of the pier, watching the dark, gray smoke clouds cover every inch of water, trees, and houses in their path, what none of us asked out loud was, if the fuel lines at the marina did indeed explode, where was Mrs. Renaud? For as long as I could remember, she sat in her umbrella chair at the edge of the dock—cash box in her lap, bottled Coke in her left hand, and a lit cigarette in the right. Every time we idled up to the pump on a Saturday morning, skis and hydro slide stashed in the back of the boat, she would toss us kids a free candy while Daddy fueled up. On our way out of the river, hours later with our arms and legs turned to Jell-O from tricks on the hydro slide and crashing into the water with each failed attempt at slalom skiing, we waved at Mrs. Renaud, still seated in her usual perch.

"Lauren, Jules, lower the boat," Daddy said, "Matt, Garrett, we'll need fuel."

Lauren, Matt's wife, and I rushed to the hand cranks while Matt and Garrett, Kate's husband, ran back down the pier.

"You're going over there?" Mama grabbed Daddy's arm and turned him to face her.

"We've got to," Daddy said. "Kate, get the first aid kits from the house. Jules, you, Matt and I will head over to the Marina. I want all the kids in the house. Nobody goes outside until we get back. Lauren, you and Garrett are going to take lookout. Mama, you grab the radio. Maybe they'll report something."

Lauren and I nodded to Daddy while turning the cranks. The 21' boat strained against the straps and cables while I tried to match my turns to Lauren's. If we got out of sync, the boat could slip from the sling and crash against the sandy bottom. Without the boat…well I prefer not to think about that. What I couldn't stop thinking about were the hot spots forming on my hands from the rough metal crank.

As the boat inched toward the choppy surface, Matt and Garrett returned with two red gas cans.

"This is it for gas until next week," Garrett said. A silent and collective panic caused all of us to pause for the briefest moment.

"We'll make do," Mama said. And that was it. The decision was made, not that any of us felt like we had much of a choice.

As soon as the boat bobbed in the water below, Matt, Daddy, and I loaded the supplies in the boat. Miraculously, the motor sputtered to life on the first try.

"Be careful!" Mama told us as we drove out of the boathouse and away from the pier. "Inside for the Rosary," were the last words I heard Mama say as we sped away.

With Matt at the helm and Daddy standing next to him, I sat in my usual spot—the cushioned, vinyl-top, live bait well in the bow facing the open water ahead. Matt pushed the throttle forward, forcing the boat to plane and pick up speed. Few places in the world ever felt more secure to me than my seat on the live well with Matt and Daddy behind me. But on that day, the ride felt different. I had no idea what we were heading for, as we bounced from wave to wave on the choppy bay.

A few minutes later, we reached the channel marker at the mouth of Fowl River. Matt veered right into the channel. Rumbling and cracking noises escaped the marina, hidden behind a jut of trees. The noises were low at first and then rose to a thunderous crash. The boat rocked violently back and forth in the growling mouth of the river. I fell off the vinyl seat, landing hard on the fiberglass bottom. Wedged between the hull and the side of the boat, I reached my hand up to the metal handrail and gripped the steel bar.

"Hold on!" Matt said, trying to steady the boat against the tall swells escaping the river.

I stared straight ahead, peering over the bow as we made the last turn into the marina, around the trees and metal bulkheads. A flock of pelicans in their V formation flew low over our heads, fleeing the scene. Broken boards, a bait bucket, and a life vest floated around the bend in the river. Trying to avoid the larger boards, Matt yanked the wheel to the right, then the throttle back, causing the back end of the boat to lurch sideways. The boat turned, nearly in a circle, allowing the horror before us to flash into view and then away again.

"What the hell?" Matt looked from Daddy to me and then tried to steady the boat so that we wouldn't end up in the water with the splintered trees, remains of small skiffs, scatterings of fishing equipment, and broken pieces of a bridge.

The Fowl River Bridge was gone, just gone. What had been a two-lane bridge arching over the marina and river was in ruins—nothing more than a series of broken columns and huge, jagged chunks of concrete bobbing up and down in the ink-black water. Mangled rowboats listed in the waves caused by the bridge tumbling into the water. A car, red, maybe a sedan, slowly sunk beneath the surface. An ambulance—probably the only ambulance owned by the Fowl River Volunteer Fire Department—sunk back end first, hood damaged and smoking as the water overtook it.

With the motor on idle, I heard the screaming.

"People are in the water! Pull closer!" I pointed to a man hanging on to his capsized rowboat in the middle of the black river.

"Jules, take the wheel," Matt ordered. When we reached the

man, I saw burns down his left side. Matt leaned over the side of the boat and pulled the man from the water, dragging him over the rails.

The man, exhausted from fighting the waves, cried, "I was under it," and then, in hysterics, "I was under it. Somethin' exploded."

"Pull up to the dock and tie off," Daddy said. I understood what he was afraid of; that if we drifted around any longer, we'd end up with a hole in the hull.

"There she is," Matt said, pointing to Mrs. Renaud standing on the dock.

Mrs. Renaud shouted to us as we tied off next to her. "The boys are in the water trying to get everybody out, but they could use help. Somebody blew up the damn bridge. Just balls of fire shootin' out of the damn thing till it fell in the river!"

Daddy grabbed the first aid kits and handed one to Mrs. Renaud. Together, they immediately started working on the man we pulled from the water. Matt and I kicked off our flip-flops and jumped in the water. We swam over to the first people we saw, a woman and a little boy holding on to an overturned kayak. We dragged the mother and her son out of the water along with two other pairings. After several minutes, and exhausted from fighting the panicked and wounded, I pulled myself up to the dock and tried to catch my breath before heading back into the water.

"See who's hurt," Daddy said and handed me gauze and tape.

Next to me on the dock was the first woman I pulled from the water. Her shirt was shredded, and her right arm was a blistered mess. I wrapped her arm with the gauze, unable to remember if I was supposed to wrap burns or not. I tried to be gentle, but the woman wailed with every touch.

"Who would do something like this?" she cried, clutching her son with her uninjured arm. The little boy, eight, maybe nine or ten, hadn't stopped crying since I pulled him from the water.

"I don't know." I checked the boy for any visible injuries. He barely had a scratch on him. "The bridge exploded?" I asked, wondering what was powerful enough to shred concrete.

Looking around, I saw injured anglers and former bank tellers, grocery store clerks and former factory workers turned survivalists. Before the conflict started, we all led ordinary lives, or so I thought. Naïve, really. To think, we were all happily rolling along while radicals prepared to burn this country to the ground. One of Mrs. Renaud's boys laid a tarp over someone, and I squeezed my eyes shut.

"Yeah, just fire shooting out of it, from under it," the woman said, shaking her head and staring at the scorched columns jutting out of the water. "The whole thing fell, almost on top of us. I heard cracking and then it fell." I left her with her son, rocking him back and forth as if he were an infant.

"Jules," Mrs. Renaud called to me, "Go in the shop and grab whatever cloth you can find and the jar of moonshine under the register. Hurry now! I need to clean these wounds."

Inside the aging store, I filled a basket with souvenir T-shirts. I grabbed a few bunches of twine and what looked to be a stack of sheets ripped into hand rags. Ducking under the counter, I found the moonshine. As I stood, the door crashed in and four soldiers rushed into the store, causing the bottle to slip from my hand and shatter as it hit the concrete floor.

"On the floor! Now!" The soldier nearest me pointed his rifle at my chest.

I dropped to the floor and felt him press my chest into the floor with his knee. He grabbed one of my wrists and then the other and pulled my arms behind me. Moonshine stung my eyes and shards of glass dug into my bare knees as I struggled to free myself.

"Stop!" I yelled as the soldier zip-tied my hands together behind my back. "Stop! Please!" My eyes blurred from the grain alcohol. My knees burned with cuts. Glass dug into my feet. "Please," I begged, but he ignored me.

"Outside!" the soldier yelled as he dragged me through the door.

Under the haze of dissipating smoke and the rising sun, oyster shells tore at my feet and buried the little slivers of glass deeper under my skin. The soldier pushed me down next to a woman and ordered me to sit on my knees.

"You, too, old lady," the soldier demanded.

"My knees don't bend like that no more, young man." As my eyes cleared, I saw Mrs. Renaud next to me, waving her cane at the soldier.

"On. The. Ground."

"Just get down," I pleaded, hoping the soldier would move on to someone else if we did what he told us to do.

Mrs. Renaud winced as she lowered herself to the ground, pressing her right hand against the oyster shells. She laid her cane between us and ducked her head, shielding her face from the gray dust floating in the wake of the soldier's heavy boots as he stomped away.

I craned my head over my shoulder, trying to look at my feet tucked under me. Tiny red rivers cut through the gray dirt and shells.

I snapped my head around toward the sound of Daddy's voice. He was still on the pier, kneeling next to an injured person. A soldier grabbed Daddy by the back of the collar and jerked him to his feet. Matt, on the dock as well, launched toward the soldier, but the soldier overpowered him. Within seconds, soldiers dragged Daddy and Matt to the parking lot, their hands bound behind their backs.

I winced and diverted my gaze back toward the dock. The woman I pulled from the water earlier clung to her son's arm, trying to stop a soldier from taking the boy from her. Her cries were louder than all the soldiers and the other screams of the wounded. "Don't take him! No!"

"Ma'am, the medics must treat you," a soldier yelled back at her, finally breaking her grip on the boy.

A medic cut away the rest of her shirt and the gauze I had wrapped around her arm, exposing burns covering her entire arm and most of her back. I did not know her injuries were so severe. I had pulled whomever I could reach out of the water, but I didn't look at any of them for too long. Now on my knees, I turned back to the crowd gathered in the parking lot, unable to look at the woman's burned body or her face contorted in agony.

In the parking lot, the soldiers segregated us with the men and boys on one side near the store, the women and girls on the other side of the lot near the boat slips. All of us sat on our knees with our feet tucked under us and our wrists tied together behind our backs. Several seagulls circled overhead, crazed over the chaos on the ground and in the water. The sounds of the wounded blended with the shrieking of the gulls. I shut my eyes and tried to block out the horrendous chorus. Tremors pinged through my body.

If my hands were free, I could wrap my arms around myself and squeeze until the panic faded. I couldn't make it stop. And I knew why. This was too much. Too soon. I was too raw. Losing Jacob with no warning stripped me of all my defenses. How could he leave me right before the world fell apart? How was I ever to be strong enough to think through this? Mama would tell me to, "Breathe. Focus on the water. Listen to the water," as she did for every nightmare of my childhood. How could I listen to the water when I can't hear it over the birds and crying? Why wouldn't they stop crying for two damn minutes so I could think? If Jacob had been there, he would've told me what to do. But he wasn't. It was just me.

Mrs. Renaud's voice broke through my panic. "Hey! Soldier boy! This girl needs help."

"No, Mrs. Renaud, I'm fine," I said after I realized she was directing the soldier at me. "I'm fine," I told the soldier, praying my knees stop burning and my feet stop bleeding and, for God's sake, make the tremors stop.

"Nobody's fucking moving or getting a damn thing until we find out what the hell happened!" the soldier closest to us told Mrs. Renaud.

"Well, the bridge blew up," Mrs. Renaud snapped back at him. "What does it look like?"

"Not the bridge, old lady! On the road! What the hell just happened on the road?" demanded the soldier.

"How would I know?" Mrs. Renaud said.

"Shut your damn mouth, lady," the soldier said. Turning to the rest of us, "One of you bay rats knows who just blew us up on the damn road and you're gonna tell us who it was."

"On the road?" I asked and immediately regretted opening my mouth.

"Yeah, on the road. On the road! Somebody blew us up and now two of my friends are splattered across the damn asphalt." The soldier paced back and forth in front of us, waving his rifle like he wanted to spray us with bullets. "Now, which one of you was it?" The soldier stopped right in front of me. He extended his rifle toward me, holding the barrel inches from my mouth.

"I swear I don't know," I said, inching backward on instinct. Tears poured down my cheeks as I stared at the barrel of his rifle. Two of his platoon were gone. Forever. "It wasn't me. I swear. We just came to help." I shook my head back and forth, staring at the soldier, praying that he wouldn't pull the trigger. "Please, please." I tucked my chin to my chest, trying to protect myself any way I could in case this soldier's emotions got the better of him.

"She doesn't know anything," Daddy yelled, pulling the soldier's attention and rifle away from me.

As the soldier stomped toward the men's side, my heart kicked in my chest, matching the throbbing in my feet and knees.

For a half hour, I kneeled on the oyster shells, trying to breathe through the pain. I softly rubbed my knees side-to-side. It hurt like hell, but I eventually pushed the shells to either side, revealing smoother dirt underneath. The blood on my feet and knees mixed with the dust from the oyster shells and formed grayish, ruddy sludge all around me.

I watched the soldier watch us, pacing back and forth in front of us while chain-smoking. As soon as one cigarette burned down to the butt, he stomped it out with his boot and lit a fresh one. His hands shook as he fumbled with his lighter. His rank showed that he was a specialist. In the Army for two, maybe three years. Even with all the grime and sweat, the plume of smoke casting a gray haze over his face, I could see how young he was. A baby of twenty, maybe twenty-one and finally able to enjoy a legal beer. But a baby all the same.

"You." A different soldier motioned to me. With his gun pointed at me, he ordered me to stand. I did and limped toward him. The oyster shells found undamaged skin, eviscerating the soles of my feet.

"Sit." Inside the store, the soldier motioned to a chair placed between the cashier counter and the empty racks that used to hold sunscreen and chips.

Another soldier snipped the plastic band free from my wrist and handed me a towel and a bottle of rubbing alcohol. "You'll want to clean those scrapes."

"Thank you," I said. The solution burned like hell and revealed dozens of cuts on the balls of my feet and deep in my heels. So much broken glass.

"What's your name?" the soldier asked, screwing the cap back on the bottle.

"Jules Jones, um Jules Martin."

"Which is it?"

"Jules Jones, my maiden name is Martin."

I looked up from tending my feet and saw an Army captain standing in the doorway. His nametag said Johnson, and he sported hoo-ah tabs on his uniform—Ranger tab, dive bubbles, airborne wings, combat patch. *Badge hunter*. Jacob's signature sarcasm slid into my mind. That was exactly what I needed.

"What happened to your feet?" Johnson asked me.

"I dropped a bottle when your soldiers busted in here," I said. "They slammed me to the floor and hog-tied me like a criminal." I did my best to keep my voice flat. Whatever badass I tried to be in that moment wasn't very convincing.

"Uh-huh," Johnson said, seemingly unaffected.

"Then they dragged me across oyster shells and forced me to kneel on the ground. Is that what you've trained them to do?"

"Are you an EMT? Out fishing this morning? Working for the Renauds?" Johnson asked. "What business did you have here?"

"We heard explosions and saw smoke from our pier. We came to help."

"Who's we?"

"My dad, brother, and me."

"So, you all just loaded up and rode over here just in case someone needed your help? That's awfully generous. Awfully *fortuitous*."

Ignoring his sarcasm, I said, "I'm sorry to hear about your guys, but we had nothing to do with that. Whoever did this had access to a lot of explosives, which we do not. So why don't you go fuck around with someone else?" The skin around my cuts began to dry, intensifying the pain, which clouded my judgement and made it nearly impossible to be anything but enraged.

"Ms. Martin, I'm not fucking around. I've got two dead men. That's two letters I've got to write. Two mothers to notify. So, pardon me if your cuts and scrapes aren't my top priority right now." Johnson stepped toward me. "Who did this, huh? Tell me. Who?"

"I don't know. I told you that already."

"Yes, you do, Miss Jones."

"No, I don't, Johnson."

"My name is *Captain* Johnson." He spat his name and with it, little beads of spittle landed on my chin. Then he turned to one soldier. "Get her out of here. She doesn't know shit."

A soldier pulled me from the chair. As my feet touched the floor, pain surged up both legs, and I fell. The shards of glass felt like nails driving into my feet. I gasped for a few seconds and crawled toward the door, preferring to be back on the shells than inside the store with Captain Johnson for one more second.

"Stop," Johnson said. He stepped over me and opened the door in front of me. "Martin! Come get your girl! Cut him free!" I looked up to see a soldier cut the ties from Daddy's wrists. "Is that your brother with your dad there?"

"Yes," I said.

"Cut the son free, too." Johnson stooped down to look at me eye-level. "Tell your father not to go anywhere tonight. I'm going to want to speak to him. If he runs, I'll know he's my guy."

"You're looking in the wrong direction. Your culprits are across the river, not up the shore."

Matt scooped me off the floor and carried me to the boat, carefully lowering me onto the back seat. Daddy cranked the motor and pulled away from the marina into the open water of the bay, the midday sun hanging hot overhead. Every few seconds, he looked back from the helm, his deep brown eyes softening when he looked at me. After a few minutes on the choppy waves, I leaned my head over the side and vomited.

———

"Perhaps if I show you my knees and feet, you'll remember me." I say to Captain Johnson, who seems more preoccupied with the swarming gnats than trespassing on private property and eyeing the lookout like a box of Krispy Kremes. "Or do you injure so many people in your pursuit of law and order that I'm just one of many?"

"The shop. At the marina," he says, and stops swatting at the bugs, perhaps out of the smallest bit of recognition.

"Yes, the marina," I say.

"Why didn't y'all ever arrest the guys who did that? It seems fairly simple to me." Matt's tone increases the tension in the air and my desire to beat Johnson with my paddle. Matt gives me a look of *don't*. "Either Liberty's Guard has more folks down here, or The Knights came into a cache of explosives, or they're working together now. Those are the only folks I can think of to pull off something that big."

"There's more to it than just comin' up with a theory, no matter how valid your suspicions," Billy Roberts says.

Captain Johnson eyes his subordinate, as if Billy revealed some juicy secret. But everyone knows. If the Army didn't blow the bridge, that left Liberty's Guard—another nut-job like Clayton Vancleave—or The Knights. But Liberty's Guard disappeared months ago. The Knights, however, had set up shop just across the river on Mon Luis Island in the shadow of the bridge.

"The bridge explosion and roadside bomb that killed two of my men are why we're here today."

"As I explained to you on the day the bridge exploded, we had nothing to do with that. Or are you here to arrest us for something we didn't do?"

"No, ma'am, we know your family had nothing to do with either bombing. You've been cleared of all suspicion on the matter."

"Well, hallelujah for that," Matt says.

"We're here today to walk this land and Goat Island," Johnson says.

"Why?" I ask. "We're not hiding anything out here, if that's what you think."

Billy reaches out and touches my arm. "It's not like that, Jules. We need a satellite base of sorts."

"And you're thinking that our property is up for grabs?" Matt asks.

"No," replies Johnson. "This is County property. Hunting on a piece of land," Johnson says, motioning toward the useless mist net, and then, "does not equal ownership."

"Well, a deed does," I say.

"Do you have that?" Johnson asks.

"On me?" The pitch in my voice raises to almost a screech. *Dial it back,* Jacob's voice coaches. *Calm. Low.* "I'm sure Daddy can produce it for you."

"Is your dad home?" Billy asks.

"Where else would he be?" Matt replies.

Billy lets out an exhausted sigh and smiles at me. "Why don't we go see him and talk about this? We'll clear all this up."

The last time I saw Billy Roberts was at Sunday mass just after our senior year in high school. Every Sunday, Billy and his family sat a few rows in front of us. I spent most homilies staring at the back of his head, wondering what it would be like to kiss him. Two weeks before Senior Prom, I conjured up every bit of courage I had and walked into the now empty mom-and-pop grocery store. Billy was stocking canned tuna alongside the other potted meats. I'm not sure what ridiculous words came out of my mouth, but he said yes. At midnight on prom night, I got my kiss and a world of disappointment. Sloppy kisser I could've worked with, but that kissing-your-friend feeling of *no feeling at all* was a deal breaker. I practically heard the air hiss from my balloon of anticipation. Billy skipped the after party and one month later genuflected before entering his family's usual pew, his head freshly shaven. The next morning, he left for basic training.

"Daddy bought this piece right after you left for basic, Billy," I say, and he glances at me with the boyish face that made frequent appearances in my teenage daydreams, prior to that one kiss at prom, of course.

"Well, we'll figure this out," Johnson says, swiping through the air at more gnats, then pulling bug spray from a cargo pocket of his uniform pants.

"The sprays don't really work on those things," I tell him. "If you're around long enough, you'll get used to them."

"They're driving me nuts." Johnson allows a split second of a smile, then quickly returns to his *mission first* posture. Glancing at Matt, he asks, "Do you have a permit for that weapon?"

The Army tracks everyone's weapons, trying to ensure that guns land in good hands, or at least *approved* hands. Matt's permit, fished from his front shirt pocket, satisfies Captain Johnson. Whereas we've never thought to carry land deeds around with us, Matt learned early in martial law to keep his hunting, fishing, and gun permits handy.

Overhead, the sun is in full bloom and the air feels like a wet blanket stuck to my face. "If that's all you need from us, we need to get this net down and get back home," I say.

"Do so. We need this area cleared of all snares and traps. Anything you've got out here will have to go," Captain Johnson says.

I glare at Johnson, wondering what part of the great green line convinced him that harassing civilians was part of his mission. "I'm not doing it for you. I need to repair it. What you need to do is get ahold of the assholes across the river. My money is on them for damaging this net and blowing up the bridge."

Billy shoots me a look as if to say, "Shut it, Jules." I crack a half smile in his direction then move to the next knot. Billy says something to Johnson too low for me to hear, then they both walk away without another word.

"Jules, what the hell was that?" Matt asks, sure that Billy and Captain Johnson are well out of earshot, having disappeared through the trees.

"What can I say? I didn't like his attitude."

"What happened to 'They can do plenty' and all that from this morning? Now, you want to poke the bear? You don't know that guy or how he's gonna react."

"I know that guy plenty." I stare at Matt as the last knot falls free from the pole, and the net drops to the ground. Matt stares back at me. "Oh, just say it."

"Say what?"

"Say it. 'Jules, you're acting irrationally. You've got to get it together, Jules.' I know that's what you think of me."

Matt jerks one end of the net off the ground. "I said nothing like that, *Jules*. I know you're hurting. I know you've lost more than any of us, but I didn't say a damn word."

"Well, maybe you should." I feel the flood gates weakening with months and months of rage pressing them open. "Maybe if someone, anyone, in this family, would talk about him. I'm not so fragile that the mention of his name would crush me." I wait for Matt to respond, but he doesn't. His silent pity is more than I can take. "You know, Matt, maybe too many months of living like a damn pioneer has used all my patience and politeness and every ounce of my damn grace. Aren't I allowed at least one year of inappropriate behavior? I've no way to blow through life insurance money or drink into oblivion or hike the damn Alps in search of my true self, so yelling at anyone and everyone who shares responsibility for screwing up my life will have to do."

Matt drops the net and wraps me in his arms. My body shakes as weeks without allowing a complete breakdown rush out. I glance down through my tears. "You're standing on my net."

"I'm pretty sure that net is the least of our problems."

Shrugging my agreement, I break out of Matt's bear hug and take a deep breath. He stares at me with all the compassion a little brother can give his older sister. "Stop that, Matt. Message sent, message received. I'm broken and you're determined to fix me."

4

B ack home and with my kayak securely hidden and tied in the rafters of the boathouse, I cut through the main house on my way to the garage to check my dwindling fishing line supply. The mist net is probably a goner, but for the love of eating something other than fish I'll try a repair.

"The lights are on?" I ponder when Alabama Power restored the electricity and how long power will last this time. One day or one week or will the A-holes finally blow the grid for good? And how long before we run out of linemen and repair persons altogether?

"Yes," Kate says, and bumps me out of her way with her hip.

In the kitchen, Mama and Kate flit around in their special brand of crazy, busy preparing dinner. Most nights during the week, dinner is a chore, but every couple of weeks, Mama and Kate plan something special, even if all we have worth celebrating is a working stove and AC. I would never admit this out loud and certainly not to them, but I love their frivolous party prep. It's one relic of my old world that's alive and well in my new world. I refuse to say "new normal" because none of this is normal and never will be. Don't ask me to say it. I live in a country that put a man on the moon, but it can't control the anar-chists and fear mongers. I swear the extremists are in a foot race to prove who's more insane by torturing the rest of us with power outages.

"Did I see soldiers out front with Daddy?" Mama asks, her face red with the stress of party prep. There is a distinct *what-now-sweet-Jesus* in Mama's voice.

"Matt and I ran into them at the lookout. They're taking the land."

The heat in Mama's cheeks moves to her voice. "Did you tell them we own that land?"

"Yes, but ownership doesn't matter."

"Why not?"

"Because if the federal government needs your land for national security, they get to use it. As long as martial law—" Mama's face contorts like she wants to slap me with something hard; anything within hand's reach will do. "Mom, I'm just the messenger." And an idiot one at that. When will I learn Mama ran out of patience and logic months ago?

"Fine. Fine. I don't have time for this today. I need to get this in the oven before we lose power again or it will be skillet spoon bread for birthday cake again. Is Jessie's present ready?" Mama's gaze shifts from angry with other people to *you best say yes or it's a plate to the back of the head.*

I love Mama to the moon and back, and she would stand in front of a moving train if it meant the train misses me. But no one has ever accused her of having complete control over her emotions. She might be the international queen of sweating the small stuff, such as a birthday dinner and present in the middle of the apocalypse.

"Yes, ma'am. I just need to wrap it," I tell her and take a step back, out of arm's reach. "Which I'm going to do right now."

Today is Jessie's birthday, my first niece, the one that made me an aunt. She is twelve today. Typically, the twelfth birthday is when girls in the Martin clan have their ears pierced, but without a salon or tiny gold studs, that won't happen. It's just as well. Jessie shed anything remotely girlie as soon as she could rip her dresses off at age three. So, weeks ago, I talked Mama into letting me dismantle two of her Dooney and Bourke handbags to make Jessie a present, one befitting her and no one else. After three weeks of punching holes through the leather and lacing skinny leather strips through the holes, I created a patchwork backpack for her, reminiscent of my punk days, where nothing was to look new or mass-produced.

My punk phase comprised a bunch of Southern, middle-class tweens and teens trying to recreate the punk movement that stormed through London and New York ten years prior to all of us in Mobile, Alabama. I discovered the Ramones, The Clash, and the Sex Pistols, and the music felt like a revolution, a profound revolt against the constraints of Catholicism. Great taste in music. Piss poor timing being born.

The strap of Jessie's bag is the belt I wore to Jacob's last promotion ceremony at Fort Stewart. It was wide, braided leather and looked quite stylish, paired with my forest green geometric design dress and knee-high boots. A few of Jacob's old carabiners dangle from various straps and seams, ready for necessities or frivolities—her choice. I hope Jessie will have the chance to leave this place, to explore the world beyond Bellefontaine as I did. Maybe she'll fill the bag with her essentials, toss it over her shoulder, and head out to make her own adventures. One day. Maybe.

"Jules," Mama says to me, and a bit sharply, might I add. "Did you hear me? I asked who the soldiers are? Did you meet them?"

"One of them is Billy Roberts. He's back, stationed here now. The other—"

Kate cuts me off. "Really? How does he look?"

"Older," I reply.

"Does he look married?" asks Kate.

"He looks like a soldier," I say, hoping the inference of *I'm not trading one dead soldier for another soldier* is clear.

"Girls, we don't have time for this. Power." Mama points to the working overhead light while heading to her familiar, pre-party state of spinning around like a top, so I head toward the door.

"Jules," Mama calls to my back, "Check the chicken coop. I think we're missing one or two."

This stops me cold. "Was the lock on the coop when you got the eggs?" I ask, turning to see her cracking eggs into a mixing bowl.

"Yes. I might have miscounted. Just check it, okay?" Mama wipes her forehead with a towel, glares at me, then looks back inside the bowl. "Dammit, how many eggs was that?" She drops the towel and counts the shiny, yellow yolks in her bowl, pointing one index finger at each golden blob.

————

At dusk, Mama and Kate light the torches around the picnic tables out back, to fend off the mosquitos and for light. The grid went dark again about a half hour ago, which means everyone is annoyed. We always hope for more time with the lights on, even if the lights attract bugs of all kinds. At least Mama and Kate had finished with the oven by then.

Seven place settings adorn the adults' table and six on the kids' table. Down the center of the adult table, Fiestaware platters display the night's feast of fried fish, greens and baked cornbread. Bottles of Mama's homemade wine for the adults fill the spaces between the platters. A jug of diluted blackberry juice sits in the center, waiting to dispense refills for the kids.

Seated at the head of the adult table, Daddy makes the sign of the cross and bows his head, silencing everyone, even little Mallie. "Bless us, oh Lord and these, your gifts, which we are about to receive from your bounty, through Christ our Lord. Amen." I stifle a laugh at the thought. *God, if you would, put a little more effort into your bounty.* Mama and Daddy would be so disappointed with my inner monologue.

Getting food, kids, and adults to the dinner table, weaving around lit torches and a pot of still sizzling oil, is a feat of timing and fire-prevention, but Lauren does her best to threaten the kids. "The first one of you to move off that bench gets to pick out the switch." I think the kids know she'd never use a switch on them, but they do a good job of acting intimidated.

Lauren needn't worry. No one's leaving the table tonight without devouring every crumb. Tonight's feast is special and not just because of Jessie's birthday. Matt and I bartered eggs, wine, and a sack of dried fish for cooking oil, baking powder, chocolate, white flour, and cornmeal. I felt awful trading shriveled, salted fish for the last of an old woman's baking powder and chocolate, but she agreed to the deal. By the looks of her, she needed the protein. Tonight, my first bite of Mama's corn bread pushes that nagging guilt right down my throat, and a sip of blackberry wine washes away any pesky guilt residue. Garrett fried the mullet to a crisp, which makes it surprisingly appetizing. It could use some lemon, but the lemons aren't ripe yet. And later, there will be cake. Not spoon sweet bread, close-your-eyes-and-pretend it's cake, but real, honest to God, chocolate cake. With icing, or something that looks an awful lot like icing. Chocolate icing.

"Matt, you're going to eat yourself sick." Mama can't hide the smile on her face as she mothers her youngest baby, her only boy.

Matt grins and piles a second helping of the cornbread and two additional pieces of fish on his plate, having gobbled down his first helping in record time. He turns to Daddy, chewing while he speaks, "Are we going to talk about what the Army wants with our land and why they think it's theirs for the taking?"

"Not much to discuss," Daddy says. "They want the lookout and surrounding land. So, they're going to pay us for it." Daddy reaches out and pops Matt's hand as he goes for a third helping of bread.

"Hey! I'm a growing boy, Daddy."

"You ain't getting any taller, son." Daddy gestures to Matt's non-existent belly, as if any of us need worry about weight gain when at any moment the food could run out. Perhaps if we had a reliable refrigerator or a way to store leftovers, we would save food for tomorrow. But, we don't. So, when food is available, we eat all that we can. No wasting food around here. On nights like these, when the serving platters and wine carafes overflow, we all breathe easier even though we know a slim day, week, or month could be right around the corner.

"You're selling the land to them?" Garrett swallows, then continues. "What do we need with money? It's all worthless paper now."

Daddy chews and swallows a big bite of fish before answering. "Propane and gasoline. They are *renting* the land in exchange for propane and gasoline."

"How much?" Matt asks.

"Twenty-five gallons of each a week. Enough that we won't have to worry about blackouts anymore. Enough that we can use the boat more."

"We could run the fridge," Lauren says, smiling at Matt.

Even with a plate full of fried mullet and greens in front of me, I salivate at the idea of never having to eat canned or dried fish again. Once the blackouts became frequent, the refrigerator became useless. Everything we catch, we cook immediately or dry and store.

"They want to use the lookout?" asks Matt. "For what?"

"From the top of the old deck, you can see the whole marshland, all the way to the mouth of Fowl River," I say. "They'll have a straight shot of the old bridge." Floating bodies and burned, jagged columns flash in my mind. That utility truck bobbing in the water comes to me, too, and a section of concrete dragging a skiff under as it sank to the bottom of the river.

"We'd be a lot safer with them there," Daddy says. "It'd put the Army between us and Mon Louis Island."

"Does this mean they've finally identified The Knights as a threat?" I ask.

"They didn't say, but I imagine that's who they'd be monitoring. It'd be pretty easy to watch comings and goings on Mon Louis Island from the lookout."

"What's to keep them from *keeping an eye* on us?" Matt exchanges a look with Lauren, then grabs the last bite of cornbread off her plate.

"Matt, stop. We've got enough to worry about without looking for trouble." I turn back to Daddy. "What about the land around it? Can I still use it? That's prime hunting ground." For me, hunting equals a chance to get away, a respite from my loving but sometimes suffocating family.

"No, we'd have to stay clear."

"Can we still use the water around it?" Matt asks.

"They didn't say," Daddy replies. "But I'd bet they want all civilians to stay clear."

Garrett, out of reach of Daddy's hand, grabs another piece of fish from the platter. "So, in exchange for some fuel, we lose our land and possibly fishing grounds? I vote no."

"Garrett, that's not how martial law works," I say.

"Now, wait a second," Mama chimes in, "this fuel could really help. The rations just aren't enough."

"Your mother is right. We can run the fridge. Twenty-five

gallons of gasoline will run a car, the Gator, and the boat. And we wouldn't have to trade for it anymore."

"We're giving up our land for it. I'd say that's one hell of a trade," Garrett says. "You sure it's worth it?"

"Mama and Daddy will give up land for it, Garrett." For the hundredth time, I glance from Kate to Garrett and try to figure out what she sees in him. Garrett—a thousand-acre peanut farmer turned vegetable gardener, apocalypse prepper, and guard dog— knows my mother well, which buttons to push and how to keep her happy. Give her what she needs to keep the wine barrels bubbling, the food cooking. Give her what she needs to love her family, and she's set right. Garrett knows Mama so well that when he and Kate decided it was no longer safe to stay on their farm, Garrett stopped at every grocery store between Silverhill and Bellefontaine and bought every pack of yeast in stock, wine yeast or otherwise. One day, I'll remember to thank him for his foresight. But tonight is not that day. I can see his wheels turning, grinding through the ways to manipulate Mama until he gets what he wants. The problem is, he isn't exactly forthcoming with his desires, choosing instead to twist words and bend circumstances to his advantage, and I swear I don't know how my very smart sister can't see it.

"Again, Garrett, this is a reality of martial law," I say. "What Captain Johnson wants, he gets. Honestly, Johnson doesn't have to give us a thing for the land—"

"So, we just roll over?" Kate asks me.

"More like bend over."

Kate elbows Garrett. "Vulgar!"

I drop my fork onto my plate and glare at Garrett. "Can we please just eat in peace? There is not a thing you, Garrett, can do to stop this, so please just accept it and shut your mouth. I, for one, am very grateful for this meal and everyone who contributed to it and would love to eat without all the combativeness."

"Combative?" Garrett snaps.

"That's enough from you two," Daddy commands.

Mama perks up, her wheels turning, and clearly not about Garrett and my most recent butting of the heads. "Would they be willing to throw in cooking oil? What we've got now is tasting burnt." Even amid a crisis, she is the eternal bargain shopper.

"I'll see about negotiating the terms," Daddy says.

"Now, hold on." Matt swallows a big bite of fish, then continues. "You don't think all this extra fuel will draw unwanted attention? Everybody around here knows exactly how much fuel each family is supposed to get."

"Yeah," agrees Lauren, caressing her husband's forearm with her thumb. "Matt's right."

"We'll store it in the shed, son," says Daddy. "There is no reason for anyone outside of us to know how much fuel we have."

"Well, we'll have to set up security rotations," cautions Matt. "We're already losing crab traps. The net is practically shredded. I'm sure everybody 'round here would love to get their hands on more fuel. We had a boat full of Knights scoping out the house this morning."

"We had what?" Mama asks.

"Don't worry," Matt says. "Just some jackass Knights hoping for an easy catch. I don't think they'll be back. Unless, of course, Jules gives 'em cause to."

"What is that supposed to mean?" Mama asks.

I kick Matt in the shin beneath the table. "Somebody needs to get control over them." Standing, I reach over Kate for the wine and top off my glass. "The way they were eyeing the fish and the entire property this morning was creepy. They were definitely casing the place."

Daddy glares at me. "Julianne, you have no proof of that. We don't know who is doing this, stealing from us or otherwise. But we know we can leave that up to the Army. If something needs doing, they will do it."

Mama piles on. "You said it yourself, Jules. We don't need to go looking for trouble."

"Agreed." Daddy leans forward, resting his elbows on the table. "We'll need more security. Shifts from everyone, got it? Round the clock." Daddy waits for a nod from all of us. "We need more fuel, and I'd rather get it this way than trade for it at Market Days."

"Going to Market Days is fine, Daddy," I tell him.

"No. It's just a matter of time before something happens there, and I don't want you there when it does." Daddy still makes me feel twelve sometimes.

"And how will it look when everybody sees soldiers all over our land?" Garrett asks. "As soon as they set up shop, we are no longer neutral in this…whatever it is. We'll be on their side."

"Who's side?" Mama asks.

"Theirs. The Army's. The Knights will portray us as supporting martial law and against everybody else. That's what all of this is about. All The Knights want is to be left alone and live freely. And I gotta say, I'm tired of the curfews and rations and all this shit. I can't blame them for being angry enough to do something."

"Garrett," I say, "How are you being inconvenienced by the curfews? Do you have somewhere you need to be? Places to go late at night?"

"Yes, I do. I need to be back on *my* land. My farm. Instead, I'm here helping all of you. Who knows what I've got to go home to?"

Kate intercedes. "Corners, you two."

"Garrett, we all know what you've given up for this family, and we are grateful." Mama reaches across Kate to squeeze Garrett's hand.

"And you may be right about looking like we've chosen a side, but like I said before, we don't have a choice. Mama and I have to let the Army use the land. All I can do at this point is to negotiate the terms." Daddy wipes his mouth and hands with the dish towel in his lap, then sets it beside his empty plate.

The rat-tat-tat of gunfire halts the conversation and stiffens each one of us. I try to calculate the location and distance, but sound is unreliable at best out here.

Matt breaks the silence. "That was a good two miles away."

For months, we've lived out of sight and mind of the Army and homegrown militias, happily isolated from the rest of the world. But as the chaos of Mobile spilled into the county lands and crept down the shoreline, the realities of martial law became the new normal. Road blocks and vehicle inspections. Curfews and rationing. The law of the land went from Sherriff Department uniforms and State Trooper cruisers to camouflaged combat uniforms, tactical gear, and up-armored Humvees.

Army patrols started, sparse at first with a couple of Humvees rolling along Bay Air Road once a week, driving through the ditch to avoid resident-made barricades built of old tires and pier boards to keep the bug men out and the home-owners alive. One day, when the thunder became so loud, like a lightning crash right on top of us, we couldn't pretend the explosions were thunder anymore. Someone was setting IEDs in Bellefontaine. That's when the Army patrols increased to every few hours and the barricades came down. The Knights' signature K began appearing on hulls, doors, and random road signs. Or maybe it was the other way around. I can't remember which I noticed first.

"If the soldiers are to the south of us, then we only have to worry about trespassers from three sides." Daddy spoke in a gentle tone, defending his actions and reassuring us that entering an agreement with the Army was the safest play.

"No, we have plenty more to worry about," interrupts Garrett, "Trust me, you don't want to start this."

My brother-in-law's fears are valid. Getting friendly with the Army will surely make us the enemy of others, but Daddy shakes his head and takes a deep breath, exhaling slowly. "There's no more discussion needed on this. There is no vote. The Army needs the land, so the Army gets the land. There's no fighting this." Daddy sips his wine, grimacing at the tart concoction. "Matt, make sure the kayaks and green bottom boat are ready for church in the morning."

"Yes, sir," Matt says.

Daddy stands and takes Mama's hand in his. "Let's walk out on the pier," he tells her. Then, to the rest of us, he says, "Call us when y'all are ready for dessert."

Once Mama and Daddy are around the corner, Garrett starts up again. "Come on, Matt, do you really want the Army all over our land?"

"No, I don't," says Matt. "But that much fuel is awful tempting."

"Daddy's right about the perimeter," I say. "And the need for security shifts."

"Yeah, sure, we won't have to watch the south for trespassers anymore, but we'll damn sure have to watch for soldiers. What's gonna keep *them* from trespassing?" asks Garrett, clearly agitated. "And you know there's more than one way to get here from there. Mark my words. With soldiers all over the lookout…well that's just gonna make us targets." He swallows, finally, then repeats, "*Targets*, Jules."

"Well, add that to your list of shit we can't do a thing about."

"Language, Jules," Kate warns. "The kids can hear you."

"Yes, by all means, I'll watch my language." *While the fucking world burns.*

I volunteer for the first night shift on the pier. With the power out again, the house is a hotbox, so I jump at the chance to spend the evening on a swing on the end of the pier with a nice breeze blowing around me, a shotgun at my side and a few shells in my pocket. I don't intend to shoot anyone. The chk-chk of the pump action should be scary enough.

Around 2 a.m., a soft thud startles me. In the dark, the figure near the locked gear closet is too short for a full onslaught and I prefer the "ask questions first, shoot later" approach. I cock the shotgun and that signature *chk-chk* freezes the small shadow where it stands. The assertion that cocking a shotgun is as effective as shooting a shotgun is accurate. I'm counting on that.

When the figure turns toward me, my stomach drops as a grave reality hits me. I am pointing a loaded gun at a child. A boy. A skinny, short boy with light colored hair and big round eyes above rounded, full cheeks. Definitely a kid. This is my life now. Holding a kid at gunpoint.

"Go. Please don't come back. Just go."

The boy scurries to the crab pier, down the ladder, and into a small skiff he'd tied off the crab pier. I lower the gun, but not my gaze. I keep that on the boy as he rows away, and he keeps his gaze on me.

No way I'm falling asleep tonight.

5

EFFECTIVE IMMEDIATELY: Unauthorized personnel are prohibited on Goat Island and the surrounding waterways. Pass-through traffic limited to residents with proof of residency. No POVs. All fishing, crabbing, and hunting on Goat Island and the surrounding land and waterways prohibited. VIOLATORS WILL BE DETAINED.

"Shit," I say then shove the flyer into my pocket.

"Watch your language, young lady." Matt walks up behind me then grabs ahold of my shoulders. "You're in a church, for God's sake."

"I'm in the parking lot. Look at this."

Matt glances over the flyer.

"Not so funny, huh?"

Matt hands the flyer back to me. "What's a POV?"

"Personally owned vehicles. It means we can't drive anything —cars, trucks, boats—through the area. They'll have it all marked off limits."

Minutes before this discovery, we stood together, the entire Martin clan, inside St. Philip Neri Church listening to the priest's final blessing. A distant *whop, whop, whop* outside grew louder and louder, nearly drowning out Father Morgan's prayer. Like little prairie dogs, all six of my nieces and nephews looked straight up, trying to peer through the yellow pine ceiling. Without raising their heads, four parents placed a hand on the child closest to them. Their gentle touch warning against adding to the distraction.

Whop, whop, whop. Deafening. Close. Helicopters. I knew the sound anywhere. I grew used to their constant percussion while living on Fort Hood, an ever-present background noise. Nightly, Jacob and I sat on our back porch, heads craned to the sky to watch the pilots train in the Black Hawks—a perfectly choreographed, loud-as-hell ballet.

But these helicopters, the ones circling over Bellefontaine now, their spinning blades ear-splitting, are not training. They are doing. What is baffling is that they need to be doing what they trained for here, in their own country.

As a child and teenager of Bellefontaine, helicopters flew over the coastline surveying damage after each hurricane, another indication that a bad storm had passed through. The helicopters were a welcome sight to the hardest hit—bright orange Coast Guard choppers, dark green Army Hueys and Apaches. They flew from just south of Downtown from Brookley Field to Dauphin Island, passing over Dog River, Hollinger's Island, Bellefontaine, Mon Luis Island, and Alabama Port along their way. They brought supplies to those cut off by flood waters, downed trees, and debris. They showed up a day or two after each storm, then disappeared one, two, or three weeks later, once recovery had begun in earnest.

Now, the *whop, whop, whop* signals patrols and flyer-drops, medical evacuations and an "eye in the sky." They watch all of us. Watch us until it's time to be among us, and that's never a good thing. Their flyer drops deliver bad news—warnings, new rules, various hits to constitutional rights we took for granted, or used to before all this. Anything that a sane person wouldn't want to tell someone face-to-face. Today's flyer makes one thing clear: The Army controls Bellefontaine—at least optically. Sure, Daddy still technically owns his land, but the Army is officially lord of the serfdom, our ever-present overseer.

"Come on, guys, let's get home," I say, stooping to pick up a couple of flyers from the ground. "Mama, Daddy, we need to go." I don't want to be in the uproar this latest prohibition will surely cause. Because it doesn't matter that Goat Island wasn't a favorite hunting spot for many people here. It's the fact that the Army is now ensconced here. No more flying over to check in on us then fly home. They will live right here with us.

Mama, assisted by Mrs. Renaud ignores me, choosing instead to de-litter the parking lot of Army flyers. Her every bend toward the asphalt announces itself with a sharp inhale and slow exhale.

Daddy motions for everyone to move toward the walking path, which will lead us back to the boat and kayaks and home. "Jules is right. Let's go."

"Well, Daddy, let me check the Tabernacle." Mama clearly underestimates the situation as she heads back up the church steps.

I tug on her arm, trying to reroute her. "Mama, we need to go."

"What if Father Morgan forgot to lock it? Anyone could just walk in the church, open the Tabernacle and take whatever's in there. Then what'll we do next week? You know we're running low." With that, she disappears into the church.

When the world was normal, nuns in some far-off place made the communion wafers, or *Host*. That was then. Now, no deliveries. The wine deliveries stopped even faster, within weeks of Clayton Vancleave's poison attack. Truckers simply refused to drive through Mobile. Once word of that reached Bellefontaine,

Mama went to work on wine and communion wafer recipes, claiming it was her sacred Catholic duty. However, no matter how much Mama loves the Lord, she doesn't trust all of God's creations, not even our parish priest. So, each Sunday morning before we leave the church, Mama goes behind Father Morgan to doublecheck the old man did his job properly. One day, St. Peter's going to question Mama about her lack of trust.

Mama's even a bit suspicious of Father Morgan, swearing to smell wine on his breath prior to Mass one Sunday morning. "This is the Eucharistic wine." She tells him that every Sunday now. "I hope there'll be enough for this week and next."

"Matt, help me get everyone moving." I shove two more flyers into my pocket and count Martins. *Two, four, eleven, twelve. Dammit, Mama, come on!*

We need to get far away from here. God will forgive the litter, but these amped-up rednecks won't be so gracious. No one with the last name Martin or a drop of Martin blood needs to be in this parking lot when this crowd realizes that Goat Island is now in the hands of the Army. It's one thing for the Army to use the land. It's entirely another to ban use of a waterway. *Thou shalt share the water* might as well be the eleventh commandment.

"We really need to go, Matt," I say, watching Garrett stomp toward us, waving a flyer in each hand. "Now."

I turn away from Garrett, hoping he takes his frustrations elsewhere, or bottles them up for the first time in his life. My gaze goes across the street to the original church, a tiny wooden chapel used for youth services. The white paint is nearly chipped clean, revealing weathered, bare wood. One of the forest green doors hangs cock-eyed on a broken hinge and has a large K on it, tagged for The Knights with spray paint.

Rumor is that if you want to live under the protection of The Knights, all you need do is sit on the steps of the wooden chapel and wait. Someone will be around shortly to escort you to their compound. Those steps will fill soon with the desperate and the hungry. Restrictions rather than trust. Limits rather than support. Flyer drops rather than real communication. The Army's actions will only strengthen allegiance to The Knights.

"Did you see this? I told you! I told you the Army doesn't need to be on our land." Garrett's voice sounds an alarm.

"What part of Daddy had no choice do you not understand?" I try to keep my voice low, but within seconds, confusion turns to anger, and the crowd ignites.

"Hey, Martin," the younger of Mrs. Renaud's two sons calls out to Daddy, "Did you sell your land to them?"

"Are you two happy?" Garrett whispers to Matt and me. "The whole damn town is gonna be against us in about two minutes."

"You're not helping." I give Garrett my best shut-the-hell-up look and reach for Matt's arm but the nudge of a metal cane pushes me aside.

Mrs. Renaud, barely five feet tall but every inch salt water and spitfire, calls out to Daddy, "Matthew Martin, what on Earth is going on here?" She waves her cane in the air and nearly smacks me in the face. "Did you do this? Did you put me in the crossfire? Everything I got left in this world right in the middle?"

"Mrs. Renaud, we didn't involve you in this at all." As soon as the words escape my mouth, I know I made a mistake.

"Didn't involve me? Girly, did you forget where the marina is? Or, rather what's left of it? Right between your Daddy's Goat Island and Mon Luis. You think The Knights are—"

I cut her off before she finishes the thought, whatever she was going to say about The Knights. I have no idea how many Knight sympathizers are among the crowd. "I apologize. I just meant this is nothing to worry about, really."

The Renaud family has been in Bellefontaine for generations. As a child, I flipped through Daddy's old photo albums, looking at pictures of Daddy as a teenager with his cousins and the

Renauds jumping off my Paw Paw's pier. We buried Mr. Renaud one month after Clayton Vancleave gassed Mobile. Mrs. Renaud swears he died of a broken heart after seeing what Clayton did. The rest of the Renauds survived by running the filling station and marina store, flipping burgers and frying shrimp in the small restaurant. Then shipping stopped—no more burgers and fries if drivers refuse to drive south of Birmingham or east of Baton Rouge. Blackouts began. Rumors of foreign attacks and home-grown radicalism. Then, the Fowl River Bridge exploded, destroying most of the marina with it. Now, the Renauds scrape by with Market Days, the brainchild of the older son. Saturdays are trading days. After giving a portion to the Renauds, we trade whatever we have for, hopefully, what we need.

"Matthew, ain't no way I can keep Market Days going now," Mrs. Renaud inches her way within cane-striking-distance of Daddy. "Did you think on that? Who's gonna come with the Army lookin' over their shoulder the whole time?"

Daddy reads the flyer again as if new information to explain the order will magically appear. The Army had no right to move on this without the deal being final. And with no warning to Daddy.

"What'd you do, Martin?" someone yells from the crowd.

"We need to get him out of here before they tear him apart." I jerk Matt by the arm.

Instead of leaving, Daddy takes two steps up the church steps then addresses the whole crowd. "I will talk to the soldiers tomorrow about all this. Give 'em your concerns. Just go on home now. I'll let you know what I find out."

Matt reaches for Daddy as Mama yells above the crowd, urging them to listen to her husband. The whole scene is pure chaos, and I swear the crowd has grown to well beyond how many attended mass. *Where did all these people come from?* Mama drops from my sight then I hear her cry out.

"Alright, back up!" Clem Richardson, local politician and semi-celebrity, shouts over the crowd, reducing it to a whisper while Daddy helps Mama to her feet. Little red spots spread on the knees of her pale-yellow pants and on the palms of her hands.

"I'm fine. I'm fine. Stop fussing over me," Mama says. The center of attention is not Mama's sweet spot.

Daddy looks the crowd over and does his best to calm them down. "Listen, all I can do is speak with the Army tomorrow. But nothin's gonna get done today. Tomorrow. *Nobody* is to do *anything* about this today. Except clear a path so I can take Marianne home."

The crowd splits, a total parting of the Red Sea, and Daddy guides Mama through. Small favor paid to the woman who's served as Eucharistic Minister to two generations of St. Philip's parishioners. Mama's cheeks flush, and she ducks her head as if embarrassed, which she shouldn't be. The assholes that shoved an old lady to the ground are the ones who should be ashamed.

"Alright, alright," Clem Richardson says, waving his long arms over the crowd. At well over six feet tall, standing on the church steps makes Clem appear to be a giant. "Now we have been given a bitter, bitter pill on this blessed mornin'. These DC folks are trying to take another piece of liberty from us. But are we to act like animals in the street? Trampling each other in rage and pushing dear, sweet Missus Martin to the hard pavement?" He motions to Mama—visual aid number one—making her way toward the path home. "No! The good people of this community are better than that!" He nods toward the crowd as if waiting for approval and sure enough, the crowd buys his act. Clem the Puppet Master works his charm, as he's done in every local campaign since before I was born, molding and moving the crowd with his syrupy tongue and calculated gestures.

Clem's audience erupts, cheering their homegrown hero. The sizeable armpit stains on his golf shirt add to the absurdity. Years of Gulf Coast sun has hardened his boyish features, and his former football quarterback body is soft and round, leaving only a glint of his belt visible under his belly, but his appeal remains intact, at least in the eyes of Bellefontaine's older women. And, of course, his glory days will keep him popular with the old men until his death and beyond. God help us all.

"The people of this community are strong." More shouting from Clem. More applause. "We have survived great adversity, and we will continue to survive!" He pauses for more clapping. "Why, I say we will not only survive, but thrive! Soon, the Army will realize the folly of their ways and leave Bellefontaine to the will of the people. 'Cause here in our neck of the woods, we are *real* Americans. Hard-working, good, salt-of-the-Earth folks with no use for their woke agendas. Once they realize who they're dealing with, the Army will run away with their tails tucked between their skinny legs. All we have to do is wait." After a moment, he waves both hands above the crowd again, this time as if releasing a calming potion into the air. "Now, my boys and I had a great morning on our beautiful bay. We've been blessed with more than we could possibly eat ourselves." He motions across the parking lot to a dually. His son, perched on the tailgate, waves at the crowd. "Dave has a bed full of mullet and shrimp to share. Please help yourselves." Then he adds, "Before the Army shows up and steals our rightful bounty, too."

Dave smiles at me. I don't reciprocate. His white grin makes me a bit queasy. It's as if his teeth are unnaturally white or maybe too many in number or maybe I just don't want the asshole son of the town liar to smile at me. Then Dave shifts to allow someone behind him to whisper something to him. He ducks his head then looks up again. Smiles at me again. Then I see the man from the boat yesterday. Same dirty white cap, same stringy hair. He smiles, too.

"Looks like your boyfriend's back for another try."

"Fuck off, Matt." With that, I turn and stride toward the beach pathway, calling to Matt with my back to him, "I'm done. Make sure everyone gets to the boats."

———

Trauma is a funny poison. It seems to remain in your cells for inconsistent lengths. Once upon a time, I could escape danger then put it out of my head as soon as the crisis ended. Now, I fear my traumas fracture my brain. Memories come in flashes. Solutions and remedies appear as flimsy band-aids at best. The *what-nexts* my imagination conjures are pure terror. That's how the last months feel—fractured, fleeting, frightening. My fight-or-flight reflex is stuck on max output. Surging adrenaline lingers.

Right at this moment, my arms find an Olympic-worthy pace as I paddle my kayak toward home. I grow the distance between the angry crowd at the church and myself but feel no distance will be barrier enough. No matter the effort, the punishing burning in my arms, I keep paddling. The more I paddle, the more open water there is, and the water opens my memory until the night of my return to Bellefontaine comes crashing from my mind's vault.

"Here, baby, eat these." On that first night of my return, in shock on the sofa, Mama handed me an opened sleeve of Saltines. For Southern mamas, Saltine crackers are the cure for many ills, but I didn't want them. I shook my head 'no' and dug deeper into my corner of the couch. "Jules, you have to eat something."

Mama stared at me and, with one hand, tried to brush my hair out of my face.

"Mama, stop it." I closed my eyes and pulled on the blanket wrapped around me. "It's freezing in here."

"I think you have a fever." Mama pressed the back of her hand against my forehead. "Kate, go get her another blanket. Just grab the one off my bed. Jules, you need to eat a little something, then rest."

With my eyes closed, I felt Kate move past me and focused my mind on Preach's voice coming from the hand-cranked radio.

Get ready, my devoted listeners. The whole world is about to shut down. Soldiers are on their way here, and you know what that means. Hold your loved ones tight tonight 'cause the body count on this thing is risin'.

The voice changed directions and started to fade. I opened my eyes and shot straight up as Mama walked toward the back door, radio in hand. "Mama, bring that back."

"Jules, you need sleep."

"Bring it back!" My throat burned, reducing my yell to a scratchy whisper. Through swollen lids and around the over-stuffed suitcases forming under my eyes, I glared at her, daring her to keep walking.

"No one needs to hear this. When I think of those poor souls at the docks. Downtown—" Mama shook her head, fighting back her own tears. "No, Jules. We've heard enough of bombs for one day."

"I know, Mama, but please," I begged for the radio, hoping a softer tactic would work.

Kate handed me another blanket. "Jules, just rest."

"I need to know what happened!" I snatched the blanket from her and tossed it over my legs, shoving the edges down into the crease between the upholstered cushion and me.

"Fine, honey," Mama said, walking back to the couch. "I'll leave the radio, but only if you'll eat."

"I'm not hungry."

"Then no radio."

"I'm. Not. Hungry." A fresh round of tears burned my eyes.

Mama folded her arms, holding tight to the radio with one hand.

"Fine!" I shoved a cracker into my mouth and crunched down, sending bits of salty crumbs to my lap. "Happy?"

"Not at all." Mama set down the radio and walked out of the room. I reached one hand out of my self-made cocoon and turned the volume knob as far as it would go.

I've been warnin' all you for years that somethin' like this was gonna happen. I hope to Gawd you listened and are ready. If you didn't, please for Gawd Almighty, listen to me now! The Army's showed up and these ain't local boys. Reports have it that the Alabama National Guard is non-existent. They can't get any of 'em to report for duty, so DC sent regular Army and they look like they mean business. They're sayin' they're here to turn the lights on, but I'm not sure how all the tanks and armored vehicles they brought with them are supposed to help repair the power lines. Hell, as I'm talkin' to you, I'm watchin' a cargo ship pass by out front with even more equipment. The bay's a damn traffic jam of military ships.

I grabbed the binoculars from the coffee table and stood. My legs wobbled as I crept to the window. Peering through the black tubes, I found a large ship on the horizon with several smaller vessels flanking it.

"What do you see?" Kate asked me.

"One large ship, several smaller ones. The big one's carrying tanks, Bradleys, Humvees and several stacks of metal containers, maybe five high."

"What's a Bradley?" Kate asked.

"An armored vehicle meant to carry infantry troops."

"What do they need those for?" Kate's pitch rose as she tugged at my sleeve for her turn with the binoculars.

"What do you think they need them for? I guess they don't have all the bad guys yet." I walked back to the radio and moved the antenna back and forth, searching for a signal. "Maybe they think we're the bad guys. You have no idea how bad it is out there." I shoved from my mind the images of my trip home. Brunswick, Jacksonville, Tallahassee, they all showed the wounds. Burning vehicles, demolished transformers, building after building with brand new holes blasted into their historic facades. Stores ransacked with the remains of their wares strewn across parking lots. And bodies. A female bloating in the sun near DeFuniak Springs, Florida. The charred remains of a driver and truck in Crestview. *Friend or foe*, I wondered. A woman cradling a bloody man in Pensacola. I heard her screams through my closed windows. Was there anyone left to help her? Who will bury the dead, tend to the wounded, give aid and comfort to the survivors?

I didn't help. I didn't stop. All my convictions dissolved as I cared only for self-preservation. I drove on until Bellefontaine. So, I swallowed the images down, away from my mind. Shoved them deep into my stomach to digest later if at all. On my parents' couch, I pushed the woman's wails from my ears and pulled the blanket tighter around my shoulders. I concentrated again on the radio, adjusting the antenna until the static cleared and the voice broke free again.

Make sure you follow their rules. Curfew at sundown, carry identification and gun permits at all times, and, for God's sake, keep your shit in order in the ration lines. Each family is eligible for fuel, water, flour, and rice every week, but you gotta come prepared with proof of household and be able to transport every-thing you get. Unfortunately, the Army don't make home deliver-ies, but they will make house calls if you give 'em cause. Maybe even if ya don't. I'll update you as soon as the distribution centers are ready to go. In the meantime, stay vigilant and make sure that rifle you killed a buck with last year is loaded. Only Christ himself can protect your ass if you don't.

Kate sat next to me on the couch and wrapped both of her

ivory hands—Mama's complexion—around one of my tan hands. "I'm so glad you came home. And that you got here just in time."

Kate can be a lot to deal with, what with her insistence on being right all time and surety that she is the smartest person in the room, but she has her fiercely loving moments too. Paddling far ahead of the others now, I stop so they can catch up. My kayak undulates on top of the light chop. Scanning the shoreline, wild with neglect, I laugh to myself. Kate doesn't even know how right she was that night. I came home just in time all right. Just in time for what's left of my life to dissolve into nothing.

6

The right loves to call us communists, don't they? Just because we expect our government to work for all of us, not just the white, Christian male. All of us. I promise you this: Until these extremists are rooted out and made extinct like the dinosaurs they are, I welcome the Army to our little town. They can stay as long as it takes to get the job done because I am sick of trying to explain what equity really is and why the truth of the past matters and why I shouldn't be treated as a second-class citizen.

Libby Lefty's voice floats from the hand-cranked radio. It's an undeniable combination of smoky bourbon and raw honey. Thick, sexy, and so smooth I feel wrapped in its plush weave. Her voice could coax blue crabs into the traps—no bait necessary. Where Preach will scare the bejesus out of listeners with his brand of the truth, Libby Lefty lulls the audience into a calmer state of scared shitless with her husky, soulful voice. I swear she turns the apocalypse into righteous poetry with every syllable.

For a time, the right and the left stood as reeds in the wind, able to withstand the warming water, the onslaught of wind, the rising tide. Until they couldn't. Like reeds in a hurricane, we splintered, shredding ourselves in the storm until all that remained were fragments of our former selves. Fragments that could never come together to be whole again. Because do we really want to be one with racists, misogynists, and homophobes? We are in the endgame now, my darlings. It's time to use the harsh words.

After last night's argument and the fiasco at the church, I'm preserving my sanity by hiding out in the garage. To purge my mind of Clem Richardson, The Knights, and Garrett's paranoia, I found our local liberal DJ on the radio, and she was coming through surprisingly clear considering the wind that moved in this afternoon.

I like to switch it up—my radio shows, that is—to get a healthy dose of full-range crazy from Preach to Libby. America First versus Burn the Patriarchy. And Libby is on fire today.

We found our tipping point, darlings, and Liberty's Guard—the right's muscle—found the bug men of our nation's port cities. The bug men found their big, sagging balls and gassed neighborhoods in every major port from Galveston, Texas, to Baltimore, Maryland. Rather than ridding their cities of mosquitoes, they went for other pests in their lives: people of color, the poor, the liberal, and anyone who had the misfortune to live nearby. Yep, the Bug Man was radicalized, make no mistake about that. And who do you think inspired them to murder thousands of our own? Liberty's Guard, that's who. You cannot deny who is at fault here. The Bug Man cometh and I will not stop talking about this until every last red asshole responsible pays for their atrocities. Because if you think Liberty's Guard isn't working here in our own backyard, you're dead wrong.

Libby's a bit of a guilty pleasure for me, since I fancy myself a feminist on hiatus. The hiatus will last as long as I have to forage for food. No one can fight the man on an empty stomach. Alone in the garage, I listen to her thick alto. Her voice conjures an image of a woman with a red bandana tied over a buzzcut, freshly washed skin with hard-earned crow's feet about her eyes. She rages but rarely raises her voice, which brings a sinister and sexy element to her propaganda. And, let's be honest, I'm strapped for entertainment.

All the red state fearmongering prompted 50 percent of this country to unleash their arsenals. And these were serious preppers, my darlings. They spent their weekends attending gun shows to build their caches and shopping at Costco to supply their bunkers, probably even learned how to turn piss into potable water. While they waited for their moment in the sun, their chance to shine as pseudo-military, zombie-killing patriots, we made them the butt of our jokes. Well, I'm not laughing anymore. If my gut is right, and it usually is, The Knights are nothing more than Liberty's Guard 2.0. And those man-babies are itching to make daddy proud.

"It always comes down to ego, doesn't it, Libby?" I ask as if Libby can hear me through the radio.

The other 50 percent—us—we ignored what was happening while making fun of the preppers. We begged for cooler heads to prevail. We decided to hold our collective breath until all returned to normal only to discover foul air upon exhaling. Yes, my darlings, we share in the blame. We may not be committing flat-out murder, but isn't complacency as bad as negative actions? And Liberty's Guard wasn't done. Not by a long shot. The bug men were only the beginning. Phase two was just as terrifying. What about phase three? What will that bring? I'm sure The Knights are planning—

"Well, that's not working," I say to no one and flip the radio off. All Libby's smooth talking did for me today was raise my blood pressure. That's the main problem with her show. She provides a supersized helping of rehashing what got us to this point with only a dash of useful information for surviving this "endgame."

That "Phase Two" she spoke of was Liberty's Guard's "burn it to the ground" plan. It brought attacks on military bases, mass shootings, car bombs, even a couple of mortar rounds shot into Fort Jackson, South Carolina. Jacob died, blown to bits, oblivious as he stood next to a trunk of explosives in a Fort Stewart, Georgia, parking lot. Was he guilty of a damn thing other than defending his country? No. Attacks on power stations became the lead story every night on the news, if you were lucky enough to have power and Wi-Fi to get any news.

With rumors of martial law circling, I bolted home to live out the rest of my days on my parents' couch in a corner of the world I know better than any other, but now can't recognize no matter how hard I squint. That is why I can't hold it together right now. I didn't just lose Jacob. I lost my whole damn life.

More than anything, I want to scream at every single person I see that "You don't know my pain!" That this shit is for real and could last forever or at least the rest of our lives. That I lost the very person that made living through crap like this worth it. And I know Jacob would have made this manageable. Together we got through bad shit so often that bad shit was kind of our jam. But without him? Without him I'm just suffering, lost, without. There're no intervals of laughter at the absurdity. There's no sex as a distraction or sex as a comfort or sex period. There's no getting wasted for the hell of it because you're bored but you're together so why the hell not?

But I don't scream. Because I know I'm not the only one. I. Don't. Scream. Maybe I should scream. Maybe that would help, but there are others like me out there—grieving, bewildered, lost.

But my family members, the people closest to me, aren't among them. They still have their people and know exactly where they ought to be. I am the outsider of my inner circle. That was made clear to me last night and reinforced this morning after Mass. But I don't scream.

Perhaps I should take a break from the radio for a bit. *Thanks, Libby.*

———

After dinner I peek through the kitchen window and see Daddy sitting on the patio by himself.

"Daddy," I say, craning my head and neck around the front door. "Want company? It's just me."

"Sure."

In the chair next to him, I prop my feet up on one of the green footstools. Painted from their original white to brown to deep forest green, the stools survived over two decades of hurricanes and tropical storms. Various pieces of outdoor furniture came and went over the years, but the stools remain.

"Jacob loved this porch," I say, remembering how I'd find him out here with a cup of coffee after a morning run. *How many holidays did we spend here?*

"Yeah?"

"He liked the peace and quiet. He'd stare at the water, not saying a word."

"That's a good quality in a man." Daddy picks up his glass for another sip of wine, wincing with the gulp.

"Not as good as bourbon and water, huh?"

"No, it's not."

"I won't tell Mama you said that."

We exchange a smile and sit in silence for a few moments,

gazing between the white columns of the expansive porch, beyond the brick steps then green lawn to the water, now flowing charcoal in the moonlight.

"Looks like no one's out there tonight. I guess everyone's observing curfew now that the Army is coming to stay." The mention of the Army hangs in the air for a moment, and I regret the comment. In my defense, Daddy can be hard to talk to. He's weirdly smart, Mensa-level smart, and he doesn't go for small talk. I, on the other hand, have reached the stage of widowhood in which I crave solitude but need chaos—everyone screaming around me with hurricane force wind blasting every cell of my body so that I can't slow down. There is a comfort in chaos, one I don't understand fully yet. When silence hangs in the air, what I want is to run or fill the space with noise.

"So, Julianne, what's on your mind tonight?" Daddy's the single person in my life who ever uses my given name.

Since I was little, he always knew something was wrong without me saying a word: jelly smeared on a couch cushion, failing grade, breakup from a dirt bag, dead husband. Daddy always sees what I try to hide. But I'll never know all that he's hidden from us over the years. From the deep creases around his eyes and his natural frown, I'd guess he's hidden more than I want to know.

"Can I go with you tomorrow? To see Captain Johnson, wherever you're going to meet with them?"

"Julianne, Matt and I will go and work out the details."

"But Daddy—"

"Jules, you don't need to go talk to a bunch of soldiers or walk around an Army camp. No, Matt and I will go."

"I'll be fine." Trying to shrug off his concern, I put on my best Army Wife voice, the fake confident tone, fully supportive of the load of crap I'd just been handed, no matter what that crap may be. "I speak their language. I could help you talk to Captain

Johnson about the land usage. Make sure Mama gets her cooking oil."

I haven't set foot on an Army post since Jacob died. I haven't seen or spoken to any of our friends since the explosions in Savannah started, well, with the exception of our friend Aiden. I spoke to him. I can't deny that, no matter how much I refused to hear what he had to say.

"Daddy, I paid attention to everything Jacob ever told me about his time in the desert."

"This is Bellefontaine."

"I know that. But if Garrett and Mrs. Renaud are right, that the Army is here to stir up more trouble, maybe I could figure out a few things by whatever's happening there."

"No, I think you should just stay here. I'm sure you have plenty to do."

"Daddy, please. Matt doesn't know a damn thing about what soldiers do, what their typical actions are, what equipment may or may not be there. I could tell a lot about this whole situation if I could get a look. I know when officers lie or sugarcoat what's really going on. When all they're offering is the Public Affairs-approved load of garbage. If something big is building up, shouldn't we try to find out what? I'm the one of us who can do that without asking. The Army is one thing I actually know. I know the Army a heck of a lot more than Matt does."

"No." He stops rocking for a second and looks at me, disbelief panned across his face at the force in my voice.

"I need this," I say. The honesty almost chokes me. "I need to do this. I can't hide from this anymore and I can't pretend that Jacob didn't exist. I don't want to. And the Army was a big part of him. So maybe going with you will make me face this. Hiding here is killing me, Daddy—"

"Fine." He reaches across the small, iron side table and squeezes my hand. "Fine. You can come. Matt will stay here, but you get to break the news to him. Hopefully, they'll have fuel we can have immediately. We need it." Daddy gulps the last of his wine, makes a gagging face for my benefit, then reaches over to tickle my knee, causing my entire body to flinch. His joints crunch as he rises from his chair. "Remind Garrett that we need the truck. It'll take less gas than the boat. And we'll need a tarp and bungee cords. We should have enough gas to make it around the swamp and back."

"Yes, sir. Thanks, Daddy." I smile at him, risking eye contact for a split second before turning my focus back to the water. Daddy might change his mind if he sees how nervous I am at the thought of driving onto an Army post again. A glimpse of my old life could send me back to the days on my couch in Savannah crying out to no one. Bargaining with God. Praying to Jacob, for Jacob.

Or maybe it will cleanse me of a bit of the trauma running through my veins.

"Lock up after you come inside."

"Yes, sir." I suck in a big gulp of soupy air. "'Night, Daddy."

Over the kitchen sink, I wash my face by candlelight and pull my hair up in a high ponytail, then change into a T-shirt and old gym shorts to sleep in. I know what will happen as soon as I close my eyes. The ever-present lightning in my veins will throb, igniting micro explosions just beneath my skin. The breathing exercises won't help. Four seconds inhale, eight seconds exhale. Four seconds bullshit, eight seconds terror rising. So tonight, because I'm exhausted and have fought it too many nights in a row, I let it be. Jacob's face appears and I give into memory.

In my mind, I trace my finger along his face, across his dark brows, down his nose, along the smile lines just starting to appear near his mouth and finally across the roundness of his bottom lip. *I miss you, Jacob. I miss you. I miss you too much.*

"Where is he?" I screamed at Aiden months ago, three days

after every house along MLK Boulevard in downtown Savannah was drenched with poison and the power grid fried by a few men with a ton of ammo. Aiden stood on my front porch and told me about the explosion that killed Jacob. Aiden swore that Jacob's death was instantaneous, no pain, as if that made his death easier to accept. In a moment, Aiden went from being Jacob's best friend to my pseudo-Casualty Assistance Officer and worst nightmare.

"Jules," said Aiden, as gently as he could, "he's gone."

"I'll go get him." Adrenaline pumped through my veins like wildfire.

"Jules, there's no one to get. There's nothing left."

The visual of Jacob's perfect body being torn apart flashed. "You promised to look out for him!" I shoved Aiden hard, pushing him toward the front steps. "Where were you? You were supposed to protect him!" Aiden stumbled then stepped to me and tried to wrap me in his arms.

"Get out!" I pushed him again. This time he stepped backward down the stairs and landed hard on the sidewalk.

"Jules, please." Aiden looked up at me from the concrete, tears filling his eyes.

"Why was he at the gate, Aiden? Why wasn't he with you?"

In that moment I didn't care about anyone's pain but my own. I hated Aiden for speaking, for breathing. I hated that I could touch him, push him, hit him. I hated him for being alive. I would have traded him to the devil for my Jacob without a single second of a pause. I retreated, slammed the front door and sunk to the floor, curling into the cobwebs in the corner of the foyer. With that door closed, nothing on the other side of it was real. I'd make it so. I cursed God and the Army and Aiden and Jacob. Especially Jacob. How dare he leave me?

Alone, I crawled to the kitchen and ransacked the house, dumping junk drawers and searching through every nook and cranny, praying Jacob had stashed a pack of smokes. All I wanted to do was sit on the couch, drink the contents of the bar and smoke until my body stopped shaking. I had no luck finding cigarettes. Instead, I spent two days guzzling a handle of Jack Daniels. Every few hours, I passed out on the couch, unable to even look at our bed. The house was still, the world around me silent. The silence was like a second explosion. So, I sobbed loudly, pushing the sound out with my diaphragm. I tried to scream myself to death but with all my effort the silence around me grew.

That fucking silence. My chest heaves with the memory of it.

Three days after Jacob died, I shot out of my comatose state at the sound of an eruption, too close to ignore. The walls shook with undeniable force—a thunderous, violent warning to stop hiding.

On the third boom, the gilded mirror above the fireplace crashed to the floor, and with that I was sober. Terrified to sobriety. Peeking through the blinds of the front window, the streets looked abandoned. Smoke rose over rooftops, just beyond our neighborhood. My cell phone was dead and the power was out, so I ran to the garage, plugged my phone into my car charger, and cranked the car. I counted down the seconds before the Apple logo filled the screen. Then, a shelter in place emergency order flashed on the screen. All caps and an exclamation point. I pulled up the Savannah Morning News app, and to my surprise, those badass journalists were doing their job. Five car bombs detonated in three neighborhoods in Richmond Hill, the tiny Savannah suburb I called home, popular for families of Fort Stewart. My hiding time was done. No way in hell was I going to shelter in place, waiting for the next fully loaded van to pull into my driveway. Fight or flight? To me, in that moment, fleeing was fighting.

I tore through each room for anything of value. I packed the non-perishable food in a plastic tub and filled every water bottle Jacob and I owned, hoping the water was safe to drink. I dragged

Jacob's footlocker of Army gear from the back closet to the garage. Naively optimistic that internet access and the power grid would become stable again, I packed our laptops.

I dumped my dresser drawers into a suitcase and my shoes in another. I just couldn't leave my shoes behind. In the bottom of one Louboutin boot, I hid our few pieces of expensive jewelry. The red soles, polished leather, and sleek design made them the most beautiful boots I'd ever seen, my one and only frivolous purchase. The stiletto heel made them useless in a crisis, but I packed them.

Continuing my pillage, Jacob's buck knife, climbing rope, bungee cords, toolbox, and other random items all fell into a reusable shopping bag with *Live, Laugh, Love* printed on the side.

Flashlights, batteries, candles, lighters, blankets, and towels went into a large cardboard box leftover from our move from Kentucky to Savannah. The moving company inventory sticker was still stuck to the side — BOX 132. *How many stickers did it take to inventory the life of Jacob and Jules?*

I grabbed the only gun Jacob and I owned, a Red Ryder BB gun that Jacob used for target practice in the backyard. Even with a pitiful toy with no sight, he proved his expert marksmanship. On my last dash through the house, I grabbed the Army Survival Guide and our wedding album, both on the bottom shelf in the office.

With the garage door closed, I loaded my SUV. I placed my purse, a baseball bat engraved with our wedding date, the BB gun, and a box of BBs on the floorboard of the passenger side. Lastly, I dropped my rosary in one of the cup holders. Truth be known, I hadn't prayed the Rosary in years, and the air pump BB gun would be too slow, but I hoped for a little extra protection from both.

At noon, the engine purred with one turn of Jacob's key. Turning up the volume on the radio, I listened for a minute to the same emergency message displayed on my cell. Ignoring it again, I opened the garage door and backed down our driveway, not bothering to close the door behind me. Let the looters have it all. I had no plans to return.

"Alright, Mama," I said out loud to no one. "I'm comin' home."

7

New checkpoints went up this morning, so make sure your papers are in order if you're going out. Just another day in the good 'ole USA! Land of the free? Sure, if you live in Cal-ee-forn-i-A or with those godless crooks in DC. Don't be fooled by what you see. Them boys' uniforms may say US Army, but they ain't us. We lost this country with that illegal election. Those Army boys don't care about you, and they don't know a damn thing 'bout our home. Hell, I got half a mind to drive 'em out myself. There's still some fight in these old bones. In the meantime, I'm hitting my knees. And I need each of you prayin' with me. Pray for our country and—

Daddy punches the audio power button on the truck's dash, silencing Preach. "That's enough of that."

"But he'll probably list the new closures and checkpoints," I say in protest.

"We're not going on the main roads, Julianne." Daddy adjusts his sunglasses and then rolls down the driver's side window. We don't waste gas on AC anymore. Without another word, he lifts his right hand and performs the Sign of the Cross. "I believe in God, the Father Almighty, Creator of Heaven and Earth…"

I follow suit—what choice do I have—and recite the Apostle's Creed with Daddy. Praying the Rosary is not optional in my family. Whenever Mama or Daddy begin, all of us join in, regardless of belief in the power of the Rosary. Sure, in my most desperate moments, I've turned to Mother Mary a few times, begging her to take my troubles into her outstretched arms. I've done that several times in the last nine months, but I'm feeling ignored. I don't like being ignored. Also, I take issue with God, placing the ultimate blame for Jacob's death squarely on his shoulders. And please don't give me that "God only gives you what you can handle" tired line. What God gave me is too much, and he didn't even have the decency to give me a goodbye kiss or even a glance the morning of Jacob's death. Jacob left for PT two hours before I woke. So, the fifty-three *Hail Marys*, seven *Our Fathers*, and all the *Glory Bes* and creeds may come out of my mouth, but my heart isn't in it. I know each prayer will go unanswered, so what the hell is the point?

Daddy shoots me a look as if he can hear the insincerity in my voice and *does not approve.* Then, he turns the wheel out of the driveway. The truck whines a bit as we leave the safety of our property. While chanting the prayers, my mind goes to its primary responsibility—searching the road and surrounding woods for potential dangers. This is the job of the passenger. The driver steers while the passenger scans the area for roadside bombs, suspicious debris, and hidden combatants. Jacob, through all his deployments in Iraq had trained his eyes to do this well. Now it's my turn.

Riding down our street, Daddy nears the end of the first Joyful Mystery of the Rosary as I spot a flash of yellow on the lowest branch of an oak tree.

"Daddy," I interrupt and feel him take his foot off the gas. He doesn't break the truck or pause the current *Hail Mary,* but he does look in my same direction. "Never mind. It's nothing." That was a lie. It wasn't nothing. That flash of yellow was a boy, a blond-haired boy perched on a branch.

While Daddy creeps forward along the road, I hold the boy's gaze. The same gaze I'd held on the pier two nights ago. He must be the same boy, but I keep my mouth shut. The look on the boy's face is unnerving and for several moments I debate my instincts. Surely a child can't pose a threat—an unarmed child. Wild scenarios flash through my mind of child soldiers, child spies. Is he watching us for someone else or waiting for our property to appear deserted enough for the little thief to get to work? Or is he hungry and alone, living as we all are on instinct and foolish prayers?

I have little time to ponder these questions because the truck whines again, brake pads protesting, as we leave our paved street and drive onto the gravel road that skirts the swamp. Several trees at the start of the road display crude signs, nailed cockeyed and waving in the early morning breeze. "Are you still free?" one sign asks. "End martial law now!" demands another. Maybe the poster board was from a school project some child never completed. No one is making craft-store runs to Mobile anymore. "Self-Rule: the true American Dream!" is spray painted on a sheet draping the remnants of a battered chain-link fence nearly overtaken by honeysuckle vines.

I wonder why the soldiers let these signs stay here? I ask myself, while chanting *Hail Marys* along with Daddy. *First Amendment, I guess. Or maybe they're too busy to notice. Or maybe Captain Johnson doesn't know that as a commander under martial law, he makes the rules around here and could just order the signs removed. Shouldn't he want to dampen hostility toward the Army?*

We finish the Rosary just as we coast up to what looks like a hastily constructed guard tower at the entrance of the Army's newest camp.

A few dozen people wait to get through on foot. Their stares move from my face and down the expanse of the truck as we roll past the line. Our suffering is mere discomfort compared to that of others. I catch the gaze of a woman clinging to the hands of two toddlers, bellies swollen. *Are they sick? Or starving? It's only been nine months.* The woman's eyes wet with tears, and I look away. Her matted hair and yellowed complexion are too much.

Growing up, my middle-class family was wealthy, according to the low-rent standard of Bellefontaine. While my parents—Daddy an engineer and Mama the head teller at a local bank—scraped together Catholic school tuition and prepared us for college, our neighbors hoped for decent hunting seasons and taught their children how to fish the water with gigantic nets rigged to patched shrimp boats. The events of the months following the election had done nothing to even the playing field. The poor grew poorer. The rich still exerted their power. The middle class, for the most part, learned how to survive and prayed for isolation from the fringes.

I spot the Renaud sons in the pedestrian line. They wave flyers from the day before and yell at the armed soldiers blocking the entrance to the camp. The wrinkled, white papers jerk back and forth against the blue sky. Again, I look away. One more time and I'm on par with St. Peter, denying my own.

"We're here to see Captain Johnson," Daddy tells the soldier at the gate as the truck comes to a stop under the awning. In front of us, a chain-link gate on metal castors and two more armed soldiers, in full battle rattle, block our entry. They must be about to pass out from the heat.

"Identification, sir," orders the soldier. He takes Daddy's driver's license. "Your passenger?" The soldier bends over slightly to look through the open window at me. Reaching across the cab, I hand over my military ID. After staring at the card for several moments, the soldier hands our IDs to another soldier. "Step out of the vehicle. You too, miss."

"They're probably searching vehicles, Daddy. It's no big deal. Just turn the engine off and pop the hood." I press the button on my armrest to unlock the doors as I had on countless occasions upon entering one military base or another. Soldiers searched every nook and cranny of my car every time, but as far as I knew, the privacy invasions Jacob and I came to expect were new to Daddy. He's never experienced suspicion just for showing up somewhere.

Three soldiers search the truck, digging through the glove box, center console, and toolbox. They shine flashlights down in the shadows of the engine and walk the entire perimeter of the truck with mirrors attached to long poles, looking for odd objects in the undercarriage.

"What business do you have here today?" asks one soldier.

"We need to see Captain Johnson. I'm Matthew Martin, Sr. and this is my daughter Jules, Julianne. And I own this land."

"You're not on the list for today."

"We need to see him. As I said, this land you're standing on belongs to me."

Then the soldier approaches me. "Hold your arms out to the side." He demonstrates by holding his arms out, forming a tall T. "You, too, sir."

This is new. I'd never had a pat down to go on post before. The soldier runs his hands down both of my thighs and up and down my back. When he pats down my chest and stomach, he turns his hands over, so the palms of his hands don't touch me, a lame attempt to make being felt up by a total stranger easier to accept.

"This is expired. You'll need to get a new card," the soldier with my ID tells me and waves my military dependent card in my direction.

"And how would I do that now?" I say, unsure how to do that without Jacob.

"Will you let Captain Johnson know we are here to see him?" Daddy asks.

"We are doing that now, sir," the soldier says to Daddy but then turns his attention back to me, "Ma'am, do you have another form of identification? I can't accept an expired card. Your sponsor will have to accompany you to update this one. Building 2015 on Brookley."

"He can't accompa—"

Daddy cut me off before I could tell him that my sponsor can't accompany me anywhere anymore. Instead, Daddy tells the soldier, "We have an urgent matter to discuss with Captain Johnson. Is he here? If you show us to his office, we can wait for him there."

"Yeah, yeah, everybody's got something 'urgent' to discuss." The soldier hands my ID off to yet another guy in fatigues.

There are so many of them, and they all look the same in their camo-printed garb, body armor, and helmets. I don't know who searched the car, who has Daddy's license, who has my ID, or who is going to take us to Johnson, if at all. I do, however, know which one needs to have his attitude adjusted, and that is the soldier standing right in front of me. I glance at his nametag and choke on the absurdity displayed before me.

"Sir," Specialist *Tude* starts up again. No joke. That's his last name, as if his ancestors were total pricks in the line at Ellis Island and the immigration clerk was feeling salty that day.

"Civilians are not permitted through the gate without proper identification. Unless her sponsor can vouch for her, your daughter's gonna have to stay here."

"My sponsor is dead." The words fly out of my mouth. I think the words a million times each day, but to hear them from my mouth shocks me. "Sir, I'm a widow, my husband was active duty when he died. Captain Jacob Jones. Fort Stewart. Maybe you heard of him." Of course, he'd heard of Jacob. TV news outlets plastered Jacob's DA photo and sparse details of his death for weeks, until of course the news outlets went the way of fast-food drive-thrus, schools, and shops—boarded up or burned to the ground.

Specialist Tude stares at me with an expression somewhere between deer in headlights and brick to the face.

"So, you have heard of him, and what happened to him?" No one handed me a flag or took pictures of me seated, barely recognizable under a black veil and dark sunglasses, or sprawled over his flag-draped coffin because none of that existed for Jacob. No coffin, no flag, no funeral. But I am what I am regardless of pomp —a widow, the person everyone in the mighty military family dreads speaking with because I represent their greatest fear. I am untouchable, unwelcome, and soon-to-be unhinged if Specialist Tude doesn't get the fuck out of my way. "Yes, I should have an updated ID card. One that says Jacob is dead, so you gate guards have to be nice to me."

"Ma'am, I'm so sorry." The soldier stammers for a second, presumably searching for the politically correct way to deny my request for entrance. "Ma'am, I'm…"

And then he gives me the expression, the trite gesture I hadn't seen yet. His face falls and his eyes avoid mine. Aiden was full of pity but didn't have this particular look when he told me about Jacob because Aiden doesn't have a wife. He never understood why Jacob stayed in the Army with a wife after his first tour, much less four. "You should get out, man. Don't put Jules through this again," Aiden said time and again. My family has never given me that look. Oh, sure, they hate what I'm going through, what I went through. But I don't represent their worst fear like I do for military family members. I am the only Martin who ever watched their spouse disappear into a plane, not knowing if I will ever see him again. This soldier gets it. He and his wife have legal wills at age twenty-two. Just like Jacob did every time he left, this soldier promised his wife he'd make it home to her. No one ever plans on dying, blown to smithereens, but here I stand. I am proof that the unthinkable happens all the damn time.

The soldier turns his wedding ring. I'm sure it's some unconscious prayer that he won't leave his wife and kids like Jacob left me. "Ma'am, I'm sorry…I just…I didn't mean to offend you."

As Specialist Tude continues his pity and penitence dance, Captain Johnson appears from behind the gatehouse. "Mister Martin, Miss Martin, good to see you." He sounds much happier than he did a few days earlier.

"It's Jones," I tell Johnson, flush burning in my cheeks.

"Oh, yes, of course. My apologies. Missus Jones."

"Why don't you just call me Jules? That will suffice." Two years into my marriage, with Jacob 20,000 miles away, I finally changed my last name to his. It was an act of pride in being his wife. What the hell do I do with the name now that "till death do us part" arrived?

"Follow me. We'll talk in my office."

"Our IDs," I say to the soldier, hold out my hand, and stare at his acne-pocked face and into his plain, brown eyes.

Driving through the camp, with Captain Johnson's Humvee leading our two-vehicle convoy, the smell of exhaust fumes and cut pine mix in my nose. Then I see it, the expanse of a clearing with tents erected and dozens of armored vehicles parked in neat rows. A pile of fresh-cut pine trees lay on the ground.

"Why didn't I know they would do that? Of course, they would do this." I climb down from the truck dumbfounded, my one option being to stand, mouth agape. I don't need to see Daddy's face to know his reaction. I can hear it in his breathing.

Captain Johnson hops out of his Humvee and strides around to us.

"You never mentioned cutting down, what?" I glance over at the pile of felled trees. "Twenty pine trees?"

"It was necessary for our mission here." Johnson projects his voice over the cacophony of generators, chainsaws, and hammering.

"No, it was the simplest, least creative solution you came up with, so who cares—" I cut my words off with the feel of Daddy's hand on my forearm. The look on his face tells me to keep in mind our mission here today. Payment. Fuel. Cooking oil. In exchange for the apparent rape of Daddy's land.

"This way." Captain Johnson gestures toward a white trailer at the end of a row of white tents. It was something between a FEMA trailer and a cargo container. "To my office…of sorts."

"I can see why you've enacted such strict restrictions around here. I wouldn't want civilians peeking around at all this either." Walking past the tents, I match Johnson's pace stride for stride.

"Yes," Johnson says, craning his neck to direct his response to Daddy, two steps behind us. "You can see why we're so grateful to you for the use of this land. To keep peace in this area, we needed better access than having to drive back and forth from Brookley for patrols."

"Sure, sure," I say, then, "but the Bradleys? Do you really need Bradleys? Does a martial law situation really require you to transport an entire infantry platoon in one vehicle? And an armored one at that? Seeing one of those things rolling down the street is going to scare people half to death."

Johnson stops and stares at me. I brace for his reply—*that's the point, Miss Martin.* Instead, he says nothing and opens the door to the blinding white trailer. "The Bradleys, being so large, are more practical for transporting platoons than, say, a Humvee. It's nothing to concern yourself over, just practicality."

Johnson pops the window AC unit with one balled fist. "Only twenty-four hours old and this thing is already acting up," he says, maneuvering the tight squeeze between his desk and the wall with little effort.

"It feels good in here to me," Daddy says.

Johnson's response, the right response, comes quickly. "Really, I'm thankful to the Army that they provide the AC units at all and the generators to run them. Others aren't so fortunate right now, are they?"

Perhaps he's not as dumb as he looks. He motions for us to sit in two folding chairs tucked against the wall opposite his narrow bunk. Johnson sits in the big, black vinyl, I'm-the-man-in-charge chair wedged behind the desk.

"So, Mister Martin, how's your family holding up? I saw a few little ones running around your yard the other day." Johnson's desk, made of the standard-issue metal and painted the standard-issue brown, lies somewhere beneath mounds of paperwork, maps, and mechanical pencils—every square inch overrun except for two inches of bare space surrounding a framed photo. In a field of sunflowers, a pretty blonde around my age poses with Johnson and four mini Captain Johnsons, all in camo pants and white shirts. She's even in the day's uniform, made sexier with what looks to be a bedazzled belt and makeup to rival any Insta queen, which means I hate her and her overdone face. To be fair, though, I hate everyone who remains happily married to a living person.

"We're getting by," Daddy says.

I wonder how long it will take Johnson to realize that this is not a social visit and Daddy won't take his bait of idle chitchat. Daddy doesn't have time or patience for social visits and never wastes time on small talk. *Minutes matter, Julianne.* I heard that one my entire life.

Johnson leans back in his chair, the posture a man takes when he's trying to look powerful, even though all three of us know a lowly captain was far from running this show. Some colonel or general somewhere signed an operation order and Johnson saluted, clicked his boot heels, and now he's here.

"We need to discuss the rental agreement," says Daddy.

"Okay. Well, as you can see, we've taken possession and so far, we're pleased with what this position will offer us to maintain peace in Bellefontaine."

"I can see that," Daddy says. "So, what I am here for is to work out the lease and the first fuel payment."

"Yes," Johnson replies, shifting in his seat. I wonder if this is how Jacob appeared, shifting in his seat while negotiating with Sheiks in Iraq. Land for internet access. Land for an improved power grid. Land for whatever the Sheiks wanted so long as they didn't blow him up on the road. Cash for what the Army blew up on the road.

"And, Captain Johnson, when we discussed the use of the land, the surrounding water was not part of the deal. People here fish wherever they please. Wherever the fish are biting. That's the way it's always been. I fear restricting waterways is the Army asking for trouble."

"What good would the land be without water access?" Johnson asks.

"Why can't both the Army and civilian boats use the water? And you would still have the road," Daddy answers. "So, what is the water worth to you?"

"Mister Martin, the water is part of the deal. Obviously, we cannot have just anyone coming freely in and out of a combat outpost. That would put your family in danger and might hinder our mission. Until the engineers finish the temporary bridge at the marina, we need to keep watercraft traffic to a minimum."

"*Combat* outpost?" Daddy asks.

"Outpost, I mean, outpost. I shouldn't have said combat."

"My property includes one hundred feet from the land out into the water. So, use of that will be an extra charge or available for our use. You tell me which."

Johnson leans forward, resting his elbows on his desk, a damn good attempt at "powerful yet sympathetic." Are we negotiating strategic territory or a new car lease? The air in here is rank with forced civility.

"The outpost and surrounding water *are* restricted areas. I'm surprised you allow your family out here at all, so close to… well you understand. You and your family will need to stay clear of the lagoon. As will anyone else you allow to fish these waters."

"I don't police fishing around here. Never have. No one here owns the water."

Johnson shifts again in his seat. A loose thread must have caught his eye because he spends the next several moments trying to tuck the thing back into the seam with the tip of his ballpoint pin.

"Burn it with a lighter," I tell him.

"What?" Johnson asks me.

"The thread. Jacob used to burn all those off with a lighter. They drove him crazy."

"Yeah, these new uniforms don't hold up for—" Johnson stops short, then looks at Daddy. "Sir, we are not policing fishing, but we will enforce boundaries for the safety of everyone."

"In that case, water access will be an additional charge." Daddy wastes no time negotiating a better deal. "I would expect you to double the proposed fuel amount in order to hand over water access."

"Double? We can't double the fuel. Absolutely not." Johnson sets his pen back on the yellow legal pad lying on his desk.

"Yes, I think you can. I'd also like cooking oil to be added to the agreement," Daddy says, stating his terms.

"There's no way. I don't even have access to cooking oil. I

mean, maybe the DFAC, the dining facility, but that's on Brookley."

"We know what a DFAC is, Captain Johnson. So, go to the DFAC on Brookley and get some oil, vegetable or peanut, your choice. Or I go to Brookley and tell your superiors that you moved onto my land without an agreement intact and that I plan to sue the US Army."

Johnson's breath is audible over the sound of the window unit. In and out. In and out. "Give me some time to work it out with the DFAC and the motor p—"

"Great. Figure that out and I'll deliver the news to everyone that the restrictions are final. Maybe they'll take bad news from me better than reading it off another flyer." Daddy appears to relax into the folding chair. "Look, the Army clearly has the resources for this deal. Propane, gasoline, cooking oil. Just tell me what you think the land and water access is worth. And keep in mind, folks around here aren't happy about you being here, so very close to home. So, this agreement is going to cause tension between my family and this town. We should be compensated accordingly."

Johnson waves one hand. "I'll increase the propane and gasoline by ten gallons a week, but I will have to check on the cooking oil."

"Make it fifteen. We'll wait here while you check on the cooking oil." Daddy leans back in his chair, appearing pleased, maybe because of the AC, more than likely because he never loses a debate and really loves winning, except against Mama. He'll happily lose to Mama.

Johnson lets the door close behind him. Hard. Outside, he yells to someone nearby. I make out the name *Sergeant Roberts*, but not much more. A moment of guilt rises in my throat. My intention was never to put Billy Roberts in the hot seat, *jammed up* as they say on all the procedural cop-and-lawyer shows I binged when Jacob deployed or left on some training stint. I push the guilt down with all the other feelings I refuse to acknowledge. Billy's a big boy; he can fend for himself. I look at Daddy and then at the door as an argument ensues just outside.

"You know, in Jacob's Army survival guide, there's a section on dealing with local populations." I recite the memorized passage. "*The population of many countries, especially politically hostile countries, must not be considered friendly just because they do not demonstrate open hostility. Unless briefed to the contrary, avoid all contact with such people.*" I pause and then, "He should have avoided us locals."

"Perhaps Captain Johnson should have read that manual," Daddy says, chuckling.

"Maybe I should be kinder to him in the future. He doesn't actually have to negotiate at all with us. Legally, he can just take the land without paying us a cent or single gallon of fuel."

Daddy and I wait in the office for an hour. When Johnson returns, his cheeks are flush and he's sweating buckets, but he delivers. We agree to forty gallons of propane and twenty-five gallons of gasoline per week, and four gallons of cooking oil each month. In return, the Army will control the lookout, land, and the lagoon, with deep-water access to Mobile Bay. And Daddy will try to explain all of this to our neighbors and friends and everyone else in Bellefontaine with a half-cocked shotgun and a bucket of shells.

8

"I'm not a part of this world anymore, am I?" I stare out the truck window and watch the soldiers busy at work. Their actions are familiar, but I don't know them anymore. I don't feel the kinship I used to feel. I am an intruder now. No longer a spouse, a member of the team, I am someone who came through the gate to sneak a glance at their world, take what I need, then get the hell back to where I belong.

"No, honey, I guess you're not." Daddy glances at me and the sympathy in his eyes nearly breaks me. A sob in my throat fights for release. "Do you still want to be part of this?"

"I want Jacob. I want our life back." The gates open, both the floodgate of tears and the gate to the Army camp. "I'm sorry," I choke out between sobs. "It was hard at times, but it was ours."

Daddy pats my knee. "He was your husband. You two were supposed to…you had so many years taken from you. Of course, you want things like they used to be."

"I want Jacob back every day, but I don't want his world. I don't know if I ever wanted that world. He was supposed to do his twenty, and then we could live. Act two was supposed to be mine. I agreed to support his dream because his dream job was really important. But that didn't make my day-to-day any easier. As soon as I felt settled, made friends, found a community, Jacob would get orders to move, and I started the whole process again in a new town with new people because I didn't want to miss any possible day with him. Through the deployments, all the times we were separated, I stayed for him. I kept a home for him. I got some BS entry-level job and not just to keep myself from going insane from the loneliness, but also because despite what a lot of people think, officer pay isn't great the first few years."

"Oh, I remember." Daddy reaches across the cab of the truck and holds my hand, which makes me choke on my words again.

"The first two years, we pretty much lived on hot dogs and Walmart boxed pasta. So, I tucked away my dream of actually using my degree, and I got the minimum-wage job because that's what our life called for. I'd work my way up, and then we'd move, and I'd do it all over again. For what? Every time he deployed, I kept everything straight—money, bills, the house, care packages, letters. I obsessed over not missing a single phone call from him because what if it was the last time… I did all of it because I wanted his life to be easier somehow. If I could make just a little bit of his dream easier to have, I did it. I did every-thing except keep him safe. That's the one thing I couldn't do." I squeeze Daddy's hand and try to pretend that I'm fine, but pretending is hard. Pretending is exhausting, and I feel a new fissure open deep in my core. This one has teeth and heat, and I can't ignore it, so I don't ignore it. Instead, I let the words out. The ones I try so hard not to say. "I'm so mad at him for leaving me."

Some days, I don't want to be fine. Some days, I want to grab a sledgehammer and bash skulls. I want to make the world pay. I want to make Jacob know what he did to me. I want to beat some-thing until bloody. But some days, all I want to do is sleep. Out the truck's windows is an untamed world. The ground looks soft, lush with grass so tall it waves at me in the breeze. Maybe I could just lay down in that grass and sleep for a week. If I lay there long enough, maybe the grass will envelope me, hide me from the world, and I can sleep for twenty years or more. Rip Van Winkle this whole catastrophe.

Like me, this world has changed through neglect. The pristine lawns and magazine-worthy decks and boathouses hide behind untamed honeysuckle, kudzu, and grass. The flora is so tall and thick that nothing less than a bushwhacker could cut it back. The vines and weeds—several stems the width of a child's arm— threaten the road as if whispering, "We're coming for you." I wish it would.

The homes abandoned early in this transformative world now provide shelter for squatters and nomads who hope the bay will provide sustenance. We know strangers linger there, behind the overgrowth. Built in the eighties, the ranch style homes were abandoned within days of Clayton Vancleave's poisonous escapade. Longtime residents deserted their homes in search of somewhere safer. Maybe north to Chicago. Maybe west to Sacramento. I haven't heard anything about bug men there. Somewhere without domestic terrorists hosing down neighborhoods with deadly toxins. We used to know every inhabitant on Bay Air Road. I knew whose yard I could cut through and whose I needed to steer clear of. I knew where the sweet, playful dogs lived, where the grandpa dogs stretched out on porches, too old to be of any harm, and I knew which houses to avoid because Cujo himself lived there.

Away from the exhaust fumes of the Army camp, the air opens to pine trees, wild berries, and lemon trees all mixed together into air so fresh it seems untouched by human hands. I encourage my mind to wander through the beauty of this wilding and my anxiety eases a bit. I take a mental note of wild blackberries growing near the end of the dirt road. *They'll be ripe for picking in a week or so.* Wildflowers have become just that, wild. One purple type of flower flourishes. With blooms and leaves like lilies, the purple flowers stand nearly two feet tall with dozens crowded in a grassy patch the size of the truck.

If only the wildflowers and vines would grow so thick, no one could enter or exit our property. But, as alone as I feel, my family will not be left alone—no matter if we demand it, pray for it, or beg for blessed isolation. In our driveway, at the end of the long path flanked by Crepe Myrtles with blooms as pink as Barbie's Dreamhouse, the dropped tailgate of a dually truck provides seating for two men I don't recognize. Clem Richardson—I certainly recognize that jackass—stands under the carport speaking with Matt. Three more men mull around near one of two large storage sheds. I recognize Dave Richardson and the gross man from the boat, but not the third.

"Daddy, were you expecting a visit from The Knights?"

"No, but I'm also not surprised." Daddy turns the wheel and steers the truck down the driveway, inching along beneath the bright pink canopy and closer and closer to the uninvited and unwanted visitors from our local militia group, The Knights.

The Knights of Fort Gaines, named for the decrepit Civil War Era fort on the east end of Dauphin Island, began as a Mardi Gras organization. Each year until this past one, on the Saturday before Fat Tuesday, The Knights decorated their flatbed trailers, dune buggies, and golf carts with Mardi Gras paraphernalia, got stinking drunk, and paraded down the main drag of Dauphin Island throwing moon pies, candy, and trinkets to the crowd. As a teenager, and then college student, I viewed the insurance and real estate agents, fishermen and crabbers, rig workers and local politicians of the island as harmless, just a bunch of pervy men who rode the entire parade route trying to entice drunk women to show their boobs for a string of cheap, plastic beads.

Over the last year, as martial law continued month after

month, the carnival group morphed into a militia, but I'd venture to say that their political disenfranchisement began long before martial law came to south Mobile County. Nowadays, they recruit new members north along Dauphin Island Parkway, claiming the land and people of Alabama Point and Bellefontaine as loyal subjects or at least Knight sympathizers. Their goals are simple: End martial law, force the Army to leave, and for the people of Bellefontaine to live under The Knights' protection.

Rather than stay on Dauphin Island, they moved a bit north to their newly claimed commune on Mon Louis Island, directly across the river from Fowl River Marina. The Knights hate any outsider who tries to enforce new rules in their territory. Of course, if these people loved authority figures to begin with, they wouldn't have moved to the southernmost tip of Alabama, connected to the mainland by a solitary two-lane bridge. And to be fair, until all this started, they really were out of sight and out of the minds of anyone living north of that bridge. Much like Liberty's Guard, I have no idea how long they've been waiting for this opportunity or how far they are willing to take this.

"Wonder what they want?" Daddy asks as he pauses in front of the carport, waiting for Clem and Matt to clear the space.

The Knights show up when they want something or want to do something to whomever they're visiting. I'm guessing the two big men on the tailgate are enforcers. They both look like they lift heavy things for a living, or at least used to.

"They probably want to discuss the new restrictions. You don't think they found out about the deal already? If they get a look in the back of the truck—"

"Don't remove the tarp until they're gone. And pray they go quickly."

"Yes, sir." Daddy pulls into the carport and puts the truck in park.

"Matthew, good to see ya. How's the family holdin' up?" asks

Clem Richardson through Daddy's open truck window, tilting his head to the side displaying his faux concern for our well-being and safety. "Can I offer you a beer? Fresh from our latest batch."

As Daddy climbs out of the truck, Clem's son Dave hands him a mason jar of pale liquid. It looks nothing like the ice-cold Miller Lite I'd been craving. Dave is the official president of The Knights organization, but I suspect his daddy, Clem, is the person calling the shots.

My father sips his beer and nods, "What brings you up here today?"

"Well, Dave and Troy here," Clem motions to his son and the gross man from the boat, "were wantin' to know how your meeting went with that new captain today. I'm hoping you're gonna deliver some good news." The top of Clem's head is pink with sunburn. Perhaps it's time he trades in his signature visor for an actual hat. Troy adjusts his own visor over scraggly, blond hair and winks at me, and I finally know why he looks familiar. The flashes of memory—too many beers, a post-high-school bonfire, a clearing in the woods, my friend Kimmie crying. I remember Troy looking smug and triumphant emerging half-zipped from the trees, winking at me then, too. The memory burns under my skin but unleashing on Troy would surely make this situation worse.

"Well, Clem," Daddy says, "I can't say it looks good."

"No?" Clem asks.

"No, it doesn't."

"Well then, guess I'll just have to pay that young feller a visit myself."

"Go on if you like," Daddy says, "maybe you'll have better luck than we did. He was in his office when we left a few minutes ago."

"Oh, now, Martin," Clem says, smug with arrogance, "you know luck's got nothin' to do with it. Ya just gotta know how to talk with these gov'ment people."

"Well, if anyone knows how to do that…" Daddy says, his poker face spot on.

"It's the least I can do." Clem tips his visor in our direction. As if anything he does is an act of service.

"Alright," Daddy says. "If there's nothing else, the kids and I have work to do."

"Just one more thing, Martin," Clem says glancing at the other men. Two men cross behind Daddy and lean against our truck, too close to the extremely generous amount of Army fuel hidden under a tarp. "Sweetheart," Clem nods at me, "You wanna run along now while I talk to your daddy?"

"No, thank you." I run my finger under the leather string tied around my neck. With my key, I can be in the garage in seconds. Just a couple seconds more and I'll reach the rifle I stashed in Jacob's footlocker.

"What do you want, Clem?" The mason jar in Daddy's hand vibrates a little, betraying a bit of the neuropathy he tries to hide from all of us, but it rears its ugly head when stress builds in his body.

"I want to know that you're on our side in this. It'll be much more impactful if we make a unified stand against these restrictions, these impositions being placed upon us, don'tchya think? All this business with Martial Law and the curfews is bad enough, but now they're telling us where we can and cannot fish? I'll have none of that and I'd think you'd have a problem with it too. We're ready, but having you and Junior and that son-in-law of yours standing with—"

Daddy cuts Clem off. "I've told you before. Leave my name and my family out of whatever it is you've got planned."

"Y'all don't want to be left out here on your own, do ya? It'd be a shame if somethin' was to happen." Clem removes his visor and wipes his forehead with a dingy handkerchief.

"Are you threatening my family, Clem?"

"No, no. No one's threatenin' anybody. I just know how bad things can get 'round here. Real fast."

"The answer is no, Clem. Now you get your boys off my property." Daddy tosses the remainder of his beer out on the grass and then hands the jar back to Clem. "Thanks for the beer, but I got a lot of work to get done before sunset."

"So, that's it?" Clem asks.

"That's it."

"Martin, I'm assuming you didn't have a choice in the Army using your land, but you got a choice now. Stand with us or stand with them. The choice is real simple."

"Clem, I've done all the talking I plan to do today. You best be on your way."

"Martin, you mark my word, this ain't the end of it." Clem tosses the jar to Troy and hops in the passenger side of the dually.

"Not by a long shot, Martin," yells Dave, jumping in the truck behind the wheel. The rest of The Knights load into the back of Dave's truck. They speed out of the driveway, spitting up gravel behind their tires.

"What a bunch of jackasses," Daddy says, watching them leave. "And their beer tastes like piss." He turns to us and motions to the truck, "Store that fuel in the shed. Use that tarp to cover it and padlock the door. Where's Mama?"

Garrett, already loosening the tarp, calls over his shoulder. "She's on the pier with everybody."

"Y'all get that put away quick. Nobody needs to see it." Daddy leaves us in the driveway and heads around the house to the pier.

"So, what happened?" Garrett asks, lifting the red containers out of the truck.

"Well, Daddy made the deal, obviously, and he got Captain Johnson to raise the price. This is just for one week."

"Holy shit!" Garrett stares at the rows of containers.

"Yep. Now are you on board?" I ask.

"Whatever, Jules. It's done now." He grins at me, grabbing the two containers of cooking oil. "Kate is gonna love this."

"What did it look like out there?" Matt asks.

"Busy. Crowded. Cleared."

Matt's right eyebrow ticks up.

"They mowed down a bunch of the trees out there to make room for everything. They've already got trailers and tents and a whole battalion of vehicles and equipment and more generators than I've ever seen in one place."

That got Garrett's attention.

"The whole camp is one big exhaust cloud. And I'm not thrilled by the arsenal they appear to be building."

"See, Jules, this is why you can't trust the Army. They've got us beggin' for shit while they're stockpiling." Garrett snatches the cooking oil canisters out of the truck and carries them to the shed. A lifetime of farm work has sculpted the muscles along his forearms and through his shoulders so he moves the canisters with little effort, as if he could toss them from the truck to the shed.

"Garrett, you don't know that. All we can do is just wait and see and try to stay under the radar." I heave a propane tank from the truck bed. "And I never said I trust them."

"Then why are you supporting this, Jules?" Garrett grabs the last propane tank from Matt and sets it in the shed.

"Well, you just put one reason in the shed," I tell Garrett, which makes Matt snort.

"There's a hell of a lot we could do about this." He stomps off toward the main house, leaving Matt and me alone. I guess Garrett doesn't find me funny.

"We're not doing that, Garrett," Matt calls to Garrett's back, who doesn't turn or pause or acknowledge Matt in any way. "We already decided. And you heard Daddy, we're not joining them."

"What are you talking about?" I ask Matt as he secures the

pad lock on the shed door. "Garrett wants to join The Knights? What the hell good does he think that will do?"

"Nothin', Jules. It's nothin' cause it ain't gonna happen."

"Does he know anything about groups like The Knights?"

"He knows what we know."

"Obviously not. If he did understand these militia groups, he wouldn't want a damn thing to do with them. Perhaps he should stick to farming. That's what he knows."

"And what? Leave the warfighting to you?" Matt chuckles at his own sarcasm. "Look, I need help with a busted trap. Looks like somebody tried to snatch it but couldn't get the rope untied. They did a good job of twisting the trap to Hell and back though."

9

*G*ood morning, darlins. Libby Lefty here and I've got the scoop for you. It took a hot minute, but our boy in DC has finally accomplished two critical items. Number one: He found his old nuts and decided to use them, and, number two, he increased US Army troops in South Mobile County. We now have our very own military base. My sources tell me it's about damn time.

For months, The Knights have gone unchecked in South Mobile County. Led by Dave Richardson, son of long-time County Commissioner Clem Richardson, The Knights have been terrorizing, manipulating, and intimidating the people of Bellefontaine. They claim to want freedom and the good ol' American way of life —a return to the good old days. Join them, and they will hook you up with all the mullet and crab you can eat. They'll put a roof over your head and a Bible in your bedroom. But, my darlins the good old days weren't all that good for those of us with ovaries.

Libby's words conjure the image of a corseted woman staring at her needlework by firelight and contemplating stabbing her abusive husband with a fireplace poker. No, the way-back-when is not for me.

The Knights' food and shelter come at a hefty price. To retain what little power Dave and his lieutenants have acquired, they've put an archaic structure in place. The men do the fighting and the plotting, the hunting and the fishing. The women tend to the children, cook meals, and service their men. Women do not leave the compound on Mon Luis Island. One source, on the promise of anonymity, reported to me that she has not seen or heard from her daughter or grandchildren since they moved onto The Knights' compound three months ago. My source even tried to visit her daughter on the compound but was turned away by heavily armed guards. Now, if this group was truly on the up and up, why do they need heavily armed guards? Why restrict access to family members? Is this a homegrown militia or a cult? Both, I'd say.

I urge you, dear sisters, to keep the faith. Screw your courage to the sticking post and we shall not fail! Lady M knew how to get things done, didn't she? She knew tough times beget tough times. And, no, I am not telling you to go out and kill the king or anybody else. Leave the violence to the other side. The next few months will not be easy. But we are women, and women do tough every damn day. I ask you now, if you see anything or hear of anything that The Knights are planning, you must have the personal courage to report that information to the Army. They are our best chance of ridding Bellefontaine, and Mobile as a whole, of this far-right aggression. Then, after, maybe we can return to some sense of normal. But not until every one of these Neanderthals are purged from this Earth.

The slamming of a door triggers every reflex in my body. I grab my buck knife and spin around, ready to fight.

"Whoah, whoah," Matt says, hands held high as if I'm pointing a gun at him. "If ol' Libby is telling you to slice up your one and only brother, maybe she's not the girl for you."

"Woman." I pause for effect then, "If you knock before ripping the door open, you might reduce your chances of being gutted." I release my grip on the knife, allowing it to fall to the worktable.

"She's just as bad as Preach with all her crazy talk and burn the patriarchy. And what is she trying to accomplish? A world of nothing but women? That would be short-lived, don't ya think?"

"I'm sure we'd keep a few men on hand, you know, to answer questions like 'Is that snake poisonous?' 'How deep is that hole?'"

"You are sick and twisted," Matt says. "Which is why you're my favorite sister. Now, can we go before everyone else wakes up and we have to talk our way out of here?"

Minutes later, I lower my kayak into the water. "Got it?" I whisper to Matt, standing below in the still, waist-deep water.

"Yeah," he whispers back, "go ahead with the other one."

Lying on my stomach I feel the weathered pier boards through my threadbare T-shirt. Matt reaches up from below, grabbing four bottles of blackberry wine, one at a time off the crab deck. Next, I hand our small bag of supplies containing water, tennis shoes, and dried fruit chips down to him. He lays his rifle and two paddles, one for each of us, in his kayak, rocking gently on the calm surface. I secure a note on the busted crab trap Matt discovered last week: *Matt and I will be back soon. No worries. Love you, Jules.* Once someone notices the kayaks missing, or notices Matt and I are gone, I hope they'll run out to the pier to investigate and see the note and forgo worry.

Rung by rung, I ease into the cool water until waist deep. On instinct, my toes dig into the rippled, sandy bottom and search for the soft black clay that lies beneath. I triple check my buck knife on my hip and slip over to Matt and my waiting kayak.

"Ready?" I ask, hoisting myself butt-first into my kayak and swinging my legs into the bow.

"Ready. You're sure you want to do this?" Matt floats on the still water, skimming his paddle back as means to fight the current.

"Yes. Now move."

We paddle in silence for the first five minutes, weaving in and out of the abandoned pylons along the shoreline. Shadows camouflage us from anyone lurking on the shore. The rising sun will aid in our escape also, shining beyond us, turning our green and orange kayaks and adult bodies into ambiguous, dark silhouettes against a shimmering, watery background and blazing sun.

Once we reach the first coastal point—each protrusion along the shoreline is a point—Matt eases his pace and turns back to me, "Daddy's gonna shit a brick, you know."

"Yeah, I know, but he can't really expect us to stay locked up in the house forever."

"Those were his orders."

"And we always do what Daddy says?" I ask.

Matt's half-laugh and paddling through the shadows reminds me of our days as teenagers sneaking booze from the liquor cabinet. How many nights did Matt and I spend on the crab pier, passing a bottle back and forth between us in the dark, talking for hours about what we planned to do as soon as we were out of the house and away from Mama and Daddy's rules? Neither of us ever mentioned living at home in our thirties, me as a widow and Matt with a wife and kids.

"This might turn out to be the dumbest thing we've ever tried." I paddle faster for a few strokes until we're side-by-side. Coasting alongside Matt feels safer than trailing behind him.

Every part of this scheme is brimming with hazards. Going against Daddy when we both know we're not supposed to leave the house will cause serious trouble. Especially when he finds out that Matt and I snuck out to go to Market Days at the Marina. And yes, that is an irritating feeling because I am a grown woman capable of making her own decisions, dammit. I'm thirty-two, not twelve. Next, what if the kayaks get stolen while we're searching Market Days for wire? That's a grave possibility and one that would require us to enter Army-occupied land. What is the punishment for trespassing on government property under martial law? And then there's this: Market Days is sure to be crawling with soldiers. Stuck between the Army—the green guys—and The Knights—the crazy guys as far as I'm concerned—is not a place anyone should be.

"Yep. Real dumb." Matt grins at me, the same grin he'd given me every time I devised some careless, teenage plot. And, like all those times, I didn't have to work too hard to convince him to go along with me.

As we paddle further along, the sun illuminates a school of porpoises going through their morning circus tricks. One small, curious creature swims toward us and pokes his rounded snout out of the water. He flips his tail and darts off in the opposite direction.

No matter the time of day, the sliver of shoreline between Bay Air Road and Goat Island, is mysterious, almost creepy. All sorts of strange items float up on the deserted strip: bottles missing their labels, etchings worn away by the waves. Odd parts of sunken shrimp boats, downed by human error or an almighty terror. Once we even found a child's bracelet. Had it been swept off a small wrist by the pounding waves of a tropical storm or tossed into the sea by an angsty adolescent? As kids, Matt and I concocted stories for every item we found washed ashore.

As we near Goat Island, Matt slows his paddling and lifts his binoculars to his eyes. It's early but I can clearly see soldiers milling about the triangle of land.

"Matt, put those away and keep rowing." Matt was mostly a smart guy, but sometimes Jacob's words echoed in my mind, *His children will be pretty, but dumb.* Each time, Jacob's insult earned him my knuckles in his bicep. But, sometimes, such as when my baby brother is actively spying on an Army camp, I agree with Jacob. "Are you trying to get us arrested or worse? I'm fairly certain they won't like us snooping." The difference between Matt and me as teenagers is that I never got caught. Matt did. All the damn time.

"What the hell are those?" Matt asks, ignoring me, still staring through the binos.

"What?"

"Those, those," Matt says and passes the binos to me. "Those cannon looking things."

Peering through the binoculars, two field artillery canons come into focus, both parked on the southern edge of the island with their huge gun tubes pointed toward Fowl River.

"Go, Matt, go," I say, handing the binos back to Matt, then digging my paddle into the water, in and back, in and back, in and back.

To think Martial Law requires field artillery canons is laughable. Almost. Maybe I could laugh if I knew without a doubt that Captain Johnson had no intention of ever loading his cannons. And, without Jacob's knowledge of weaponry, I have no idea what those things shoot. Mortars? Guided missiles? Packs of gummy bears and T-shirts with "I survived the worst year ever" printed across the chest? What seemed laughable twelve months ago is now plausible. All of it.

"How about there?" Matt asks, pointing to a break in the reeds leading to a sloping piece of land.

"Looks fine." I follow him through the gap. With the reeds blocking the wind and chop of the bay, the sounds of Market Days rise in my ears. I often wonder at what point in this goat rodeo will we lose our social norms and stop being polite, swapping sugar and feigning concern for each other when what we really want to say to each other is, "Why do you look better fed than me? How is it that your hair looks clean? What are you hiding from the rest of us, you selfish piece of shit?" And not that money works around here, but I'd give up every dime I may still have in the bank to see Mama forget her manners and slap the snot out of Clem Richardson. Knock that visor clean off his sweaty head.

The clearing Matt spotted looks deserted enough so we tie off the kayaks under the remnants of an old dock, hidden away from anyone with a knife sharp enough to cut the ties. On solid land, I slip on my tennis shoes—still dry, thank goodness—and grab the supply bag. After a few minutes of picking our way through the thick pines and undergrowth, we stand at the edge of the woods to survey the marina parking lot turned marketplace.

Several vendors are ready for business with a handful more setting up their wares, using the backs of pickup trucks for inventory and folding tables for storefronts. It looks as it has for several Saturdays now, except one glaring feature—a fence enclosing the entire lot, leaving one way in and one way out. Army Humvees with gunner on top form startling barricades at the entrance and exit. Four armed soldiers pace around each Humvee.

"Shit," Matt says, stopping in his tracks and gesturing with his rifle, "No way they're gonna let us walk around with these."

"I told you they would be here. The Army's not going to leave a mass gathering like this unattended," I whisper back. "You'll just have to stash the rifle here."

"Fine. But if my rifle gets stolen, I'm gonna be pissed."

"I know, I know."

Matt stuffs his rifle into a blackberry bush, nearly picked clean of berries by whomever beat us to the harvest, then covers the opening with vines. "Okay. In and out as fast as possible. Stay close to me. We'll work our way through the vendors and then to Missus Renaud."

"Matt, I've been to the market before." I smile at him as I stroll toward the lot. "Let's see what we can get for Mama's wine." That sounded way more convincing than, *Two Humvees, a dozen or so armed guards, crazy tall fence, what the ever-loving fuck are we doing?*

"Help me remember where I hid that." Matt frowns at the bush, picks up a fallen branch and lays it on top of the mound.

"It's fine, Matt."

We ease along the edge of the fence to the first entrance. Heading through the gate, a soldier grabs my arm.

"We're just going to the market," I tell him and present the bottles of wine as proof.

"I can see that," he says, "What's in the bottles?"

"Blackberry wine," I say, "Wanna make a trade? My Mama makes it herself. Best in town." In lieu of a hair flip, I toss my ponytail over my shoulder and smile at the boy-faced soldier.

"Um…no thanks. Hold out your arms."

Matt and I sit the wine bottles on the ground. Matt and I stretch out our arms forming two T's. The soldier examines my arms one by one, pushing my sleeves up.

"What are you looking for?" I ask, attempting a Jedi mind trick to stop the pat-down.

"Anything you might consider smuggling in here, ma'am," replies the soldier. He runs his fingers along the underside of my right arm.

"That tickles," I say and pull my arm away from him before smiling at him again while he moves on to search Matt.

"They're clean," he yells, to no one in particular, as far as I could tell. When his gaze drops to my boobs and the corner of his mouth rises a bit, I know he's too green to be of any harm to us.

The soldier hands me two bottles of wine from off the ground. He makes no attempt to pick up Matt's bottles. "Maybe I could sample that wine later on," the soldier says, "if you don't find any takers."

"Maybe," I say and walk through the entrance, making sure my ponytail swings back and forth like a damn cheerleader.

"So now you're flirting with Private Dipshit over there?"

"Just being friendly. It can't hurt."

Matt rolls his eyes at me and tucks the bottles high up under his arms.

Market Days at the Marina is no HGTV-inspired hip, open-air market where you can purchase a Victorian-era chifforobe for ten bucks then transform it in a day with a jug of chemical stripper and a can of spray paint. Picture the worst flea market you've ever visited then add the stench of dead fish and a body-funk cherry on top. Finding the wire we need will involve digging through piles of junk thrown in the backs of pickup trucks and breathing through my mouth. Lots of breathing through my mouth.

Matt and I stroll from vendor to vendor, searching for wire to repair the busted crab trap—thick, moldable, but not too weak. As mangled as the trap is, I'm dumbfounded that we all slept through the theft attempt. Whoever tried to steal the trap had to create quite a lot of splashing and noise trying to rip the trap free of the pier. And what kind of looter doesn't carry a knife? I'd think a knife for cutting rope would be standard issue when attempting to steal something tied to a pole. But the rope wasn't cut. Whoever tried to steal the crab trap, tried to untie the rope from the trap or tear the trap free of the rope. Either way, he failed in stealing it but succeeded in mangling the wire, even breaking it in a few places. Just not where he needed to. The rope was still attached to the trap on one end and the pier on the other. Perhaps it was that kid again. Should I be grateful that he came ill-prepared? Probably, but the looks Matt and I receive from each vendor and passerby diminish my ability to be grateful for anything at this moment.

To many people in Bellefontaine, Matt and I are privileged, and they're right. First, we're Martins and that means we went to parochial school, not public. Private school speaks to the whole money thing, but being more than dirt poor isn't much. Of course, I can't really expect our neighbors to know that. Second, Matt is legendary for his fishing skills, consistently placing in the Dauphin Island Fishing Rodeo every year since he was old enough to compete. Third, the section of bayfront Mama and Daddy purchased has an added and envious bonus: the bottom of the Bay surrounding our pier is smooth, except for gentle ripples created by the current. Cedar stumps and jagged, barnacle covered rocks litter much of the bay floor along the western shoreline. Walking through the water is a fool's errand and one that will tear up your toes, heels, and shins. In several sections of shallows, the sand is so thin that the bottom is really just swaths of black mud. But not ours. Our piece of paradise is perfect for nighttime floundering or wading about with a cast net.

So, what do all these strikes add up to? We're not starving, and we're out. Out of the common thread, out of good favor, and out of luck, as far as the wire hunt goes.

"You know you love Mama's wine. I see you smile every week in church after just one sip," I say to Ms. Fontenot after retrieving a partial spool of wire from the open trunk of her car. "You know you want a bottle for yourself. It would be such a treat for you." I offer her my best good daughter, mild mannered, young lady smile, extending the bottle of Mama's finest to her. "There's maybe a yard of wire there, not much at all, for a whole bottle of wine."

"Now, Jules, you know I loves yo' parens, but I cain't sell that to you t'day. You best just run on now. Run on." Ms. Fontenot shooed me away from her booth as if I had smallpox. So much for *love thy neighbor*. And screw her the next Sunday she asks me to turn pages for her at the organ because "'dis weather's got my arth-a-ri-tus flarin' up." *Turn your own damn pages.*

The next row of vendors react as Ms. Fontenot did. We are shopper non-gratis.

"They don't want anything to do with us," I tell Matt. "Do you think Clem and Dave have put out some order against us? Told everyone not to trade with us anymore?"

"Hey," a man said in a low raspy voice, "y'alls the Martin kids, right?"

Matt and I spin around to find him standing directly behind us. His proximity—the fact that I can smell the salted fish on his breath—is unsettling.

"Yeah, I'm Matt and this is Jules."

"Yeah, yeah," the man says, brushing off the introductions with one dirty hand. "Listen. I know yer Daddy. I know he ain't got a thing to do with all this. All this mess goin' on. But y'all ain't so welcome around here right now. Ya hear? People see you walkin' round they gonna think you're spying for the Army, now that y'all's in cahoots and all."

"Wait a second," I say, interrupting, "We're not 'in cahoots' with anyone. We didn't have a choice in the matter. When the federal government says they're going to use your land, they get the land."

"Alls I'm saying is there's a whole lot of people none too happy with y'all right now. Y'all be much safer at home. And, we're safer not doing business with you all. 'Least till this all blows over. I'm just doin' the Christian thing, trying to keep a neighbor safe." The old man eyes the bottle in my hand.

"Till what blows over?" Matt asks.

"Thanks for the heads up." I hand the man the bottle, and he scurries away, trying to hide the bottle under his T-shirt.

"Old drunk," Matt says then turns on me. "Why are you giving shit away? Especially to him?"

"Because he was willing to speak to us at all. Look around, Matt. Nobody wants us here."

I wave to one of the Renaud boys. He sits in a lawn chair, the old, plastic webbing style that as soon as one strip of plastic breaks, the lounge-ee sinks through the seat, one butt cheek at a time. The chair and the Renaud son perch atop a vintage Winnebago, the kind in every 1980s road trip film ever made. "Is your mom home?" I ask by way of yelling to him. He nods then peers through his binoculars again.

One year ago, that exchange would've played out much differently. The Renaud, whichever one this is, would have stood, climbed down the aluminum ladder affixed to the rear of the RV. He'd offer me a beer or a Coke, something cold to kick off the first of the two topics of conversation worth having: It's so freaking hot the air feels like mashed potatoes and the fish are hiding. He'd turn to Matt and inquire about fishing spots and the elusive, gigantic blackfish Matt and Daddy have been chasing around the Bay for years. Now, the Renaud remains at a safe distance and we from him. We retain suspicion. We watch.

Mrs. Renaud peeks through the tinted glass of the camper's door. She opens it, just enough to glance around the parking lot. "Matt, Jules, come on in and shut the door. Come in. Come in. Hurry up now."

Matt and I scoot through the door and huddle together near the captain's chair behind the steering wheel. Mrs. Renaud moves quicker than I've ever seen her move, sliding windows shut and pulling down blinds until the only light comes from the windshield. It casts a dim, yellowed glow about the living-dining-kitchen combo.

"Sit, sit," she says, pointing to a built-in love seat covered in orange plaid, a tweed so stiff my skin itches before my legs bend to sit. "I figured y'all'd be paying me a visit today." She hands us two glasses of sweet tea, lukewarm with a circular slice of lemon in each. "You'll have to make do without ice in your sweet tea."

"Thank you, Missus Renaud. This is a treat, ice or no ice." I take a sip and try to make my face match my words, but the shock of sugar proves too much and I am sure she witnesses a wince.

"So," Matt says, "How long have you been living here?" The assumption that the Renauds have left their home, one mile down river, to ride out this mess in the RV is easy to make with the mussed sheets on the full-sized mattress in the rear, dishes stacked near the sink, and the lived-in odor assaulting my nose.

"We still got the big house for the boys and their wives and the grands, but I'll be here till this is done. No way I'm leaving what Mister Renaud's built to the looters. Well, what's left of it." She glances down at her hands—liver spots covering crooked fingers and knotted joints hidden by skin so thin a good breeze could tear it.

"You stay here by yourself?" Concern is thick in Matt's voice.

"Young man, I am not as fragile as your face thinks I am. But, no, I do not. The boys take turns staying here with me. And before you ask, they're none too happy with me staying here, but I'll tell you what I told them. I am not leaving. Not as long as the Army points those cannons in our direction. If they want to bomb anybody 'round here, they're going through me first. And I'll be damned if I turn this spot over to the squatters or anybody else."

"I don't think they would use those cannons." I adjust in my seat to move my thigh away from a particularly spikey section of tweed.

"Of course, you don't think that. Young lady, we're all sure your Jacob was a good man, although none of us got to know him well, seeing as you rarely made it home for the church lawn party, much less Christmas and Easter each year."

"Yes, Jacob was a good man. And I'm here now with no plans to go anywhere any time soon." *Why the hell should she care how often I came home?*

Mrs. Renaud rests her glass on the laminate table bolted to the floorboards in the middle of the conversation-lounging-eating area. "Jules, you should know people 'round here are startin' to put two and two together. First, you come home, right after Clayton Vancleave gassed those poor souls in Mobile."

"I came home because Jacob died."

"Then, the Army starts patrolling and hanging around you."

"Hanging around? I'm not hanging around with the Army."

"Well, you and Billy Roberts were spotted chatting it up on Goat Island with that Captain Johnson fella and then the next day Army equipment starts rolling in like their settin' up to fight the Nazis."

"You're missing a lot of details—"

"Details don't matter. Only thing that matters is what people see and what people believe, and they all believe you are the one working with the Army, that they came to you, and you convinced your Daddy."

"None of that is true." The lack of ventilation in this RV becomes pointed the longer I listen to Mrs. Renaud's nonsense.

"And don't think we don't all remember you and Billy Roberts making goo-goo eyes at each other every Sunday coming back down the aisle after Communion. And Mister Greer reminded me just yesterday about a teenage *you* waiting around his grocery looking for Billy. So, I don't think it would be a stretch to say that little crush has rekindled since he decided to come home."

"Billy was assigned here. Soldiers don't choose their orders, they just follow the order."

Mrs. Renaud snorts. "Parading around in that uniform, waving his rifle before his own people. The shame his mother must feel right about now."

"Why should she feel ashamed?" I ask, my pitch too high to hide my true emotions. Matt presses his arm against mine, but I shrug him off. "Missus Renaud, I am not working with the Army in any way. You need to get your facts straight. Yes, Matt and I ran into Billy and Captain Johnson on Goat Island. Yes, I was happy to see Billy, but there is nothing going on there. And everyone needs to know that when the Army says 'we're taking this land for a while' that means they're using the land whether we want them to or not." I stand too quickly and bang my head against an overhead compartment. "Shit!"

"Watch your language, young lady."

"Excuse me," I say through clenched teeth. Rubbing my scalp, I will the dizziness and pain away, then glare at Mrs. Renaud. "Before all of you start blaming this mess on me and my family, you may want to look across the river. My money's on The Knights for blowing up the bridge and all the bombs and causing the Army to have to come here in the first place. I can't prove it. Yet. But trust me when I say those are the people you shouldn't trust."

Matt stands and nudges me toward the door. "We should probably be getting home."

"Fine." I turn to unlatch the door, then remember the wine. I sit three bottles on the table. "This is from Mama." *Try not to choke on it.*

10

S lamming the door on an RV does not satisfy me. The flimsy thing pops right back open after I slam it, leaving a framed image—Mrs. Renaud still in her chair breaking into a bottle of Mama's wine. Cocktail hour starts early at the marina.

Back on the asphalt, the air is better than inside the RV, but a crowd at the market entrance has gathered since we first entered. Several of the men waiting in line shout at the soldiers, taunting them with accusations of being *commies* and *occupiers*.

"Since when did being a soldier become a bad thing?" I ask.

"Since the soldiers switched sides."

"Excuse me?" I cut my eyes at Matt, the urge to explain the Constitutional duty of the military almost too strong to deny.

"To all of them, the Army are persecutors, not protectors."

"Well, they are wrong, Matt." The catch in my throat is too familiar, as if unstable is my constant state. Why do I care what anyone thinks of the Army anymore? That part of my life is over.

"Maybe the fam hasn't noticed we left," Matt says as we move through the entrance, skirting the thickest part of the crowd.

"They've noticed. By now they're—"

A blast knocks both of us to the ground. Maybe we dove. I

don't know. The force of the sound jolts my insides. I can't hear. Oh, I can't hear. I open my mouth and taste dirt and metal. Blood. My mouth is bleeding.

"Matt!" My throat pushes the sound forward, but I can't hear his name. On my knees I scramble to him, on the ground a few feet away. "Matt, Matt." I grab his shoulder and roll him over.

Matt's lips form the words *I'm fine, I'm fine* as he spits dirt and dust out of his mouth, but I still can't hear anything save a ringing akin to an icepick to the ear. Metal scraping metal, looping, rising, piercing.

I clamber to my feet and look back at the entrance to the market. The chain link fence is mangled, with sections twisted into sharp claws reaching toward the sky. People litter the ground. Some curl into balls, trembling. Some writhe and reach for bloodied limbs and lacerated faces. Some don't move at all.

My ears pop and for a moment the release of pressure is heavenly, but then I can hear. I hear everything. Screams and cries escape the wreckage. A woman grasps my ankle. Her hand is bloody. She has a gash above her eye. Several yards away, the ground is scorched and what is left of maybe two people lie motionless on the ground. They must have been standing too close to the explosion because neither corpse has legs.

Soldiers, their tan combat boots covered in soot, move through the wreckage. They bend to assess injuries and yell commands over the screams and cries. I turn in a circle, uncertain of which direction to move, when someone hits me. He slams into my back, knocking me to the ground. His shoe comes down, barely missing my face as I roll onto my side. From the dirt, I see a man running away from me, down the path. On my hands and knees, I strain to identify the man who just mowed me over. Before the man dashes into the tree line, a flash of blonde hair flaps from under his baseball hat, revealing exactly who he is.

I crawl toward the path, trying to get my feet under me to run after the man. "Matt! Matt, that's Troy! Matt!" I call again as I rise, propelled as if someone throttles me into the air.

I hurdle a fallen pine tree and then another, cutting through the thicket to make up time on the winding path. Pine needles prick skin as I block the larger branches with my forearm.

"Jules!" Matt yells from somewhere behind me, but I don't stop.

I run straight toward the shore, trying like hell to catch Troy. The asshole from the boat and our driveway runs ahead of me, disappearing into the tree line. In my gut, I know why he's running. If I could catch him, drag him back to the soldiers, this could end. The Army would have proof of who The Knights really are. If I can just run faster.

Out of the woods, I see him again. Several yards from shore, swimming. Two men grab him by the arms and pull him into a boat. The motor roars as the boat heads east, straight out into the bay. My head and ears pound and I squint, making out the gold K painted on a blue shield on the back of the boat.

"Jules! What the hell are you doing?" Matt asks, now standing next to me, a rifle in his hand.

"That was Troy!"

"So what?"

"He did this!"

"Did you see him plant the bomb?"

"No, but he knocked me to the ground as he was leaving. Why would he be leaving so fast if he wasn't trying to escape? If he didn't have some reason to run?"

"Looks like he had a ride waiting for him."

"Uh, yeah. A bomb goes off, Troy takes off running, a waiting boat speeds him away. Doesn't take a genius to see suspicion in that."

"Also makes sense that you don't tear off after him like a damn maniac."

"We should go back and help." I step toward the path to the marina, but Matt stops me.

"No, Jules. We need to get home."

"I need to tell the soldiers what I just saw."

"No! Home, Jules. We're going home."

"But we know who did this."

"We're going home." Matt stomps toward the kayaks, leaving my mouth agape on the shoreline. "Jules, right now we need to go home and figure out how to get all of Bellefontaine to stop thinking of you as the enemy."

"One way is to tell Captain Johnson what I just saw. Tell him that Troy did this."

"You still don't get it do you, Jules? To most of the people here, the Army is the bad guy. Which means you are the bad guy by association. Which means we," Matt gestures to us both, "are the bad guys."

"So, let's go help them! Some are already dead for all we know!"

"No, Jules! Stop! Right now, you can't fix anything." Matt bends to untie a kayak.

"Why are you so pissed at me?"

"What were you planning to do if you caught Troy? You alone? Unarmed?"

"I don't know, Matt. Something!"

"Something? You could've gotten yourself killed running after him."

"I'm fine!"

Matt snaps back at me. "Let's get the hell outta here before somebody blames us and strings us up from the nearest tree." Matt steps into the water, shoes and all.

We keep close to our neighbors' piers on our way home, scanning the boards and pylons as we glide under each one. After seeing the Fowl River Bridge and market destruction, it wouldn't surprise me if private piers became their next target. Unless they're aiming for the Renauds, which makes no sense at all. Why blow the bridge and the market gate, if the real goal is the Renauds? They could just incinerate Missus Renaud in her RV with at least one of her boys, blasted out of his lawn chair, and then they'd be done with it. Yet how much bad luck can one family endure? A sinking feeling tells me that we, the Martins, are responsible for today in a significant way: Soldiers never guarded the market before we gave them our land.

None of this seems right, and every time we hit a section of open water, I feel exposed. Troy and his friends could come at us from any direction. I concentrate on my strokes, somewhat, but fear pulls focus. Growing up here, in the middle of middle-of-nowhere-adjacent, the worst crimes were all petty theft and foolishness: a couple of fishing reels stolen off a pier, a chalice stolen from the church, and drunk teenagers who took the curve on Bay Air Road too quickly and ended up in our neighbor's back yard after taking out his mailbox. Bombings are what happens in far off pockets of the world, not here.

But now, the body count is rising. Bombings are a part of my world now, too frequent to cast off as isolated acts. The woods that used to hold my fears of alligators and bobcats now hide so much more. Knights who aim to harm us. Soldiers who want adherence to rules and peace at all costs, even if it means terrifying a community. I am afraid that we, like the people fishing under the bridge that day or the people in line at the market, are in the middle. Blamed, ousted, exiled from both sides. In too many ways, we are the middle, that tract of battlefield where two sides collide. Red coats versus blue coats, drenched in blood until only one color remains. But we, the Martins, are not wearing the color of either side. Not if anyone around here bothers looking.

Paddling through the last pier near our stretch of Bay Air Road, I see Mama pacing back and forth near the boathouse, Daddy off to her left. When she sees us, she stops pacing and folds her arms across her chest. Mama's pursed lips pull me from my rabbit hole.

"Shit," Matt says.

"Yep, they look pissed."

To be more accurate, Daddy isn't looking at us at all. He's rocking back and forth in a swing, staring straight ahead at the open water.

"Where have you two been? Were you in that?" Mama yells at us, points to smoke rising over the shoreline. "Get your butts up here, now!"

"Yes, ma'am."

"Don't you '*ma'am*' me, young lady!"

Climbing up the ladder, I take the first kayak from Matt, who stands in the water below. Mama continues, "Your father gave you a direct order not to leave this house. And what do you do? You run off, completely ignoring him. That's what you do!"

Standing in the shallow water, Matt lifts the second kayak over his head. I grab one end and heave it up onto the deck.

"You've scared us all to death!" Mama pulls me close and wraps both arms around me. "Stupid, Jules! So stupid!" Over her shoulder, I see Lauren running to us, flip flops popping against the pier boards. She's followed by Kate, Mallie, and Jessie. Mallie's blonde curls bounce with her small body as she holds tight to her mother and jostles around on her mother's hip.

Matt tosses the loose paddle up on the crab pier and climbs up the ladder.

"Well, where have you been?" Mama asks again. "Answer me!"

"The marina," I say and glance over to Daddy. He stares straight ahead, which is alarming in its dismissiveness. His sunglasses hide his eyes, but I don't need to see them. I know he's as furious as Mama, probably more.

Lauren shoves Matt and then grabs him. She hugs him tightly, wrapping her arms around his neck. "What the hell were you thinking?" Tears pool in her eyes and run down her cheeks.

"We needed wire," Matt says, pulling out of Lauren's embrace.

"Wire?" Mama snaps.

"Yes, Mama, wire," Matt says, "and we were trying to find out what's going on around here. Don't you want to know?"

"Do not speak to me like that," Mama says, unfolding the note I left earlier. "And what was the meaning of this?" Mama waves the scrap of paper at me. "I know this is your handiwork. 'Matt and I will be back soon. No worries.' Do not insult me with your patronizing, young lady." She turns to Matt. "Daddy and I don't need you to find out what's going on around here. And we don't need five traps. Four is enough. But you…you…you just run off on your own! And I'm not supposed to worry?"

Mama's pitch and volume scares Mallie. She cries and reaches her arms out to me. "Ules, Ules! Pease!"

"I'm sorry, Mama," I say.

"Ules boo-boo." Mallie touches her bottom lip, then pats it. "Boo-boo Ules."

"I'm fine, Mallie. It doesn't hurt." I wince when I touch my lip, busted from my fall. "I'm fine. I promise."

"No, you're not." Daddy finally speaks. He grabs Mama's hand, pulling her into the swing. "If you were, you wouldn't have left this house. You wouldn't have put yourself in danger. You wouldn't be looking for ways to get yourself killed."

"Daddy, we're fine. We weren't hurt." I glance down the shoreline at the smoke still hanging over the marina.

Mama, while grasping one of the chains that connects the swing to the rafter above, says, "Julianne, you cannot go off like that."

"Mom, Jules and I can take care of ourselves. We're careful," Matt says.

"We heard the explosion!" Mama sobs but doesn't break her gaze with us. "For all we knew, you were in that."

"So," Daddy breaks his silence again, "You went to Market Day."

"Yes."

"Which was bombed?"

"Yes, sir." I can barely make eye contact with Daddy. With my knees scratched and my palms raw, I know it was a stupid move.

"Which I told you would happen, right?" Daddy asks.

"Yes," I whisper.

"Speak up!" Daddy demands.

"Yes! Yes! You're right!" I glare at him from my swing, unsure of who I'm angry with: Daddy for treating me like a child or myself for being so freaking stupid as to walk into such an obvious target?

"But you chose to ignore me?"

"Yes."

"Well, what did you get for my wine?" Mama asked. "I know you took four bottles."

"Nothing from the vendors," I say. "None of them will trade with us."

"They're all pissed at Jules."

"Matthew Junior!" Mama snaps.

"We didn't get anything from the vendors," I say, silently begging Matt to keep his mouth shut. "But, Missus Renaud was willing to speak with us."

"And?" Mama asks.

"They blame me."

"For what?"

"Everything."

11

*G*ood afternoon, Patriots. And let me be clear, by Patriots I'm talking to all of you who cherish what is truly American in our struggling country. If you're some lib, happy that the Army is here and you don't mind your constitutional rights being stolen in the name of protection from some unknown boogeyman, go on and hop on over to Libby Lefty. I'm sure she'll coddle you and wipe your little butt and make you feel that the Army is here to save you. But you, my fellow Patriots. You know the real deal. The Army is a warfighting organization. And they're here to fight us.

The radio spits and sputters with static so I jiggle the antenna until Preach comes through loud and clear again.

That's their sole purpose. So, if not to wage war on Americans, why are they here? If they're here to protect us, then they are doing a piss poor job. I lost count of how many people were injured this morning at the marina, but I do know that five innocents lost their lives, and the Army did nothing to prevent that. Oh, they're doing illegal body searches and have limited our access to the market and fishing and hunting while we're trying to feed our families and keep our community unified through this mess. But, let me assure you, they are abiding by DC's liberal agenda—

Static spills from the radio again, cutting off Preach's rant so I cut off the radio. Thank sweet, baby Jesus for small favors. How can I explain the tangled mess that is my brain? Well, first, my head is pounding, but if I sit still or lay down, a low hum fills my ears. Maddening. All morning and into the afternoon, Mama forced mint-sage tea on me. That's mint and sage leaves crushed in hot water, so I don't think it's technically tea. There's not a single tea leaf on the Martin property. So, maybe it's broth. But I think broth indicates meat and there's no meat in it. But I guess you could consider it vegetable broth. Oh, who knows? Who cares? What I do know is that Mama thinks the concoction will soothe my headache. Something about natural remedies. I also know that the concoction is revolting—mint sauce with a hint of rotted foot.

After the noxious tea and forced reclining on the couch, I'd retreated to the stifling heat and dingy smells of my workspace; first to hide from the rest of the family, but mostly to try to salvage something, anything good from this day. I had nowhere to escape except the garage. Hunting with Matt is out of the question. A peaceful outing in my kayak is a no-go. Mama and Daddy will never agree to let me take a kayak out on my own, possibly ever again. Lauren and Kate are also angry with me for running off, putting myself in harm's way, and dragging Matt along with me. They know whose scheme we'd played out.

My heart aches at the thought of the Army being villainized because they are following the orders of their Commander in Chief. Do I want the Army here? No. But, it's not because I am afraid of them. And why would anyone believe I'm all gung-ho Army when they're the reason Jacob is dead. And, yes, I know the Army didn't kill Jacob, but he's dead because he was in the Army. Is Captain Johnson a total ass-hat? Yes, but that doesn't mean he aims to hurt innocent people. And, why isn't anyone villainizing the person responsible for yesterday's bomb? The person that creates explosions around here is the enemy, not the soldiers doing their jobs.

That brings me to what has me so full of dread that I laid on the couch for an hour replaying the scene in my head: Troy being hoisted into a boat with the Knights' emblem painted on the side and staring at me while they sped away. I'm no detective, but that behavior screams "perpetrator." So, what do I do? Do I go to the camp and inform Captain Johnson of what I saw? That would be the right thing to do, except Mrs. Renaud claims that someone is watching me and reporting who I talk to and where I talk to them. How did I not know someone was lurking in the woods that day Matt and I ran into Billy and Captain Johnson? That was maybe two or three weeks ago, but it feels like ages and the world feels chaotic and I feel like I should go on the run like Harrison Ford in the *Fugitive,* only I don't know what crimes I'm running from as I haven't committed any.

If I do report Troy, and he is arrested, what then? Surely The Knights will retaliate. They could come here. Plant bombs here. That puts everyone at risk. Jessie will never leave this place for her own adventures. Mallie will never grow up, never learn who she is to become. But, are they safe if I do nothing? Troy could come after me to make sure I can't report him. That brings me back to running. But unless I tell The Knights "I'm leaving, so chase me and don't hurt my family," leaving isn't the answer either.

I want Jacob. I want my old life. I want Monday through Friday of a soul-crushing job and to fall asleep watching TV. I want weekend date nights and quick getaways. None of this should be happening and that thought makes me curse myself because it's so stupid and pointless. Jacob is dead, dammit, and he's never coming back. This shit is happening, and there's nothing I can do to stop it. So, reminding myself over and over again that all of this sucks seems masochistic.

I pick up my hammer and chisel and pound the seam between the red sole and black, polished leather of my Louboutin boots. The glue and stiches rip apart. The destruction feels good. My fingers tear into the broken seams—splitting, devastating, ending a thing of beauty.

Another half hour of hammering and ripping, and I don't know the sweat on my face from the tears. I toss the hard foot-bed and sharp heel aside and rip my blade along the back seam of the boot shaft. The leather is perfect—black, shiny, supple—worth every penny I paid for it in a world filled with karaoke nights and work lunches. Like everything else in this world, my boots are toast. *Good riddance. I've no use for beautiful now.*

I drop the leather to the table and sit on Jacob's trunk crying into the back of my hand, trying to muffle the sound. A few seconds were all that separated us from that bomb, the violent burst of fire and metal. In exile in the garage, I cry without fear of interruption or judgment. Because the truth is I'm scared. And the guilt of knowing I put my baby brother, my best friend, in danger is too much. Sobs stick in my throat every time I think of having to live without him. And if Matt had been one of the five, Lauren would know my constant pain. His children would grow up without a father. I would have no one left in my corner.

The image of Lauren running into Matt's arms plays over and over in my mind. I will never feel that again, to be so close to another living being that his flesh is an extension of mine. I will never be so scared that half of me won't come home or feel the elation of wrapping my arms around him when he does. I hate her for still having those moments, and I hate myself for the envy burning my skin.

With several deep breaths I dry my face on my T-shirt, not giving two shits that it's filthy. Let the grime mix with the tears and sweat. All that matters, I decide, is the project laid out on the worktable before me. *One moment, one task at a time. Breathe. Focus.*

The leather slices easily under my blade. Any resemblance to my sleek boots is gone in seconds. I run my knife lengthwise along the boot leather, cutting a long strip. Beads of sweat drip off my face and dot the leather. No matter. The leather is utilitarian now. Its purpose is strength, not style.

Would Jacob, the man I chose, even recognize the calloused, primal woman I've become? Would he want this version of me? One who chased after criminals alone with no thought to her own safety or the safety of her family? Was that what Jacob did, in the moments before he died? Did he run toward the danger without any thought of leaving me behind, or was he just caught in the middle?

I grab two straw brooms, pliers from Daddy's toolbox and two wired, beaded necklaces from the bottom of my shoe bin. With the pliers, I tear the broomstick clean of straw. Breaking the clasps off both necklaces, the beads slide into the toolbox, freed from the wire. They bounce around the plastic compartments like pretty, painted jumping beans. I grab a handful of long drywall screws and secure two screws to the broom with the wire. I wrap the wire around and around the broom and screws until the wire is so tight it slices the palm of my right hand. The pain is an awesome sensation —real, present, visceral. And the cut is well worth the pain. The screws point out from the broomstick, their sharp tips ready to plunge into whatever comes their way.

I secure one end of a long strip of boot leather with a tack hammered into the wooden broomstick then wrap the end of the broom, covering the wire. A few inches of metal stick out from beneath the leather and beyond the end of the broomstick, like three serrated blades attached to a spear and perfect for stabbing a flounder with the sharp, pointed tips. I repeat the process with another broomstick, more screws, more wire, and another strip of the soft leather. Droplets of blood fall onto my work, so I wrap my hand with a scrap of fabric. The blood easily smears away but leaves a dull streak across the leather. No matter. Soon enough, I'll cover the entire gig with blood. My functional artwork is a thing of beauty to behold—one perfect, useless pair of boots reincarnated into two new flounder gigs.

12

With everyone else sound asleep thanks to a little help from Mama's finest, Matt and I scan the water for bottom feeders. Tonight is perfect for floundering—low tide, clear water, and a big bright moon. Any snagged stingrays, spots, and croakers will bait the crab traps. Blue crab, ground mullet, and especially flounder, we'll eat. As soon as I showed the gigs to Matt, he was ready for nightfall and floundering. Chomping at the bit, really. Why he feels he needs his rifle slung across his back while floundering, I'll never understand.

I hold tight to my new gig ready for my first strike when a hardhead catfish brushes by my ankle. I jerk my foot up. "Shit."

"What was that?" whispers Matt.

"Catfish."

"Yeah, I'm afraid that's what stole my bait earlier tonight. Nasty bastards."

These are not the catfish that, when filleted and fried, taste like my Granny rose from the grave to prove to the fast-food industry how fried fish should taste. Although, I'd devour some rectangular fried anything from McDonald's right now. No, the catfish in Mobile Bay have venomous barbs along their spines and taste like…well, I don't know what they taste like. We don't eat them. Period. And, we try like hell not to step on them. If stuck by a barb, the swelling is serious and the pain severe. I can't see a catfish without remembering Mama writhing on the beach, screaming at Daddy to get a barb out of her foot. Daddy scooped her up and ran to the car, yelling at us to stay put until he got back from the hospital.

Matt and I stalk our prey in silence, shuffling our feet through the sand—the best way to walk and not get a catfish or stingray barb in your foot. With the moon to light our way, I bend close to the water and peer through the surface looking for any shadow or mound of sand that could be a flounder, our most desired target.

"Gotcha!" Matt sneers after several minutes of our slow, silent stalking. "Jules, the net. The net!"

I grab the net out of the tub, dropping my own gig in the water. It starts to float away, but stops as soon as the twine connecting it to my waist tightens. Without hesitation, I scoop the net under Matt's gig and pull his prize out of the water, which nearly fills the net. It flops and flails at the end of the gig, struck right between the eyes.

"Holy shit! Look at the size of that thing!" Matt forgets for a second to be quiet.

"He's got to be two feet long."

"Hold the tub still. I don't want this baby falling back in the water."

"That's no baby." I lower the enormous fish and net into the tub, holding the floating bucket steady with my free hand. With one hand on the fish and one on the gig, Matt tears the screws out of the fish, shredding its face.

"I guess I should have used nails instead of screws," I say, staring at the bloody mess.

"Well, this guy was never bound for beauty pageants." Then, presumably remembering that floundering is a quiet endeavor, he whispers, "But he is bound for my belly!" Matt's smile flashes in the moonlight, and I can see the boy who taught me to flounder decades ago. For now, we are those two kids again, awake well past our bedtime, relishing a playground few children ever know.

With the water rising, our tub heavy with fish, and the moon creeping behind approaching clouds, our night of floundering comes to an end. "Might as well go in," I tell Matt, "I think we're past our fair share of flounder. And I don't want anyone to think we've run off again."

"Yeah, you're probably right." Matt pats me on the shoulder. "You've gotten much better with the gig."

"Desperation is the spark of determination."

"Don't tell me you miss *buying* your food," he teases.

"Yes, Matt, I miss overpriced, plastic wrapped steaks and little Styrofoam trays and rude cashiers. I miss all of it."

"Steak…and cheeseburgers. I'd gig you right now for a cheeseburger."

"Hey!" I say and kick through the water, spraying his shorts and T-shirt.

Matt splashes back at me, spraying the light salty taste into my mouth. "Yeah, do you think we'll ever get back to the way things used to be?"

"I've no—" A faint shimmer moves across the water near our pier. On second glance, the object appears rigid, catching the fading moonlight as it glides past the barnacled pylons of our pier. "Matt," I whisper, grabbing his arm, "what is that?" I point to the object.

"What the hell?" Matt whispers back and quickly unties the bucket of flounder from his waist. "Jules, take this." He hands me the rope and pulls his rifle around to his chest. "This is why I wanted the rifle. Get behind me." We crouch down into the water, our chests just above the rising tide. Matt holds his rifle in front of him, just above the surface. On our knees, we inch closer to our pier through the shadows of the old, weathered pylons.

"Stop!" Matt yells as he jumps to his feet and runs toward the pier. A small skiff floats into a pool of light. One of our crab traps rides in the stern. "Stop!" With his second warning, Matt fires one shot in the air.

I drop into the water, shocked by the loud bang from Matt's gun. Brackish water splashes into the mess of flounder, but the tub stays afloat without letting any of its precious cargo escape.

Looking across to our pier, I see the skiff flip over. The sound of splashing fills my ears as Matt runs through the water to the skiff

"I won't miss twice," Matt yells as he reaches the skiff. "On your feet!" He points his rifle toward the skiff, waiting for its pilot to emerge.

Dragging the tub of flounder behind me, it takes me twice as long to reach the overturned dinghy. "Matt, stop!" A small blond boy turns to face us. From head to toe, he's nothing but skin and bones, all 'knees and elbows' as my Pawpaw would've said. Even in the poor light, shadows appear under his rib cage and gapped teeth behind rounded, pink lips.

"It's you."

"You know this kid?" Matt asks.

"You shouldn't have come back," I tell the boy.

"Come back? What the hell, Jules?"

"You're trying to steal from us again? Why?"

The boy says nothing. Instead, he stands frozen, staring at me. Then, he takes one step backward.

"Stop. You're not leaving this time."

"Jules, seriously, how do you know this kid?"

"Matt, I caught him out here once before, a week or so ago. It's not important."

"Uh? Yeah, it is. Is this who's been stealing shit from us?"

"I don't know. All I know is that he tried once before," I tell Matt, then turn back to the child. "How old are you?"

The boy looks up at me. A buck knife sticks out from the waist of his cutoffs.

"So, you found a knife, huh?" Rather than answer my question the boy shifts his gaze from me to the tub of flounder.

"You better hand me that knife, son," Matt says, pointing his rifle directly at the kid. Slowly the boy pulls the knife from his shorts and hands it to Matt. "And get your hand off my crab trap, you fucking thief."

"Matt! He's just a kid," I say, smiling at the boy, trying to ease his distress, although he seems unaffected at having a gun pointed at him. "What's your name?"

No response.

"Do your parents know you're out here?"

The boy closes his lips around his overbite and stares at me.

"Who do you belong to?" I ask.

"Hey, kid," Matt snaps, "we're being awfully nice to you since I'm guessing you're the little shithead that's been stealing stuff around here. So, are you gonna answer her or not? Who do you belong to?"

"Me," the boy says.

"Well, that clears things up now, doesn't it?" Matt grabs the boy by the arm and drags him toward the ladder.

———

Matt's cleaver crashing against the cutting board wakes me with a jolt. He smiles at me, his sneering smile that says *I'll let you live but this might get painful.* Another chop and he whacks the head off a flounder. The stench of fish guts waft over me as I unfold from my swing and glance at the opposite swing and its contents

—a pintsize thief sleeping soundly through Matt's hacking and chopping.

"He's still here," I say, stretching my arms toward the metal roof.

"Yep, the little shit didn't escape. No help from you, of course. You snore, by the way."

"I do not," I say. Then whisper, "What should we do with him?"

"String 'em up by his ankles until he gives me back the shit he stole."

"Matt, be serious."

"I am being serious."

"Nobody's stringing anyone up. We don't even know his name. We don't know where he came from or who he belongs to— nothing." I pad over to Matt, trying to stay upwind of the flounder.

"Exactly." Matt waves his cleaver toward the sleeping boy. "Maybe he needs a little incentive."

"Maybe he's on his own? He doesn't look exactly cared for. What kind of parents let their kid run wild through the woods?"

"Maybe." With his fillet knife, Matt pushes the deboned strips of milky, pink fish to the side of his board, and then dumps the skin, spine, tails, and head in a corroded ten-gallon bucket. "Wait. Woods? I thought you caught him out here."

"I did. The night Daddy told us about the deal with the Army. But…" I paused, bracing for impact. "I saw him the next day in the woods off the road."

"What? Why didn't you tell anyone?"

"Because he wasn't doing anything. He was just perched on a branch."

"Like a lookout? Jules, dammit, I don't know where your head is at sometimes."

"Matt, how much damage can a child do?"

"Plenty. To date, we've lost one long-handled net, two very expensive reels, one cast net, a flounder gig not made from your damn boots, and about a week's worth of salted fish, stripped right off the drying lines. He's gonna have to tell me how he pulled that one off and what he did with all my stuff."

"You don't know if he stole those things or if someone else did. All we know is that he was trying to steal a crab trap last night."

"And that he was standing right here a couple of weeks ago, probably trying to break into that shed." Matt points to the closet-sized shed in the corner. "You know the same shed that we lock now because a whole lot of fishing equipment walked away not too long ago. And like you said, no parent is going to let their kid run around the woods by themselves right now. So, my guess is that little shit is the lookout for someone else or reporting to someone else. At the very least, he's following someone's orders."

"And if he's gotten himself wrapped up with bad people, don't we have an obligation to help him?"

"I'd bet the 'bad people' he's wrapped up with are related to him. I don't know. But, he will tell me." Blood drips between his knuckles as he points at the boy with his cleaver.

"Matt, we have to do something. If he's on his own, how long will he survive? And if someone is sending him out to steal from people, again, how long will he survive? And what if his parents don't know where he is and are searching for him? Freaking out thinking maybe he's dead or kidnapped?"

"Jules," Matt says bringing his cleaver down on his next victim, "you seem awfully concerned about some thief's well-being rather than finding out the whereabouts of all the gear he's stolen from us."

"What makes you think he's the one responsible for all of our missing gear? Trust me, he's not the only desperate one around here."

"And here we go. Jules Martin Jones. Defender of the downtrodden."

"People wouldn't have to steal if they had access to necessities! And he obviously doesn't have what he needs."

The swing behind me creaks and I turn to see the boy, fully awake, blue eyes shining in the morning sun and boring a hole in my face. "Good morning," I say, uneasy with his steady stare. "Are you hungry? You must be hungry."

He doesn't answer and I'm not surprised. Last night, after an hour of Matt's fruitless interrogation and me urging him to at least tell us his name, he fell asleep on the swing without giving up an iota of information. I guess I fell asleep shortly after. Judging from Matt's mood, he stayed awake for the rest of the night, contemplating fileting us both.

"Still don't feel like talking, huh?" I ask and flinch as Matt's cleaver finds its way through another flounder. "Pay no attention to him. Matt's harmless."

"You'd like to think so, wouldn't you?" Matt asks, brandishing his bloody cleaver just below another wicked grin.

"Matt, stop it." I turn back to the boy. "Well, maybe you'll feel like talking after breakfast." I turn toward the main house. "Let's see what we can scrounge up. Okay?"

"That's right, Jules, feed the criminal."

"Would you like me to bring you some breakfast, Matt?"

"No, no, I'm fine. By all means, the rat should eat first."

The boy hops off the swing to follow me, jumping at the chance to either eat or to get away from Matt. I can't tell.

To the tune of *Camp Town Races*, Matt sings to himself while freeing another flounder from its head. "Little bastard stole my shit, do-dah, do-dah. Little bastard stole my shit. He's gonna give it back." Whack!

The boy and I both jump at the hard thud and the blood and guts spraying from the fish.

"Let's go. Matt's not right for public consumption today." I toss Matt a healthy dose of side-eye and guide the boy down the pier. "Everyone else should still be asleep." Back on solid ground, I lead the boy through the front door and into the great room and point toward the barstools tucked under the kitchen island. "Have a seat. I'll see what I can find for us to eat."

Breakfast in the Martin home is never exciting: bread, jelly, if we have it, and fruit, if we have it. In our mad race against the heat of the day, we always eat quickly to get the harder chores done before the sun hangs high over us. Protein and lengthy conversations are for midday and evening meals.

"Eventually," I say while slicing a day-old loaf of bread, "you're going to have to tell me your name."

The boy doesn't look at me this time, just at the bread.

"Do you like strawberry jelly?"

He gives me a curious look and then watches me as I unscrew the lid.

"Well, do you like strawberries?" I ask.

"Who doesn't like strawberries?"

Well, at least he spoke. I spread a thin layer of jelly over two slices of bread and offer one piece to him. "Here you go." He takes it and in doing so, I see black dirt under his fingernails. I should have made him wash up before eating. Adults are always saying those kinds of things to children. *Wash up for dinner. Wash your hands. Remember to use soap.* And, whereas I am an adult who lives with several children, I am not their caretaker. So, with two, small, dirty hands, he shoves half the bread and jam into his mouth.

"Careful, you're gonna choke."

"No, I ain't," the boy says between hurried bites. Then, he smiles. And when he smiles, little bits of bread and dark pink jelly peek through gaps between his teeth. He devours the bread in three huge bites then gulps down the cup of water I poured for him.

"Can I have more?" he asks.

"More bread or more water?"

"Both. That jelly is good. Where'd you get it? It ain't like Greer's is open."

"My mother and sister made it."

"Well, it's real good."

"How about another piece in exchange for your name?"

"Huh?"

"I'll give you another piece of bread, if you give me your name."

"And more jelly?"

"And more jelly," I agree, knowing I would give the boy whatever he wanted with or without information in return. What I don't know is why. I should be suspicious of this boy, but I'm not. I search every cell of my being and can't find an ounce of suspicion.

The boy gazes at the ceiling, as if considering my proposition for a couple of seconds. "Deal." He holds out his hand, not offering a handshake, though. Rather, his arm is outstretched with an open palm.

"Name first," I say, holding the bread out of his reach.

"Cole. My name is Cole Aarons."

"Aarons, huh?" I ask, filling his cup from the large container of drinking water. Then, I sit on the stool to his right. "That's like a character from a favorite old book of mine."

Cole's face betrays him for a moment and the faint smile tells me I'm on a good path.

"Perhaps you've read it. *Bridge to Terabithia*?"

Chewing, he shrugs.

"The main boy is named Jessie Aarons. He's pretty quiet and

shy at first but then creates this whole fantasy world and learns—"

"He doesn't do it all by himself. Leslie's there too."

"So, you do know the book?"

"Yes, and he doesn't create Ter-bithia because he's shy. He creates it so him and Leslie have a place to go because the world is dumb sometimes." He glares at me with eyes even bluer than earlier on the pier.

"Did you read the book for school?"

"No. At home."

"Oh. That's a pretty complex book for a reader of your age. What, like, ten?"

"I'm eleven. And I didn't read it by myself. My mama read it to me and sometimes we read it together."

"So, where's your mother now?"

"Can I have another piece? I mean I can go find something to trade you for it, but that shouldn't take long around here."

"Payment isn't necessary, and I think if I let you go *find something*, Matt will toss you on the cutting board with the flounder." The boy shudders. "I'm just kidding! I won't let him do that." I grin so that he knows I'm teasing him, and then caution, "let's wait a minute and see if you're still hungry." From the looks of him, he stays hungry, but I don't want him puking on Mama's floor. "So, where are your parents?"

"Heaven, I guess. Least that's what Miz Martha says."

"Oh. Oh, no. I'm so sorry."

Cole shrugs off my concern but the silence thickening the air tells me his parents haven't been dead for long.

"And Miz Martha is?" I ask.

"The old lady that checks in on me every few days. She used to live next door to us before Mama and Daddy died and the soldiers came and cleared out all the houses. They told us nobody can live in our neighborhood anymore because all the houses got poison in them."

"Poison?"

"Lady, you sure ask a lot of questions."

"My name is Jules. You can call me Jules not *lady*. And when a boy creeps around alone in the middle of the night trying to steal a crab trap, I develop a lot of questions. Now, who do you live with on a daily basis?"

"Nobody. I can take care of myself. So, I do."

"I'm sure you can, but being alone isn't the safest thing to be right now."

"Like I said, I take care of myself."

"So, where do you do all of this caring for yourself?"

His lips purse again, as if he's reached his limit of questions for the day. He eyes the jelly jar, fingers drumming the granite counter as if he was planning to snatch it if the jar ade a run for the pantry. "Henry and Miss Martha, they let me sleep on their porch, if it's raining. Miss Martha gives me bread sometimes too, but she don't have no jelly."

"Maybe you are still hungry." I walk around the counter. Cutting a third piece, I ask, "So, where do Henry and Miss Martha live?"

"Bellefontaine Boulevard."

"So, not too far from here."

Cole takes the third slice from me and slides off the stool, taking the bread with him.

"Careful," I say, "you get jelly on that sofa and Matt's cleaver will be nothing compared to my Mama's wrath."

"Your mama lives here with you?"

"My whole family does."

Cole holds the bread closer to his bare chest, careful not to bring it close to any object in the living room. He examines each piece of furniture, glances over pictures, and smells Mama's flowers as if investigating every item for its worth and use.

"These don't smell like nothing," he says, pulling his nose back from an orchid.

"No, they're just pretty."

He gives me a curious look.

"They make my mom happy. So, who cares if they smell or not?"

"Flowers should smell." He moves around the living room, not touching anything, just looking as he nibbles on the bread, sucking on each sweet morsel. Stopping at the open toy box, he stares at Jessie's bucket of Legos.

"Those belong to Jessie, my niece. She's about your age."

"Is she the redhead girl?"

"Yeah, how do you know she has red hair?"

Cole points to the console table. "Well, her picture's right there… and I seen her on the pier and…"

"You have?"

"Yeah, I seen her with a couple other kids."

"Do you come here a lot?"

"Sometimes. Mostly on real calm days. It's hard to row in the big waves. If the water's rough, I just stick to the land. But, I'm a good rower," he says, as if I questioned his ability to paddle his little skiff up and down the shoreline.

"When you finish your breakfast, we can play with those Legos if you want."

Cole shoves the remaining bread into his mouth then lifts the bucket of Lego bricks from the toy box. Still chewing the huge bite, he carries the bucket to Mama's cream rug and plops down in the center. He rubs his dirty, bare feet on the soft carpet, digging his toes into the long shag. Dumping the bucket, he spills little red, yellow, blue, black, and green pieces onto the floor.

Cole connects a few pieces, then looks up to me, frowning. "Matt is your husband?"

"No, he's my brother."

"Oh." He appears to contemplate that for a few moments. Then staring at the Lego pieces in his hands, he says, "He wants his stuff back, doesn't he?"

"Yes."

"I don't think Miss Martha will give it back."

"Miss Martha?"

"Yeah, I already ate the bread," he says.

"You ate three pieces," I say and sit in front of him, the bucket of Lego between us.

"Not the bread you gave me, the bread she gives me."

"Do you steal stuff and trade with Miss Martha for food?"

"Yeah, Miss Martha… others, too. But Miss Martha's my main customer."

"But it wasn't your stuff to trade." I pick up a couple of plastic pieces, snap them together and wait for him to speak. He doesn't. "Cole, it's not right to take other people's stuff. That's stealing. No matter the reason, it's still stealing."

"Well, then, is Matt gonna give me my knife back?" he asks. "He took that from *me*."

Mama and Daddy's bedroom door creaks and footsteps on tile sound from the hall. Cole quickly shoves the pile of Lego toward me and jumps to his feet. Mama and Daddy stop short when they see the wiry boy standing in the middle of the great room.

"Jules, I didn't realize we had company," Mama says pulling her cotton robe closed over her nightshirt.

"This is Cole," I say, glancing down at Cole standing next to me, "Cole, say 'hello' to my parents, Mr. and Mrs. Martin."

Cole stiffens and closes his mouth, returning, once again, to his silent defense.

13

"Mine," Matt says, tugging on a rope knotted every two feet or so and tied to a large branch of the most beautiful live oak I'd ever seen. The tree conjures fairy tales and storybooks with ivy covered limbs and wisteria-draped branches. "Mine. Mine."

I turn to see Matt holding a gig and net. "Matt, stop it."

"You stop it. You may have some weird soft spot for this kid, but what I see is a thief." Matt glares at Cole. "I'm taking my shit back."

"Cole," I say and stoop to speak to him eye-to-eye. "Is this where you are living?" I know the answer by the makeshift campsite littering the ground and the blanket draped across the biggest branch of the tree. Staring up at the branch, I ask, "Is that where you sleep?"

"Only on nights when the ground's too wet."

"This can't be safe. Living on your own out here can't be safe."

"I do just fine on my own," Cole says, straightening his belongings as Matt pilfers the campsite.

Matt snatches a green fishing lure off a table constructed of broken pallet boards with soccer ball-sized rocks for legs. "Yeah, you seem to be doing just fine. Mine!" Matt shakes the lure in Cole's direction.

"He's not fine!"

"Yes, I am," Cole says, but he doesn't raise his voice, doesn't lose his cool. He states his case, plain and simple. "I take care of myself."

"What if you get bit by a moccasin, or a boar or bobcat come up on you? What would you do then?"

"If you leave them alone, they leave you alone." Cole's resolve reflects a much older person. What kind of child is unafraid of the teeth of a wild boar or fangs of a snake?

"Cole, do you remember in *Bridge to Terabithia* when Leslie decides to go to Terabithia on her own? Do you remember what happened to her?" The boy nods at me, frowning because any true fan of Terabithia hates thinking about what happened to Leslie. "Living in the wild like this, alone, it can all change on a dime, and no one will be here to help you." Cole shrugs me off and climbs his tree, three branches up and a worrisome distance from safe ground.

Hours before, Daddy, Mama, Matt, and I stood around the kitchen island discussing the "Cole situation." Cole played with Lego bricks on the floor with Lauren's and Kate's kids. It hadn't occurred to me how bored with each other they must be until I saw them welcome Cole into their playgroup. Not one turned up a nose or gazed on Cole with suspicion. To them, he was new, wild, a living embodiment of the Swiss Family Robinson.

Cole relaxed in their presence as well, locating pieces for the roof of a miniature cottage for Jessie and smiling as Mallie pinched his cheeks. He sat on the floor with his chin resting on his bent knees and chatted with them, Jessie mostly. I strained my ears to hear their conversation, to learn what secrets he felt he could share with Jessie but not with me.

But I couldn't hear what Cole told Jessie because the adults were talking. No, not talking. Arguing. The adults were, per our usual, arguing, and this time we were arguing over the best course of action for a deserted child. Matt and Mama pushed to take the boy directly to the Army camp and turn him over to the authorities. Daddy argued taking him to the church so Father Morgan could turn him over to Catholic Social Services. What, if anything, they could do for Cole in the middle of this mess, with the world around us so unsettled as crises hide behind every turn, none of us knew. As for me? I want to keep him. I know that sounds insane, knowing that I've known the kid less than twenty-four hours and that I know exactly two things about him: He is an orphan, and he does what he must to survive.

"How do you know he won't hurt one of us as soon as we fall asleep?" Mama asked.

"Sure, Mama, cause that's what he is. A little Ted Bundy in the making."

"Jules, our first priority is to this family," Matt stated.

"As long as we're safe, to Hell with everyone else? Real Christian, Matt." Well, that was the straw that broke the back of that conversation. Mama suggested I walk away before judging anyone's faith, at least not in this family.

In the end, I decided that we, Matt and I, would escort Cole to wherever he was hiding out. Setting him free with no idea of how he survived on his own was out of the picture for me. Turning him over to the authorities as a criminal was also out of the question. That would only result in a kid lost in the system, and, well, Mobile has enough lost children right now. Matt agreed for the reason now on display: Screaming *mine, mine* like a harpy and snatching and grabbing his stolen gear. Mama and Daddy agreed because Matt would protect me as I am obviously, in their eyes, weak and incapable of taking care of myself. Thank goodness for Matt or I surely would fall victim to the twelve-year-old serial killer. I agreed that if any of us caught Cole doing anything else illegal, I would turn him over to the Army myself.

"When that guy killed my mama and daddy, I was at school. I stayed late that day 'cause I had robotics club and when my mom never showed up to get me, my teacher finally drove me home." Twenty feet up, Cole straddles a big branch, laying on his stomach with his arms wrapped around the fat limb. "I remember I got out of his car and Miz Martha came running over, telling me not to go in the house. I think the only thing that saved Miz Martha from the poison was her flower ladies. She had one of her flower meetin's that day. And the meetin' was in Mobile, so she and her man Henry wasn't home when it happened."

"What happened? Do you know what happened to your parents?" *Easy. Don't push too hard.*

"I's told the bug man came. Sprayed all the houses. But the bug guy comes 'round all the time so I can't figure how that time was different."

"Clayton Vancleave?" *Keep him talking. Ease him down.*

"Maybe, but. Nah. Not Clayton. I mean, I don't know." Cole's gaze shifted forward as if peering through the thicket of trees just beyond his small clearing. "This was a couple months after Clayton done what he done and I'm pretty sure he was already dead. Least that's how people were acting, like Clayton's dead. I remember when Mama and Daddy died it was after Halloween, and Miss Martha wouldn't let me go in the house even to get my Halloween candy, and I got two full bags this year."

"That's too bad. What was your costume?"

"Psycho zombie clown."

"Oh! I bet you looked very scary." I glance at Matt who rolls his eyes at me. So stubborn. Then, something Cole said struck me. "Cole, did you know Clayton?"

"Yeah. He lived a few trailers down from me. Was friends with my daddy."

"Oh." *Holy shit. Welcome to our fucked-up world, young man.*

Clayton Vancleave had killed himself almost nine months prior to this boy looting his way into my life. So, two months later, maybe three, another bug man sprayed Clayton's neighborhood. Why would someone do that? How had we not heard of this on the radio? At the very least, the gossip mill should have been humming.

"So why aren't you living with Miss Martha now, or maybe a relative, a family member?

"I ain't got family. It was just Mama and Daddy and me."

"So, Miss Martha?"

"I'm not gonna live with her. I tried that already. Her man's mean, and I don't want to be anywhere near him. He took a belt to me. Only reason he lets me sleep there when it's stormin' out is because I bring him and Miss Martha stuff they can trade for food. I even bring 'em food sometimes. So, if you don't let me be or if you're thinking you're gonna leave here and turn me in, Miss Martha'll starve to death without me. They're old and Mister Henry's got a bum leg. They will starve without me."

"Cole, I can't just let you be. Out here? Alone? That's not how good adults care for children."

"I'm not a child."

"Sorry, kiddo, but in the eyes of the law, you are a child. And children without families need to be placed with a family who will care for them."

Cole sat up, straight-backed and defiant. "I won't go. And if you make me, I'll run. I made it away from the Army when they came—"

"When the Army came?"

"To my old house." Cole looks at me, annoyed. "Mobile. D-I-P." Everyone in Mobile knows Dauphin Island Parkway as DIP. We also know some of the roughest neighborhoods in the city line that highway. "Ain't you been listening to me? You are from here, right?" Cole pointed north toward the Mobile suburbs. "I used to live over that way. And after the bug man came, a bunch of soldiers showed up, wearing these mask things on their faces. They said we all had to leave the neighborhood immediately. They tried to load us all in their trucks, saying we couldn't take nothing not even our cars cause the whole neighborhood and everything in it was poison."

"Oh."

"Well, I knew better'n to get in no Army truck, so I took off for the woods and hid out there for a couple of days. Then I saw the firemen show up, but they didn't come to put out fires, least not at first. First thing they did was start fires. Every trailer burnt. Only the trailers didn't burn all the way. So, they hosed the burnt pieces and then big trucks came and took all that away so now there's nothing left."

I sift through memories, trying to recall a fire in that direction. And it'd have to be a big one, but smoke is commonplace nowadays so who can distinguish one smoke cloud from another.

"Few days after that, Miss Martha found me. She and Mister Henry got an RV set up in the trailer park a little ways from here. I went with her, but after a couple weeks, I couldn't stay there no more. My mama told me if anyone ever put their hands on me, I was to run like hell to safety. Well, Mister Henry's belt might not be a hand, but it hurt like one, maybe worse. That's when I decided I's better off alone. No bug man is gonna spray my stuff with poison in the woods. He'd have to find me first and no one's found me yet."

"I found you."

"Only 'cause I let you."

"Cole, you're alone."

"Yeah, but out here is a lot safer than being where you are." Cole gestures in the direction from which we came, in the direction of our home. "Too many peepers 'round there."

"Peepers?"

Cole straddles the branch and scoots on his bottom closer to me. "Now who's not being safe? You ain't noticed the people in the woods by the swamp. I see the same two guys there all the time."

"What are they doing?" The hairs on my arms stand up.

"Just hangin' out I guess. I don't know. Listen, just leave me alone alright? I promise I won't steal stuff from y'all anymore."

I look at Cole for several moments, noticing how he doesn't break eye contact with me. He doesn't withdraw behind the tree's trunk, trying to avoid me or hide. He has stated his case and is at peace, steadfast even, with the decision he's made. How can this boy be only eleven? "How about you check in with me every other day at my family's house, just so I know you're safe, and let's go with 'not steal from anybody anymore' because people shoot looters around here. I can give you food and whatever else you might need." Matt offers a random noise in my direction, a grunt or cough or some other blast of derision. "Ignore my brother. *I* will help you."

Cole stares at me for at least ten seconds, locking his gaze to mine.

"Cole, agree to my terms, or I'm letting Matt have you. And if that happens, no one will talk him out of dropping you at the Army camp. You'll be arrested, probably jailed, and then who knows what will happen to you. I don't want that for you, but you're leaving me no choice. And just so we're clear, if you don't check in with me when you're supposed to, I will be back here. I know how to find you now."

Cole's jaw tightens. "Okay. But just so you know, I'm doing this for you. I'm not afraid of the Army, and I'm not afraid to be alone, and I'm not afraid of the woods."

"You best be afraid of me," calls Matt, tired from all the

pillaging and now resting against another tree at the edge of the clearing.

"You don't have to be afraid of Matt. His bark is way worse than his bite. Come by tomorrow to check in. I'll scrounge up a food bag for you."

"Fine."

"Well, don't sound too excited," I tell him.

"Good, cause I'm not."

Call me a smitten kitten because this kid, this crooked-teeth, sass-talking, dirty, no-good looter, is perfection. Pure, blessedly independent, fearless defiance behind bright blue-green eyes and spot-on instincts.

"Matt, do you want me to list what's not going to happen?" I ask, following Matt's lead over a felled pine tree.

"No, but I'm sure you will—"

"I will not turn Cole over to the Army for theft. I will not return him to that abusive Henry and his manipulative wife Martha. I will not allow Cole to starve or feel like he has nowhere to go once life out here becomes too hard."

"Fine. But you're giving him your share. Not mine or Lauren's or anybody else's. Yours."

"So, again, Matt, I've got to ask. When did we start caring about us and only us and everybody else be damned? That's who we are now?"

"Jules, we are already killing ourselves—you and me—to keep this family fed and now you want to add another mouth, one we don't know. One that stole from us. You have officially lost your damn mind, Jules."

"Matt," I say, stopping short of the next rotting log on our path back home. "What is the point of all the church and all the prayers if we don't reach out to those in need? Isn't Cole among the weakest of us? You're telling me you're fine with him starving? Alone?"

Matt stares at me. He says nothing. Not a word. Sweat beads roll down his forehead. "Lots of people are hungry right now."

"But we know this one. He has a name. We might not be able to help everyone, but we can help him."

Matt shrugs. He's either out of arguments or tired of them.

"You're fine that he has no choice but to keep stealing, so he can make his deals with Martha hoping she'll give him a few crumbs?"

"Of course I'm not okay with that. That woman should be arrested. And Cole does have choices. You're refusing to see that, sis."

"Starve or steal. Those are his choices as *he* sees them."

"You know, Jules, I've always loved your bleeding-heart side, but I don't have the luxury of helping every stray that wanders into the yard. I've got to do what's right for my family, my wife, my kids." He takes a few steps forward, then pauses. "You don't have those luxuries either."

"I know."

Matt may think he's suffering while he and Lauren worry together in the bed they share. When the bed is gone, along with the person who is supposed to be in it with you, that's a suffering I would never wish on my baby brother. I can see that suffering in Cole's eyes. He's surviving, but for how long? He's coping, but how well and when will he use up the last dose of coping he's stored away? He's lonely. I saw that when he chose to lower his guard with Jessie and Mallie and the other kids. I wonder when his loneliness will ruin him. I wonder the same for myself.

"Okay, Matt, here's an offer. Tomorrow, we go find this

Martha and explain to her that she is not to trade with Cole anymore. That if she does, we will turn her in for peddling stolen goods and child endangerment. In exchange, I feed Cole. We have enough to feed one more kid. And won't threatening Martha bring you a scrap of vindication?"

Matt turns in a circle, exhaling a long stream of air. "Fine. But if I catch him snooping around again where he doesn't belong, his ass is mine."

———

In so many ways, grief is a hurricane. Brace for the storm surge. Endure blinding wind and rain for hours or even days on end. Seek higher ground when the water rushes toward you. Marvel at the stillness of the eye, that moment when the wind and rain and waves subside and all you're left with is quiet. Yet you know that peace is only temporary, and you don't know how long or short the calm will last. Without warning, the wind whips around and comes at you from both sides. The southern eyewall pummels you while the northern edges of the storm whip back around to remind you of what came before—fear, grief, pain, loss. Grief is not a singular wave. It is a series of onslaughts. It is a cyclone, capable of reminding you in the harshest ways if you stay in a state of calm too long.

I lay on my parents' couch trying to sleep. Begging for relief from the backside of the storm. Cole—meeting him and talking with him and leaving him alone—gave me a blessed distraction and a worry outside of my usual troubles. For a few moments, I forgot what I needed—Jacob's miraculous return to me—and concentrated on the needs of another. And that other person, that *new* person, has no connection whatsoever to my old world. His only connection is in the present. No memory of Jacob lies in his expression. Cole can only be part of the present. So, for the transgression of forgetting my rage, my sorrow, I will pay. The cost? One decent night's sleep for forgetting my dead husband for a couple of hours.

14

"Don't." Peering down at Jacob's footlocker, I fight the urge to run my fingers over the remains of his life, piece-by-piece, for the thousandth time. A picture of Jacob kayaking in North Carolina, broad-shouldered and smiling, the sun tanning his skin. His Dress Blues jacket, the one that reminds me of how the sight of Jacob walking into a room told everyone everything they needed to know about him—confident, intelligent, with a smile that drew people to him. Why can't I be on his arm just one more time? Feel the strength of his posture for one more hour? An hour, because one minute will only make me want another.

The mist net, still in need of repair, calls to me from my work-table, but working alone in here is the last thing I want. Today I want to run from the grief, those invisible prickles covering my skin and screaming of loneliness. They've grown too loud.

"Let's go-o!" Lauren, in her best mommy sing-song, breaks the silence. Her voice floats through the open door of the garage, drawing me away from Jacob's trunk.

Peering around the door, I find Lauren standing in the carport, several small baskets in her hands. Her oldest, Jessie, five-year-old Lucy—Kate's middle child—and little Mallie trail out of the main house. Mallie's round cheeks and blonde curls bounce beneath a lilac sunbonnet.

"Where are y'all off to?" I ask Lauren.

"Blackberries and pole beans," she says, handing baskets to the girls, giving the smallest to Mallie who wraps both pudgy little hands around the handle.

"Do you have another?" Picking berries and beans isn't the chaos I crave, but it will get me out of the garage.

"Have mine." Lauren smiles and offers me her basket. "Mallie and I will share."

Unlike the women with whom I share blood, Lauren doesn't hold grudges. She expresses anger and sorrow and worry as she did two weeks ago on the pier, then she lets the ugliness go. On the contrary, I carry around a mental shit-list of those who've done me wrong. As does Kate. We learned to do so from Mama. And, before you think I'm blaming Mama for my ability to hold grudges, don't. I'm grateful. My shit-list has served me well. I remember every person who ever dared misjudge Jacob or underestimate his abilities as a commander, friend, and just all-around good human being. I remember every man before Jacob and the lies and slights they tried with me. I remember every situation where I felt belittled or tricked. My list informs my instincts, so I keep it close.

Lauren tilts her head and softens her eyes. "I didn't know if you'd want to come." She hands me her basket and glides one hand over and down the length of her golden ponytail. Everything about Lauren is golden—skin, hair, heart. How did a sarcastic man like my brother convince this Disney princess to spend her life with him? Yes, I'm grateful for this, too. Along with holding grudges, Mama is the one who taught me to count my blessings, especially on rough days. Lauren is a blessing.

"I need a good distraction," I say, taking the basket from her and feeling the woven reeds, rough against my callused hands. I attempt to grab ahold of Mallie's hand for the walk down the road to the garden, but she bobs and weaves, keeping her footing in that way toddlers do—somehow finding their balance just before disaster strikes. Mallie toddles up to Jessie and Lucy, proclaiming her big-girl status. Her white basket bounces back and forth at her ankles, her only care in the world to keep up with the older girls' much longer strides.

In the garden, in a single-file line, we walk between two rows of ripening fruit. The garden is an impressive sight. More impressive is how quickly Garrett transformed the empty plot of land into this cultivated mass of life sustaining food. Before planting a single seed, Garrett and Matt spent a week driving tall stakes into the soil and connecting one to another with wire so that a fence surrounds the garden, and rows of stakes hold vines of precious cargo—blackberries and pole beans, tomatoes and strawberries. Mama's greenhouse, once shelter for orchids and other moody flowering plants, now holds a steady rotation of seedlings. Once one harvest is complete, we transplant the next crop of vegetables into the garden.

How did Garrett and others know we would need a long-term solution? I didn't. For the first six months I held out hope. We all believed this mess would end and quickly, that everyone would come to their senses and drop the anger and bad acts. But not Garrett. His natural cynicism saved us from malnutrition. While Garrett planted seedlings, I clung to hope. I live day-to-day, believing my mantra, "Tomorrow we will return to normal." My brain tells me that one night's sleep isn't going to rid our corner of the world of the militia groups, con-artists, radical psychos, and traitors, but I do enjoy a good dose of "ignorance is bliss."

"Lucy and I will get the beans," I say, shaking off my tangled thoughts.

"Okay, that means Mallie, Jessie, and I are on blackberry duty. Mallie, I'm watching you," Lauren says, stooping to look into

Mallie's round face beneath the brim of her hat. "I better see berries in that basket and not in your mouth. Your Nana needs these berries."

Mallie giggles and bounces off toward the closest bush teeming with blackberries the size of gumballs.

One row into the beans, my basket is half full, and the tension knotting my shoulders and stomach starts to ease, although my lower back aches from the stooping and standing and standing and stooping, low stem to high stem for almost an hour. Perhaps I can get Mallie to jump up and down on my back when we get back to the house. Work out these knots for her favorite aunt.

In this place, where a garden exploded from nothing but grass and dirt, I confirm that a simple repetitive task like harvesting pole beans in the sun allows my mind to go blank, void of whatever is plaguing me. No whispers of Jacob. No nagging of the boy who lives in the trees. I concentrate on the process alone: check the bean stalk for ripeness, pick the shoot off the vine, drop it in the basket, and repeat. Check, pick, drop, repeat. Check, pick, drop, repeat. On and on, filling our baskets to the sounds of little girl giggles and cicada songs. I stand, stretch and prepare for the next squat.

My legs freeze as my eyes register a figure at the end of the row. "Lucy, run on and get your Aunt Lauren," I stare at Troy and try to keep my voice level. The sight of him, a member of The Knights trespassing in our garden, sets my nerve endings to Code Red. "Go, honey, go." *Remain calm. Breathe. Dogs can smell fear.*

"But that man…" Lucy moves behind my leg. I keep my breathing steady hoping my panic doesn't seep through my skin and infect my niece.

"It's okay," I tell her. "Just go on to Aunt Lauren while I speak with the man." I guide her to a thin spot between two stakes and watch her crawl through and run around a row of berries, out of sight. When I turn back, Troy's closed the gap between us, now standing ten feet from me.

"Troy, I don't know why you are here, but you need to go. This is private property."

"I know that." He chews on a piece of jerky dangling from his mouth, then takes the whole piece into his mouth, chews, and swallows. "So, Miss Julianne Martin, did you finally remember my name?"

"Yes, Troy, I know who you are. And you need to leave."

He walks closer to me, and the breeze blows a sour, boozy smell my way. If I had to, I'd guess corn mash moonshine. Nauseating and toxic, especially if you consume the first batch out of a still, which to my dismay Troy apparently didn't do.

"Now, why would I want to leave before we get a chance to catch up?" Troy spits on the ground. "You know, when we seen you and ol' Matt with that bucket of mullet a couple weeks back, I thought that was you, but I thought ain't no way she's still looking that good, but I was wrong. You look as tight as you were back then."

"Move on, Troy." My voice holds conviction as I stare him down. Out of the side of my eye, I see Lucy's escape path and wonder if I will fit, if I will need to.

"Don't be like that, Jules." Troy takes another step toward me. "The way you was chasing after me at the market, I figure you're itching for us to spend some time together. Figured I'd let you catch me this time."

"Last warning, Troy." I reach for my knife, but his hand catches my wrist, fingers closing around my arm so tight I think it may break. "Let go!" My voice is unlike any sound I've ever made. Loud, low, primal.

Troy throws my knife to the ground and pulls me into his chest. "But ain't this what you wanted yesterday? You weren't chasing me for something else, were you? You're not that stupid, are you?"

The stench of sweat, dead fish, and moonshine burns my nostrils. "Let go!" My legs flail as he lifts me off the ground then slams me hard onto my back. Scrambling in the dirt, I back away, but not fast enough. He's on me, and his hair is falling into my open mouth, and his arms pin me to the ground.

Troy's knuckles are in my stomach as he yanks at the waistband of my shorts. And then they're down. *No. No. No.* I tug at them but he yanks even harder and I feel the hard ground through my panties and his fingers on my inner thighs as I drive my heels into the ground trying to back away. He presses one forearm onto my throat, pinning me even more, stopping my escape. He's heavy, more so than he looks, and I struggle to breathe. No. This can't happen. He shoves one knee between my legs and grabs my right thigh.

"No!" My voice is a low rasp with his arm still against my throat.

"Hold still, bitch," he pants in my ear, his tongue so close I feel its dampness.

"Hey! Get off her!" A voice pauses Troy. He laughs.

I tilt my head back expecting to find Lauren charging down the row. Instead, I see Jessie. In one fluid motion, she plants her feet, extends her right arm back and her left shoulder forward. Like Matt throwing from third to first, she releases a rock. She is indeed her father's daughter as her aim is as true as his ever was. The rock ricochets off Troy's forehead, splitting his skin on contact.

"Fuck!" Troy rolls away from me and onto the ground. Blood runs into his eyes and down his nose. "You little bitch."

"Run!" One word is all I find as I scramble to my feet and pull up my shorts. I reach Jessie then Lauren runs toward both of us, practically dragging Lucy and Mallie behind her. She scoops

Mallie into her arms and heads toward the gate. Jessie holds a second rock, still facing a writhing Troy. Pole beans from my spilled basket litter the dirt in all directions. Jessie stands her ground and with the back of her hand wipes a strand of curly red hair from her eyes.

I grab Jessie by the back of her shirt and pull her toward me. "Run!" We reach the gate several yards behind Lauren and the little ones. Halfway down the road, I turn to see if Troy follows. Nothing. He's not on the road. No one stands in the garden or walks near the fence. Nothing. There's no one there, and the only sounds are the heaves coming from my chest and Lucy and Mallie's cries. The fly on my shorts is torn and won't fasten, forcing me to hold my shorts up with one hand as we run.

———

"Try to hold still," Mama pleads, her eyes wet as she cleans the scratches on my legs.

"Here." Kate offers me a clean button-down, oversized, the kind of shirt worn for comfort alone. "Give me that shirt and put this one on."

I remove my tank top then wrap myself in the soft, baby blue cotton. As I slide my right arm into the sleeve, I see the imprint of Troy's hand on my wrist.

"I'll wash this," Kate says, examining smears of brown and black and green on the cotton.

My shoulder blades feel singed, rubbed raw against the ground. "Burn it," I tell Kate. My fingers tremble and the buttons on the shirt won't go through the small, stupid holes.

Mama cups her hand over mine and glances at the ruined tank top. "Let me look at your back first. Then, we'll fool with those buttons."

"I can get the stains out," Kate says.

"Burn it!" Tears fall from my eyes, finding tiny cuts along their way past my nose to my chin.

"Of course," Kate says. "I'll burn it."

"Kate, will you take the kids outside?" Mama asks. The question is really an order. She's soft with her words and soft with her touch, but I want it all to stop and I want to put a shirt on and I want to scream and I want to kill Troy for trying to do what he was trying to do. I flinch, causing my shoulder to bump Mama's cool, damp cloth, and I yelp as a new, sharper pain is released.

"Who wants to go for a swim?" Kate asks, coaxing Lucy and Mallie away from me. Lucy leaves my side, but only because Kate pulls on her hand. "Let's give Aunt Jules a few minutes of quiet."

Mallie clings to my leg. Her soft arms wrapped around my calf. "Ules boo boo?"

"Yes, Ules has a boo boo." I reach down and pat her head.

"You be okay. I kiss." Mallie stands on her tiptoes and tries to kiss me.

I suck back a cry. "Yes, baby, I'll be okay."

"Bad man gone?"

"Yes, baby." That's a lie. I don't know if the bad man is gone, but I won't have Mallie terrified. She's too young for such emotions.

Kate comes back and frees Mallie from my leg. "Come on, Mallie. Let's let Auntie Jules rest so her boo boos will heal." Kate squeezes my hand with her free arm and takes Mallie outside.

"We didn't see anyone out there," Garrett calls as he, Matt, and Daddy come through the back door and I pull the shirt around my exposed torso.

"Did you check the swamp?" I ask. Mama's fingers make quick work buttoning my shirt, as if my brother, brother-in-law, and father catching a glimpse of my bra would be embarrassing. The bruises are humiliating and they're everywhere. They prove that Troy put his hands on me, tried to rape me. Who gives a shit if my family sees my bra? But, I do. I really do. I want to be head-to-toe covered. Never mind the heat. Give me a blanket, a burka, something I can wrap around my whole body and hide from everything and everyone. I stare at the floor, so I don't have to look at anyone.

Crowded around the granite-top island in the middle of the kitchen, Lauren recalls to the others everything she remembers of the man: tall, blond hair, tattoos, wife-beater tank.

"Troy. It was Troy. He made sure I remembered him."

"Remembered him?" Mama asks.

"From high school. We weren't friends, but he hung around some of the guys from church." Back then, I thought being the only Catholic school girl at the public-school parties made me so badass, so mysterious, desirable even.

"Why would he do this?" Mama asks. She looks to Daddy, "Was this a warning? Some sort of punishment for the Army using our land?"

"I don't know," Daddy says. He stares through the kitchen window, apart from all of us, his jaw tight.

I push down Cole's warning of *too many peepers* around our little slice of paradise. "Troy was drunk. This was nothing more than Troy being drunk." I glance at Matt, begging in silence for him to keep his mouth shut. *Don't connect those dots, Matt.*

Yes, this was a warning. Punishment. Retaliation for being in Troy's way at the market and for chasing him for killing and maiming so many. If I reveal that Troy has good reason to want to hurt me, we could have a lot more blood spilled around here than just a few scratches on my back, arms, and legs.

"We'll find him. He couldn't have gotten far." Matt unlocks the hall closet and retrieves two boxes of ammo. He hands one to Garrett and keeps the other for himself. "We'll search the swamp and the woods between here and the river. He can't have gone far."

And that's the whole plan. Nothing about what they'll do with Troy if they find him. No plan to take him to the Army or inform Clem Richardson that one of his boys attacked me. Not even the best way to castrate the asshole. Just find him. Shoot him. Make him pay.

None of us, not even Daddy, stops them. No one tries. No one objects to the use of gasoline to hunt the man down, least of all me. My silence encourages their brand of backwoods' justice and seems to heighten their adrenaline as they run out the back door—rifles in hand and pockets full of ammunition, ready to defend my goddamn honor. I hope they do find him, and I hope they don't shoot on sight. *Please, Mary, please. Don't let them shoot Troy before I get my chance to beat him with a brick.*

"Jessie." I glance around the Great Room and spot her seated on an ottoman. "I don't know what I would have done if…thank you."

"I had to do something. He was hurting you." She speaks as if her actions were natural, normal, and without consequence. She doesn't know yet that there are adults who wouldn't do what she did or that this unfaltering family allegiance imbedded in her genetic code may become a burden to her. She doesn't know that, because of her actions, a target is now on her pretty, red head.

"Daddy, you and the boys need to finish the fence. The entire property, fields and all, need to be enclosed." Mama has transitioned from nurse to commander.

"The garden is enclosed." I search my mind but can't remember if I closed the gate or not after we first entered the garden.

"Then add barbed wire to the top." Mama's voice hurts my ears and my heart. Anguish fills every syllable.

"This place is going to look like a prison," I say.

"I don't care how it looks." Mama's voice cracks. She tries but fails to choke down a sob. "I just want it safe. Just make it safe, Matthew! Hire laborers if you need to. Just get it done."

Daddy squeezes Mama's shoulder then moves one hand up and down her back, trying to calm her. "I'll start looking for barbed wire today. Maybe the Army will spare some."

I see Mama's wheels turning. "Lauren, you and the kids need to spend a couple of days fishing. Catch as much as you can so we can pay the laborers. I'm sure they'll work for food."

"Marianne, the boys and I can get the fence up and barb-wire the top ourselves. I don't want anyone we don't know around this house." Daddy glances at me, his eyes offering a sorrow I don't want. There's something else there too, in his expression. Does he know we aren't safe, no matter how many fences we build or how close the Army is? Does he know Troy will come again if he's not put down? Whatever it is, I look away. Being vulnerable in Daddy's eyes is one degradation I won't accept today.

15

Matt and Garrett went out early this morning, rifles loaded, to search for Troy. I told them that the only place they'll find him is on the Knight's compound, and that's a place none of us may visit per Daddy's latest orders. Troy is a predator who deserves to have his tiny balls sliced off, but he is not an idiot. Even so, Matt and Garrett are about as interested in logic and common sense as I am right now. So, they will search the swamps and woods from dusk till dawn while I touch my cheek and feel the scruff of Troy's jaw, his breath in my ear, and the weight of his soiled body on mine. The pressure of his arm on my throat remains. His foul odor sits in my nose.

"Jules, honey," Mama says, standing in the side door of the garage—open only for air circulation, not as an invitation to visitors. "Why don't you come inside with me. Kate and I are making hoe cakes."

"Generator, Mama. You're going to have to speak up." I glance at the mist net in my arms. Perhaps repairing it will bring me some sense of forward movement.

Mama steps through the doorway, closer to me. "I don't think it's good for you to be by yourself right now."

"I said, 'I'm fine.'" I try like hell to make my expression one of stoicism rather than rage. I know what I need. What I need is quiet. I know who I need, and I need his arms wrapped around me so tight the vibrations stop. He is not in that damn house. He is bits and pieces on asphalt four hundred and seventy miles away. The thought of that chokes me.

"Do you want to talk about what happened?"

"Not at all."

"It will help."

More staring. *Focus on Mama's blue eyes that I didn't get in the genetics giveaway. Breathe. Keep the angry words inside.*

"It'll help, Jules. You can't keep all of this—all of this anger—"

"Mama, I can barely hear you over the generator." I can see the irritation on her face.

"Your anger! I can see it. You need to talk to your mother. This, what happened to you."

"*Happened to me*? Let's not say *what happened to me*. If we have to talk about it, let's give it real words. Accurate words. Troy attacked me. He tried to rape me—"

"Not so loud," Mama cautions and glances toward the open door.

"Not so loud? Why can't I be loud about this? I couldn't fight him off. My entire life I was convinced that I would never be the victim, the anonymous woman mentioned on some guy's rap sheet and the nightly news. Not me. But I was wrong, and now I'm locked up here." I motion to the garage and the clutter of random memories, tools, and scraps. "So, please, let me get on with my punishment in peace, okay?"

"You're not being punished, Jules."

"Oh really? I'm not allowed out, so what would you call it?"

"I'd call it—"

"So, Mama, how long will my grounding last? One week?

Two? Am I grounded for the month? Maybe if I'm really good, I can go to the Homecoming Dance?"

"Your father and I want to keep you safe." Mama's words are sharp, heavy with exacerbation. She exhales. "I don't mean to…I keep seeing him hurting you. In my mind, I keep seeing what it must have looked like, and I won't be able to get rid of this terrible picture until he's caught."

"That makes two of us."

"You can't just wave this off with sarcasm, Jules. And stop treating me like I'm the person who hurt you."

"I can and I will for as long as I want to." *Dammit*. That came out far harsher than I intended and now Mama looks like she's going to cry. "I'm sorry, Mama. I didn't mean that."

When did she become old? When did her skin become lined with age, this former Jackie O beauty? Is it just the stress of recent events and her worry for me or the fact that every part of surviving like a damn pioneer is exhausting? Is that why her cobalt eyes seem to be fading to a hazy cornflower blue?

"I'm sorry. Really. I didn't mean…Can we talk about something else?"

Mama hesitates, then her face concedes. "Fine. New subject. Have you seen Cole in the last couple of days?" Mama leans on the worktable.

"He came by yesterday before I…he came by and picked up a basket I'd put together for him."

"Hmm hmm."

"Don't worry, I didn't give him too much."

"I didn't say anything of the sort, Julianne. I think it's good you're looking out for him. Somebody has to, or that boy is going to end up in jail or worse."

I nod and pick at a knot in the mist net, one of ten lines I need to free if I'm to have any hope of repairing this thing. "I'm sure Matt is still angry with him, but how could I ignore the fact that there is an eleven-year-old boy out in the woods on his own? And, before you say I should turn him over to the county or state, he promised me he would run if I do that, and I don't doubt him for a second. He's already run once."

"You seem to have decided to trust him rather quickly."

"What other choice do I have? I know he's out there. I know he can't go on stealing from us or anybody else, so I'm going to make sure he doesn't have to steal."

"You get this from your Daddy, you know. The need to help any foundling that comes your way."

I look at Mama with my best *you're kidding* expression.

"I'm serious. When I gave birth to Matt and the doctor told us I couldn't have any more babies, your daddy was crushed. Why do you think we had so many pets when you kids were young? Dogs and birds, a rabbit, a turtle, that hamster. If Daddy couldn't have more kids around the house, he was going to take in every pet from here to Timbuktu. I had to cut him off from going to pet stores. He begged for years to adopt kids, too, but I couldn't handle more than the three of you and the zoo he kept bringing home so I refused. Maybe I should have given in." Mama fingers a corner of the mist net then looks at me like she's searching for exactly the right words. "I think God's given Daddy and I all we can handle right now."

Kate calls for Mama from what sounds like the back door. The sharp *Mama!* is heavy with irritability.

"Sounds like Kate is ready to fry up the hoe cakes," Mama says without stepping toward the door.

"And she's tired of waiting on you."

"Well, your sister struggles with patience." Mama turns to go but pauses and says, "You may find that baskets of food and a visit every couple of days isn't enough. Cole may need more from you. You need to decide now if you are willing to give him everything he needs. There's no halfway with parenting."

"Who said anything about parenting?"

She smiles and leaves, and now I'm angry, hurt, and dumbfounded. How am I supposed to know and provide everything that boy needs? Yes, he needs parents. Every kid does. He needs to be in school, not that schools are open right now, but soon, maybe. He needs a roof over his head and clean water to drink and soap. Definitely soap. More than anything, he needs someone, anyone to help him survive. Mama's acting like if I help him at all, I better be ready to adopt him. How about I start with ensuring he doesn't starve to death?

———

Mobile, Alabama, is known for its proximity to water. Rivers cut veins through the landscape, the salty Gulf waters are minutes away, and then there's the bay—beautiful, contentious, necessary. Mobile Bay and the long-ago battles fought on and for the water captivate naval battle enthusiasts. Perhaps the brackish water has grown bloodthirsty again. Maybe the ghosts of Mobile Bay don't like how we've stewarded their tomb—dotting the horizon with gas rigs, clearing its wild, lush shoreline to make way for condos and mansions, and allowing factories and commerce to pollute the water and air. Maybe the ghosts unleashed Clayton and the domestic terrorists and The Knights on us—the Bay's way to playing the long game to total human elimination. Maybe we deserve it.

These thoughts swirl in my mind as I walk the perimeter of the Martin property, which now feels more like a compound than a home. I walk to the far back of the property, which most people would consider the front yard because it faces the road, but in Bellefontaine the front yard is whatever side of the yard faces the water. The back is whatever side faces the road and the rest of the world. That's how this place works. We look to the water for everything—solace, sustenance, survival. The water is why we came here, my parents with my siblings and me in tow when we were too young to have an opinion. If the Bay, the front side, provides life, the backside of the Martin property holds the mystery and mystique of Bellefontaine. As I near the road, I hear the swamp with its thousands of species of reptiles and insects and wildlife of every type from poisonous frogs and snakes to small bears and bobcats. I scan the tree line for the web of a banana spider, and spot one big, yellow-and-black creature stretched out in the center. I listen for the brown owl, probably older than I am and the size of a small child. With my eyes closed, I soak in the sounds of Bellefontaine, prior to the noises of unrest becoming the norm.

"Jules!" A deep voice behind me throttles me from my thoughts. Billy Roberts is_standing three feet from me. Several yards behind him, on the road, is a parked Humvee with two soldiers leaning against the hood smoking cigarettes. "Are you okay?" Billy asks. "I called to you several times, but I guess you didn't hear me."

"I'm fine," I say, embarrassed and wondering how I didn't notice the rattle of the armored vehicle or someone calling my name. I smile in a sad attempt to appear normal. "Do you need my dad? He's probably out on the pier."

"No. I came to see you."

Great. From the look of the *poor, pitiful Jules* expression smeared across his face, I assume someone told Billy what happened yesterday. "So, is this a social visit or official?"

"A little of both. Your dad came to the camp this morning. He told Johnson about your assault yesterday. I'm so sorry that happened to you. Thank God your niece got Matt's ball skills and acted before anything really bad happened."

"No. Nothing really bad." I look at Billy and all the kindness oozing from his freshly shaven face and want to punch him in the throat. *Nothing really bad. Nothing but my dignity and sense of security stomped into the ground.* Shouldn't I be happy that Daddy told the authorities what happened? I've always been on the side of women going to the police so their attackers can be identified, arrested, and punished. My convictions reduce into a pile of seagull shit now that I'm the one with the soon-to-be scars and very present humiliation. But, isn't this my story to tell? It's certainly not Daddy's.

"Did he do that?" Billy asks, gesturing to the scrape on my jaw line. Billy steps closer and zeros in on my neck. "Jesus, Jules, your neck."

I bring a hand to my neck to cover the bruises, an urge too strong to deny. "You say that like I haven't noticed."

"Jules, you don't have to be embarrassed."

"Who says I'm embarrassed?"

"Jules, I know you. I know it's been a while since we've spent much time together but you're not the kind of woman who would be okay with being attacked like that."

"And what kind of woman would be okay with this?" I snap at him, harder than I should, but what a dumb thing to say. "No one is okay with being assaulted, Billy."

"That's not what I meant. I'm just surprised Troy's walking around with his balls still attached, that's all."

"Believe me, I'm considering alternatives if I can find him."

"Jules, that wasn't a suggestion."

"Have y'all caught him? Are you going to arrest him?"

"No, we haven't found him yet. Johnson distributed a description of him to all the guys so we can look for him on patrols. That's why we're out here now. We're increasing patrols of Bay Air Road, DIP, and the surrounding side roads."

"Troy's not so stupid as to wander down one of the roads, Billy. He's either hiding out at The Knight Compound, or he's taken to the woods and making his way north. You'll never see him from the road."

"We're doing what we can in the middle of this. It's all fucked up."

"What is?"

"This. All of this. The fact that I'm trying to maintain peace in my own hometown. That's fucked up, Jules."

"So, if you know that, why are y'all here? Why not leave us be?"

"Jules, for once in your life, you don't know what's going on."

"Enlighten me then."

"For one, this crap is happening all over the south, and DC's putting pressure on the Army to squash groups like The Knights. Do you know a group calling themselves New World Order kidnapped the mayor of Savannah and lynched her? Strung her up in Forsythe Square for being an enemy of the people."

"No, I haven't heard that."

"The same thing happened to a couple of journalists in Charlotte. And they're finding little cells all over the place going after infrastructure targets. We don't have proof yet, but we're pretty sure The Knights cut the fiber-optic line. We've identified one Alabama Power lineman and two cable guys living on the compound."

"Why would anyone want to live without a line to the rest of the world?"

"There are benefits to cutting yourself off. No one out. No one in."

"Hmm hmm. I don't know if The Knights are good enough to find that line, dig it up, then cut it."

"These are the guys that would know how to do that. Hell, they may have been the guys that laid that line in the first place."

"So, the same men who are grabbing whatever power and

territory they can around here are the same guys that caused this? I don't think The Knights started this, Billy."

"Maybe not. But, maybe they were waiting for the opportunity. Waiting for everything to be bad enough. That's what these homegrown militias do. They dream up scenarios where only they can save the country. Create chaos. Dismantle every institution to rebuild according to their own jacked-up ideology. You don't think guys like Dave Richardson and his buddies would jump at the chance to make this place exactly what they want it to be? Bring back the glory days? Online chatter with these groups has been escalating for years. They were ready."

My mind reels with the events of the last few months. "Do you know how fast everything went to shit around here? As soon as the panic started after Vancleave poisoned all those people, roadblocks went up. People freaked out that the bug man was going to poison us here in Bellefontaine so they blocked the roads with tires and old furniture, broken-down cars. You couldn't get past the T except on foot, but who's going to walk to Mobile all the way from here? People cleaned out every shelf in Greers and the Chevron, even Dollar General was picked clean. That's what Mama and Daddy told me. Then, soon after I came home, the bridge blew up. But, maybe that wasn't The Knights. That's what I assumed, but why would they blow up something so close to their compound?"

"Was that when The Knights, all of a sudden, became the answer to a lot of prayers? You need food? We've got it. You need shelter? We've got that too. You need protection? We'll do that. That's how these groups work."

"For months, we've been trying to piece together any clues from Preach and Libby Lefty about what's going on outside of Bellefontaine."

"Jules, you won't get shit from them but propaganda. You know that."

"Of course, I know that, but what else are we supposed to do? According to you, The Knights are controlling the flow of information around here. The only thing they can't destroy is radio waves."

"But how do you know those two are telling the truth? Shock jocks aren't known for their ability to fact check."

"I honestly don't know either way, but the Army isn't exactly forthcoming with information, now are they?"

Billy stands silent, frustration growing in his face.

"That's what I thought. Maybe if y'all would repair that cable, we could get the truth. Maybe even get some real help down here. Or, at least find out if it's safe in Mobile yet."

"Mobile's pretty much a ghost town right now. As soon as the check points went up on I-10, people were too scared to move around. What we were told is that a lot of people got out of Mobile right after Vancleave poisoned Midtown, then another mass exodus started after the looting began. And there's no one left really to clean up the mess. Looks like a deserted warzone."

Every nerve in my body wants to run. To where, I don't know. But, I stay and listen and try to digest what Billy says.

"I think they're gearing up for more." Billy glances back at the Humvee. He turns his gaze back to me and lowers his voice. "I think the safest place for y'all to be right now is right here. You're protected here. Here." He points to the ground. "Out there? It's going to get worse before anything gets better."

"It doesn't sound like there's much left out there."

"I mean anywhere else in Bellefontaine. When the market reopens, don't go."

"Or you could just arrest the people responsible for the market bombing?"

Billy ignores me. "I know your parents will insist on going to church, but I don't know if even the church will be safe for much longer."

"They're not going to give up church, Billy."

"They need to."

"Well, Billy, what are we supposed to do? Hunker down until The Knights control everyone here? Tuck our heads between our knees and pray? If you're not going to do something about those assholes, and I mean immediately, why did you want our land?"

"Jesus, Jules, I came here to tell you to be careful. Don't go anywhere by yourself. We need time to find Troy. Figure out if The Knights are connected to the market attack and your assault, or if this was just some random act of a drunk. Bottom line is The Knights may be working with some of these other groups around the South, at least influenced by them if they've figured out a way to get information."

"How long have y'all suspected that?"

Again, Billy's lips close.

"Days? Weeks? Months?" I wait for an answer, but Billy offers nothing. A chill wraps around my neck at his lack of response. "How long has the government been watching these groups? Did they know about them before my husband was killed?"

"That's above my paygrade, Jules. I promise you I don't know that. What I do know is that if you step off this property, you're not safe. That I feel in my gut. Troy's going to try again if he gets a chance. Your family is a big target now—"

"Thanks to the Army and eminent domain."

"Dammit, Jules, stop it. I'm trying to tell you that taking out any one of you would send a pretty powerful message, don't you think? That The Knights will do anything to protect what's theirs, even kill a Martin."

That stops me. "He came here to warn me. To punish me for chasing him out of the market after the bombing."

"You did what?"

"He was running and knocked into me. Hard. Then he took off again so I chased him. I know it was him that planted that bomb."

"Do not go near him again. Do you hear me?"

"I'm not your child, Billy."

"No, you're not. My kids aren't so dumb."

"Now you sound like Matt."

"Matt knew Troy was there?"

"Matt was with me."

"Did you see Troy plant the bomb?"

"No."

"Did you see him doing anything suspicious?"

"Always."

"I'm serious."

"The bomb went off and he ran into me while *clearly* escaping. A boat was waiting for him offshore."

Billy stares at me, shaking his head. "I'm taking this back to Johnson, but you are not to do a damn thing about it. Simple truth is you don't know why he was running away. He could've been really freaked out by the explosion. That could be all that was. Then you go off after him half-crazed."

"Are you blaming me for him attacking me?"

"Of course not, Jules. You're twisting this all up. What I mean is you don't see everything, Jules. People are hurting and scared and, yes, all it took was a couple of bad months and bad shit happening. Do you know how long people have been this angry? Years, Jules, years. We don't know what they're planning or who carries out the plan. All we know is the chatter from around the country." Billy steps closer to me, so close I hear his softened volume loud and clear. "Civil war, Jules. No shitting around. That's what they want. And if you're not careful you're going to end up a casualty."

I'm tired. Billy is tiring me out. This conversation is tiresome. I do not have the energy to discuss the possibilities of civil war. I take a long swig from my water bottle and savor the liquid as it coats my throat. "Like I said, Troy was drunk, and I don't have anything to do with your war. Forget everything else."

"I can't do that. He was looking for you. That much I know. Maybe for payback for the market, maybe because your family is working with us."

"We weren't given a choice on that were we?"

"That doesn't matter to them."

"Then why didn't you protect me from them? If y'all know so much, why did you let this happen? Why don't you tell Johnson to find a different piece of land to use?" The dam threatens to break as my voice cracks with a strangled sob.

"You know I don't have the authority. Where Johnson is concerned, I can yell till I'm blue in the face. It won't make a difference."

"So, something else I just have to swallow? My husband is gone. My pride is gone. Why not throw away any semblance of safety too?"

"Do y'all have somewhere else you could go? Maybe y'all should leave. I already sent my wife and kids and mom away. They're at our hunting camp, so hopefully The Knights won't know to look for them. Maybe you should get out of here too. You could go there. There's plenty of room. Soon enough, The Knights will screw up and we can shut them down. But I don't think you're safe here. Not if they're following the same play-book as the other groups."

"Billy, I'm not going anywhere." Cole's crooked smile flashes in my mind and just like that, in the micro-moment of that kid's face appearing in my mind, I have reason to stay. "I'm staying."

"Then, at least promise me you won't go anywhere by yourself."

"Daddy's already taken care of that. I'm grounded."

"Good. And you've got to be observant even when you're

home. I could've grabbed you and been halfway down the road with you before anyone around here heard you scream."

"I needed a moment to myself."

"Well, *moments* get you killed."

"Yes, sir!" I say and pop my hand to my forehead in a Barney Fife style salute.

"Jules, I'm being serious." He closes the distance between us by another step, so close that his shadow falls on my face.

"Fine, Billy. Fine. I didn't think I mattered to you that much." I need him to back away. But, it's Billy. Why should I fear Billy? In my head I know I'm just on edge because of yesterday, but every cell in my stomach, leg muscles, and bones scream *Run!*

"You're my friend. You've been my friend my entire life. Of course, you matter." Billy's face softens and I wonder if he can feel how anxious I am being so close to a man. He rocks backward on his heels, giving me air and space. "Just because it didn't work out with us, doesn't mean I stopped caring about you?"

"Prom didn't exactly go as I'd hoped."

"Really? What were you hoping for?" Billy grins at me, the same grin that made me walk into that grocery store and ask him to prom in the first place.

I feel my cheeks pinken. "I'm not saying that," I say and nudge him further away from me.

"Doesn't matter. I recovered." He tilts his head and looks at me, the kind of look I swear men see in a Rom-Com then perfect in front of their high school bedroom mirrors. "Some guys can get over you, you know. I mean, it's possible. I may be the only one, but I'm here to tell you," Billy clicks his heels together and raises his right hand as if swearing an oath, "I have recovered from a crush on Jules Martin. I joined a support group. Found healing. Got my chakras right."

"Oh, for God's sake, stop it. Fine. I'll be careful. I will stay put. And I'll come to you if I see or hear anything from Troy again."

Billy's radio, small and black and clipped to a loop on his shoulder comes to life. I recognize Captain Johnson's voice. It orders Billy to report to Bellefontaine Boulevard, about two miles north. I can't make out everything with all the Army code-speak and acronyms, but what I can make out isn't good. Not good at all. Really freaking awful.

Billy takes a deep breath then looks at me. "An Army boat ran over a civilian in a kayak. Shit." Billy reaches out and squeezes my hand before rushing back to his Humvee. After covering half the distance, he turns back to me. "Oh, I almost forgot. We've heard about some kid stealing fishing gear up and down the shoreline lately. Supposedly he's got blond hair and is about four and a half feet tall, skinny, blue eyes. Keep an eye out."

"Will do," I say and watch him jump into to the Humvee and speed away. *Dammit, Cole. You are going to get yourself arrested.*

16

*T*his is a heartbreaking day for all of Bellefontaine. Our thoughts and prayers go out to the Gradney family. To lose a child is the worst pain a person can endure.*

Libby Lefty's voice is softer than her usual determined vibrato. News that a sixteen-year-old boy has died should have me wrecked, but it doesn't. And because I'm serving as my own grief counselor, I've decided my inability to feel pain for others right now is because my heart is carrying everything it can handle. Rather than sadness, what I feel is dread.

My heart also goes out to the driver of the boat, one of the soldiers from Goat Island. The guilt he carries for this tragic accident must be heavy. To know you've taken a life, accidentally cut the future of such a young, vibrant boy seems too much.

"Jules," Mama pokes her head around the propped-open front door. "You've got a visitor out back."

"Who?" I ask from my seat on the porch steps, watching Mallie pick wildflowers in the front yard. The contrast of her blonde curls against the green grass is an image I'm hesitant to break away from. I cut the radio off and stand.

"Cole. He's at the end of the driveway by the gate. I'm not sure how long he's been there, but I'd guess he's waiting for you. Go on. I'll look after Mallie."

"Thanks, Mom. You okay?"

Mom blinks several times. Her eyes are red. "Of course, of course." She lowers herself down onto the stoop and sits next to the radio. "Have they said anything else about the Gradney boy?"

"No. The details are still pretty sketchy. All they know is that somehow the patrol boat hit his kayak."

"I don't know what I would do if I lost one of you. A part of my own body would be missing." Mom looks down at the solitaire diamond on her left hand and twists it back and forth around her finger. "This is why Daddy and I pray the Rosary. To keep all of you kids safe and healthy."

"I know, Mama," I say, with as much compassion as I can muster. Everything comes back to the church with my family, and I'm losing my ability to respond. I'm grateful for their faith, and maybe even a bit envious. But my personal relationship with the Almighty right now is tepid at best.

I cut around the house and stroll down the driveway. I want to run to Cole and warn him that the Army has received reports of a kid matching his description stealing fishing gear. I want to caution him about patrol boats and run down the list of boating safety measures every Martin kid could recite by age twelve, rules to follow whether in a twenty-one-foot ski boat, a dinghy, or a kayak. But, I don't want to spook the kid by charging at him, so I force my feet and legs to relax.

"Cole," I call to him. "Hop the fence and come here. I know you can."

As Daddy and Garrett are still on the hunt for barbed wire, the makeshift, six-foot gate offers little obstacle to the tree-climber, and Cole scales it in four easy steps. He lands softly on his feet.

"Come with me," I tell him and rush to the garage, away from the road and possible patrols, out of sight of onlookers, blood-related or not. Opening the door, I usher him inside. "Stay here while I find you some breakfast."

That word—breakfast—brings a slight smile to Cole's face, so I know he's hungry. When I return with two pieces of bread with strawberry jam smears, I find him fingering the mist net, unfinished, the repairs abandoned again yesterday.

"What's this?" he asks, holding up one corner of the net.

"It's a mist net. It's used to catch birds. Big ones though, preferably geese when they migrate through here. That's why the squares are so big. Small birds aren't worth eating, so they can fly right through, but the big ones get caught up in the lines."

"Why is it here? You ain't gonna catch geese in no garage."

"You *won't* catch geese in *a* garage," I offer. Cole accepts my correction with a click of his tongue. "It's here for two reasons. One, the geese finished migrating for the year weeks ago. And two, it was slashed so I need to repair it."

"Slashed?"

"That's what it looks like. It was hanging in the woods just south of here but when Matt and I checked it the last time, it had two big cuts, almost from the top all the way to the bottom. I need to tie all the broken strings together so it will be ready in a few months when the geese come back through."

"Oh," Cole says then turns his focus to the bread sitting on the corner of the table. "Is that for me?"

"Yes."

He bites into one piece then holds the other out to me. "No, no, I already had breakfast. Those are both for you."

Cole does a quick survey of the workshop. I've no idea what he's looking for until he grabs a scrap piece of fabric from a shelf behind him. "Can I have this?"

"Yes, but what…" I abandon my question when he lays the fabric flat on the table and wraps his second piece of bread in it. *Oh.* "I've got a better idea. Why don't you go ahead and eat that now and I'll gather up some supplies for you to take back to your camp for later? Maybe some fruit and fish?"

Cole crams a too-big bite into his mouth and through half-chewed bread and jelly says, "That'd be awesome."

———

The garden, once a treasured escape, is now a labyrinth, one I do not wish to enter. My eyes no longer see the beauty. I see hiding places and blind spots. Cole stands next to me at the garden gate. My right hand is slick with sweat as I grip my basket, the basket I intend to fill with fruit and vegetables for the boy, but my left-hand refuses to move the latch. *Rip the Band-Aid off, Jules.*

"Somethin' wrong?" Cole asks.

"No, no. Of course not." *Rip it off.*

"Then why are you shaking?"

The boy is right. My left-hand rests on the latch but instead of lifting the iron bar, it trembles.

"Somethin's got you scared." Cole looks around, turning in a circle and peering through the wooden slats of the gate. "I don't see anything."

"I'm fine. Just checking." *Rip. It. Off.*

"My Daddy used to say when somethin' scares you, you gotta rip the Band-Aid off."

I glance down at the boy, whose eyes fix on a row of strawberries. "Your daddy sounds like he was a pretty smart man." *And way too in my head for me today.* I open the latch and push the gate wide.

Cole darts through the opening and straight to the row of strawberries. The first few yards are packed with fruit, our harvest day cut short the way it was. Cole snatches three fat, red berries off the vine then stops. "I'm sorry. I guess I shoulda asked before I grabbed those."

"You're good. But only pick what you know you'll eat. We don't waste food around here. So, maybe two or three or twelve handfuls of the strawberries. That should get you through a few days." Cole flashes me a smile, appreciative of my generosity and sarcasm.

The rows of pole beans still show evidence of Troy—large boot prints in the dry dirt, green bean shoots littering the ground, soon to spoil. I wish it would rain and wash all of this away. Toward the end of the row, shadows shift beneath passing clouds.

"The green beans really need to be cooked, so I'm going to skip those. Do you like cucumbers?"

"Don't really know."

"I think you'll like them. They're best with vinegar and a little salt and pepper, but they're fine on their own. And they've got a high water content, so that will be good for you."

Cole calls from the row of peppers. "Can I have a few of these bell peppers?"

I walk to his row and see him squatting in front of a bush of green bell peppers. "I wouldn't have guessed a boy your age would be drooling over bell peppers."

"Mama used to stuff these with ground beef and rice and cheese. They were so good. I guess I can't stuff them, but—"

"How many do you want? Two?" I hesitate to give him more than that as I doubt he's ever eaten a raw bell pepper.

Cole nods and grins, flashes his crooked teeth at me then reaches for a pepper.

"Wait, wait." I grab my knife off my belt. "Garrett's taught me that bell pepper plants are kind of fussy. If you grab the pepper off, it could damage the stem. So, it's better to cut off the pepper with a little bit of stem. That way the plant can repair faster and grow more peppers." I cut off two big peppers and drop them in the basket along with the cucumbers and strawberries. "Now, how do you feel about tomatoes?"

A half hour later we return from the garden with a basket of cucumbers, bell peppers, strawberries, and cherry tomatoes. Cole pops a cherry tomato in his mouth and grins at me again. A bit of juice drips from the corner of his mouth, but I swear with his big blue eyes, thick tuft of blond hair, round cheeks, and tanned skin, he looks as if someone drew him. I hear the creak of the garage door, and Cole's smile falls into a frown.

Matt stops short when he sees Cole. "I'm going to check the crab traps." Matt eyes the basket of produce on the table. "You're not supposed to go the garden by yourself right now, Jules. How many times do we have to tell you?"

"First of all, I wasn't by myself. Cole was with me. Second, you are not my warden, Matt."

Matt scowls at Cole then saunters away.

"I think he's still mad at me," Cole says, watching Matt disappear around the corner of the house.

I squeeze Cole's hand and am surprised that he lets me, almost as surprised that I made the gesture at all. "Matt should be grateful the world doesn't judge him for his past sins and maybe pass that same courtesy on to others."

Cole glances at me, and I swear I see regret in his eyes.

"Cole, you don't have to apologize to any of us anymore, got it? You know stealing is wrong." He nods in agreement. "And you're keeping your promise of being on the straight and narrow. No more trading stolen goods with Martha?" He nods again. "So, now you must forgive yourself. What's done is done. Matt will come around eventually."

"Okay."

"And I don't want to scare you, but you need to know this. The Army is looking for you. We didn't report you, I promise, but someone did and the description they gave of the alleged thief is a really accurate description of you."

Cole swallows a cherry tomato, staring at me. "What should I do? Hide?"

"I think your camp is plenty hidden enough, but stay clear of the main roads. They're doing extra patrols since—" How do I explain my attack to a child, even the oldest of an old soul child? I can't find the words because the words probably don't exist, so I move on. "There're extra patrols right now, so they'll be up and down the roads. But I doubt they'll go into the woods to look for you. They seem attached to their vehicles."

"How d'you get those scratches? Did someone try to hurt you?"

"Um…" Do I lie? Sugar-coat? I decide to be truthful but leave out the nasty details. "Yes, a couple of days ago a very bad man tried to hurt me."

"And this bad guy, did he hurt you in the garden? Is that why you didn't want to go in there?"

"Wow. You don't miss much, do you?"

"Nope. I don't."

"Smart kid," I mutter to myself. "Yes, a bad guy in the garden tried to hurt me, but I'm fine. See," I turn in a circle then wave my splayed fingers at Cole, "Ten fingers and ten toes and both my arms and legs. Perfectly fine. Nothing permanent." That was a lie, but I think I told it convincingly enough. "But still, you have to be careful and know who may be lurking around you at all times."

"I do. I am careful."

"And I guess if you stick to the trees, no one is going to sneak up on you." I ruffle his hair and feel dirt and sand on his scalp. "How about a shower before you head back? We've got an outdoor one with walls and a door so you don't have to show your bare butt to the world. But be fast because the pump will only give you about a minute of water. And the water will be lukewarm. No hot showers around here. And no cold showers unless it's January."

Cole laughs and tosses another cherry tomato in his mouth.

"After that, we'll get you some salt fish before you head back to your camp."

17

I'm trapped. Seriously, freaking trapped. To the left of me is a wall, specifically one interior wall of St. Philip Neri Church. To my right are Mama and Daddy, Matt, Jessie, and Lucy. Kate, Garrett, Mallie, and Lauren are in front of me. Getting out of this pew will be no easy feat, but escape seems key to self-preservation. In front of me, at the pulpit on the altar, stands Clem Richardson in all his blustering glory.

"You know me, good people, and you know I won't lie to you. I'm not gonna insult your intelligence with fairytales. I'll leave that up to those politicians in DC. So, you can trust me when I say our way of life is on the verge of destruction. That's why I had to come here today and speak to you. I'm so grateful to Father Morgan for the opportunity to share my concerns with all of you."

Where is the eject button on this pew? Father Morgan should install eject buttons.

"The Knights and I need your help. We must end martial law in Bellefontaine. I wish those Army boys well, as any good American would, but they do not belong here. They are only here to further the dangerous agenda of our supposed president, although I don't know a single soul that voted for him."

Stop it, you bald jackalope.

"They're telling us the Army is here for our safety, but do you feel safe?"

I did until I was attacked by one of your "good Americans."

"I sure don't. Really, I want to know. Are we better off than we were a year ago? How long will the Army command our daily lives? Is it American to live under military rule? No, it is not."

The Army is here because of your boys, asshole.

"A year ago, I could fish where I wanted. I could drive my boat wherever I pleased with only the tides telling me where to go. I'd gas up at the marina, grab a burger and a beer and be on my way. Now, what? It has been weeks since the Fowl River Bridge was blown up, but the Army hasn't arrested anyone for that horrible and deadly act. I wonder if they're even looking for the guilty party." He shakes his head and purses his lips then turns to the Renauds' pew. "Missus Renaud, our thoughts and prayers are with you while you piece your life back together. You let me know if there is anything I can do to help you."

You could tell The Knights to knock it off with the explosives.

"Tomorrow, the Gradneys will bury their son. I'm sure many of you know the family and share in their grief. My thoughts and prayers are with each of you who are hurting right now."

Clem bows his head, squeezing his eyes shut, and the display makes me grateful that the Gradneys are not in church this morning.

Clem opens his eyes and the shift from feigned sympathy to fear-peddler is a master class in politics. "That boy's death proves the Army has no business being here. How are they supposed to protect us when they can't even drive a boat without dire consequences? Their recklessness will only cause more harm. I promise you all that I will not rest until the Army leaves and we can once again live free in our beautiful community. I will not rest until whoever killed one of ours, ran over him like he was nothing more than a buoy bobbing on the water… the guilty party will be brought to justice. I promise you that."

I knew this would happen. The Gradneys have nothing to do with The Knights or vice versa. The accident that killed the boy was just that—an accident. Still, The Knights will use his death to further their agenda.

"And the Army is guilty of more than killing one of ours. They are here illegally. They are determined to take our guns so that we can't defend ourselves. Today, we have to register our guns—shotguns and twenty-twos—while they are armed with bazookas and rockets. Tomorrow, they could take what little protection we have left. We are told where we can and cannot drive our boats. They are destroying our land. The number of trees, trees that stood through decades of hurricanes, that they have chopped down is a crime against nature. No one is holding them accountable for any of the damage they're causing, and it is time that stopped. This is turning into a country I don't recognize. Everything about this is just plain un-American."

The collective adrenaline in the church is rising. If anxiety and rage had a presence it would be the air inside this church—hot, thick, and sour. So is Clem's hypocrisy, not that anyone seems to mind hypocrisy nowadays. A giggle escapes my throat at the thought of Captain Johnson running amuck with a bazooka on his shoulder and the absurdity of Clem's line of bull. Daddy shifts in his seat. When I glance down, his left-hand twitches on his lap.

"If we let this go on, not a trace of the America we know will be left. We're heading straight into fascism and the only way to stop this is to stand together as one Bellefontaine!"

Applause rises from the audience as the corner of Clem's mouth twitches upward. He is fighting that grin of appreciation, that adoration of the spotlight, so hard. He breathes in and out, long and full and slow, then grips the podium with his leathery hands. These people, with the constant unknowns of their daily lives, have developed a critical need to follow. They are hungry, thirsty, bewildered and beaten down. In the absence of purified water, they drink in Clem's dangerous tonic. Why is it dangerous? Because Clem wants to pin us against the Army. He wants us to take the bullets for him.

"Good people, you know my thoughts and prayers are with you every day as I try to lead you through these uncertain times. But I promised the good Father that I would keep this short. So, as soon as he releases you—"

Clem pauses to glance at Father Morgan, who meets Clem's wink with pure stoicism. Morgan's either riding the fence in self-preservation, or maybe—*please, Jesus, let this be true*—I'm not the only one in this church who knows Clem Richardson, his son Dave, and The Knights, are not our saviors.

"My boys and I will be in the parking lot. The missus and all our other ladies have been baking up a storm this week. Come by the truck for a free loaf of bread or maybe one of Lurline's black-berry pies. So delicious you'll slap your mama."

Daddy stands, followed by my Mama.

"Matthew, good to see you, friend. Did you want to add some-thing this morning? Maybe something about the destruction on Goat Island? All those trees. Gone. I'm hoping you will pledge your support to help us rid Bellefontaine of these misguided soldiers."

"I'm just waiting for the final blessing from Father Morgan." Daddy motions to Father Morgan who hops-to, scurrying from his throne to his place behind the Credence Table.

I stand and squeeze Daddy's hand. *Christ Almighty. I do love my Daddy.*

Father Morgan smooths the linen tablecloth and flips to the appropriate page of the Missal. As Clem saunters off the altar, Father begins. "The Lord be with you," he says, extending his arms to us.

"And with your spirit," we respond. *But not yours, Clemmie Boy.*

I hang in the pew for a moment as the church empties, feigning a moment of piety and prayer.

"I know you're not praying, so what's going on?" Matt asks, sliding next to me on the hard pew.

"I'm asking God if Troy's in that parking lot, and if he is, for forgiveness in advance."

"Clem and Dave aren't dumb enough to let him show his face around us."

"But what if they don't know?"

"Jules, how could they not? According to you, he left the garden with a gash in his forehead."

"Like he's going to say, hey I tried to rape a Martin but the redheaded girl stopped me." A cry catches in my throat at the word rape. *Breathe. One. Two.* "He might not have gone back to them at all. We haven't seen him. Billy hasn't found him. There seems to be an awful lot of people looking for one guy that's nowhere to be found."

"Good. Maybe he disappeared. He should be running, if he knows what's good for him. But you shouldn't be hiding. That wasn't your fault." Matt squeezes my hand then pulls me out of the pew.

"According to Billy, we all should be hiding. He doesn't even think church is safe anymore."

"No one is going to do anything to us in here, except torture us with speeches."

"How can you know that?"

"Jules, I have to believe there are still lines none of us will cross."

At the front doors of the church, propped open for the sake of the breeze blowing off the bay, Dave Richardson meets me with a loaf of bread and a pie. My throat seizes with the proximity of his body so close to mine. "Jules, I tucked away a loaf and Mom's best pie for you."

Matt steps between us. "Dave, we're good on baked goods for now. Thanks." Matt looks around the parking lot, scanning for scraggly blond hair and tattoos, I'm sure. "Where's your boy?"

"The kids are at home this morning."

"Not your kids, Dave. Your boy. Troy."

"How should I know where Troy is? I'm not his keeper."

"But he does your bidding, right?" I ask, looking Dave in the eye. "Are you hiding him, Dave?"

"I'm not hiding anybody. But maybe I should be hiding him from you."

"He deserves whatever happens to him." I step right to slip past Dave, but he shifts and blocks the exit.

Dave lowers his head, moving his lips close to my ear. "It's my understanding that he didn't do a thing to you."

I feel Matt standing at my back. "Not for a lack of trying, Dave. Now move out of Jules's way before I kick your ass in a church."

"I thought that redhead fought Jules's battles for her? She put quite a few stitches in Troy's forehead. Pretty clear to me who the victim in that little scuffle was."

"Scuffle?" I ask, keeping my voice low to not roil the crowd in the parking lot. "Troy assaulted me, and for all I know, you ordered it. Now, I don't know if this was payback for working with the Army or maybe you two don't like the fact that I know Troy planted the bomb at the market—"

"If you know so much, why not run to the Army? Tell your buddies everything you know."

I hesitate and from the smirk on Dave's face, he knows he got me.

"Jules, you don't know shit and you can't prove a thing."

"Either way, you tell Troy to stay the hell away from me. If I see him again—"

"You'll what, Jules? Run to your good pal Billy?" Dave leans forward and whispers, "For all you know I did give the order to Troy. And maybe it won't be my last." Dave shoves the baked goods in my arms and turns, descending the steps two at a time. "Enjoy the pie, honey."

Every word of warning and concern from Billy yesterday rings in my ears. Exposed. I am exposed.

"So, asshole is a Richardson family trait, huh?" Matt asks.

All the air rushes from my body, as if with the slightest touch I'll tumble down the stairs. "Billy was right. None of us are safe. Dave Richardson is determined to punish us for Goat Island and Troy getting hurt and—"

"He did kind of show his cards, didn't he?"

I look at the bread and pie in my arms. Carbs have never looked so unappealing. "I need to give these to someone. No way I'm taking it home for us. Maybe the Renauds could use it."

"Or Cole?"

I stare at Matt. "Did Jessie hit you in the head, too? I figured you'd rather string him up by his toenails than help him."

"I'm not completely heartless. And I'm fairly certain that kid will eat anything no matter who made it. I'm even more certain that if I walk into the house carrying Clem Richardson's handouts, Mama will have my head." I consider the ramifications of Matt and I going off together again, instead of straight home with the family and decide feeding a homeless child is worth irritating my parents. "You in? I don't think I should bring this to him by myself." Matt looks over at Lauren and the rest of the family. "Tell Lauren that we're bringing this to Cole and let's go. Before I lose my nerve and any of them can stop us."

———

The boy can eat the pie and bread unaware of how tainted the baked goods are. So, Matt and I walk through the woods, hoping to find Cole. If I remember correctly, his campsite is about halfway between the church and our house. After twenty minutes, we find the camp and Cole, perched in a tree. A woman below him on the ground orders him down, but the boy is as stiff and tight-lipped as ever.

"You must be Miss Martha," I say, stepping out of the thick of trees that surround Cole's small clearing.

A portly woman, Miss Martha stands about five feet tall. Her silver hair is like tinsel—thin, brittle, and loose in the breeze. Falling a few inches below her knees, her blue cotton moo-moo is shabby in places, suggesting decades of wear, and sweat wets the fabric below her breasts and around the collar.

"Yes, I am," she says with a start. "And you would be?"

"This is Jules," Cole says, shifting from a perch to a seat on the branch.

"Cole and I met a couple of weeks ago. He was stealing one of my crab traps."

"Now, I don't know anything about that," Martha says, taking a step away from me. "You know how little boys can be. They just run off. Do whatever they want to." She reaches up to Cole, attempting to grab one of the boy's bare feet. Cole's too quick for her though. "Cole, hon, come on down now." Martha's voice modulates to sticky sweet. "You must be starved. I've got supper cooking at home."

"No need," I say, glancing at Cole and extending the baked goods in my arms to him. "I've got it covered. Fresh bread and blackberry pie."

"Well, thank you, um Jules?" Martha says, still slick and sticky as maple syrup. "That will make a lovely dessert, but I've got a proper meal for Cole at home. Growing boys need their protein and veggies."

"Would you stop that?" I ask, done with the charade. "I know exactly who you are and what you've made Cole do. What I don't know is what you plan to do with him now. Or should I say, I don't know what you plan to have him do for you because your little enterprise is done, at least Cole's part in it."

Martha glares at me then turns back to Cole. "Cole, get your butt down here right now. We are going back to the trailer and that's that. Don't make me—"

"Do what?" Matt asks, his voice low, almost menacing. "Go get your man Henry and beat on the kid?"

Martha spins around to face Matt. "My Henry knows how to handle a boy like Cole. You've no idea the trouble this boy has caused us."

Cole drops his head and looks at his legs straddling a branch. His lips close over his crooked teeth.

"Cole may have his troubles, but what you've done to him—"

Martha cuts me off mid-sentence. "What I've done to him? Kept him clothed and safe after his parents died? Gave what precious little my Henry and I have to keep him fed? Lady, you've got a lot of nerve saying to me, 'what you've done to him.'" Martha turns back to Cole. "Cole, for the last time, get down and let's go. You got a lot of missed days to make up for. And making me traipse all over these damn woods looking for you? You're gonna learn your responsibilities, boy."

"Cole has no responsibility when it comes to you. Not anymore. He's not going to be doing anything else for you, Martha. No more stealing and looting. No more sneaking around. No more depending on you for a damn thing." I walk between the old lady and the tree. Cole's feet swing very near to my shoulder. "And if you're smart, you'll stop your little black-market game all together. The Army is looking for Cole for theft. A lot of thefts. If they find him, I'm giving them your name as ringleader of the black market around here. And I'll give them Henry's for child abuse. Hell, I might even escort them to your RV. After all, I know where you two live. Why shouldn't I see my civic duty to completion?"

Martha stares at me as if daring me to blink first, then spits on the ground inches from my right shoe. "Fine, boy," she says to Cole. "Good luck with this broad and whoever the hell that man is who can't even be bothered with introducing himself. Good luck getting them to care about you. Try not to starve to death, you little shit." Martha stomps away into the trees.

Cole moves a couple of inches closer to the trunk and drops the knotted rope down. It bounces and swings as if shaking out stiff muscles.

"Cole," I say to him, sensing his urge to chase after what he knows. "You do not need her. We will take care of you. I promise. Haven't I kept my word so far?"

Cole glances in Martha's direction again then slides down the rope. "Blackberry pie, huh? Can I have a piece now or do I have to wait?"

"It's yours," I say. "Eat it whenever you like."

Cole pinches off a piece of crust and pops it into his mouth.

"Matt, slow down." I dodge a branch jutting out into our path through the woods. I hadn't expected meeting Martha today or that convincing her and Cole that parting ways is best would take so long. So now, we're late getting back to the house, and Mama and Daddy and Lauren are probably worried again.

"Walk faster," Matt says. "Dad's gonna be pissed if I make him wait much longer."

"The busted pipe will still be busted whenever we arrive." I two-foot it over a rotting log, after Matt leaps over it entirely, easy as pie.

"I know how that conversation's going to go, Jules. 'Matthew, where have you been,'" Matt says, putting on his best Daddy voice. "'You smell that shit, boy? Cause I sure can. Your poor mama had to go lie down 'cause that smell was too much for her.' That's option one, Jules. Option two is we show up late as hell and Mama, Kate, and Lauren are knee deep in shit with the outhouse scattered in pieces in the yard. If that's happening while we're strolling through the woods, then I get the couch for the next week cause no way Lauren's letting me sleep with her. You can sleep on the damn floor." He affects a high, snipped tone, representative of my dear sister Kate. "'You two are never around when we need you.' Yep. Any kindness you've gotten from Kate in the last week will be long gone if Daddy makes her get anywhere near fixing the outhouse. I'm not in the mood to clean up shit and take it from Kate in the same day."

"Matt," I say and lunge forward to grab his shirt and stop him cold. "Don't move." I point at a trip wire tied across the path.

"How the hell did you see that?"

"Shhh!" I glance around, scanning the trees and brush. Turning in a circle, I see a hint of light. Not light per se, but something light where one would expect only dark green or brown. The mystery glimmer moves.

"There!" When I point to a bush about twenty feet down the path, my feet run before my mouth has time to catch up. "Troy! Matt, it's Troy! There!" I call to Matt again as I hurdle another fallen tree. Rounding a rock formation—a larger rock balancing on a smaller rock as if placed by divine hands—I'm gaining on Troy.

"Jules!" Matt yells from behind me, but I don't stop. I run toward Troy, trying like hell to catch my attacker, but he increases the distance between us.

As I run out of the woods and onto the paved road, I see Troy again, clear as day. He leaps onto the back of an ATV. The engine revs. It picks up speed and heads west, farther away from me. Away from home. Out of reach of my need to hogtie Troy and beat him until my fists bleed. Beat him until I'm spent, every bruise and scratch on my body avenged. But he has escaped, thanks to Dave Richardson, the getaway driver.

"Dammit!" Exhausted, I bend at the waist, plant my hands on my knees, then give up altogether and collapse in the dirt.

"Jules! What do you think you were doing?" Matt asks, standing next to me.

"That was him! That was Troy!"

Matt stares at me without saying a word.

"I almost had him," I say, pointing toward Troy's escape route. "Dave was waiting for him, and I almost had him."

Matt continues his stare.

"This proves Dave and Troy are working together for more than baking damn pies and catching fish. What? What?" I yell.

"What were you planning to do if you caught him? Alone? Unarmed?"

"I don't know, Matt. Something!"

"Something? You could've gotten yourself killed running after him. Especially if he wasn't alone!"

"I'm fine!"

"Clearly, you're not. What would you have done if Dave Richardson got off that damn ATV and came at you?"

"Then, I'd beat the crap out of him too."

"Really? Jules, I'm starting to think Mama and Daddy are right. You aren't safe away from our property."

"None of us are."

"No, Jules. You! You."

"I'm not some fragile, little girl in need of defending. I can take care of myself!"

"You're not thinking right. You keep going off half-cocked, flinging yourself into one danger after another. Not thinking at all about consequences."

"That's who I've always been, Matt."

"No. You were never this careless. Never this dumb. Before."

"Before what, Matt? Before Troy attacked me? Before Jacob died? Or, before Jacob entirely? Back when I was only a Martin girl and followed all the rules?"

Matt laughs, a half-frustrated laugh. "Jules, you never followed rules. But you did care whether you lived or died. You had some common sense rather than a death wish. Now, I don't know what you'll do from moment to moment."

"Troy was waiting for us, Matt. He set a trap and was waiting. Shit," I say, remembering what or rather who is on the other side of the trip line. "Cole. Do you think they know about him? They could go after him. Or, Cole could trigger whatever that line leads to." I turn around and walk toward Cole's camp.

"Jules, stop. We're not done here."

I pause near the rock formation. "Maybe being with Jacob did change me. Maybe caring about somebody else and doing everything I can to protect the people I've got left is what's keeping my head above water."

Without a word, Matt turns and stomps back into the woods.

"Where are you going?" I ask.

"I'm going to check that trip line and disassemble it if I can." Matt takes his Leatherman off his belt and opens the blade.

"Matt, you don't know a damn thing about disassembling trip wires. What if it's attached to a bomb?" I envision every war movie I've ever seen. A soldier on patrol. The enemy was in the area earlier and may still be nearby. The soldier chats with his buddies in a whisper and doesn't see the trip wire near his boot. The soldier along with his buddies are blown to bits.

"Hopefully, all Troy wanted to do was slow us down enough to jump us. If it's attached to something sketchy, I won't touch it."

The trip line was only that, a trip hazard. Matt cuts it off the trees, winds it, and puts it in his pocket. By the time we reach Cole's camp, he's gone. We head to the shoreline thinking maybe the boy went for a swim. But the shore holds far fewer hiding places than the Amazonian woods of Bellefontaine. Again, I am exposed. Of every feeling I've had since Troy forced himself on me in the garden, this feeling of exposure is the hardest to stomach. I never knew my confidence, my sense of self-power, was so fragile, as if it was never real to begin with. Taken away by one man in one act.

We keep close to our neighbors' piers on our way home, scanning the boards and pylons as we duck under each one. Our eyes sweep the water for approaching boats, jet skis, anything that could lead to someone getting the jump on us again. Every time we hit a large section of beach, those precious, undeveloped bits of waterfront property, I feel exposed. Troy and his friends could come at us from any direction. Would they make two attempts in one day?

Yes, it is crazy. I know this now, but a part of me still felt protected here after Troy attacked me in the garden. That part was tiny, but it stood its ground. Now, the vulnerabilities of my home, my life, my body find light. They reveal themselves in cruel intensity.

Our pier stands a short distance away. Home. Or, at least home for now. Mama and Daddy and Kate and all the others. I want to run the remaining distance, but my legs aren't in it. For a few more minutes, Matt and I trudge across sand and through shallow water until at last we climb the rocks and find Mama standing on the front lawn. I go to her. Wrap my arms around her.

"Jules, what is it?" she asks. Mama always knows when of one her children hurts. She may not get our names right when calling to one of us, but she knows when we need extra love. She knows when the monsters have grown too big and come too close.

I speak into her shoulder, unwilling to let her go. "We saw him. Troy. He's still here. He didn't run. He was waiting for us, there was a trip wire, and Dave Richardson was with him. They sped off before I could reach them. Billy was right. And if he was right about Troy—"

Mama squeezes me tight then breaks the embrace. She turns and marches toward the house—mama bear on a mission. "Daddy! Matthew!"

Once Daddy hears what happens, he and Matt are in the truck, gravel spraying behind them as Daddy peels down the driveway. I want to be with them heading to the Army Camp, but I am "not to leave this house under any circumstances." Matt will bear witness to what and who we saw. Daddy will relay to Captain Johnson the urgency of arresting Troy for what he did to me and Dave for aiding him in the second attempt. But will Captain Johnson listen? Will he act? Will our safety matter when it really counts? My gut says no.

19

Thirty-five years. That's how long Mama and Daddy have been saying, "I do." Thirty-five years. We should be celebrating this feat of love and compromise in a grand way—a family vacation to some exotic locale, a party with glitz overkill and a signature cocktail, at the very least an overpriced restaurant where everyone raves about the food while silently wishing their lamb chops with mint sauce would transform into a cheeseburger and fries.

Thanks to our cooking oil score, we do have fries tonight. French fries with fried fish and fried hushpuppies. I think Garrett was ready to throw anything and everything in the hot grease, excited as he was to don his fish fry master apron, but he stopped at potatoes, mullet, and globs of damp cornmeal mixed with onions and bell pepper. We're also enjoying a big helping of *don't talk about that* and *good God, ignore that subject.* And wine. Plenty of wine.

Tonight, we celebrate Mama and Daddy and all the love that brought us into the world and kept us together. We won't speak of Troy or that shameful *almost* that I shouldn't feel shame over but still do. The shame and anger escalate to teeth-rattling rage if I allow them too much space in my head. Troy was able to pin me to the ground. Me. On the ground. And no amount of *it's not my fault* will change that. So, yes, tonight we celebrate Mama and Daddy and that is what I focus on—their marital successes—as I watch Father Morgan bless their marriage under an arbor of greenery Kate constructed for the occasion.

"Well, if we can't go to the church tonight, I still want them to feel special. And a focal point always sets the mood." Kate told me this while she cut magnolia stems from a tree twenty feet away from the makeshift altar. The ceremony was lovely, and Kate was right in her insistence of having the arbor. If only Father Morgan hadn't cut his eyes so many times to Garrett at the fryer under the carport while performing Mama and Daddy's vow renewal.

"Let's eat!" Daddy grins after Father Morgan's final blessing, then kisses Mama again and squeezes her so tightly she pushes him back.

"You're not going to make it to thirty-six years with me if you keep clutching at me like that." Mama blushes, as pretty as pie as she pats Daddy's chest.

"All right," Kate orders, assuming her role of party planner extraordinaire, "Father Morgan, will you lead the buffet line?"

Well, who knew the old man's legs could move like that? Before anyone else thought to grab their plates, Father Morgan presents his empty plate to Garrett, pausing to allow a second and third filet to be added before moving on to the fries and hush-puppies.

Father Morgan is wasting no time, so before Kate and Garrett make it to their seats, he offers a quick blessing. Peace falls over the group. Both tables—adults and kids—are quiet, the only sounds being the smacking of lips, licking of fingertips, and the occasional pop from the citronella torches surrounding the carport turned ballroom.

I nearly choke as a figure appears from the darkness. "Someone's there," I say, rising from my seat and silently calculating how quickly I can retrieve a rifle from the garage.

"Billy?" Matt calls to the man who now shows his face to the light, helmet tucked under one arm and rifle loped about his chest. "Everything okay, man?"

"Yes, yes," Billy says, a big helping of awkwardness in his reply. "I apologize for intruding. I let myself in through the gate. Matt, you need to shore up that thing. It's too easy to jimmy it free. But, I can come back tomorrow." Billy shifts as if to leave, all the while clearly trying not to eye the buffet spread. "I didn't mean to interrupt."

"Nonsense, stay," Kate says. She nudges Garrett who hops up and retrieves another camping chair. Kate is apparently skilled in telepathy because in no time she nudges me closer to Matt and squeezes Billy between her and me. "We've got just enough room for one more. If you don't mind putting that rifle down. We follow a strict, no guns at the table policy here."

Billy places his rifle at his feet as he sits looking hungry and embarrassed. But mostly hungry.

"I didn't mean to cut the party short," Billy says, helping Lauren and me clear the table. Mama and Daddy retreated to the house after Garrett and Kate left to escort Father Morgan to the Rectory before the 9 p.m. curfew. I'm not crazy about them being on the roads after dark, but Mama insisted Father Morgan not drive alone. I'm sure she doesn't want *Priest Murdered by Marauders!* or *Old-as-the-Hills Priest Drives Car into Mobile Bay!* on her conscience. Calculating every possible risk for what used to be mundane no-brainers is our life now.

"Oh, no, no. You didn't. We don't make it long past sundown these days." Lauren takes a stack of scraped-clean plates from Billy. She places them in a tub of water and a look of disappointment crosses her face, as if the number of dirty dishes will test her will to live. "I think I'll let these plates soak until I have some daylight."

"Lauren, I've got 'em." I bump her aside with my hip and light the grill to heat a pan of water.

"Well, then," Lauren says, grinning. "Time to get the littles in bed and for me to sleep off tomorrow's hangover." She smiles at Billy, then at me with such matchmaker twinkle I could smack her. *When did all these damn Catholics forget about Billy's marriage vows to his wife?* "Matt, I'd love your help with bedtime tonight." With that she makes her exit with Mallie on her hip and her husband in tow.

Steam begins to rise from the pot of water and for several moments I can feel Billy staring at me.

"What?" I ask him. "You've never seen anyone wash dishes during the Apocalypse?"

"Just not sure what exactly you're doing."

"Well, we ran out of Palmolive several weeks ago, so now we scrub the plates in regular water, heat water till boiling, dunk the scrubbed plates in the hot water and pretend everything ends up sanitary."

Billy's face reveals a bit of shock.

"Regretting crashing dinner?" I ask.

"No, no. It was delicious and I'm sure the boiling water will—"

"You can stop tap dancing, Billy. These plates, which may or may not end up clean, are really a metaphor for the absolute absurdity of this whole mess aren't they? Mama and Daddy's thirty-fifth anniversary is today, so of course we had to celebrate. And why shouldn't something as amazing as a thirty-five-year marriage be celebrated? No matter the circumstances. No matter the fact that in doing so, we ignore that nothing about the celebration will be normal, from burning citronella candles for ambience not because of the mosquitos but because the lights are out again, and we have no other candles left. We use the real, fancy plates rather than easy-clean-up paper plates because we ran out of paper plates four months ago. Just as well, because we can't spare any paper products. I'm not looking forward to the day we run out of paper entirely because the bathroom situation around here will be unfathomable."

Billy lets out a nervous laugh. "Well, I admire your innovation. With the hot water and all."

I pull on a pair of silicone potholders and dip the first scrubbed plate into the boiling water. "Desperate times and all that." We stand in silence as I dunk the next three plates. "I guess that's what I'd like the Army to know. Everything about our lives right now, us civilians, everything is odd. And it's odd to a point that it's really stressful. This has been dragging on for so long and the longer it does, the more stressful everything is. It all piles up like dirty dishes until we have to do something about it or just eat directly out of the pot like a trough. Animals rather than human. We're trying to preserve the tiniest bit of dignity."

"That's why I came here tonight."

"To preserve my dignity? That ship sailed and crashed into an iceberg."

"No. To give you an update. We haven't found Troy, but we've got guys out all over looking. Land and water. We'll find him."

"So." I take a breath, hoping something polite comes to mind but at the mention of Troy, my ability to be polite sails away with my dignity. And, honestly, I don't give a rat's ass about being polite anymore. Polite sucks up energy I don't have. "You don't actually have an update other than *we're doing our job*. Troy's still out there. As far as we know he's standing right behind that tree right there watching me again and trying not to laugh." I suck in a gulp of air, a pathetic attempt to hide the panic rising in my throat.

"I know you're scared, Jules. Anybody in your situation would be."

"I'm not just—"

Billy cuts me off, stepping closer to me. "I also know you. The idea that some shithead perv would pin you to the ground is stuck in your head, isn't it? The unbreakable, kick everybody in the throat Jules Martin, was pinned to the ground and you can't get that out of your head. Am I right?"

"Yes, but—"

"And you've been turning over every word I said the other day to find a solution to this whole mess?"

"Well, of course, but how—"

"And you're tired of waiting for someone else to deal with it, right? Because let's face it, patience has never been your strong suit, and you're a total control freak, so—"

"So, you came here to insult me and tell me that you haven't found the boogeyman. And we're still a go for Civil War two-point-O. Thanks. That's helpful."

"I came here to tell you that we're looking and *I* won't stop looking until I find him and to tell you not to do a damn thing but stay put. No wandering around the woods, even with Matt. No kayaking by yourself. No bringing food to little orphan boys hiding in the trees."

"How do you know that?"

"Because we know things, Jules. That's how."

"So, everyone has spies out now, huh?"

Billy blows past my question. "And absolutely no going after Troy yourself."

I tap my potholder hand to my forehead in a quick salute. "Yes, sir!"

"Quit it with that shit, Jules." Billy takes me by the shoulders and holds me at arm's length in front of him. "You're my friend, Jules, and I don't have many of those left. Do you understand me? I need you to be safe. I need one good thing to come out of this shit."

When the flicker of torchlight catches Billy's eyes, I can see he means what he's saying. Tears pool in his eyes and his grip tightens on my shoulders. "Billy, I'll stay put. I promise."

"That's all I'm asking." He releases me and takes several steps backward. He grabs his rifle and helmet. "I've got to get back."

With that, he leaves, and I'm alone in the darkness, the imprint of his hands still alive on my shoulders.

———

"Jules."

On the couch, I open my eyes to Kate, her eyes filled with tears. In fact, tears stream down red cheeks. "What happened?" I sit up, fully awake. Awake and knowing that whatever Kate will say next will be bad. Very, very bad. Because Kate doesn't cry. Not often and never openly.

"Get your shoes on. It's Billy." Then, she tries her best to swallow a sob, but it escapes her mouth, and the sound of that gasp is worse than the look in her eyes.

In the glare of the morning sun, rising directly behind the boat house, I see several people standing beneath its tin roof. Kate hurries down the pier and I follow. Why would Billy be back already? Did he find Troy last night? And why would he be on the pier? Did he come by boat? Possible but strange. "Kate, what's going on?" I ask while trying to catch up to her. I step into the shadow of the boathouse, still several feet away from her. With the sun angled behind the roof I see something. No, not something. *Someone.* Someone hangs from a rafter. Swinging slightly. Dangling. Turning on the breeze. "Kate?" I ask again. My ankles go numb, and my knees hit the boards.

20

Billy dangles above me, his face bruised and gray. His mouth is open, just enough so that a sliver of something shows between his swollen lips. Cruel gashes and deep purple contusions mangle his once bronze skin. Flies buzz around open wounds and land in the black tar letters across his chest: *TRAITOR*.

"Get him down," Mama says. "Somebody cut that rope." Her voice sounds sedated. Soft and uncertain. "Please."

Garrett searches the boathouse then his eyes land on me. "Jules, do you have your knife?"

"We can't," I say. "We can't cut him down yet. Not until Captain Johnson—"

Daddy helps me to my feet and walks me to a swing but the last place I want to be is sitting so close to my friend's body dangling from a rafter, so I instead lean against the railing. Daddy squeezes my shoulders, the way he always does when something terrible has happened. Daddy squeezes my shoulders in the same places that Billy held me last night. His hands had felt warm. "Matt and Lauren have gone to the camp. They should be back with Captain Johnson soon."

"Okay." I glance at Billy. I don't want to, but I can't stop myself. His uniform shirt and undershirt have been cut off his body, with strips of fabric left limp from his wrists and belt.

T R A I T O R. I can't look away from the word.

"What about his mother? She doesn't need to see this. And his wife. He has kids. Had kids." I correct myself. And the correction sends me spinning as if the waves have taken the boathouse and thrown it into a waterspout and everything around me spins except Billy. He hangs in the most still silence. "They're at a hunting camp. Billy moved them there."

"Someone beat the shit out of him and hung 'im like a fucking animal," Garrett says, staring up at the man he barely knew.

"Not someone, Garrett. The Knights." My head ceases spinning and in place of the whirling, a fire ignites. "The Knights did this and you know it. So, you can stop pretending that they mean well and just have a few bad apples. They did this. This is what happens when we ignore who they really are. And this is what happens when someone tries to help us."

"We don't know that for sure," Kate says.

"And where were you last night, Garrett? You were supposed to be out here. It was your shift."

"I wasn't feeling well."

"You weren't feeling well?" I ask. "So, what, you just took the night off?"

Kate steps between Garrett and me. "Jules, back off. This is upsetting for all of us. Billy was a friend to all of us. I just can't believe someone would do this to such a kind man."

"Don't you dare," I tell her. "Don't you dare make this about you, as if you knew him. You knew who Billy was and that's it."

"That doesn't mean I can't grieve him just the same."

"What the hell do you know about grief?"

Two thoughts charge against each other in my brain, wrestling for space: blame and Billy's wife. That's where our minds go, us forever military spouses. We go to the wives. Regardless of race, background, or religion, one thing unites us as military wives—the likelihood of becoming a military widow. Billy has a wife who will know how he died, where he died, but not why. Not completely. I gasp and bend over, dry-heaving toward the wooden planks. I know her pain, the all-consuming pain that will be hers. He was my friend, but he was her everything.

Kate strokes my hair and stands me upright. "Jules, maybe you should sit."

"No. I need to know where Garrett was last night."

"Hey! I didn't do this. Stop acting like this is my fault."

"You were supposed to be on guard duty, and you obviously weren't. Had you been out here where you were supposed to be—"

"It's a blessing that Garrett needed the outhouse last night," Kate says. "If not, then whoever did this would have probably killed him too. Is that what you want, Jules?"

"Of course not, Kate," I say, and I decide that Daddy was right —I need to sit before the spinning causes me to vomit. "But, please, can we stop pretending we don't know who did this? Who else would paint *traitor* across Billy's chest, lynch him, then hang him on *our* pier? Our pier! This is a message to us." I suck in a gulp of air because my lungs feel like they will explode and then I will explode. Little bits and pieces of me all over Billy's body and the boathouse.

"Because he had dinner with us last night?" Mama asked. "No one would kill someone over dinner, Jules. Please, someone get him down from there."

"No. Not until Johnson gets here. And I think they would. Kill over a dinner. The Knights. I think Troy would. He's not stable. He'd kill for a lot less than a few fried flounder and a glass or two of homemade wine."

Kate nods in agreement, even though I don't know if she's ever laid eyes on Troy.

"I saw something in his eyes in the garden and again in the woods. He's messed up. But I don't think anyone could do this alone." Billy's last words to me—*I need you to be safe*—ring in my ears. "Billy came to warn us. He told me to be safe. He made me promise that we would all stay safe. But no one kept him safe."

Mama reaches out and grabs my hand, squeezes it just before I retreat.

"But he had his rifle with him." Mama turns her back on Billy. I can't blame her. No one wants to have this conversation here, next to the black-haired boy that took such care bagging Mama's groceries every week at Greer's. Back in our blissfully ignorant teenage years when all of this was as plausible as a sci-fi movie.

"Mama, sometimes one gun isn't enough." I look toward the house. "Where are the kids? I don't want them to see this."

"I put them in the garage. I hope you don't mind—"

"Of course not," I say. "I don't want them wandering out here."

"I told Jessie to keep them locked in there until we come get them."

I nod at Mama and then see Matt and Captain Johnson appear around the corner of the house. Johnson is halfway down the pier when he sees Billy. He slows to a deliberate stride and closes the gap between us.

"What time did you find him like this?" Johnson asks no one in particular. He slides past me and stands before Billy, seeming to stare at his wounds. Three more soldiers have followed Captain Johnson. One of the soldiers can't handle what's in front of him. He does what we all want to do—hangs his head over the railing and heaves his undigested breakfast into the bay.

"Sir, we can be ready to go in thirty," another says. "We need to find who did this."

"I want to get him down. Take his body to the camp. I've got to contact his wife. Then, we need to…" Johnson's voice trails off as if his list is incomplete but the train of thought is lost. "What time did you find him?" Johnson asks again.

Daddy speaks first, "About an hour ago."

"He must have been put here somewhere between 3 and 5 a.m.," Garrett adds. "I was out here before that." Garrett glances my way, but I just shake my head and squeeze past the soldiers and through the gate of the boathouse. I need to be away from Garrett, Billy, all of them.

In the front yard, my legs give way under me, and I stumble to the ground. I turn back to the water, wanting to curse God and everyone involved in whatever the officials are calling this. Is this a civil war? Brother against brother? Domestic unrest? But I can't find the correct description. I kneel in silence and my face floods with tears. Did we all just let it happen? Ignore the warning signs? Dismiss the last several months as isolated incidents, rage that will fizzle with time?

A small hand covering mine interrupts my sobs. I grip the grass between my fingers, but Cole only tightens his fingers around mine. "Jules, you're going to be okay."

What is he doing here? Looking at him through cloudy eyes, I can't register his expression. "You shouldn't be here."

"Trust me," he says. "You're going to be okay."

"You don't know that. How could you? You are a kid, Cole." Lashing out at Cole is unfair and wrong but what else can I do in this moment? "These are the kind of dangers I've warned you about. That could easily be you out there."

Cole shrinks away from me a bit. "Never gonna happen."

"I'm sorry. I didn't mean to…it's not safe for you here. I don't know where you'll be safe, but it's not here and not with me."

"That ain't true. Nothin's gonna happen to me. It's like I've got an invisible shield. You're the only person who actually saw me and then caught me. Why do you think I got away with stealing for so long? Nobody notices a kid, especially not this kid."

I nod. On the dock lies Billy, nearly unrecognizable for the swelling around his eyes, nose, and mouth. My old pal, my teenage crush, my friend, my one and only friend here in Belle-fontaine ruined, branded a traitor, blood and dirt covering his body. My mind, my heart couldn't take it if Cole were next, beaten to death by The Knights and because of me.

"You shouldn't be here. You need to stay away from me. And you shouldn't be out here for this. Seeing this," I tell Cole. "Kids shouldn't see stuff like this." I look to him for confirmation but get none.

"I've seen a body before. Two."

"Oh. Yes. I guess you have. Of course. But—"

"But, Mama and Daddy were just lying all peaceful on the floor. They didn't look like that." Cole points to the end of the pier, which snaps me into the present. The real present. The here and now and one very real threat to Cole who is about to walk this way.

I jump to my feet. "You can't be here."

Cole stands, his lips parting in protest.

"No. You can't be here. If Captain Johnson sees you, he'll arrest you. He'll snatch you up and I won't be able to help you." I grab Cole by the hand and drag him around to the back of the house. "Go. Go straight back to your camp and stay there. Got it? Go, go." I grab his shoulders just as Billy had grabbed mine. "Stay out of sight. Hide. Got it?" And, just like that, Cole sprints to the end of the driveway, hops the ditch, and disappears into the trees.

My own shoulders burn with my last memory of Billy, of us,

friend versus friend trying to get through to each other, trying to solve what seems like utter bullshit now, arguing over something we agree on—the world is garbage and no one knows how to fix it. I want him to breathe, stand, smile, anything but lay dead, killed by men who call themselves patriots. Lynched. The ultimate degradation.

Billy is gone. Taken. How many have been taken now? Jacob was taken from me. Jacob was a good man. Both Billy and Jacob donned the uniform to serve, and that uniform got them killed. Fuck that uniform. How many did Clayton Vancleave kill? How many other bug men all over this country poisoned their countrymen in the name of patriotism? The removal of Civil War statues and names of racists on elementary school buildings is why Clayton did what he did, because he felt he was being erased with every toppled statue and renamed building. So, he made an orphan out of Cole and how many others? Fuck Clayton Vancleave.

The Knights killed Billy because of proximity to the Army and to us. Whether The Knights control Bellefontaine or not, we remain under the control of the US Government. Does this scrap of power justify murder? How many soldiers died on guard duty —check an ID and then get blown to bits? Jacob's wasn't the only post hit. Liberty's Guard and offshoots like The Knights have one common goal: Create anarchy and watch the country burn. As long as they hold onto their seats of power, the rest of us can burn, too. So, most of all, fuck The Knights and every other home-grown militia in this country filled with overgrown brats playing soldier.

I suck the cry down my throat and head back down the hill toward the pier. I watch as Billy's body is moved to a stretcher and carried toward me, as if by four pallbearers.

"McManus, Grimes, get your teams and search this whole property and perimeter, the dock, outbuildings, house, the whole thing." Captain Johnson rattles off orders as they pass me. I am the lone observer to this funeral parade. Everyone else has a purpose, one that requires more than watching. "No one gets in or out. Got me?" The soldiers nod in agreement.

"You can't do that," I tell Johnson.

"I most certainly can. My soldier was killed on your property. We will search every square inch of this place."

"But we didn't do this."

"Miss Jones, I'm going to need a statement from you. Later. Don't go anywhere."

I follow Billy's body around the house and watch as the soldiers load it into the back of a Humvee. Without another word or goodbye or even acknowledgement to me standing in the carport, Johnson climbs inside the truck with Billy's body and pulls the doors closed. A cloud of dust follows as it speeds down the driveway, turns onto the road, then turns again out of sight.

"I never would have pegged you for a smoker." I stand near Johnson's trailer on the camp. Near us, a handful of soldiers mill about, performing what looks like pointless extra duty. The one with a shop broom pushing debris from side to side of the dirt path between Army trailers seems exceptionally useless. Two days have passed since we discovered Billy's body. Two days without the follow-up I expected from Johnson. That's what lands me here today, next to a junior captain who smells like wrath and feet.

"I don't," Johnson says and takes a drag from the lit cigarette in his right hand. He turns his face toward mine, glaring at me for several uncomfortable seconds from his seat on his trailer steps. "So, to what do I owe this visit, Miss Jones?"

I let his tone slide. He looks like he hasn't slept since Billy's murder, so punch-drunk is expected. And, to be honest, my fight-face is exhausted so I don't have the energy to call him on his attitude.

"Do you need something?" Johnson asks, this time softer.

"I just came to see if—"

"Billy's still dead? Oh, he's dead." He takes another drag and blows it out before tucking his head between his knees. "His wife just left. She was my fifth notification since arriving in this hell-hole. I hate to admit this, but I'd really hoped the note I sent would be enough. But she showed up. Just showed up. Kind of like you."

"Well, I'm here to give a statement. You'd said—"

"I know what I said, Miss Jones. I'm not a complete moron."

"I'm not saying you are. Are you okay?"

"I'm great. And I don't need your statement."

"What? Why not? Did you catch who killed him?"

"No. But we know it wasn't you or your family."

"How do you know that? I mean I'm glad you know that, but how?"

"We found drag marks along the crab pier, like Billy was pulled from a boat onto the crab pier then into the boathouse."

"Oh." *How did I miss those?*

"I'm surprised you missed that. The drag marks. I thought you were more observant than that."

"Observant," I scoff. "That's apparently what I'm worst at lately. Of everything—"

"Let's not do this, okay?"

"Do what?"

"The bonding over self-loathing and mutual failings. Let's not do that."

"So, you're not okay. I mean, of course, you're not okay. Why would you be? One of your guys was just murdered."

"Not 'one of my guys.' The guy. My right hand. What kind of

shithead commander can't even protect his First Sergeant?" He drops the cigarette and stomps it out with his boot, rising to his feet in the process. "When I find out who did this, I'm stringing 'em up by their balls." A bloodied piece of paper lay on the step next to where he was sitting.

"You know who did this," I say.

"I do? Who then?"

"The Knights. Who else?"

Johnson cuts his gaze at me. "I know The Knights, but I don't know which ones."

"Why does it matter which ones? They're all guilty."

"That's not how we do things."

"So, how *do* you do things?"

"We investigate."

"Investigate?" I ask, incredulous. "That's not enough and you know it."

"Stay out of this, Miss Jones." He picks up the paper, crumpling it in his closed fist.

"What is that?" I ask.

"I mean it, Jules. Stay out of this. This is not any of your business."

"The hell it isn't. Billy was my friend. I have known him my entire life, and he died on my pier. And you know and I know who's responsible for this. And you know it's time to end this. Wouldn't it be best for everybody to get rid of all of them whether they strung Billy up or not? Who cares how they got their hands dirty!"

"There's procedure."

"Screw procedure. The Knights sure as hell didn't follow procedure when they beat him and painted *traitor* across his chest and strung him up like some blue-ribbon marlin! And crammed that paper in his mouth!" I point to the bloodied paper. "There's blood on that. Is that what was shoved in his mouth? I saw something peeking out of his mouth on the pier. Is that it?"

"This is not your business, Jules."

"He was your friend, too, wasn't he? He didn't just work for you, right? You Army guys always talk about brotherhood. Well, your brotherhood just got lynched. Now tell me you're going after them."

"Jules," Johnson stands and turns toward the door. "Stay out of it."

"They're recruiting, you know. More every day."

"You don't think I know that?" Johnson snaps around, charging me this time. "I know that. I know what they're doing and how bad..." He stops himself as if one moment of honesty will blow this entire crap show of a mission.

"What's on that paper, Johnson?"

"I will not discuss this with you."

"What's written on that paper?" I reach out, grabbing his arm.

"Go home!" he says, brushing me off.

"Wait," I say, following him up the steps and into his trailer. "That note is why you know we had nothing to do with Billy's murder, isn't it? Who the hell cares about a few drag marks on the crab pier? It's all on that, isn't it?"

Johnson eyes seem to catch fire as he spins around to face me. "Tell me how Billy's last night went. I am curious. He left here alone, without authorization and never made it back. Sometime between leaving here and ending up fucking dead, he went to see you. What time did he leave your house?"

"I guess about nine."

"Okay, so he left your place at nine, then got strung up on your pier between then and 6 a.m. Do I have that right?"

I nod, regretting my decision to be in such a tight space with Johnson.

"So, that's what I know. That and what's on this," Johnson

says, waving the bloodied note at me. "So, tell me where he was between 9 p.m. and 6 a.m. Because that I don't know. But I do know that he wasn't just my friend or just worked for me. He was *my responsibility*!" Johnson clinches his fists together like he wants to punch something or someone and lets out a loud moan. "I had a responsibility to his wife and kids, and I let them down."

"I don't know where he went. He ate dinner with us, we talked for a bit, and then he left."

"Huh," Johnson mumbles, wheels clearly spinning. "And which way did he go when he left? Right or left out of your drive-way? Did you watch him leave?"

"I think right."

"You think?"

"I'm pretty sure. Umm, yes, right."

"You're *pretty sure* he went right. And that's the information that just couldn't wait any longer, so you paddled yourself on over here *alone*—"

"Matt's with me. He's waiting with the kayaks—"

"Oh, good. Matt. So you and Matt just had to come give me this critical piece of information? Thank you. 'Pretty sure he went right' is the exact information needed to crack this whole case. That's the missing piece to this mission of keeping as many of you alive as possible. Because that's why we are here, Miss Jones. We are here to keep all of *you* safe."

"That's what's written on that paper, right? They're coming after all of us? Anyone they deem a traitor, right? My family." My stomach roils at the thought of The Knights going house-to-house, dragging out anyone and everyone they think betrayed them, chose the wrong side. Unpatriotic. Snowflake. Sympathizer. "Because you chose us and our land, they're coming after us."

"I'm ordering you to stay out of this."

"That's my family out there, not yours."

"And this is my job, not yours."

"Then do it. Do something."

Disgusted, I break through a group of soldiers gathered, no doubt, to listen in on the *Jules vs Johnson show*. As I charge between the few pine trees left on Goat Island, I wish I could beat both Johnson and myself with my paddle. I'd like to smack Johnson for being such an ass, which shouldn't surprise me in the least because he's been an ass since I first met him, and myself for letting him get to me. One good, hard whack to his face and mine should set us both straight.

21

"Matt, we've gotta get home now." I grab my safety rope from Matt and shove my kayak into the water. With one hard push of my paddle against the soft bottom, I'm off. "They're coming after us. The Knights. We're next."

The reeds stand tall and still, carrying the tell-tale water line of low tide—pale, sun-soaked above the line, darker and spongy below. I hope the water beyond the lagoon isn't too choppy. Paddling against the waves will slow our progress.

"How do you know that?" Matt asks.

"Johnson just confirmed it. I'll explain everything later. Right now, we just need—"

I dig my paddle into the water and coax my kayak around the final turn of the tall grass where the swamp meets the bay. The water is flat. No chop at all. Four of the biggest stingrays I've ever seen glide through the water next to me. One brushes its angel wing against the left side of my kayak and breaks the surface. It pauses for a second and looks at me with one bulging eye, as if to say, "You coming?"

I flinch, watching the barb on the end of his tail cut through the water. Then more rays surface and surround my boat. *Could it be?* Surely it is! The most wonderful phenomenon stirs around me. With a tight grip on my paddle, I slash through the water, furiously pulling at the water as fast as I can. *Right stroke, left stroke. Right stroke, left stroke.*

"Holy shit, Jules!"

"I know. I see." I can barely get the words out as I paddle harder, faster.

Then, I hear them. The bells! Bells ring out from every pier and dock we pass along the western shore. This was what we'd been waiting for. Hoping for but dare not pray the word aloud. All summer we watched the water. Begged in silence. Pleaded. And now, finally, a jubilee!

A jubilee! That explains it: the hot, shallow water, the still air, the gigantic stingrays having left their sandy, safe bottom to linger on top of the water. *Jubilee*, a word synonymous with celebration and festivity because that's what one is—a rare and wonderful occurrence as if God tells us, "Stop trying so hard. Allow me to provide. Today, I give you all the bounties my wonderful sea has to offer." There is a complex scientific explanation for jubilee— an occurrence that happens only in Mobile Bay and Tokyo Bay— but belief in miracles runs deep here, and on days like today, the soul needs a miracle.

The mystique of jubilee goes far beyond a sudden change in the salinity of the water causing the appearance of the fish, crab, and shrimp in mass quantities. Creature behavior changes during these fleeting moments. Their skittish ways dissipate. A fish that normally darts off at the slightest contact with a human being becomes unnaturally depressed, as if they swim here to die and choose to make their death easy and quick. And not just the fish. Crabs line up for suicide. Climbing up tree stumps, rocks, and pylons, they wait for their ultimate demise.

"Jules!" Matt calls to me from the ladder as I near our pier. He ascends the ladder and pulls his kayak to the deck as I paddle the last stretch of open water.

Looking across the water, I see every member of the Martin clan. Kate and Mallie rush down the pier, as fast as Kate can carry the toddler. Garrett scales the rock bulkhead, five-gallon buckets in each hand in lieu of gig and net. Mama and Daddy stand in knee-deep water, a metal tub between them. Lauren, surrounded by children, shouts directions to the little ones to grab crabs by the back of their shells.

"Don't get yourself pinched, now!" she calls.

I will ruin their day later, after the Jubilee. For a few precious moments, we will believe that the world is safe, and life is sustainable.

Matt wastes no time in tying a rope from his waist to one handle of a large metal tub and drops into the water below with his cast net slung over one shoulder. Matt is in full Jubilee form, with a gig in one hand and a scoop net in the other, ready to grab and snatch and sweep up everything in his path.

"It's a Jubilee, Jules! A damn Jubilee!" Matt's grin fills his face. "Take this." He tosses the gig to me sideways. "I'll do better with the cast net."

Matt throws the scoop net back up to the dock and trudges through the water, around the pier, back toward the shore. He winds the cast net's leash into a loose lasso with one hand. Then, he drapes part of the large circular net over one shoulder while collecting the rest of the net in a neat bunch with his other hand. The iron weights sewn in the hem of the net sound like the hi-hat of a jazz percussionist. Matt becomes one with his net. He holds the center point of the net between his front teeth then leans forward on his left foot and rotates back on his right hip. Twisting forward, he releases the net, casting a shimmering circle of light blue nylon. The shiny, wet strings pause in mid-air before falling into a perfect circle on the water's surface. With a sharp tug on the leash, Matt closes the net around a school of unsuspecting fish.

Toward a breaching sandbar, a throng of oxygen-deprived flounder skulk to breathable water. The deeper water betrayed them, as it does on occasion in Mobile Bay. The salinity of the water is now too dense, forcing the fish to shore in search of breath. But the flounder find no reprieve today, only the prongs of my gig.

I snag two flounders, both a good eighteen inches long and run over to Matt, ripping my first and second treasures from the long screws. They land in the tub, flopping and gasping.

Near the rock bulkhead, Lauren, using a small net, scoops blue crab from the sandbars, collecting them into another metal tub as more wet sand emerges from the retreating tide. "We've got soft shells!" Lauren yells to me, referring to molting female blue crab. A jubilee in late July when the crab is molting is so special, it almost repairs my relationship with God.

My stomach rumbles with anticipation of fried soft-shell crabs, my favorite seafood delicacy. Deviled crab, deep-fried crab balls, stuffed flounder roasted over an open flame, today would bring all of this. As I pierce my next flounder, my mouth begins to water.

Kate, on the end of the pier, holds Mallie up to our brass bell. Mallie's chubby arms, still plump with baby fat, yank up and down on the bell's rope, banging the clapper against the corroded walls of the bell. The clamor beckons everyone in earshot. *Jubilee!*

Standing knee deep, I watch both neighbors and strangers appear from all directions to our anointed stretch of land. Within minutes, the people charge from the tall grass, woods, and swamp that surround our small haven. As they swarm the shore, rushing to the water before the feast disappears, I scan the tree line. At last, a boy with a glowing mop of hair appears on the beach. Barefoot and bare-chested, he plows into the water. I watch as he grabs a flounder barehanded and tosses it up on the beach.

Jubilees don't last long. Just as quickly as the phenomenon appears, the wind could shift, sending any missed treasure back to deeper water. I grab a bucket off the pier and splash through the water to the boy. Thrusting my gig back into the water, I spear another flounder. Twenty-four inches of sustenance writhing on the end of my stick, and I marvel at the size.

"Cole!" I push the bucket into his arms. "Take this. And fill it up."

For the first time in a year, I am alive, as if the warm water has washed me clean of hard-fought living. Every strike of my gig, successful or not, pumps adrenaline through my veins, pushes out the fatigue, makes room for vitality. A crab nips at my little toe, but even the slight pain is a blessing. Alive! I am alive!

I hold my latest trophy high in the air, displaying my effortless catch. "Cole, look at the size of this thing!" The free-for-all pauses for a moment as cheers rise from my fellow revelers. Cole's grin catches sunlight as he holds out the bucket, ready to accept the fish.

"Matt's gonna have to teach us how to clean fish," I say as I drop another flounder, number six, into Cole's bucket.

"I'm ready to learn! Now switch with me," Cole says, handing me the bucket. "It's my turn with the gig!" The boy splashes away through the water and I think that is how every eleven-year-old boy in the world should be—free to splash and yell and spill joy and energy from every pore.

I move closer to the shore, midway between the end of the pier and the rock line. In the clear, shallow water, I see beneath the surface. Sunken logs litter the sandy bottom, making me step with care. Just before I clamber over one, a school of silver eels escapes their hiding place, forcing me back two steps to avoid their razor-sharp teeth. Not everything a jubilee offers up is worth snagging.

As I move around the log, several boats appear on the horizon. From the spray coming off the hulls, I know the boats are coming straight toward us. Normally, Matt chases away such vessels with a verbal threat or a warning shot, but today we have plenty to share. Today, we have *abundance.*

"Jessie!" I call to my niece who's dumping her bucket of goodies into a large tub on the pier, "Grab an empty tub and bring it over here."

Over the gurgling of suffocating flounder and the snipping of crab claws trudging up the rock line near me, I hear the true sounds of Jubilee. All our neighbors forget to be fearful or guarded and join the festival of fish. Elated voices rise above the water as hands, arms, backs, and legs lift from the water weeks of good, life-sustaining food.

The boats arrive and before anchors hit the water delighted families fling themselves overboard with cast nets, gigs, buckets, and scoops. One man foregoes the use of a bucket entirely. Instead, he scoops fish from the water with his bare hands and tosses them directly into his boat.

Farther down the beach, squatters and cave dwellers flood the pale sand north of our house. Without a single piece of equipment, a man and a teenage boy charge the water to grab the moribund flounder two at a time. They toss the fish to a woman nearby on the beach. Standing guard over her loot, she catches each fish before adding them to the growing pile between her bare feet.

I return to my pillage, gathering softshell blue crab into the hem of my T-shirt, my improvised bucket. Just as my shirt threatens to overflow, Cole appears, and I let each precious crab slide from my shirt into the bucket.

"Thanks. Jessie should be on her way with another bucket, if we have any empties left." Cole hands me the gig and crosses the sandbar. I swear to you the boy was skipping. *Skipping*! Jubilees are indeed pure magic. I sink to my knees and let the water lap around my hips. My arms are tired and I've no idea what we will do with such a harvest. Feast or famine, right?

I realize the bell has stopped ringing, so I look about, hoping to catch a glimpse of Mallie in her first jubilee. In the water, near the end of the pier, instead of Kate and Mallie, I see him. Blond. Dirty, wife-beater tank top. Troy jumps from a boat, fully clothed, and lands with a large spray of water. He runs. Sprints through the shallow water. To Kate. Kate is right there in his path. Holding Mallie. I can't breathe. I feel the same panic that these deprived fish must feel. From behind, he snatches Mallie from Kate's arms, shoves Kate into the water. Mallie's face contorts. Somewhere near, but to my ears the sound is miles away. The sound of screaming. Kate's face is pure horror. Garrett's voice rings out, threatening, but I can't see where he is either. Mallie writhes in Troy's grip, struggling to break free, using her little fists to beat on him. Stranger danger.

My legs pound through the water as I fling a flounder off the sharp tips of my gig. I move toward Troy. Toward Mallie. My beautiful and joyful Mallie. Troy trudges through the water toward the boat. Faster and faster and screaming in a voice I don't recognize as my own, I reach them. I raise my right arm and bring it down hard. My gig finds Troy's back and I push it further into his flesh.

As blood flows into the water, encircling the three of us, he falls. I release my grip on the gig and snatch up Mallie. I run, but both of my feet lift off the ground. An arm wraps around my waist, and I feel my body rise. My toes stretch for the ground but find air instead. My back scraps against the side of a boat. Garrett is close. I see him. He's almost here. I throw Mallie to him. *Save her. Please save her*. I fall to the fiberglass bottom and my cheek crashes into something hard. When I open my eyes, I see Dave Richardson standing above me.

"Welcome aboard," he says, gunning the engine and sending me sliding toward the stern.

———

My mouth tastes like blood and cotton. I guess I cut my tongue or maybe the metallic tang is from my lip, which feels swollen to the touch. Opening my eyes proves difficult. And shifting positions sets off a series of alarms in my head. First pounding, nauseating pain. Next, darkness. Fading light glows in spots—a sliver here and there, maybe under a door. The binds around my wrists and ankles don't allow for much movement. My shoulders burn with the discomfort of having my hands held behind my back. Panic sets in with the final alarm—a rustling a few feet from me.

"Whatever you are over there," I say to the sound, "if you can just remain in your spot, I'll remain in mine. Please." My childhood fear of death by rats, opossums, raccoons, and all the other rodents of the swamp floods my mind.

I hoist myself to a seated position and try to slow my breathing while my eyes adjust. Looking around as much as I'm able, I take in my surroundings. The floor is concrete. I know that by the way it feels on my legs. The air is stifling, putrid even. Perhaps my rustling friend has a dead friend. Or, maybe it's just that I appear to be in a storage shed and something has spoiled. What little light I have illuminates stacks of boxes and whatnots. I can't read a single label on the boxes with my blurry vision. Shifting again, I slouch against something hard, metal and warm from the sun. Maybe that's a wall.

I'm only sure of two things: Dave Richardson put me in here, and I've got to get out.

"Don't pull on those," a voice tells me. "You'll only make them tighter."

"Jacob," I say, because the voice belongs to Jacob, "what else am I supposed to do? I've got to get out of here."

"They'll catch you if you try."

"So, what? Then I'll be in the exact same position I'm in now."

"They'll beat you again. Maybe worse the second time around."

The memory explodes in my mind. Arriving on Mon Luis Island. Dragged from the boat onto a pier, then down the pier to someone's front yard. Two women rushed Troy inside a house. His shirt was red with blood. A third woman ran toward me and slapped me so hard with the back of her knuckles I fell. She spit on me. The spittle hit my cheek.

That's when I started kicking. And punching. I remember flailing, trying like hell to get away then feeling large hands wrapping around my wrists and ankles and carrying me, one limb in each hand, around the house.

"That one was for Troy," Dave said kicking me in the ribs when they dropped me. "And this one's because I've never liked any of you Martins." Another strike to my ribs, which explains why it hurts to move or breathe now. "Not so hot now, huh? Little Miss Jules Martin. Tie the bitch up and lock her in here."

So, I guess whatever 'here' was is where I am now. I don't remember being moved again, but I also don't remember falling asleep or passing out or whatever happened after they locked me in here. I don't remember being zip-tied.

"Jacob," I say. "Jacob? Please, Jacob. What do I do?"

No answer. The silence chokes me. A sob escapes my mouth and fills the air with the pitiful sound. If I ever needed Jacob in my life, it is in this moment. I need him to ride in here, shoot every Knight he sees in the face and rescue me. But that won't happen because ghosts can't do that. Not even the one alive in my head so much so he'd be right here if I could just find the right lock and the right key to free him first. *Fuck, fuck, fuck. I'm going to die in this shed.*

Or worse. I won't die here. What if they take me back to our pier? String me up like they did Billy so that Mama and Daddy must witness my bloated and bruised ending, swinging back and forth under the rafters, a noose tight around my neck. No. I can't do that to them. I can't put that unforgiving and unforgettable image in their mind. Mama would never recover. What mother could? Will Billy's mother ever recover from what they did to her child?

Get it together, Jules. Think. Calm down. I'm not dead yet. So long as I'm not dead, Mama and Daddy don't have to endure the worst thing to happen to a parent. I can't let them endure that. I won't. Think, dammit. Think.

I stretch my legs as far as I can and run my bare toes along the floor. The right sweep comes up empty, but the left proves fruitful.

"What do you think of my monkey toes now?" The memory of Jacob freaking out every time I picked something off the floor using my toes brings a smile to my face, but the expression pulls at the cuts in my lips.

I pull the object toward me. Reaching for it, I can't believe my good fortune. A drywall screw! A bit rusty but retaining a few sharp threads. Thank goodness for all those years of dance lessons and yoga. I'll never be graceful, but I am flexible. I bend forward and hold the screw in my mouth. I draw my knees up to my chest and get to work on the binding around my ankles. The ties cut into my skin as I sit butterflied, and I might break a couple of teeth, but if I can cut through the plastic, I can run. If I can run, I can live.

The light shifts, the sudden whirring of multiple generators startles me, and a man clears his throat making me drop the screw.

"Jules, Jules, Jules, you're not trying to break free, are you?" Dave Richardson smirks at me from the open door of the shed. He drops a piece of bread and a bottled water at my feet. "Eat up. We don't want you passing out in the middle of your trial."

"I'm not hungry." Total lie. I mean, I wasn't hungry until Dave introduced the idea of food into this nightmare. Now, my stomach roils with hunger. I pick up the water with my bound hands and examine the unbroken seal. "Where did you get bottled water?"

"Well, see, Jules. That's just the thing. You want everybody to believe I'm some sort of monster. That me and Troy go around trying to hurt people. What we're actually doing is saving people. Those willing to be saved. And, we've got the resources to do that. We don't have to go begging the government for it."

I take a sip of the best water I've ever had. Then another sip, but instead of swallowing I swish it around my mouth trying to kill the taste of blood, and spit it out on the floor.

"Hey! Is that anyway to treat my property? You see? This is what you people do. We give you something, which you gladly take, then you spit it out and demand more." Dave looks down at me for several prickly moments then reaches to the side and grabs a folding chair—one I didn't even know was in here—and expands it in the doorway. He sits and leans forward, elbows on his knees, legs spread as if he's got something between them in need of space. "It looks like you're going to be here a while. No sign of anybody coming to get you. I guess you're not as important as you or I thought."

"They'll come."

"It's going to take a lot more than Matt and your ol' daddy to get you out of here. For their sake, I hope they don't come."

"None of us have done a damn thing to you, Dave."

"I think Troy would disagree with you."

"Just leave us alone. Let me go before—"

"Before what? The Army shows up? You think Captain Johnson's gonna ride in here, bring the cavalry to rescue you?"

"Do you really want all these families hurt? You've got a lot of people here. Living here. What happens to them if the Army does come here for me?"

Dave leans forward in his chair and whispers, "Maybe that's the plan."

Instinct sends me backward, scooting on my butt until I back into a stack of boxes. No where else to go.

"So, Miss Jules, why don't you go on and tell me what all you're taking from the Army. I know your ol' cheap daddy wouldn't just give them that land. So, what did he get for it? Did they set y'all up nice? Real comfy?"

"They demanded we follow the law."

"Oh, the law. You mean their law? But, you see, their law ain't lawful. Not according to the Constitution. That asshole in DC overstepped his authority declaring martial law. Congress never approved it."

"He didn't need congressional approval, Dave." I take another small sip of the water. I want to guzzle half of it then pour the other half over my face and head, but I don't. Who knows if Dave will ever give me another bottle.

"I'm not going to debate the finer legal points with you, honey. You've got your way of looking at it and I've got mine."

Pain flares right behind my eyes and at the base of my skull, and now this asshole wants to debate with me. "It's not finer legality or opinion bullshit, Dave. It's fact!"

Dave stands and kicks his chair backward. "Don't you raise your voice at me, bitch. Don't you talk to me like that ever again."

I cringe backward, bracing for blows. "I'm sorry. I'm in a lot of pain and I think I may have cracked a rib earlier. I really need to go to a doctor. Take me to a doctor and I'll just forget about this whole thing, okay? You let me go, and I'll forget everything that happened today."

"Oh, but that's the thing, Jules, I'm not going to forget what happened today. How can I forget you trying to murder my best friend?"

"I wasn't—"

"Don't you dare deny it." Dave crouches to my eye level. "Don't you ever deny that."

"What happened to you?" I ask. The man standing before me looks to be a man possessed, a far cry from the guy a couple years older than me telling jokes and getting happily plastered at high school bonfires. There's nothing in his eyes I recognize. "I need to use the restroom," I tell him. That's no lie. My bladder feels ready to burst.

Dave's wheels turn. He glances over his shoulder then reaches down and jerks me upright. "Come with me." He leads me to the side of the shed and directs me to piss on the ground between the exterior wall and a gigantic azalea bush.

"I can't really do this with my ankles bound."

"Figure it out. Cause you're not pissin' in my shed." Dave pushes me and I fall into the azalea bush, where I shimmy my shorts and panties down. My bladder is grateful for the relief, but the rest of me fills with humiliation.

———

After showing my bare ass to all of Mon Luis Island—maybe not literally but it sure felt like it—Dave tosses me back in the shed. I listen to the jangling of chains, the click of a padlock until, at last, the sound of fading footfalls plays sweet music in my ears. Leaning against the boxes, I work again with the screw and the zip-tie around my ankles. But a teeth-rattling crack of thunder makes me drop the screw. It disappears into the junk pile. I search again in the dark for anything to free my feet. No way I'm just going to sit here and wait for my inevitable execution.

"Jules," a whisper comes from outside. "Jules, it's Cole."

"Cole?" I scoot to the direction of the voice. An open sliver in the rusted wall allows me to see a bit of shadow. "Cole, what are you doing here?"

The rain picks up and batters the tin roof so hard I struggle to hear him. "I snuck in. I told you. Nobody notices me."

"But they will. You've got to go. Run. Now."

"Ain't nobody out here right now. They all ran for cover from this storm. Looks like a bad one. The sky—"

"Cole! Go. Please. You've got to get away from here. If they catch you—"

"They won't. I just wanted to let you know that Matt is working on it. He's going…we're going to get you back. I told him I'd find out where they were keeping you, and I did." Cole sounds so proud of himself, but pride can get a person killed. "So, you gotta hold on, okay? Don't be scared. Jules? Jules, did you hear me?"

How can a boy have more courage than any of the adults I know? A cry sticks in my throat, so I swallow hard until it's good and gone.

"Jules? We're going to get you, okay?"

"Yes, yes. I heard you. Now, please, go."

"Okay. I'm going. Matt's going to start wondering where I am anyway."

Listening to Cole go, I realize how calm he sounded. He didn't sound scared, not in the least. He sounded like he was relaying a run of the mill message. *Dinner's ready. I'm running to the store, be back in a few. It's your turn to unload the dishwasher.*

Not one iota of stress or tension or fear at all. A little excited, but aren't all kids a little worked up all the time?

And did Cole say that Matt was going to worry about where he is? My brother Matt? The same Matt that suggested stringing Cole up by his toenails? A smile threatens to pan across my face, but it's quickly chased into oblivion when Dave's words come back to me: *We don't want you passing out in the middle of your trial.* The Knights are going to put me on trial. They will put me on trial then hand out whatever sentence they deem fit because I don't think acquittal is on the table.

Then I remember Billy's warning about journalists in Charlotte lynched as traitors. Why didn't I listen to Billy that night? We could have packed up and hidden at Billy's hunting camp for months until all of this was over. Until we were safe. But no. I had to go on believing what was right in front of me was somehow wrong, an overreaction, Billy being overly cautious.

I should have insisted we leave as soon as the Army took the land. Garrett was right. How could I ever think the Army would protect us when they didn't protect Jacob, and Jacob was one of their own? I should have known this is how this would all turn out. The world's greatest authors couldn't have imagined a more perfect ending.

22

Breathing soupy air through a hood is difficult. It's morning and the rain stopped at some point in the night, giving way to a day so humid steam rises from the ground and mixes with the damp air, then swirls around my face, arms, and legs before settling on my skin.

Sweat stings my eyes. I blink over and again as—*thank you, Jesus*—someone pulls the hood away. One glance around and I wish they'd put the hood back over my head. I'm on a makeshift wooden stage with my hands and feet zip-tied, seated in a wicker chair. The mint-green chair is better suited for a lady's lanai in Destin than a trial. That's where I am, I guess. My trial.

Two men stand guard on either side of me as if at any moment I'll jump up, bust the zip-ties from my ankles and run. And I guess the green of the chair is fitting if I decide to go full turtle with my torso still bound to the chair as I make a break for the beach. Sorry, boys, I won't be adding to the absurdity today.

Before me, on the ground sit several rows of camper chairs and deck benches and even a few crocheted poufs, sure to be moldy by day's end. Every seat in the house is occupied by a looky-loo. I recognize a few faces from church, and at least two of the longtime cashiers from Greer's Grocer are in the audience. Mostly they all look fresh off a shrimp boat with sun-burned skin, tangled hair, and sweat-dampened clothing, but a few, namely three women on the front row, look fresh as daisies. I swear one has had a blow-out, which irritates me far more than it should. I should be freaking out right now rather than envying some dumb broad's hair. That's right. To my mind, they're all dumb broads right now. But I don't have the strength for petty insults or full panic mode. Insults require brain power. Panic requires adrenaline. I'm tapped out of both.

The crowd all looks to the left of me, so being a damn sheep, I turn my head as far as I can to catch a glimpse. Approaching the stage, Dave and Clem Richardson flank Troy. My assaulter-slash-victim (depending on who you ask) squeezes between blowout queen and her less attractive friend. One arm is in a sling and the two women each offer him soft, careful caresses as he sits. Blowout queen looks up at me with a shit-eating grin as if she's won something I wanted. I wanted him for dead, sweetie, not *for me*. But, I guess since he's still breathing, I've lost out just the same.

Dave and Clem march up the stairs and relieve the guards of their noble task—guarding me. Now I'm the meat in a Richardson sandwich, and I'm pretty sure the whole po'boy has spoiled.

"Good morning, good Knights," Dave says and chuckles, prompting the audience to hoot and holler in appreciation of his pathetic pun. "We are gathered on this glorious morning to ensure that which our Constitution and country are based on—Justice!"

More whooping and hollering. As I suspected, blowout queen and her friends are woo-hoo girls and let out a few whoops better suited for a bachelorette party than a trial.

"Alright, calm yourselves." Clem waves one meaty hand over the crowd. "Justice is serious business."

"Daddy's right. We want a fair, orderly trial today." Dave nods to his father, who in turn takes a seat on the stage making me wonder if Clem is the judge. My question of who's playing the role of prosecutor doesn't go unanswered for long as Dave clears his throat. "Ladies and Gentleman of the Jury, we are gathered here today for the trial of one Jules Martin Jones. Miz Jones is charged with the attempted murder of Troy Cowart." Dave removes a couple of index cards from his back pocket. Flipping one over, he turns to Clem and says, in a low voice. "Daddy, you got that pocket Bible on you?"

Clem fishes a small, red St. James out of his pocket and hands it to Dave.

"Miz Jones, place your right hand on this Bible." Dave holds the Bible out in front of me just as someone from the crowd yells, "hope it doesn't burn ya, bitch." I place both hands—zip-tied, so Dave gets both, not just the right—on the Bible. "Do you swear to tell the truth, the whole truth, and nothing but the truth, so help you God?"

"I do," I attempt to say but the words stick in my dry throat. A second attempt produces the proper sound.

"Miz Jones, three days ago during our most recent jubilee—"

"Three days?" I ask. "I've been here three days?" How did I miss a day? Or is it two? I know I slept last night, but was that my first night in the shed or second?

"Do not speak until you are told to speak," Dave orders. "On the day of our most recent jubilee did you stab Mister Troy Cowart with a flounder gig?"

I close my lips still trying to figure out what day it is and how long I've been in that shed and if my parents know I'm still alive.

"Answer the question."

"Um, yes, I saw Troy grab—"

"Yes or no, Miz Jones."

"Yes."

Dave gestures at his dad who turns in his chair and fetches my flounder gig from its resting place, leaning on the side of the platform.

Dave holds the flounder gig just out of my reach. "Is this the gig you used?"

"Yes. I think so."

"It looks homemade. Did you make this gig?"

"Yes." The leather and screws look intact, despite having plunged into Troy's shoulder.

"And, did you make it for the specific purpose of murdering Troy Cowart?"

"No, I made it for flounders."

"Yes or no, Miz Jones." Dave pounds the wooden platform twice with the gig's long handle. "So, you just happen to have this gig on you during the jubilee?"

"Of course, how else—"

"And then you waited for Troy Cowart to come to the jubilee."

"No, I was—"

"And when he came to fish with everyone else, you saw your chance and stabbed him?"

"No. That's not how—"

"And this was retaliation for his flirting with you a while back? Ladies and gentlemen," Dave says and turns full front to the crowd. "This is what happens when we allow our traditions, our culture to be cancelled, stamped out by the liberals. Suddenly, innocent flirting is cause for murder."

"Wait a sec—"

"No." Dave turns back to me, wild-eyed as the night before, or maybe the night before that. My head pounds. I've lost track of time. "Troy made a couple of harmless advances toward you, and you decided he wasn't good enough for you so you decided to kill him."

"That is absurd."

"Is it? Is it absurd? What's absurd is that Troy may never have full use of his arm again thanks to you. What is absurd is Troy nearly bled to death in my boat. What's absurd is that we didn't kill you on the spot for what you did."

Clem rises from his seat and puts a hand on Dave's shoulder. "Good job, son. I think you've laid out the case just fine."

Dave lets out a long string of air then saunters to the chair and sits. "Fine, Daddy. You finish it up."

With the saner of the two at center stage now, I jump to my own defense. "Clem, Troy grabbed my niece. Mallie. The little one. He was trying to pull her into that boat. He snatched that baby from my sister's arms. She's just a little girl, a toddler. What was I supposed to do?"

Without standing, Dave yells, "Your other niece—the little redheaded bitch—should be on trial, too, for bashing Troy's head with a rock. You Martins are nothing but a bunch of crazy bitches."

"Mallie's a toddler. What was I supposed to do when a man grabs, tries to kidnap her?"

Clem turns from me to face the crowd. "I think we have heard all the testimony we need to hear on this matter—"

"He was going to hurt that baby."

"That's enough, Miss Jones."

"You have to understand. Mallie is so little. I panicked. I was scared and—"

Heat rises from my cheek as the force of Clem's hand across my face reverberates through my skin to my bones. Through blurry eyes, I see Clem turn back to the crowd and hear the cheers from the mob, ready and waiting for their pound of flesh.

"We will have one vote today," Clem tells the crowd. "The vote will be to determine guilt or innocence."

"Guilt or innocence? The only things I'm guilty of is not wanting to be raped and—"

Clem snaps around, his hand raised for a second slap. "That is enough, Miss Jones. One more outburst and I will have you gagged!" Once composed, he continues with, "After the vote and verdict, the Senior Council will determine sentencing."

Everyone in the crowd nods at Clem as if this all makes perfect sense. But none of this makes any sense at all. I guess I do have the energy for panic after all. Five minutes doesn't equal a proper trial. There's no judge—just a village of jurors. Why do they even need to vote on my guilt or innocence when they've already convicted me and are thinking ahead to sentencing? I don't know what Cole and Matt are planning but I need them to show up now. Not later. Now. Right now.

What is Dave's preferred execution method? No matter how many generators they've got, I don't think they can power an electric chair like Big Bertha. Lethal injection seems too mild, and where would The Knights get an overdose of drugs? We Martins don't even have aspirin. *Would Dave go in for gruesome death, perhaps something medieval, capitalizing on primitive resources and sadistic torture fantasies? Will Troy get a say on the matter?* Yes. Full panic mode.

"So, please line up to cast your vote." As the crowd leaves their seats and forms a line down the center aisle of the audience, Clem doles out further instructions. "Up here, you'll find a stack of papers and a pen. On a slip of paper, each of you write either an I for innocent or a G for guilty. Then drop your vote in the box there." Clem points to a shoe box at the edge of the platform next to a bowl of paper and pens. The box is pink and bears the Jellypop Shoes logo, all swirly and juvenile. *Really? My fate rests in a box for tween shoes? Perfect.*

The best way I can describe the line in front of me is enthusiastically lock-step, as if this is the moment every member of The Knights has been rehearsing for their whole lives. And I can tell by the eager smiles how this vote is going to go.

Ridiculous, really, to carry out the ritual. Why conduct a secret vote when not one person in this crowd looks at me with sympathy? A more accurate command to this crowd would be "ready with the first stone," or maybe, "Billy Bob, light the woodpile."

Troy's up first. He glares at me, then makes a big show of having to write with his left hand. *Give it up, asshole. Even with two good arms, you'd still struggle to complete the alphabet.* He scratches out a G, which I know because he shakes the damn piece of paper in my face before dropping it in the box.

"You tried to hurt a child," I say. Troy laughs me off.

One by one, The Knights take a turn at the table. Each one marks their paper, displays it, and drops it into the box. G, G, G, G…

"Don't any of you care that a child was in danger?" I ask. I've never wanted to spit on complete strangers so badly in my life. Just one good wad right on someone's forehead. But my mouth is so dry I can't make spit.

"No talking," Dave told me, then he spit on the ground. *Hydrated asshole.*

With only a handful of jurors left, a frightfully thin woman approaches the voting box. She is the kind of skinny that makes an observer worry or at least wonder. Her cheeks are sunken so that her cheekbones stick out like boomerangs. The same can be said of her collarbones, visible thanks to a faded, pink tank top. Her eyes bulge and the emerald green against her tan skin and bleached hair creates a Cinderella meets Gollum vibe.

"I'm going to ask Jesus to save your soul," the woman tells me in a voice as thin as her body.

"Thank you," I say, surprised. "I was only trying to save my niece. I was scared."

A popping giggle escapes her thin lips. "Don't thank me yet, dearie. Only time will tell if he's listening." She points to the sky then giggles. *Fantastic. The only juror remotely in my corner is batshit crazy.*

The woman teeters back to her seat, the last to sit after voting. The crowd looks on as Dave rummages through the box, flipping over paper after paper. The breeze picks up a couple and carries them away. No matter. I don't think two votes will change today's outcome.

"Guilty," Dave announces and the crowd nods. Not solemn nods, but the nods and head jerking of a platoon eager to annihilate the enemy. A fifth-grade classroom waiting for the last bell before summer break. Black Friday shoppers foaming at the mouth to break through the doors of Walmart. Hungry. They are hungry, and I'm the lone menu item.

"The Senior Council will deliberate sentencing, which will be announced later, um, after we decide. So, I'm sure all y'all got work to do. Get to it."

The crowd lets out a disappointed sigh then saunters away. As I sit, waiting for whatever comes next, a beam of light nearly blinds me. Looking beyond the crowd, I catch the source and culprit—Cole, in a tree, holding what I assume is a mirror or some small reflective object. He grins—hard to miss with all those big teeth—then shimmies down the tree and out of sight.

———

Dave let me bake in the sun for at least an hour, maybe two. I know the sun moved quite a bit while I sat tied to my chair because at the start of my so-called trial, I felt the sun on the back of my shoulders and now it's scorching my scalp.

"Come with me," Dave says after clipping the zip-ties from my ankles and wrists—the ones that held me immobilized in this damn chair for who knows how long.

However long, I sat there long enough to realize movies lie.

The ones that feature the captured hero or kidnapped ingénue. From the moment of capture, the captured hero focuses on nothing but escape. She frantically scans her cage for anything useful to her great escape. Then, she remembers the bobby pin in her hair and voila! She MacGyvers the shit out of the pin and blows the lock off the cage. The kidnapped ingénue, on the other hand, cowers in her basement prison, crying and shaking in perpetual panic until a man with a special set of skills comes along to rescue her.

I am neither of these tropes. As I sat in the chair, I grew angry. Angry because I am tired and my back hurts from being tied to a chair. Furious at the women and children who kept walking by me and taunting me with water but refusing me a single drop. Homicidal because I am hungry. Hungry to the point that I'd eat the face off a mule if anyone around here presented me with a mule. What worries me is that I'm not panicked. I should be. I should be plotting my escape. I should search for a bobby pin or pray a knight in shining armor gallops in on his white horse, but I'm not. I just want out of the sun and a drink of water and some damn food. My insides are gnawing on themselves.

"You smell like horse piss." Dave drags me by the arm across someone's back yard. I can see the bay in the distance as we approach a white manufactured home anchored to a brick foundation.

"You don't exactly smell like sunshine and roses yourself," I tell him. I honestly can't smell anything other than myself, and I am revolting. Sweat, dried urine, dirt, and grime do not make a comely scent.

We walk around to the side of the house to an outdoor shower. A woman waits by the teak stall, seated on a bench next to a folded towel and what looks to be folded laundry.

"I'm Bethany," she chirps. She looks early twenties with a high, auburn ponytail and hoop earrings. "I'm gonna get you cleaned up, but I don't want no fussing out of you. And if you try anything at all once we're in there, Lyle here will shoot you." Lyle must be the squat man with a soul-patch beard and Oakleys sitting on a bench near me because he smiles while waving his Glock in my direction.

Dave lifts his chin toward Lyle then turns back to Bethany. "Bring her in once you're done." With that he walks away.

If it weren't for Lyle's gun, I'd make a run for it. Bethany looks about as fierce as a lovebug, petite and unaware. One punch would lay her flat. Lyle's ample paunch and short legs suggest years of video gaming, not actual sports. I could outrun him for sure. But I can't outrun a bullet. And maybe Lyle here can really shoot. I assume his trigger finger is fit enough for the job.

"Go on. Get in. Hand me your dirty clothes once you're in there." Bethany clicks her disapproval of my worn-out and filthy attire.

"There's no door," I say.

"You ain't got nothing we all hadn't seen before," Lyle responds.

"Lyle, stand over there." Bethany points to the far side of the shower stall, out of sight of the open side. "I don't want you ogling anyone's titties but mine."

I strip down, hand my clothes to Bethany, and step under the nozzle of a garden hose affixed to the top of the back wall. The lukewarm water does nothing to curb my humiliation. Naked in public and a prisoner of some bullshit, homegrown militia. For once, I'm happy Jacob can't see me.

23

Across the round kitchen table sit Clem and Dave, a platter of grilled fish and hoecakes between us. My skin prickles from the air conditioning as my wet hair falls about my shoulders and back, soaking through my threadbare, borrowed muumuu. Bethany gets high marks for affecting prison attire, and I should congratulate the whole Knight operation on their ability to keep full-house generators running.

"If this is supposed to be my last meal," I say, "I'd like to request a menu change. Perhaps fried chicken and a cheesecake."

"Eat," Clem tells me. "I know you must be hungry."

"I'll eat when you do." I shift my ankle, trying to find a more comfortable position between the zip-tie and the chair leg.

"Sweetheart, we wouldn't kill you with poison," Clem says and forks a filet, moving it to his empty plate. "Food is too precious a commodity around here." He lobs off a bite and shoves it in his mouth. "Oh, I'm sorry. Should we say grace? I know how religious you Martins are."

"No, it's fine. Your house. Your rules."

"Actually," Dave says. "This is my house. So, it's my rules."

"Okay. So maybe you can explain what's going on here. I'm sure you've decided on my sentence. Why not—"

"Patience dear," Clem interjects. "We wanted to have a little chat first."

"Oh, this should be fun. Get to know each other better before you put the noose around my neck?" I take a bite of a hoecake. There's actual onions and peppers in it and a spice blend reminiscent of waterfront restaurants.

Dave lowers his fork to his plate. "Jules, we understand you were the last to see Billy Roberts alive."

"You're not going to pin that—"

"No, but we'd—"

"Of course not. Billy Roberts was your handiwork." I reach down and slide the zip-tie lower on my ankle.

Dave slams his fork down on his plate so hard I glance over to see if the ceramic cracked.

I'm getting to him, so I press on with my half-baked be-an-asshole plan. "Do you have some lifetime supply of zip-ties? Every time you move me, someone cuts the ties then ties me back up with a fresh pair."

Dave breathes in and out slowly. His fist clinches as if he'd like to beat me to death right here. Clem gives him a Father-Knows-Best rub on his right shoulder, which seems to tame his primal urges. "You spoke to Billy that night, yes?"

"Yes, he had dinner with us. Really, the whole family spoke to him. And you didn't answer my question about the zip-ties."

"But you spoke to him privately after dinner, right?"

"Fine. Mums the word on zip-ties. So, which patch of woods do you hide in when you're spying on us?"

"What did you two speak about?" Dave rolls his fork back and forth in his hand.

"Nothing much. But couldn't you hear us from wherever you were? Why repeat a conversation you already witnessed from the…?" I lean forward in my chair as if waiting for Dave to answer my prompt.

"Did you discuss what the Army is planning?"

"Uh, no. Why would anyone in the Army discuss their plans with me? As far as I know, they will be here so long as you keep killing people and blowing shit up. Stop all that, and they'll probably leave."

"So, if Billy wasn't there to confer with you or your family, what was he doing there?"

"We're friends. Not everyone sees him as some sort of traitor just because he wore that uniform. Some of us still cared about him."

"What did you two discuss?" Dave taps my hand with his fork.

"He just wanted to make sure I was being careful, not making too much noise."

"Noise against who?"

"Anyone."

"Who?"

"Everyone."

"Who, Jules?" Dave presses the tines of his fork into the top of my hand. The points threaten to break the skin and press against the bones of my hand. "Who?" I underestimated Dave's enjoyment of causing physical pain and overestimated my tolerance.

Red droplets appear around the tines of the fork and I wince. "Groups like you. Like The Knights. That really fucking hurts, asshole."

"Son!" Clem says, and I yank my hand away.

Blood oozes from four tiny holes in the middle of my hand.

"Here, dear." Clem hands me a towel to suppress the blood. "And, please, eat, eat."

"I've lost my appetite." I press the cloth over my hand and

turn to Dave. "All over the South, innocent people are dying because of people like you. People who believe they are doing their patriotic duty but what they're really doing is murdering good people. Good people like Billy."

———

I sat there tied to that chair and freezing from the air conditioning, wet hair, and lack of undergarments, which is totally fine because I'm not into wearing other people's panties, for at least another hour. Clem and Dave questioned me about Billy and what happened when we found him on the pier and what the Army did after we contacted them and what Johnson told me about the death since then. I succumbed to a slice of blueberry pie so good I should have licked the plate clean. I had no solid information to give them. None of any real value. This fact was unbelievable to them so now I find myself back in the shed—now a roasting box of humidity and mosquitoes—to sit until I tell them what I don't know. All I want to know is what my sentence is and when they're planning to kill me because, come on, I'm not walking out of here on my own and everyone knows that.

"Time to go." The door of the shed flings open, banging against the outer wall. In the doorway stands Troy, his eyes blood-shot in the fading light.

"I'm not going anywhere with you." I scoot as far away from him as space allows, but he grasps my ankles, bound again by damn zip-ties and drags me across the concrete then dirt.

Dave steps between us and lifts me, throwing me over his shoulder. "I'm taking her."

Outside, a commotion brews with men, women, even children darting back and forth. As soon as we clear the shed, a woman rushes inside.

While Dave carries me away from the shed, I hear Troy

instruct the woman. "Make it look like she was never here. Move all that shit around. Make it look like no one would fit in there."

Dave rushes between two houses toward the water. He carries me with no concern for the bruised—maybe even broken—ribs that scream with every hurried step.

"Put me down!" Vomit rises in my throat, the hoecake and pie from earlier threatening to spew all over Dave's back. And yes, I would enjoy that. Not the vomiting part, but covering this asshole in regurgitated blueberry filling would be awesome. "Down! Please!"

"Shut up," Dave tells me as we pause near Bethany and a fire pit. She seems frantic, pushing the button on a long-nozzle lighter. "Hurry up and burn those, Bethany."

"I'm trying but this damn thing won't light."

"Then find another." Next to the firepit, my dirty clothes lay on the ground.

Dave lowers me to standing, and my ribs sing out, but the notes are sour. I teeter, gripping the ground with my bare toes as my ankles rub against the restraints. More than anything, I want to lie down. The spinning would stop. The throbbing in my side would stop. I swallow hard against my gagging.

"I'm going to vomit."

"You better not. I'm just switching shoulders." Dave hoists me over his shoulder again and I yelp, the pain too intense for silence. "You're not as light as you look."

At the end of a pier, Dave tosses me in a small, flat bottom boat, one painted to match the brackish water. Another man loosens the rope from the lower deck pylons, and Dave and I begin to drift with the current. Sitting on the rear bench, I glance behind us as Dave fires the engine.

"Is that why we're running?" I ask and point to the column of armored vehicles barreling toward Mon Luis Island. Further off, grey Army patrol boats speed south as well, their bows pointing toward The Knight compound. Matt and Cole did it. They got through to Captain Johnson and the Army.

"Hey!" I raise my arms above my head, trying to wave with my bound wrists and hands. I twist and gyrate left and right, trying to create enough movement to catch someone's eye. *Johnson, Matt, Cole, Private What's-His-Nuts. Anyone. Please notice me you sons of bitches! I'm right here!* "Hey! Hey!" Then with a sharp pain in the back of my skull, I fall between the benches, out of sight.

———

My head pounds. The sun beats down on me with an intense summer heat. I rise up to a seated position and realize where I am —Middle Bay Lighthouse. Out of commission for decades and in the middle of Mobile Bay, the lighthouse is accessible only by boat, but looking around, I see no boat. I'm not inside the keeper's house or even on the lighthouse wrap-around porch. I'm on the rickety, wooden platform that butts against the lighthouse pylons and support cables. Matt and I have spent many afternoons fishing here, tied off near this platform. However, again, I see no boat. *No boat.* No Knights and no Dave. Dave Richardson must have driven out here, dumped me on the platform, and left.

Dave left me for dead. Surely that was his plan. He wouldn't leave me out here in the middle of the damn bay with no food, water, or, currently, shelter, for safe-keeping. Right? He left me for dead. Did he hope I'd roll off the platform and drown in the bay, so far offshore no one would hear my gurgling screams? Probably. Because that sounds like something he'd do. *Asshole. Coward. Psycho.*

But I'm not dead. Not yet at least. I'm injured, but I'm alive. My hands and feet are still bound, which proves what a coward Dave is. He could have at least given me a fighting chance of swimming to safety. But no. Between my head and my ribs, I doubt I can swim the three miles to shore. I probably wouldn't make it three yards. I'd drown for sure. Definite shark bait. A tinge of panic threatens so I do my best to beat it back.

Okay, Jules, take stock. Injuries? Head and ribs, chafing on my wrists and ankles. The top of my right hand stings. Hopefully the cuts will scab over soon. Resources? Nothing, as far as I can see. Reasons to panic? My hands and feet are bound, no one except for a lunatic knows I'm out here. No food, no potable water, the punishing sun. Immediate need? Get the damn ties off my wrists and ankles. Goals? Dry land and stay alive.

I scoot into the only sliver of shade on the five-foot-by-five-foot platform. In another hour, this shade will be gone so I need to remedy my baking-in-sun predicament along with my zip-tie predicament because the zip-tie predicament is contributing to the burnt to a crisp future predicament.

The Middle Bay Lighthouse is a hexagonal, wooden structure. It sits atop eight tall pylons, which are all lashed to each other by steel cables. Extending from the platform, a metal truss connects the platform to the deck of the lighthouse. The truss used to hold the mechanics of a weather station, back when the Dauphin Island Sea Lab monitored weather changes from this spot, but it looks like someone ripped the device from its post, probably for scrap. No matter, because what I need is the truss. If I can climb it, I can get into proper shelter and out of the sun.

First things first—these ties must go. I roll onto my uninjured side, stretch out my legs and position my feet on either side of a corroded cable. I'm sure I resemble a deranged cricket, bringing my legs in and out, in and out, my abdomen on fire with pain as I scrape the plastic tie against the cable. But who cares what I look like? Who cares how loud my screams are? I am alone out here—completely, utterly, terrifyingly alone.

No. Stop. It is not time to panic. Panic leads to mistakes.

Mistakes lead to death. My death out here leads to my family and Cole never knowing what happened to me. They will live with unsettled grief, knowing I must be dead without the closure of knowing the circumstances of my death. The questions and what ifs will eat away at them.

Yes! And *holy shit that hurt.* The zip-tie snaps free of my ankles but not without my ankle dropping hard on the cable leaving a nice gash. No way I'm going in the water now. *Blood in the water!* A flash of memory fills my mind. Matt, Kate, and I as kids in the water. Our favorite game involved Matt playing the role of shark, and Kate and I the injured swimmers. *Swim faster, Jules! Sharks can smell blood!*

No. Stop. Focus. Save that memory for later.

Laying on the platform, I glance across the choppy, brackish water and imagine Jaws—cavernous mouth agape with rows of pointed teeth ready to blow through this platform and tear me to pieces. I scoot away from the edge. As a child, I had a recurring nightmare of the Looney Toons' shark. In it, I played the role of Daffy Duck chased by the shark all through the water and around the pier. I'd make it to the shore and take a relieved breath only to realize the shark chased me still. On land! He'd chase me through the house and into the backyard and kept chasing me until I woke up.

Enough. I don't have the luxury of losing my mind right now. I sit up and work on the zip-tie on my wrists. In a minute or so, the plastic snaps and I'm free. Completely free! Still alone, hurt, probably screwed and about to die, but free.

And, the truss holds. The climb is a bit precarious but the truss makes for a good enough ladder. Standing on the deck of the lighthouse, I will see oncoming boats—if any approach—much better. From the look of the once painted white, cottage-style keeper's quarters, the lighthouse has suffered the same fate as many structures in and around Mobile Bay over the last months.

The main door is missing, ripped from its hinges. Most of the window panes lay in shards of glass all over the floor of the interior. That's concerning because I'm barefoot. Whole sections of the cypress interior paneling are gone, I assume pillaged. Mixed with the glass are hundreds of seagull feathers. Bird droppings cover the deck, and I'm careful to avoid the piles laced with tiny fishbones—again, bare feet. *My kingdom for a pair of shoes.*

From the doorway, I explore the interior of the keeper's quarters. It's one open room, a big, wood hexagon, now empty of all necessary accoutrement except a blanket. Perhaps some teenagers climbed up here one night with a sixer of Natty Lite and that blanket for a boozy make-out session. I'd like to think that was the reason for the empty beer cans and blanket, rather than some nomad stealing a few hours of shelter from a storm before perishing from hunger out here. I see no dead bodies, so I assume the blanket owner left the lighthouse. Somehow. *Don't think about that either.*

In the center of the room hangs a pull cord attached to the hatch door which leads to the top of the lighthouse. I imagine the keepers of the past pulling the cord to lower the hatch then climbing up to the small windows of the perch. From there, they could manually control the light, guiding each approaching ship safely through the bay.

On the wall opposite the door, a simple message is painted in black letters. It reads *"Please leave hatch closed & protect your heritage."* I marvel at the message, almost cackling at its timeliness. Is this what happened? Did we leave the hatch open on our heritage? Did we sneak up and down the perch ladder until all our secrets revealed themselves? Did we force the gatekeepers from their eagle's nest when we demanded Congress acknowledge our sinful heritage? Is all this a result of one group hurt by a heritage that aimed to persecute them and another white-knuckling to the traditions they made and have always known as their one true way of life? Maybe this place should be swept under, along with everything else until every sin of the past is atoned. *Maybe I should shut the hell up and figure out my escape.* I need to get out of my head, but I fear I will be here too long to keep my mind focused on staying alive. The crazy is bound to sneak in and stretch out.

Jules, do something productive.

Talking to yourself isn't productive. Stop it.

I discover two alcoves or closets of sorts. One still has a door, although it's not fully attached to the frame anymore. It hangs lopsided like a good breeze is all it will take to bring it down. Inside that closet is a built-in bench with a hole cut in the center. My stomach roils at the thought of all the lighthouse-keeper-shit-eating fish I've eaten in my lifetime pulled from the water below. And now my mind is back on that no food situation. I'd love a shit-eating fish to eat right now. Kill it, clean it, shove it down my throat.

The blanket in the keeper's quarters gives me an idea and a bit of hope. The idea is twisted and is going to take every bit of nerve I have, but it's all I've got. I take one large step inside and reach forward, careful not to step on any glass. I snatch the blanket from the floor. *Thank you, Lord, that no critters were hiding beneath it.* I don't know how a critter would get out here, but you never know. Maybe they hitched a ride, stowaways on a shrimp boat or crouched under the bench of a rowboat, then scurried up the pylons to the shelter of the house. Legend has it when Middle Bay Lighthouse still had an onsite keeper, a century or so ago, the keeper rowed the three miles to shore one day and loaded a cow into the skiff. Then, he rowed that cow all the way out here and tied it off to the deck railing, where it lived so that the keeper's wife and new baby had milk to drink.

Stop stalling and get on with it.

I lay the blanket flat on the deck, spreading it out from end to end. With a triangular shard of glass, I cut the blanket in two. With the tip of the shard, I prick the end of my left index finger, wince from the pain, and draw a letter H in blood on the blanket. Each letter—H E L P—requires another finger, another cut. After all the bloodletting, I tie the corners of my banner to the outer railing and pray the right person sees it: *HELP*, written in big, bloody letters.

On the remaining piece of blanket, I lay down to rest. The throbbing in my fingers competes with the throbbing in my head and the ache around my ribs. I need water. Food. Rest. I won't last long if no one sees my banner and heeds my call. So, before closing my eyes, I offer up one short prayer. *Please, God, let my blood see my blood.*

24

There are no atheists in foxholes. I wake with that tired cliché in my mind. There are also no atheists on rickety decks in howling wind and sideways rain. That's what woke me. Not the cliché. The cliché keeps me from screaming. I'm clinging to born-again faith, praying that this deck holds and that I tied the corners of my banner tight enough that the wind doesn't blow it out to sea.

Stop it. If the banner blows away, make another. Somehow. I will prick the fingers on my right hand and paint the sides of this lighthouse if I must. Anything to get to dry land. Anything to get back to my family. To keep my unspoken promise to Cole. To see the complete and total annihilation of Dave and Troy and The Knights. Clem is an elected official, for God's sake. How could he let Dave do this to me? *I'm so fucking naïve.* Elected official has never meant "good person" in this country.

I scoot back as far as I can into the doorway of the keeper's quarters. The storm has removed any bit of light the moon may have offered, so I can't see the glass shards inside where it is somewhat dry. Inside, where I would find shelter from the wind. I will hide in the water closet. Ha! Literally a closet over water with a hole that however many lighthouse keepers set their bare rump on and let go of their bladders and bowels.

Stop. You're heading to the edge again. I cannot go inside in the dark. Inside in the dark is where I will surely end up with glass in my hands and legs and feet.

Breathe. Just breathe. *That's your one job, Jules. Keep breathing.*

I close my eyes. Focus on what is pelting my face. *Death by a million rain drops. Stop. Just stop.* Fat raindrops splash on my cheeks and forehead. I part my lips and let the rainwater drop into my mouth. That's safe, right? Water directly from the sky to my mouth is safe to drink. I think. Why didn't I pay closer attention to my high school science classes? Did Mrs. Blount cover potable water in sophomore biology? Maybe Mr. Rusten did in Organic Chemistry junior year. Safe or not, I suck down every drop that falls in my mouth.

After nearly waterboarding myself, I draw my knees up to my chest, tuck my face between them, and fill my mind with anything but the storm.

The Knights. Think of The Knights and those glorious Army vehicles charging toward their compound. The memory reminds me of a story Jacob told me about the invasion of Iraq. He and the other scouts hunkered down in Al Najaf, ambushed and out of options. Then the ground shook and a distant rumble rose in Jacob's ears. When he glanced behind him, US Army tanks crested the sand dunes. They were saved. He always told that story with such amazement in his eyes. "Jules, I swear. It was like Patton himself coming over the dunes." If only Captain Johnson had arrived ten minutes earlier. Would I have felt the ground shake, heard the rumble of the armored vehicles from inside the shed?

And what of The Knights now? Judging from the darkness surrounding me, about twenty-four hours have passed since I saw that beautiful column of vehicles barreling toward the compound. How did Dave know they were coming? Does he have a spy? Of course, he has a spy. He has spies all over. In the woods, at the market, probably even inside St. Philip Neri church, members of the parish, my parents' lifelong friends. The Knights have eyes everywhere. I need to live long enough to see the Army root them out. Them, the spies and their eyes. Every person who's helped The Knights destroy this community must pay. Every last one of them.

But what if I've lost track of time again? What if I slept for days and nobody found me, causing my family to stop searching and accept that I was lost to them?

And where is Dave? I wish I knew. He may come back for me. With my luck, a boat with a single spotlight will appear out of the darkness and I'll celebrate and dance the dance of the pitifully wounded, but then, on closer inspection, I see the truth. Dave Psycho-freak Richardson captains the boat. Dave I'm-going-to-kill-you Richardson. Dave I'm-here-to-feed-the-sharks-with-your-body Richardson. I wonder what his actual middle name is. I don't think I've ever heard it? Why would I? It's not as if we were friends. Just occasionally shitfaced at the same time in the same place. Teenage booze fests don't really make for lifelong bonds, do they?

I'm losing it. Shut the fuck up, Jules. Get it together.

Did Dave abandon me and then return to the compound? Will he go down fighting or slink off a coward? I'd bet on coward, but I've been wrong so many times. I underestimated how warped Dave's moral code is. Sure, I knew Troy was a sleaze. He wears his nastiness, like a cloak of wife-beater T-shirts and swamp butt. But Dave is a different story. I mistook Dave's actions for misguided patriotism. Somewhere along the line, he swapped knowing right and wrong for an extra helping of psychotic rage.

I'm rolling all these questions over in my head for nothing. As far as I know, the Army has arrested everyone on or near the compound. Maybe this is all over, but I'll never know the ending because I'm going to die on this deck from the wind blowing me into the water or from starvation or from infection or from a lack of potable water.

Water, water everywhere. Not a drop to drink. Or something like that. What was that line from? A poem? A nursery rhyme? I can't remember, and I should remember.

Calm down. Please. Please calm down. Breathe in. And out. In. Out.

So, it's a little rain and wind. Big deal. A local writer some time back—What year was that? Were Jacob and I living in Georgia or Texas or Kentucky? Doesn't matter. A local wrote a story for a local magazine years ago about him and his brother caught in a storm when he was about twelve. They tied off below deck and took shelter inside the Middle Bay Lighthouse—this very lighthouse. The storm he described rivaled this one. The boys lasted the night and the next day returned safe and sound to their parents. Their parents grounded them, or I think they did. I can't remember exactly. So, if a twelve-year-old can ride out a storm on this deck, I can.

I think his name was Watt? Yes, Watt Key. That was it. I wonder if he's still alive. I bet he could survive all of this. I wonder if he's writing. Maybe he's cataloguing all of this and will publish a bestseller based on the months and years of the country falling apart. But that assumes that there will be an after to all of this. Of course, there will be an after. There must be an after. And I will be in that after if I can just survive this storm.

I can, I can, I can. Please, Mama and Daddy, ground me one more time.

And what about Cole? There's a kid with the bravery of ten full-grown adults who's survived an entire list of catastrophes in the last months. First his parents die, then the government or whomever torches his neighborhood, then living in the woods and escaping Martha's and Henry's abuse. He meets me, and I bring him into my world—but now I've abandoned him, too. I never even told him that I want him to stay with us. Live with me. Let me be his family. A little family of two. Everyone needs a family, right? Maybe he feels the same. If he doesn't have the same idea —Jules and Cole vs the world—why did he risk his safety and freedom to sneak into The Knight compound to offer me a bit of hope?

Mama was right. I have wronged that boy. I gave him hope that someone cared for him. Should I have let it go? Stayed out of it? Out of his life?

Mama, if you can hear me or sense me, please take Cole into your home. If I never make it off this deck, please open your heart to him.

Daddy? Daddy, will you help him? Mama told me you always wanted more children. Cole is the child God has placed in your path. I thought it was my path, but if I die, when I die, Cole still needs us.

Cole needs me. He wants a home. I must give him that. In some form or fashion, I will give him a home.

25

At some point in the night, I must have fallen asleep, or passed out. Either way, dawn brings a headache, throbbing fingers, and calm, gorgeous water.

Decision time. Sit or swim? Die here or die in the water? Not this crap again. Death isn't inevitable. I might survive. So, do I sit here and wait for a boat or swim to the shore?

I lay on my stomach and look below the lighthouse deck. I don't see water lines on the pylons beneath, so it must be high tide or coming on high tide. If I swim, I'll have to stay afloat longer to reach water shallow enough to stand. That probably requires a superhuman strength I lack. Swimming also seems like a definite pass or fail situation. And alligators. Did Matt say it was alligator mating season? I think he mentioned that. Would that make the alligators more or less aggressive?

Shit, Jules, does it matter?

Sighting a less aggressive gator in the water while I'm in the water is going to make me panic and probably drown from the panic, so the aggression level of the prehistoric monster doesn't matter at all. And sharks. I can't forget the sharks. Lots of sharks. Hammerheads and black tips and tiger sharks and the kind of sharks that eat intruders who trespass into their territory. Isn't that all sharks? Maybe not. *For flipping sake, Jules.* Again, that doesn't matter. A shark is a shark and a bad time to see one is while flailing in the water, trying to swim to shore. I'm losing it. Definitely losing it. And right now, this moment, this is a shitty time to lose my mind. Is there a good time to lose my mind? No.

Stop it or feed yourself to the sea monsters, Jules.

Of course, sitting and waiting poses entirely different but just as disastrous risks. I could starve to death or die of dehydration before a boat spots me. I could fry in the sun until my skin blisters. Infection settling in my scrapes and cuts is almost a certainty. The seagulls and pelicans could mistake my festering wounds for a snack and by then I'll be too weak to fend them off. Pecked to death. What an awful way to go. Or Dave could come back. Maybe then death will come quickly.

That's it, Jules. Find the silver lining in the shit-storm clouds.

I gaze down at the water again, then ahead. Tiny ripples on the surface signify a northerly current, powered by the wind coming from the southeast. In summer, it pretty much always comes from the southeast in the morning. By afternoon, it will switch to the southwest or maybe the wind switches to the north. These are important things, right? If I could think straight, which seems impossible, as I can feel my pulse in my head and my fingertips and ribs, I could figure this out.

Dry land. How do I get to dry land? Because sitting here waiting for death feels like Dave winning. I don't want Dave to win. Dave is a psycho, and psychos shouldn't get what they want, right? There must be some semblance of justice here. Some way to balance the scales, put it right again. If I live, Dave loses, at least in killing me. And that particular tick in the Dave Richardson loss column is critical. Maybe not to the grand scheme of things, but it's damn important to me.

So how do I get to dry land?

Directly north is Gaillard Island. Swim three miles and I'll make it there. But Gaillard Island has nothing on it except birds stinking to high heaven, biting black flies that hurt like hell, and a center of muck and sludge—the sulfur-rich dredging of the Mobile Bay shipping channel dumped by the Corps of Engineers. It smells worse than the birds and breeds mosquitos and water bugs the size of my face. I'll call this option "pointless."

If I swim directly west, I'll reach Mon Luis Island and The Knights' compound. Whoever's left there probably won't welcome me with a smile. A whipping post, dry kindling, and a match at my feet, maybe, but not a smile.

Maybe the current will carry me northwest, just past Mon Luis Island to Bellefontaine, to Mama and Daddy's pier. Maybe I can swim five miles, or however many miles to shallow water, then walk and wade my way home. Maybe I won't get run over by a boat speeding up and down the coastline. Maybe that boat will spot me and pick me up with both my legs intact, having missed the motor blades by mere inches. Maybe that boat will have friends or family in it rather than radicalized maniacs.

Maybe.

Being from the west coast of Mobile Bay as I am, I have no idea what the water on the eastern shore is like. Depth, debris, rocks, and currents are all lost to me, as I never had a reason to explore the Eastern Shore. My knowledge of the Eastern Shore is that the cops and judges don't like speeders and loathe underage drinkers. So, guess where I didn't go as a kid? And none of that law-and-order knowledge will tell me what is in the water over there. The only thing I know about the water is alligators. Lots and lots of alligators. Somewhere along that shore is a place called Alligator Point, and I don't really feel like finding out exactly where it is or if it is, in fact, party town for gators. East is out.

I glance back toward Gaillard Island. Three miles with the

current is better than five miles fighting the current. Three miles to the island. Two miles at most from the island to the shore. By the time I get to the island, the current could drift to a westward chop. That could help. Or, I could sit here debating myself so long that by the time I make it to the island, the tide changes and I will fight the water's retreat.

Seriously, Jules, you've got to stop this. Stay positive. Stop the negative talk. In fact, stop talking to yourself altogether.

This is possible. Surely possible. That's all I am asking for: the possibility of not dying. Yes, this is possible. And dying while chanting that mantra is better than dying while doing nothing, right? I didn't survive losing Jacob and eating dried fish and using a damn outhouse for months to end up vulture meat now. Not without one last-ditch, hairbrained scheme.

My next thought makes me chuckle. Just call me Jack because this lighthouse might as well be a sinking boat. But this time around, Rose is going to make room on that door. No one's dying on or near the Titanic on my watch. Standing, I look inside the keeper's house at that beautiful cypress door hanging onto one hinge. As I tiptoe through the shattered glass and piles of bird poop laced with sharp fish bones, a plan takes shape in my mind.

The door looks flat enough. No crazy warping to cause it to list and roll. I know dried out cypress floats. Enough of it has floated up on the beach over the years for me to know that. But what if this isn't cypress? Some article on the lighthouse I read years ago talked about the wood in here being top-notch cypress. Does that include the doors?

Stop stalling, Jules.

I prop the door upright. One pin in the hinge is all that holds it in place. One pin! One ancient rusted pin. While holding the door to the wall with my hip, I bend and try to loosen the pin. I can't even get my fingernails in the crease below the pinhead. What I would give to be one of those women with long, strong nails,

nails like talons, rather than the thin, brittle nails I have. My nails are evidence of a calcium deficiency for sure. I seriously need a manicure, complete with a paraffin dip and hand massage.

You're still stalling!

Fine, I tell myself. *No more stalling.* Maybe I can rip the hinge loose.

I let go of the door, letting it drop. When it does, I hear a crack. Wood giving way to splinters as the heavy door and rusty hinge fight each other. The hinge clings to the wall, but the door pulls in the opposite direction, and I see how short the screws holding the hinge in place are. The door wobbles as if wanting to lie down. *You and me both, baby.*

Without thinking, I jump, throwing my entire weight feet first at the door. With a hard thud and splintering clamor, the door crashes to the ground and I go flying forward. My knees crash into the hardwood, but my hands find purchase on the wooden bench, saving me from face-planting into the shitter. I roll over on my backside, victorious and head spinning. *Thank you, dear sweet Jesus, that I do not have to live knowing that my mouth landed on the ghosts of poopers past. You are, in fact, a merciful God.*

The door is free of the wall. Step one of Operation Rose & Jack—every good plan needs a name—is complete. My knees are scraped and bleeding from the fall, but my lifeboat is ready for its maiden voyage.

I push the door through the keeper's house and onto the deck, using the slab of cypress to clear my path of broken glass and bird poop. I say a quick apology to Mother Nature for pushing the nasty debris over the edge of the deck and into the water, then lay the door down on the deck. I free the ratty blanket from the railing and laugh when I see that my bloody *HELP* from the night before is nothing but a ruddy stain now, indiscernible. Of course, blood on cotton is not waterproof. I examine my tender fingertips. Not the dumbest thing I've ever tried, but close.

I tear the blanket to strips and tie the strips around my knees. I take one last look at the lighthouse, then push the door off the deck. It splashes below, then bobs on the surface. The current catches it and carries it away. With no time to spare, I jump, landing in the water, short of the door, thank goodness because crashing into it would have broken a bone or two. I swim to the door, hoist myself up, heaving, pulling, and panting, but I make it atop the unsteady life raft. My stomach growls a loud protest. "You're miles away from eating so shut up with all that."

That's good. I'm talking to myself again.

On the door, I feel a surge of energy. Faraway globs of green call to me—land. But the eastern and western strips of green aren't my target. I paddle around and aim for the green blob directly north of me—Gaillard Island, the land of birds of bugs. Lying flat, my arms are just long enough to hang off either side and paddle. I scoot back, dipping the bottom of the door in the water just enough to get my feet under the surface. Slow and steady—kick, kick, kick, paddle, paddle, paddle—I move through the water and hope the current holds long enough for me to reach the shallows of Gaillard Island.

———

I look behind me and the lighthouse is smaller. The green blob of Gaillard Island is bigger. Good. I'm still on track. For now. The sun is getting high, already at a forty-five-degree angle above the horizon. Because I don't possess Matt's wizardry with Mobile Bay, I don't know exactly when the wind will change. I don't know how long it will take for me to paddle three miles like this. In my kayak, I could make it in an hour, less if I'm rested. I've paddled this distance hundreds of times, up and down the coast. Mama and Daddy's pier to Fowl River and back. That's all this is. But my arms burn. They've been burning for some time now. My skin rubs against the wood with every stroke, so it's chafing. No doubt about that. How long do I have until this becomes too tortuous to continue?

I stop paddling and prop up on my elbows. The punishing sun is showing out, scorching my skin and proving that I am, indeed, an idiot. Why did I think this would work? Paddling a damn door across open water. For three miles? And that only gets me halfway to safety. And who knows if my destination is even safe? I look left and see smoke rising above Bellefontaine. Was that there before? Is that new smoke or an old fire sputtering out? I suck down a cry because crying right now will do about as much good as telling Mama and Daddy that no, I won't be joining in the Rosary for the hundredth time this week. Futile. Useless. Not an option. Full stop.

Instead, I scream. Loud and long, I scream and scream. I am a banshee on the water. Crazed and waterlogged. In my hissy fit, I nearly flip the door. I regain my balance and look ahead. Like a beacon of hope rising above the water, there it is—a navigation marker.

Before all this end-of-the-world shit started, ships of all kinds used the man-made channel to cross the bay to the Port of Mobile. The channel, marked by bright red-and-green drums and thick, wooden pylons with signs and solar lights, is the only stretch of Mobile Bay deep enough to handle cruise and container ships, and shiny, new battleships built for the US Navy at the port. The pylon ahead with its square of green is within my reach.

With a surge of "I'm not dead yet" energy, I paddle for the pylon. Just a little rest is all I need. I tell myself that as I paddle—chanting really—and at last reach out for the bottom rung of the ladder screwed into the pylon. The ladder helps the Coast Guard or whomever change burned-out lights, but I grab the ladder as if it is the last fingerhold before plunging from the side of a cliff. Just a little rest. A bit of easy breathing. Then I can paddle again.

I lay there, bobbing with the chop in the water. The sun dries my skin and the back of my thin dress. With one hand on the ladder and the other tight to the edge of the door, I fight sleep, losing the ability to give a damn about the current or wind or distance I have left to paddle.

Then, I hear a sound other than water. The sound rises as an alarm in my ear. Thwapping and drumming. Looking right and left, I see nothing. But the sound is getting louder. Definitely louder. Something is here, coming my way. I push off from the pylon, lay as flat as I can and kick like mad. If The Knights are coming for me, they will have to catch me. Okay, fine, that won't be hard, but I am sure as hell not going to make it easy for them. I'll go down fighting. Come and get me, you sons of bitches.

Then the sound grows to a deafening level. It cuts through the dulled pain in my head and drowns out my panting. It's the sound of helicopter blades. A short distance away from me, a helicopter flies just above the water. A cry even louder than before explodes from my lungs. I sit up on my aching knees and wave my arms. Then I'm in the water. My flimsy dress tangles around my legs and floats up to my face as I scramble for the door. One or two strokes and I reach the door, scrambling back on top of it.

"Please! Please see me!"

As if in slow motion, the helicopter creeps toward me. Closer, closer, until it turns a circle directly overhead. The last thing I see are waves kicking up in the wind shear and a baby-faced soldier leaping out the open door of the helicopter. Then my back crashes into the metal ladder of the pylon. Pain erupts in my back as my door flips over and I sink below the surface.

26

"Hail Mary, full of grace, the Lord is with you."

The chanting sounds far away but near, as if coming from just above the surface. Is this it? I'm drowning and soon will give in to watery sleep.

"Blessed art thou among women."

God has a wicked sense of humor. Really? Rather than Jacob ushering me to a bright light, I get Mama and Daddy's voices praying the Rosary. Faint, but the chanting no doubt belongs to them. If I could free my hands…why are my wrists bound again? No, no, no. I freed my hands on the lighthouse platform. I know I did. I think I did.

"And blessed is the fruit of your womb."

Dave must have come back for me. He bound my wrists and left me in the water. No. Fight this. I can fight this. *Swim, dammit!*

"Jules, Jules," Mama says. Clear as day. Not a prayer. Not the words she turns to when scared or worried. Mama is saying my name.

I force my eyes open.

"Jules, honey, please. You must calm down. You'll pull your

IV out." Mama leans over me, stroking my hair off my face. "You're safe. I promise you're safe."

I try to sit up, but my muscles have no function, no ability.

Daddy cups my shoulder with his hand. "Just rest, Julianne. The doctors are taking good care of you, but you need to rest."

"Where am I?"

"In the clinic on Brookley. I'm going to tell the nurse you're awake." Mama shuffles away from my bedside, then disappears behind a light-blue curtain.

"I'm so sorry, Daddy." My body feels as if it weighs two tons, and I don't have the strength to stop the sobs. A fresh wave of panic flattens me to the bed. "I'm so sorry I put you through this."

"You did nothing to us," Daddy says. He takes my hand, but I wince and move my hand from his. "Oh, hon, I'm sorry. I forgot about your fingers."

"That's okay, Daddy." I suck in a sob. "Could I get a tissue?"

"I don't know if I could have done what you did." Daddy hands me a tissue from a nearby cart. "Jump from the lighthouse, then swim across the bay."

"I didn't have a choice. Not a good one."

Daddy's chin quivers as if he's holding back rage. "When they found you, you told them, the soldiers, that Dave Richardson left you out there. Is that true?"

The mention of Dave lights terror through my body. "Where is he? When he took me away, I saw Army vehicles coming toward Mon Luis Island. Did they get—"

"They've got Clem and Troy and several others in custody and are clearing out the compound. 'Processing it' is what I was told. That's going to take a while."

"And Dave?"

Daddy shakes his head. "No. They haven't found Dave yet."

"Matthew Senior, we agreed not to talk about that until Jules is better." Mama rushes to my bedside holding a gray lidded cup, one of those with the accordion straws. "The nurse said you can have some water." She touches the straw to my lip.

I take a sip, and the water is cool and fresh. I let a sip linger on my tongue. *Heavenly.*

———

Two bruised ribs, concussion, and bandages on my right fingertips and knees. A thick goop akin to second skin covers my wrists and ankles to heal the abrasions caused by the zip-ties. No organ damage, but the doctors want to keep me for another night or two for observation and because I am dehydrated. Ice packs every fifteen minutes for my ribs, along with rest and deep breathing and forced coughing to stave off lung infections. Pain level checks and abdomen checks and saline bags and pain meds drip, drip, drip into the IV and pumps into my veins, and I want to sleep for one hundred days straight.

My memory of the last few days comes in flashes. Some, I know, happened. Cole sneaking into the compound. That so-called trial. My too-public shower. The appearance of Troy in the doorway of the shed. Dave heaving me into the boat. Others, however, are hazy.

"Mom," I say, turning to her in the chair near my bed, "is Cole okay?"

Mom smiles and lets out a slight chuckle. "I was wondering how long it would take for you to ask about him."

"Well?" Rocks form in my stomach in the seconds of waiting for a proper answer.

"He's good. At home."

"He's back in his camp? That's not safe. Not if Dave is—"

"No, no. He's at *home*. With Matt. And, he will stay there, that is, if you still want him to stay with us."

"He's with Matt?" My throat tightens and tears threaten.

"Yes. Common goals often bring people together, even the most unlikely of people."

"Common goals?"

"Your brother and that little boy searched for you nonstop. Once they confirmed with the Army that you were not on the compound the day of the raid, neither of them rested until we received word you'd been found."

"Thank goodness for routine patrols, huh?"

There's a glint in my mother's expression. "I guess they're not all bad." Mama scoots her chair closer to my bed. "They must have used up a month's worth of gasoline searching for you. Up and down the shore while Garrett and Kate drove the gator through the woods. I don't know what made you leave the lighthouse…"

"I couldn't just sit there and die."

"That's my girl. My tough, amazing girl."

Tears flood my eyes and roll down my cheeks.

Mama rises from her chair and pads over to me. She strokes my cheek. "I can't imagine what you went through, but you're going to be okay. I promise you're safe now. We are all safe now."

I choke down a sob and resist my urge to contradict Mama. She needs to believe we are all safe. She needs to believe I will recover, move on from this. But I already know the rise and fall of every scar she will never see. The jagged lines of my being. I am forever altered. I feel that deep in my cells. I also know that until we find Dave Richardson, I will not feel safe. None of us are safe.

———

I'm not sure how long I slept. A gray-blue haze comes through the window, so it must be early. Ungodly early. And quiet. As if the entire world is resting.

With Mama in a deep sleep in her bedside chair, I check the ties on my hospital gown then rise from the bed. My muscles ache and my stomach grumbles. For the first few steps, I keep one hand on the wall for balance, the other holds the IV stand, but my legs recover to a more steadied limp. I roll the IV stand beyond the curtain and wince at the bright, sterile lights of the clinic. *Coffee. I smell coffee.* I take several careful steps toward the nurses' station.

"May I have a cup of that?" I ask a blonde in camo scrubs seated behind a large counter and two computer monitors.

"Of course," she chirps and stands. "Look at you! Up and about already. That's really good for you to take short walks. That will speed up your recovery. And just a bit of coffee, okay?" Pouring a half cup of coffee, she continues, "Don't overdo it. I don't want you to get dizzy and fall or get sick to your stomach."

"I'll go slow," I tell her. "Just a stroll up and down the hallway."

The nurse hands me the mug. I hold it with two hands and blow on the top for a few seconds. I put my lips to the rim and beautiful, black, bitter coffee fills my mouth. I try to remember when exactly we ran out of coffee. At first, all the adults of the Martin household—well, all but Kate who prefers Diet Coke to coffee and had been doing without her caffeine fix for several days by that point—considered the coffee supply drying up to be a full-blown crisis, worthy of cranky retorts, headaches, and hurt feelings. But after a couple of weeks, we all got over it. Moved on. What else did we learn to ignore?

I find my bearings and turn to see Captain Johnson in a nearby stall. He's unconscious and tubes of all sorts trail from his body to machines of varying sizes and beeps and ticking sound from the stall. The whoosh-whoosh, up-down of a respirator mesmerizes me. I walk to the edge of his stall, afraid to move closer. How long has he been here? What happened?

The nurse saddles up beside me. "Do you know him?" she asks.

"Yes. That's Captain Johnson." I try to understand the tubes and machines and the constant beeping, the stillness of his body. "What happened? Why is he here?"

"The raid the other night had some unexpected problems."

"The Knights knew they were coming."

"How did you…oh, yes, of course."

"Will he recover?" I ask.

"Where is he?" a woman's voice, loud and desperate, echoes down the hallway. The nurse and I turn toward the voice. Rushing toward us is a woman around my age. She drops her purse, and the contents spill out on the floor. The nurse goes to her, crouching down to retrieve lipsticks and tampons, a small sleeve of Kleenex, a cell phone, and more. She is a woman from a different world where objects are still owned and kept in purses. One where cell phones work, and lips are tinted with gloss. Upon a closer look, I realize the woman is the one in the picture on Johnson's desk.

The woman brushes by me. "Oh, Brandon," she says and gasps before going to his side and placing her hand on his.

Captain Johnson's name is Brandon. I'd never thought to ask him his first name. I questioned his tactics; I demanded safety from him; I blamed him for Billy dying and Troy attacking me. I expected him to solve everything, but I never asked him his name.

"You're going to be okay," the woman, Captain Brandon Johnson's wife, tells him. "You will pull through this, okay?" She leans in and kisses his cheek, but I don't know if he knows she's there or not. The woman turns to the nurse, who now stands at her side. "I left as soon as I could, but all the checkpoints between here and New Jersey. It took forever. Or at least it felt like forever. Hours and hours. Days even. I was so afraid I wouldn't make it in time."

"The doctors are hopeful," the nurse says. She strokes Mrs. Johnson's back—care for the caregiver.

I turn and walk away, down the hallway of curtains and stalls. Later, I will tell Johnson's wife what all her husband did to help us. Because he helped us, right? He neutralized the Knights, at least most of them. Later, I will thank her for sharing her husband with us, but not now.

Because I finally get it.

Yes, I'm angry over Jacob's death. I probably always will be. Yes, I'm hurt that I will never get to honor him at his funeral or visit his grave, but maybe one day I will place a marker for him somewhere. What I am most angry over, what I will never let go of, is that I never got my bedside moment. That moment when I kiss his face and tell him everything is going to be okay. I didn't get the chance to nurse him back to the man he was before the explosion. I didn't get to whisper to him that he was the best man and the best husband and that I love him with everything I have. I didn't get to hold his hand while he left this world. I didn't get my goodbye.

I never got my chance with Jacob, so I'll be damned if I interrupt that moment for another woman, another wife, Johnson's wife.

With my cup empty, I return the mug to the nurses' station. The blue haze of dawn glows through the clinic windows. Weaving through the area of stalls and mostly empty beds, I find the doors. The blue light outside with a thick fog floating above the water appears otherworldly, another outfit Mobile Bay tries on from time to time. This is her lady of mystery look, her secretive sphinx attire.

I take a few steps out of the clinic and breathe in the fresh air. Although my ribs are tender still, the natural air feels right on my skin—humid, thick, and right.

Headlights blind me in the driveway. A truck pulls forward

into a parking space. The engine sputters, then stops. The lights extinguish and my eyes clear. Matt gets out of one door of the truck, and Cole climbs down from the other side. My shoulders shake as tears flood my face for the second time, but I doubt the last time today.

Matt grins at me, striding toward me.

"No bear hugs yet, please," I tell him, bracing for one of his famous hugs that threatens to crack ribs while being lifted off the ground. "My ribs can't take it."

"Fine. No hug," Matt says, his face so full of joy and relief, an expression I haven't seen him wear in months. "This time. But as soon as you're healed." He points a stocky, calloused finger at me and waves it. "Game on."

"I know." I smile at Matt, then look at Cole standing by the truck. He looks timid, which for him is more than odd. "Cole, come here," I tell him. "Come look at this. Have you ever seen the bay this thick with fog before?"

He stands next to me, then reaches up and slips his hand in mine. "Jules, are you going to be okay?"

"I am now."

"Will you get to go home soon?" he asks.

"Yes. And so will you. With me."

27

*O*h, my darlings, where do we go from here? That's the question on everyone's sun-chapped lips. The Knights' compound is empty, at least that's the word on the street. My sources tell me that the Mon Louis Island residents are being held at Brookley. Many will face charges in connection with various criminal activities, most recently the abduction and attempted murder of Jules Martin Jones.*

My head snaps toward the radio at the sound of my name. I should be used to hearing it. Libby Lefty has talked about nothing else since I came home from the hospital one week ago. Me. My imprisonment on Mon Louis Island. My escape from Middle Bay Lighthouse. I am the lead story every day, and I must say, I am not a fan of celebrity life.

As far as the condition of the compound is concerned, your guess is as good as mine. The Army has the whole area shuttered. Old Shipyard Road is blocked. Boats aren't allowed within 200 yards of shore. From my vantage point, all I can see is dozens of uniformed personnel milling about. I assume they're processing the island as a crime scene, but who knows? What I do know is

Dave Richardson and Troy Cowart didn't terrorize this community by themselves all these months.

No, they didn't. A flash of my sham trial comes to my mind's eye. I've tried to make sense of that mob. All those people were so willing to believe Dave's and Clem's garbage. So ready to defend their boy, Troy. Eager to risk their lives and freedom for a lie. Eager to kill an innocent woman. Of course, that mob didn't believe Dave, Clem, and Troy were lying. Their belief in my guilt outweighed logic, with no room for cooler heads to prevail. How many of them are now sitting in a Brookley detention center waiting to stand trial themselves, waiting to learn when, if ever, they will live in a free society again because of their belief in their cause?

The handsome Captain Johnson is recovering from his injuries, but he won't be returning to duty in Bellefontaine. I hope he heals quickly and gets plenty of rest. Each one of us owes him a debt of gratitude for clearing out The Knight compound. That's the good news—Captain Johnson will recover. But his convales-cence means that we have a new captain to get to know. With him —I assume the new captain will be a man because the patriarchy is still flying high—with the new guy may come new regulations. So, play nice. We need to move forward, and that requires that justice be served to every person involved with The Knights and justice for each of their victims. Justice takes time. Be patient, my darlings.

My shoulders tense at the idea of The Knights roaming free. If released, am I supposed to shake their hands at the church, trade with them at market, ever feel safe again?

Moving forward requires our cooperation. Yes, another new normal is coming. I beg each of you to accept that new normal. At least for now. Haven't we all endured enough chaos?

Now for the weird news, my lovelies. My old sparring partner

Preach has not been on air since the raid. If you don't believe me, switch over to his channel. All you will hear is static. It's as if Preach never existed. Radio silence, as they say. So, I can only conclude that Preach was a member of The Knights and broadcasted from Mon Louis Island. At least now I know where his bias originated. If Preach—whoever he is—is sitting in a cell on Brookley, I hope they throw the book at him. We all know that words can inflame a situation. Preach, in my opinion, was a squeeze-bottle of lighter fluid on hot embers. He may not have committed a single act of violence, but he inspired too many to ignore his involvement.

Preach was a member of The Knights? I twist the dial of the radio over to the conservative talk radio station. I adjust the antennae, searching for a signal. Nothing but static. Maybe Libby is right. Maybe the Army swept up Preach with the other residents of Mon Louis Island. I knew he leaned more to the right in his politics, but that didn't mean he was helping The Knights. But now? If he's been silent since the raid, what else am I supposed to think? Perhaps I met him, the man behind the moniker, in the compound. He could have been at my trial, voted in favor of my conviction, supported whatever punishment Dave and Clem dreamed up for me. Then hopped on the air to preach more good Christian values and patriotism. Did Preach see Dave throw me in that boat and barrel toward the channel? I bet he didn't broadcast that.

How many people on that damn island saw me being dragged to certain death and did nothing?

My face flashes hot, and fresh tears sting my eyes. Not because I am sad. Because I am angry. I am angry that Dave is roaming free somewhere. I am angry that The Knights tried to kill me and were probably planning to kill my family, and I'm angry because I don't know if this anger will ever subside. I don't think

I can accept another new normal that includes a single member of The Knights being set free.

"Jules, are you okay?"

I look up from my worktable to see Cole standing in the doorway. He strides in, carrying Mallie on his hip and with Jessie behind him. Mallie is Cole's constant shadow. She begs Cole to pick her up and spin her around—a favorite new toy. Watching Cole and Jessie play with Mallie are the only moments my anger lifts, leaving my muscles tired from the constant strain.

"Do you want me to find a channel for you?" Cole asks, reaching for the radio.

"No, no," I say, glancing at the radio and wondering how long I stood here with nothing but static pops running down the battery. "I'm not really listening to it. You can just turn it off."

"Okay," Cole says and flips it off.

"Outside, Ules! We go fishing." Mallie smacks her lips to Cole's cheeks in an attempt to zerbert him but succeeds only in dousing his cheek in spit.

"Mallie, yucko!" Cole wipes at his cheek as Mallie tosses her head back, squealing at her gross attempt. "We're going fishing. Well, Jessie's going to teach me to use the cast net. Do you want to come with us?"

"Um, I might come out in a little bit. I have a couple of things to get done in here first."

"All right. Well, we'll be out on the pier whenever you're done in here." Cole exchanges a look of concern with Jessie, then turns to go.

"I am fine, you two. You don't have to worry about me. You just keep up with that little blonde spitter right there."

"Okay. We won't bother you anymore," says Jessie, then leaves with Cole and Mallie in tow.

"You're not bothering me," I call to them, but the doorway is empty, and I am on my own again.

I spent a full week in the hospital. My hand got infected. Those tiny holes made by Dave's fork tines proved to be the hardest injury to heal. But they are healing. And I got to keep the hand, although it tingles now and then. The tingling grows worse at night. The doctor gave me a bottle of anti-anxiety pills to settle my mind, but I haven't taken them yet. I'm trying other coping methods to calm my nerves. I pray, or rather meditate, now. Sometimes talking directly to God. Sometimes praying *Hail Marys* until the words become one long sentence and my mind is set to trance.

I'm also writing it down. All of it. Before leaving the hospital, a therapist dropped by my room. She offered me free counseling sessions, but I'm not ready for that and someone would have to go with me. Mama and Daddy did, in fact, ground me again. I'm officially on restriction. And I don't mind at all. So, the therapist gave me a notebook. She said if I wasn't ready for counseling, that I should at least write down my thoughts. That is what I am doing in this thin, spiral notebook, one I hide from Matt, or he will surely add it to the not-quite-toilet-paper supply.

So, here goes something.

Dear Jacob,

Are you at peace? I have been praying you are. I'm sorry I didn't pray for you earlier, but I was so mad with God. Honestly, I still am. And I may never get over this—your being gone from my life.

But that is one characteristic of love and grief I didn't know before you died, my beautiful Jacob. I didn't know that moving on after grief doesn't happen. I don't think grief has an after. I will move forward, but never move on. To move on would be to erase you, or at the very least, replace you. I will not do either. Years ago, when I gave my heart to you and accepted your love in return, I didn't know there is no return policy for loving a person as I love you. So, please don't ask me to get over it or to move on. Neither will happen. You know how stubborn I am, so don't even try.

I told Cole the same. He must move forward, but he doesn't have to move on from his mom and dad. Oh, who's Cole, you ask? Cole is, in some ways, my kid. He lost his parents and had no one, then I found him one night. No, he doesn't need a new mom and dad. He proved he can be quite self-sufficient, but I don't think anyone should have to be completely self-sufficient. You proved that to me. That a person can be independent and fully loved and cared for at the same time. That's what I hope to do for Cole. I hope to be his guide when he needs a guide, his comfort when he wants comfort, and his protector when this world threatens him with cruelty or injustice or self-doubt. We all need someone in our corner, and I am in his.

I am okay, Jacob. Without you. Or, I think I will be. Eventually. I just never planned there would come a day without you. But now there have been so many, and I have so much to tell you.

More later.
Love you always,
Jules

I hear Matt's footsteps outside the garage just in time to stash the notebook in my trunk. I'm not ready to lose my journal yet, even if it is 100 pages worth of toilet paper. Maybe Johnson's replacement will order toilet paper for the ration lines. Maybe grocery and dry goods shipments will return to Bellefontaine now that the main safety threat is gone. Maybe writing to Jacob can be my secret for a little while longer.

"Jules, let's go," Matt says, walking through the open door. "It's too nice of a morning to stay cooped up in here."

"Did anyone ever tell you that the older sibling is supposed to tell the younger sibling what to do? Not the other way around."

"Did anyone ever tell you that hiding out in this sweatbox of a garage isn't good for your health?"

"I'm recovering, Matt."

"And doing a swell job at it. So, grab your gear. Poles, not gigs. I think you need a break from gigs for a while." Matt flashes a wicked grin at me and cocks his head toward the door. "No excuses, Sis."

"Fine. Fine. I'll be right out."

Matt folds his arms, determined not to leave without me. Resigned, I stoop next to my trunk and pull open the heavy lid. Underneath the notebook, I find Jacob's old desert camo boonie hat. I slip it on my head and feel the shadow of the brim covering my face.

Standing, I close the trunk and turn to Matt.

"I'm ready. Let's do this."

The End.

Make sure to join our Discord
(https://discord.gg/5RccXhNgGb)
so you never miss a release!

THANK YOU FOR READING SPLINTERED REEDS

We hope you enjoyed it as much as we enjoyed bringing it to you. We just wanted to take a moment to encourage you to review the book. Follow this link: **Splintered Reeds** to be directed to the book's Amazon product page to leave your review.

Every review helps further the author's reach and, ultimately, helps them continue writing fantastic books for us all to enjoy.

————

You can also JOIN our non-spam mailing list by visiting www.subscribepage.com/aethonthrillsnewsletter and never miss out on future releases. You'll also receive three full books completely Free as our thanks to you.

Facebook | Instagram | Twitter | Website

————

Want to discuss our books with other readers and even the authors?

JOIN THE AETHON DISCORD!

————

Looking for more great Thrillers?

————

From desk agent to unexpected field agent. The safety of the world hangs in the balance. Kate Malone is an intelligence analyst specializing in Russian military and politics. When asked to debrief a Russian defector in Paris, she considers it just another routine assignment. Routine becomes chaos and leads to a desperate chase through the capitals of Europe... With no training as a field operative, Kate must learn the ways of a spy even as Russian agents hunt her down. Failure could lead to another world war, but success depends on survival. And in the world of international espionage, survival is never guaranteed. **Experience a gripping tale of international intrigue and espionage perfect for fans of Tom Clancy, L.T. Ryan, and Saul Herzog. Join Kate as she must leave the safety of her agency office behind and face the dangers of life as a field agent.**

Get Too Soon A Spy Now!

The truth shall set you free. But for one young lawyer, it might just cost him his life... A popular priest is accused of a horrific assault and tied to the murders of two other women. Jackson Price and his mentor race to uncover the motives of his accuser. At the same time, detectives uncover a checkered past of inappropriate behavior with women and mental health issues. The case may hinge on the truth of an apparition and the impact it has on everyone involved. As the case races through the criminal justice system, Jackson finds himself caught between reality and the delusions of a killer. One could end his short career; the other could end his life. Strap in and follow the investigation to the thrilling end! **The Apparition is a gripping psychological legal thriller with high stakes suspense and vivid courtroom drama. From debut author Marc X. Carlos, it's inspired by one of his real cases as a career criminal defense attorney with extensive experience in high profile crimes, courtroom technique and crime scene investigation.**

Get The Apparition Now!

**For all our Thrillers, visit our website at
www.aethonbooks.com/thriller**

ACKNOWLEDGMENTS

Writing this novel began on a kayaking excursion near my childhood home on Mobile Bay in lower Alabama. As I paddled through the reeds, listening to cicadas and frogs and all the other creepy crawlies of the marshland, I thought, "I must write something set here in this beautiful, mysterious place." I hope you all enjoy what I've created with this setting. Unlike kayaking, writing and having a novel published is far from a solo gig. I've many people to thank for *Splintered Reeds* coming to fruition.

To the team at Aethon Books, thank you for taking on this project and for giving my novel a home. You've no idea what publishing this story means to me.

To Amy Collins, my agent, thank you for being my champion, bulldog, and trusted guide. You know this industry inside and out. I don't want to navigate it without you, so you are stuck with me for the long haul.

To my writing critique group, you are stuck with me, too. Thank you for your thoughtful critique month after month as I wrestled this manuscript into the story I wanted to tell. Linda, Betsy, Mike, and Jim, your writing inspires me. I wish mountains of success for us all.

To my beta readers, thank you! Julianne, you've been a fan of this novel from our first walk through our neighborhood. I simply have no better cheerleader. Kasie, how many drafts of this have you read? I don't deserve the energy and time you devote to my work. Kathleen Rodgers (yes, I will always use your full name), thank you for giving it to me straight. Every writer needs a friend like you, brave enough to say what needs to be said and to encourage the writer to achieve their full potential.

To Mama, Daddy, Kim, Kellie, and Leo, thank you for inspiring me with your love. Thank you for giving me a childhood filled with natural beauty, companionship, devotion, and faith. How wonderful it would be to take one more barefoot walk down Dead Man's Beach in a pink gingham bikini Mama made. (Of course, nowadays, that bikini would require much more fabric.)

To my husband and go-to military consultant, thank you for troubleshooting every hair-brained scheme I had for this story. Your ability to explain military procedures while not making me feel stupid should be studied. And you "Look sexy doing it." That fact should never be ignored.

To my sweet, curious, and brave little boy, you changed this story for the better. Like Jules, you give me a purpose I didn't know I wanted before you came into my life.

To my readers, with every ounce of gratitude, thank you for choosing to read this story. Out of the millions of books out there, you invested your time and energy into my book. Thank you for allowing Jules to live in your imagination and to explore the village I love so much. I hope you enjoyed the trip.

ABOUT THE AUTHOR

Jodie Cain Smith is the founder of the Mobile Literary Festival and a Page Turner Award Winner. Her novels include *The Woods at Barlow Bend* and *Bayou Cresting: The Wanting Women of Huet Pointe.* Her short works have appeared in *The Petigru Review, Pieces Anthology,* and *Chicken Soup for the Military Spouse's Soul,* among others. When not creating fictional worlds on her laptop or planning events at her favorite indie bookstore, Jodie hangs out with her long-suffering husband and the most precious little boy ever created. Seriously, the kid is amazing, and the husband puts up with a lot.